THE
REAL
WEREWIVES
OF
VAMPIRE
COUNTY

THE REAL WEREWIVES OF VAMPIRE COUNTY

ALEXANDRA IVY
ANGIE FOX
JESS HAINES
TAMI DANE

KENSINGTON BOOKS
www.kensingtonbooks.com

KENSINGTON BOOKS are published by

Kensington Publishing Corp.
119 West 40th Street
New York, NY 10018

All Kensington titles, imprints, and distributed lines are available at
special quantity discounts for bulk purchases for sales promotion,
premiums, fund-raising, educational, or institutional use.

Special book excerpts or customized printings can also be created
to fit specific needs. For details, write or phone the office of the
Kensington Special Sales Manager: Kensington Publishing Corp.,
119 West 40th Street, New York, NY 10018. Attn. Special Sales
Department. Phone: 1-800-221-2647.

Kensington and the K logo Reg. U.S. Pat. & TM Off.

ISBN-13: 978-0-7582-6158-8
ISBN-10: 0-7582-6158-6

First Kensington Trade Paperback Printing: November 2011
10 9 8 7 6 5 4 3 2 1

Printed in the United States of America

CONTENTS

WHERE
DARKNESS
LIVES

ALEXANDRA IVY

*To Don, who kept me sane with plenty
of fresh cheese and much-needed comfort when
I was drowning in snow . . . love ya!*

CHAPTER 1

Sophia was a female who took pride in being idolized by her fellow pure-blooded Weres.

Why shouldn't they worship her?

Not only had she managed to produce a litter of four healthy daughters during a time when the Weres were hovering on the brink of extinction, but one daughter, Darcy, had managed to mate with Styx, the King of all Vampires, while another daughter, Regan, had wed Styx's most trusted vampire guard, Jagr, and a third, Harley, had landed Salvatore as a mate, the current King of Weres.

She was literally choking on royal sons-in-law.

And if that wasn't enough, her fourth daughter, Cassandra, had been revealed as a prophet, the rarest of all creatures. Although she was currently missing, dammit to hell.

Sophia took equal pride in her reputation as being the "bitch of all bitches."

It was a reputation she'd worked hard to earn and the primary reason why she'd hesitated before she'd returned to Chicago to purchase the sprawling brick house in the chi-chi neighborhood near the shores of Lake Michigan.

She didn't want anyone thinking she'd become all mushily maternal in her old age. Okay, she might be secretly delighted that her daughter Harley was expecting her first litter of children. And there might be the teeny-tiniest desire to settle into a lair near her family.

It wasn't like she was going to sit around knitting booties.

Hell, she'd just opened a high-end strip club with the finest male Were dancers to be found in the Northern Hemisphere. Sophia's Menagerie would soon be known as the one and only destination for women of discerning taste.

Human or demon.

And of course, she'd already managed to cause a stir among her snotty neighbors.

Without undue vanity she knew she was drop-dead gorgeous.

Her hair was a curtain of pale gold satin that tumbled to the center of her back. Her face was heart-shaped with fragile features that were dominated by a pair of pure green eyes. And her slender body, which was currently attired in skintight leather pants and barely there halter top, could (and often did) stop traffic.

But it was the smoldering sexuality that heated the air around her, along with the predatory hunger in her smile that made the men trip over their tongues when she was near.

And made women detest her on sight.

The flutter over her arrival had definitely added a spice to her move to the stuck-up, overly pretentious gated community.

And earned her an enemy.

Sophia shook off the unwelcome thought as she stomped across the tiled floor of her foyer to yank open one of the double oak doors that was framed by high arched windows.

"Go away," she growled.

Ignoring her warning, the tall, raven-haired Were attired in a black Gucci suit with a white shirt and blue silk tie brushed past her.

Salvatore, King of all Weres, looked like royalty with his arrogantly handsome features and golden eyes that glowed with the power of his wolf. His hair was slicked into a short tail at his nape, and his lips curved into a sardonic smile.

"Is that any way to greet your favorite son-in-law?" he demanded, folding his arms over his chest.

Sophia planted her hands on her hips, not about to be intimidated. Salvatore might be her king, but she'd already gone above and beyond when it came to duty to her people.

She was done taking orders.

"Have you found Cassandra?" she demanded, referring to her missing daughter.

Salvatore grimaced. "Not yet."

"Then you're not my favorite son-in-law and we have nothing to discuss." She motioned her hand toward the still open door. "Ta-ta."

"*Cristo*, Sophia." Salvatore frowned, his Italian accent more pronounced than usual. "Why will you not be reasonable?"

It was a tediously familiar argument.

"By reasonable I assume you mean, 'Why won't I be a good girl and allow myself to be incarcerated in Styx's dungeon?' "

The king snorted. "Hardly a dungeon. I might not like the leeches, but not even you can deny Styx's lair is the finest piece of real estate in Chicago. It makes most museums look shabby."

It was true.

Styx and Darcy's lair, which was only a few miles to the north, was a sprawling mausoleum filled with acres of marble and gilt and priceless works of art.

Her own home was half the size, but as far as she was concerned it was far superior.

The long sunken living room was decorated in shades of pale gray and silver with a glass wall overlooking the pool and distant tennis courts. The kitchen was large and airy with a breakfast nook and an attached dining room. A curved double staircase led from the foyer to the master suite upstairs, which had a bed large enough to accommodate a football team and a built-in whirlpool that would make any Were purr in pleasure.

And her bathroom . . . it was every woman's fantasy, with a shower that ran the entire length of one wall, while the tub was deep enough to drown in.

No way in hell was she giving up her comforts to hide in the basement of a leech.

Or at least, that was the story she'd given her daughters when they pleaded for her to join them.

And she was sticking to it.

"It's cold," she informed her unwelcome guest. "And it's crawling with bloodsuckers."

"Your daughters are all settled in."

"Good. They need your protection." She was genuinely relieved to know that Darcy and Harley and Regan were safely hidden. If only Cassandra was with them she could at last breathe easy. "I, however, do not."

"These are dangerous times, Sophia. Even for a pure-blooded Were."

She rolled her eyes.

Yeah, King of the Obvious.

There wasn't a demon alive who wasn't aware that the Dark Lord was threatening to return from his banishment and unleash all hell. Or that there were all sorts of nasties crawling out of the shadows.

Which was precisely why her daughters were currently being hidden in Styx's lair.

And why she wasn't about to put them in any further danger.

"I've been taking care of myself for centuries."

Salvatore studied her stubborn expression.

"You don't have to anymore," he said at last, his voice soft. "You have a family."

Once those words would have given her a rash. Now it made her heart warm with a strange emotion.

Hell, maybe she was getting old.

"A family is like medicine." She twisted her lips into a sardonic smile. "Best in small doses."

The golden eyes flared as his wolf prowled close to the surface.

"I'm also your king. I could make joining us an order."

Her smile widened, edged with a warning that made the large predator pale.

"And I could tell Harley about those nymph triplets that you—"

"Fine," he abruptly interrupted, headed toward the door. "Be careful."

"What danger could I be in here?"

"Trust me, evil can lurk anywhere." Salvatore paused on the wide veranda to glance toward the distant homes surrounded by their perfectly manicured grounds. "Even suburbia."

Sophia managed to hide her tiny shiver.

"Concentrate on finding Cassandra," she said. "If I need you, I'll call."

"Take care of yourself. . . ." Salvatore tossed her a mocking grin. "Granny."

Sophia narrowed her gaze.

Okay, she might be tickled pink that Harley was pregnant, but there was no way in hell she was putting up with "granny."

"Call me that again and the litter Harley is carrying will be the last babies you're capable of producing."

With a chuckle, Salvatore headed toward his BMW, which was parked next to her low-slung Lamborghini.

Sophia watched his departure with a faint frown.

She hadn't expected Salvatore to concede defeat so easily.

Which could only mean one thing.

This particular battle wasn't over.

Sophia's Menagerie was a two-story brick building that discreetly blended in with the more conservative businesses that lined the quiet Chicago street.

Once inside, however, there was nothing discreet about the crimson carpet and shimmering gold wallpaper. Or the Venetian chandeliers that spilled light over the padded booths that were arranged to face the low stage.

There was an atmosphere of indulgent luxury that lifted her club above all others.

Well, that and the insanely gorgeous male strippers who could send an entire audience of women into a frenzy of screaming excitement.

Entering through the back door, Sophia made her way past the dressing rooms to the main floor, a satisfied smile curling her lips as her employees scurried about, preparing for the upcoming flood of customers.

This place might be just another strip club to some people, but for her it was her tangible display of independence.

She halted a moment to appreciate the sight of Dmitri and Dominic practicing their dance routine. The twin Weres had recently immigrated from Russian and were so exquisitely handsome it was a wonder they hadn't melted Siberia.

Tall and slender with short, spiky blond hair and ice-blue eyes, they moved with the liquid grace of all pure-bloods. Combine that with the tiny fur G-strings that were the only thing covering their pale, perfect bodies . . . yummy.

Then her smile twisted as she caught sight of the man standing near the edge of the stage, his hand reaching toward Dmitri. Or was it Dominic?

Troy, prince of imps, was a large, muscular man with the build of a professional wrestler and the fashion taste of a drag queen. At the moment he was attired in silver spandex pants and a see-through jade shirt that gave a nice glimpse of his broad chest.

His long, brilliant red hair flowed down his back like a river of fire and his emerald eyes danced with a wicked sense of humor that was contagious.

He was like an exotic butterfly that oozed a blatant sensuality.

"Mmm . . ." he drawled as Sophia halted next to him, his gaze never wavering from the nearby dancers. "Delectable as always, my love."

Reaching out she slapped his hand. "No touching the merchandise, Troy."

The imp pouted, but, dropping his arm, he turned to face her. "But you know how I love them tall, blond, and furry."

"You love them any way you can get them."

"True." Troy ran his hands down his shirt, licking his lips. "A wise imp swims with the tide."

She snorted. Troy did a lot of swimming with the tide. Which, of course, meant that he had connections throughout the demon world.

And that was precisely why Sophia had contacted him a few days before.

"Did you bring what I asked?"

With a chuckle that should have given her ample warning, he gave a lift of his hand, motioning toward a nearby doorway.

"Don't I always deliver?"

Her lips parted, but her words were forgotten as a man stepped from the shadows.

No, not a man . . . a pure-blooded Were, she quickly corrected, catching the feral scent of his wolf. And so sinfully gorgeous that he made her heart slam against her ribs.

She covertly clenched her hands as he strolled forward. What the hell was wrong with her?

Her entire life had been filled with handsome, powerful men. All of them anxious for the opportunity to impress her. Whether it was to earn the right to breed with her. Or just to enjoy a few wicked nights of pleasure.

But she couldn't recall ever feeling as if she'd just stepped off the edge of a cliff and was plummeting through thin air.

Was that why she couldn't breathe?

More than a little disturbed by her unwelcome reaction, she warily studied the stranger.

He was handsome, but it wasn't the polished elegance of her dancers.

The blue-black hair was cut short, as if he couldn't be bothered to mess with it, but the severe style only emphasized the stark male beauty of his face. His skin was the rich bronze that came from Latin heat and his eyes more black than brown.

He was taller than her, perhaps six foot, but he was thick with muscles that rippled beneath the skintight black T-shirt that was matched with a pair of black combat pants.

Ruthless.

The word whispered through her mind at the same moment his potent heat wrapped around her, inflaming her blood with a pulsing awareness she hadn't felt in decades.

"Good . . . God," she muttered.

Troy cleared his throat, doing a piss-poor job of hiding his amusement.

Jackass.

"Sophia, this is Luc. Luc, Sophia." The imp waved a languid hand toward the massive Were. "Isn't he just to die for?"

Sophia's gaze clashed with the burning black gaze, her skin suddenly feeling too tight for her body.

Shit. Shit. Shit.

This Were was trouble with a capital *T* and the very last thing she needed.

Tilting her chin, she allowed her gaze to slowly skim over the body that begged to be licked from head to toe, deliberately allowing her lips to curl into a sneer.

Neanderthals like this were always hyperarrogant. An insult to his pride and he'd be out the door right quick and in a hurry.

"I asked for a bodyguard, not a stripper wannabe," she mocked.

The dark eyes narrowed, but instead of the chest-thumping and the fast exit she'd been hoping for, he stepped even closer, the rich scent of male musk teasing at her senses.

"Good, because I'm not into public displays." His voice slid over her like hot chocolate, smoothly decadent. "Of course, if you want a private performance you could ask me nicely."

Oh, she wasn't going there.

Not even in her mind.

"What I want is protection, not another pretty boy," she said between clenched teeth, shoving her hands against his chest as she prepared to leave.

Let Troy deal with the muscle-bound fool. She was through.

Only she wasn't.

Even as her palms slammed against his chest, his fingers captured her wrists in an unbreakable grip. At the same time he was spinning her around, jerking her until her back was pressed hard against his chest and pinning her arms across her chest.

"I know what you want," he growled, his face buried against her neck left bare by her red halter top.

She shivered, telling herself it was outrage at being manhandled and not white-hot excitement at the brush of his warm breath over skin or the feel of his body pressed so intimately against her.

"I'll let you two play." Troy chuckled, wiggling his fingers as he moved past them. *"Ciao."*

"Troy," she snapped in disbelief. Surely the imp didn't intend to leave her alone with this . . . psychopath?

Evidently he did.

"Don't worry, I'll send you my bill," he assured her, sashaying out the door.

"Idiot," she muttered, her wolf prowling restlessly just below the surface. It wasn't angry, it was . . . on edge. As if it sensed something momentous was about to happen. Which was as disturbing as the ease with which he'd captured her.

"Can we talk now?" he asked softly.

"Not until you let go of me."

"If you insist," he taunted, his lips brushing against the pounding pulse at the base of her throat before he slowly released his grip.

Holding her head high, Sophia refused to glance in his direction, instead heading across the crimson carpet.

"We'll finish this in the privacy of my office."

She sensed him fall into step behind her. "You're the boss."

"Actually, that has yet to be decided."

Despite his bulging muscles and impressive fighting skills, Luc wasn't stupid. Hell, until this moment he'd always prided himself on being the most intelligent Were in the room.

Now he had to wonder if he'd left his brain back in Miami.

Not that it was entirely his fault, he swiftly assured himself, his gaze trained on the finest ass he'd ever set eyes on as it swayed across the room. A man would have to be a saint to think clearly when face-to-face with Sophia.

Even warned of her lethal beauty, he'd been stunned by his first glance at the delicate features that looked as if she was barely out of her adolescent years and her slender body that was shown to advantage in her leather pants and tiny halter top.

He'd expected a hard, jaded female who would turn him off with her bloated conceit. Not an exquisite woman who attempted to hide her vulnerability behind a brittle shell. Or one whose emerald eyes held a haunted fear.

The man in him wanted to haul her into the nearest bed and teach her the true meaning of howling at the moon. The wolf in him wanted to toss her over his shoulder and take her to the safety of his lair.

It was his wolf's reaction that was most troubling.

Lust he could handle.

But possession?

It was addling his wits and jeopardizing his mission.

Grimly he shoved aside the disquieting thought.

He was here with a purpose. It was time to get on with it.

Following her into the private office, he reached to pull out the folded sheets of paper he'd tucked into his back pocket. His first order of business was making sure he was hired as Sophia's bodyguard.

Of course, he wouldn't say no to an invitation for a more . . . intimate arrangement, a voice whispered in the back of his mind.

It would certainly make it easier to keep an eye on her.

His eye and so much more . . .

His cock hardened and with a muttered curse he turned his attention to his surroundings. Anything to keep himself from pouncing on Sophia and spreading her across the wide walnut desk.

The room was spacious with wooden shelves along one wall that held a stunning collection of priceless Fabergé eggs. Across the room a marble fireplace was framed by two cream leather wing chairs that matched the low sofa beneath the window. The floor was covered by a Persian carpet. And the drapes were a soft peach velvet.

He wasn't surprised by the muted elegance of the room.

Although Sophia was currently dressed like a biker chick, she possessed an air of sophistication that was as much a part of her as the smoldering sexuality.

A lethal combination.

Directly on her tail, Luc smiled wryly as she hastily moved to put the desk between them, turning to send him a glare of frustration.

He wasn't the only one battling an unwelcome attraction.

Idiotically pleased by her reaction, he tossed the papers on the desk.

"Here."

With a frown she leaned forward, studying the papers without actually touching them. Did she fear they might bite?

"What's this?"

"My references."

She skimmed the top page, her head abruptly lifting. "Miami?"

"Fun in the sun," he murmured. "You should give it a try."

"I've been to Miami."

"Not recently," he said with absolute confidence, his gaze gliding over her milky white skin. Would it taste like cream? "I would have known if you were in my city."

"*Your* city?"

"Mine."

She studied him with a blatant suspicion. "If you're such a big shot in Miami, why would you want to travel to Chicago to become a hired thug?"

He shrugged. "It suits me to be out of Florida for a few weeks."

The emerald eyes hardened. "Female trouble?"

"Does it matter?" he demanded. "The imp put out the word that he was willing to pay top dollar for a seasoned bodyguard. I'm the best there is. End of story."

"No, it's not the end." She tossed his glowing references in the trash. No doubt where they belonged. He'd forged them on his way to Chicago. "I'm a long way from hiring you."

He moved to perch on the corner of the desk, folding his arms over his chest.

"What's the problem?"

"You aren't what I need."

A small smile curved his lips. She sounded . . . petulant. "Do you even know what you need, Sophia?"

Her jaw tightened. "I know what I don't need. A conceited ass who pisses me off."

He battled back his wolf. Now wasn't the time to prove he was a dominant male who was worthy of her respect.

He needed Sophia to believe that she was in charge.

"The imp wouldn't have chosen me if I wasn't the best at what I do, would he?"

Her lips thinned. "There's more to being a bodyguard than just muscle and fighting skills. I need someone who can blend into the background."

"I can blend."

"Is that a joke?" She threw her hands in the air. "You look like you should be invading a small country."

He glanced down at his black T-shirt and pants. He'd deliberately left his Glock and two Uzis in the car. Of course, he had his handy-dandy S & W tucked in a holster at the small of his back.

"What exactly does that mean?"

"It means that you're not right for the job." With a lift of her chin, she rounded the desk and headed for the door. "Sorry."

With a speed that was shocking even for a pure-blooded Were, Luc reached out to snag her arm, twirling her around so she was standing between his spread legs.

They were nose to nose, electricity crackling in the air between them.

A heady combination of aggression and pure sex.

"You know what I think?" His voice was husky.

She could have broken his grip. He might be physically stronger, but she wasn't helpless. Everyone knew there was nothing more dangerous than a pissed-off female Were.

Instead she met him glare for glare.

"I don't care."

"I think you're scared."

She stiffened, her eyes glowing with emerald fire.

"Let. Go."

"You're scared because you want me."

She wanted to deny the truth of his words. He could read it on her exquisite face. But she wasn't stupid. Even if he couldn't feel her telltale shivers at his touch, or see the way her eyes dilated when they slid down his body, he could scent her arousal.

"I've wanted—and had—countless men over the years," she informed him. "Big deal."

He growled, his wolf not pleased at the thought of her with another lover.

"You've never had a man like me—" he started to assure her, abruptly freezing as he caught the flicker of light out of the corner of his eye. A scope reflecting in the sunlight. *"Mierda."*

Acting on pure reflex, Luc shoved Sophia to the ground and landed on top of her, covering her with his larger body.

She cursed, but before she could try to throw him off, the sound of a gunshot echoed through the room, followed by an explosion of splintering glass.

Luc remained motionless, waiting for another shot. When nothing happened, he at last pulled back to run a searching gaze over Sophia's pale face.

"Are you hurt?" he growled.

She gave a shake of her head. "No."

"Good." With one fluid motion he was on his feet and sprinting to leap through the broken window. "Stay here."

CHAPTER 2

Stay here.

The damned Were was delusional if he thought he could order her around like a pet dog, Sophia told herself, swiftly rising to her feet and following him through the shattered window.

Okay, he'd saved her life. And while it annoyed the hell out of her that she'd needed his protection, she was willing to offer her gratitude.

But that didn't mean he was going to go around snapping out commands and expecting her to obey.

Some bastard had just tried to kill her and she was going to find who the hell it was.

Then she was going to rip out their heart and feed it to the vultures.

Or at least that was the plan.

Managing to get through the window without slicing open a major artery, Sophia paused as she realized that Luc had already crossed the street and entered the three-storied brick office building.

Holy shit, he was fast.

And wicked strong.

And so gloriously, spectacularly male that he made her ache in all the right places.

Which, of course, was why she was so twitchy when he was near. And why she was so reluctant to hire him as her bodyguard.

Even if she would rather bite off her tongue than admit it.

Realizing that the gunshot had already attracted unwelcome attention, Sophia forced herself to walk at a steady pace across the street and into the building where the shooter must have taken aim at her. Humans were always so easily spooked. A few gunshots, even when they weren't the target, and they were ready to panic.

It made her long to shift and really give them something to fear.

Muttering beneath her breath at the realization that her attacker could be halfway to St. Louis by now, she pulled open the glass door and entered the empty lobby.

Cautiously she sniffed the air, catching Luc's enticing scent that blended with the humans that filled the building. But there was no hint of another demon in the area.

Could it have been a mortal who had taken a shot at her?

Puzzled, Sophia ignored the bank of elevators and pulled open the door to the stairwell. She hesitated only long enough to make certain nothing was lurking in the shadows before moving up the metal steps tucked against the wall.

She had only a second of warning before Luc was vaulting from the top floor to land directly before her.

Show-off, she silently muttered, even as her blood stirred at the grace of his movements and the power of his male body.

Then, reluctantly lifting her gaze from the impressive width of his shoulders, she met his burning black glare.

"What part of 'stay here' don't you understand?" he snapped, his voice pitched to ensure it wouldn't echo.

She slapped her hands onto her hips. "I'm the boss here and I don't take orders from you." Her expression hardened. "Or anyone."

"Surprise me," he muttered.

"What?"

"It's my job to protect you," he growled, stepping so close that his heat seared over her skin. "And if that means giving you orders then you'll obey them. Got it?"

"Why you . . ."

Brushing past him, she headed up the stairs. She bypassed the second floor, knowing from the angle of the bullet currently lodged in her desk that it must have been fired from the third floor. Personally she preferred her kills to be up close and personal, but she was a trained marksman.

Continuing upward, she sensed Luc directly behind her.

Hell, she more than sensed him. The pinpricks of his anger were biting into her skin, warning that his wolf was prowling close to the surface.

A powerful wolf, she inanely acknowledged.

One that was more than a match for her own.

Trying to shake off her distraction at his proximity, Sophia halted on the top floor landing. Before she could reach for the doorknob, however, there was a faint squeak on a stair below them.

The sound had barely reached her ears when Luc had her shoved up against the wall, caging her with his larger body. At the same time there was the deafening crack of a gunshot followed by a nerve-shredding screech as a bullet pierced the thin sheet of metal exactly where they'd been standing less than a second before.

"*Por Dios.*" Pushing back, Luc ran a searching gaze over her tense form. Once assured she was injury-free, he moved to glance over the railing. "Stay here." He turned his head back to glare at her with eyes that were more wolf than human. "This time you'll do as I say or I'll handcuff you to the door. Got it?"

Without bothering to wait for her response, the idiot was leaping down the stairs, pursuing their trigger-happy attacker with a reckless disregard for sanity, self-preservation, and the basic laws of gravity.

Not that she should bother being worried.

Luc was obviously a trained thug who probably spent a large portion of his day chasing after crazies. If he wanted to take a bullet or two to prove he was a big, strong Were, then let him.

Except he had saved her life, a tiny voice whispered in the back of her mind.

Twice.

She at least owed him a thank-you before he got himself offed, didn't she?

That was the only reason she was pacing the cramped landing instead of returning to her club and getting on with her day.

"Pain in the ass," she muttered beneath her breath, her head snapping around as Luc jogged easily up the stairs.

"Were you saying something?" he asked, a faint smile toying at the edges of his mouth.

She ran a swift gaze over his magnificent body, refusing to allow herself to linger on the rippling muscles and the broad shoulders that were displayed to perfection by the tight T-shirt.

He was unharmed.

That was all that mattered.

"Did you find the shooter?"

"Nothing." His jaw clenched with frustration. "Whoever it was managed to enter and leave the building without leaving a trace."

"A witch?"

"Impossible to say without further information." He shrugged. "I'll do a more thorough search when the building closes for the night."

She cleared her throat. "I haven't thanked you."

Expecting him to gloat, Sophia was caught off guard when he abruptly stepped forward, grasping her upper arms as he regarded her with a fierce glare.

"I don't want you to thank me, Sophia. I want you to let me do my job."

She shivered as the heat of his hands seared against her bare skin, her wolf growling in low approval.

Traitor.

"I haven't given you the job."

His eyes narrowed. "I've heard any number of rumors about you, but none of them mentioned that you were stupid."

She stiffened. Until this moment she'd never given a damn what people said about her.

Who cared if she was known as an immoral, heartless slut?

Now she scowled at the thought he might be judging her without ever knowing the truth.

"What rumors?" she growled.

"That you're the Queen of Bitches."

"True." No point in trying to deny that. Not that she wanted to. "What else?"

The dark gaze skimmed over her face. "That you're exquisite."

"Also true."

"That you were blessed with four pure-blooded daughters. An amazing gift to our people."

She lowered her gaze. Although the word of Cassie's talent of prophecy, as well as her recent disappearance, weren't state secrets, they hadn't yet become common knowledge.

The fewer people who knew, the better.

"Yes."

"And that you're a survivor," he continued, ignoring her sudden wariness. "Which was why you were smart enough to seek help when you needed it."

She lifted her head with a wry smile. "Slick."

"Skilled," he corrected, frustration still simmering in his magnificent eyes. "And unfortunately late to the party. Take me back to the beginning." His brows drew together as she hesitated. "Sophia?"

She ground her teeth. Dammit. He was a wolf on the hunt.

He wasn't going to let this go.

"I'm not really sure," she muttered.

"Something spooked you or you wouldn't have felt the need for a bodyguard."

"It's all been so . . . childish."

His hands loosened their grip so he could run his fingers lightly up and down her arm, sending a series of pleasurable quakes through her body.

"Childish?"

She struggled to keep her mind on track. Not easy when her

thoughts were being consumed with how quickly she could have him stripped of his clothes and pressed against the wall.

The things she could do to that fantastic body.

Mmmm.

His eyes dilated as the spice of her arousal filled the air, his body tensing with an answering hunger. With a low curse, she wrenched her mind back to the conversation.

Where were they?

Oh yeah, her murderous stalker.

She shrugged. "It started with spiteful notes left on my door."

"What did they say?"

"The usual. 'I hate you.' 'Go away, bitch.' 'Whore.' " Her lips curled in disgust. "Something a juvenile human would do."

"What else?"

"My tires slashed. A dead rat left in my swimming pool." Her gaze shifted past him to the bullet hole in the floor. A few more inches and she would have been skewered. "At least until today."

His frown deepened, his expression distracted. "Strange."

"Strange that someone tried to shoot me, or strange that they hadn't tried before?" she asked dryly.

"It usually doesn't escalate so swiftly."

She forced herself to hold his questioning gaze at his unnerving perception.

It wasn't bad enough his mere touch could make her wolf pant with need, he also had to be intelligent?

"You mean the attacks?"

"Exactly." His hands shifted so his thumbs were brushing the sensitive line of her throat, pausing over the unsteady beat of her pulse. "It's a hell of a leap from scribbling a nasty note to pulling a trigger. Most people never progress to that point. And those that do take longer than a few days to go from catty to psychotic."

"Hmmm." Her expression was noncommittal. "I see your point."

His eyes narrowed. "When did you receive your first threat?"

"A few days after I moved into my new house. Two weeks ago," she promptly answered. "I assumed it was a jealous neighbor."

"Nothing before then?"

"Lots." Her lips twisted wryly. "I am the Queen of Bitches, remember? But most of my enemies have the balls to face me, not creep around like an angst-ridden adolescent."

He gave a slow nod. "Tell me about your neighbors."

"I've only met a handful." She hadn't been particularly concerned by the lack of a welcoming committee. "Most of them are mortal. Big yawn."

"But not all?"

"No. There's a vamp who has a lair directly behind my tennis courts."

His thumbs skimmed up and down her throat with an intimacy that should have made her wolf snarl in warning. A Were's neck was considered off-limits to all but their most trusted pack mates.

Instead she battled the urge to tilt back her head and offer her tender flesh to his teeth.

Christ, what was wrong with her?

"A vamp wouldn't waste their time with notes and tire slashing," he said, his gaze following the path of his fingers, a glow deep in his eyes. "You piss one off and they go directly for the throat. Literally."

"Kirsten's barely out of her foundling years," she informed him. "She's still at the mercy of her human emotions."

He seemed to dismiss the vamp, although Sophia didn't doubt he'd tucked the info in the back of his mind.

Nothing was allowed to escape this Were's notice.

Not the most comforting thought.

"Anyone else?"

"There's a nymph down the block." Sophia grimaced. "She's always polite in public, but I sense that she has no intention of becoming my BFF."

"She might be responsible for the drive-by harassments, but nymphs aren't usually bloodthirsty."

"You haven't seen how possessive she is of her current lover." Sophia shuddered. There had been a fanatical glint in the nymph's eyes when she'd introduced her boyfriend to Sophia, her hands clinging to him with an embarrassing desperation. "It's creepy."

Luc lifted a dark brow. "Lover?"

"A cur." Curs were humans who'd been bitten instead of being born a pure-blooded Were. They were capable of shifting, but they couldn't control the shifts as a Were could, and they weren't immortal, although their lifespan was greatly increased. "Well, more or less."

"What does that mean?"

"He's been turned, I can smell it, but he's a pathetic excuse for a cur." The image of his short, pudgy body and pasty face turned Sophia's stomach. "He's an embarrassment to curs everywhere. I've never encountered such a timid creature."

He stepped forward, pressing her body against the wall. "Not your type at all."

"You know nothing of my type."

Lowering his head, he allowed his lips to brush over the racing pulse at the base of her throat.

"I know I'm it."

Hell, they both knew he was it.

She was going up in flames from a mere touch.

What would happen if he actually kissed her?

Not about to stay around and find out, she shoved her hands against his chest.

"Ugh," she muttered, marching around him and down the stairs.

It was bad enough that she'd spent the day dodging bullets. She wasn't going to make it worse by becoming another victim to Luc's fatal charm.

She had no doubt there were enough of them littering the streets of Miami.

* * *

Luc finished his sweep of the office building and was pulling his black Mercedes SL550 Roadster past the uniformed guard who was opening the gates of Sophia's neighborhood when his cell phone beeped.

A glance at the flashing ID and he grimaced, knowing he couldn't ignore the call.

Turning up the car stereo, he put the phone to his ear. There were too many demons with superior hearing to take chances.

"What's up?" he demanded, sighing at his caller's response. "*Sí.* I'm headed back to her house now." His jaw tightened. "No, she doesn't suspect anything. Not yet. But she's too smart for me to fool for long." There was another burst of sharp words. "Yeah, I got it. I'll keep in touch."

Tossing his phone into the passenger seat, Luc parked his car at the end of the tree-lined street. Then, briefly considering the benefits of shifting, he gave a shake of his head and jogged toward Sophia's house.

He'd already called his wolf to search the office building. His human form couldn't begin to match his wolf senses, but while he was stronger than most Weres, he didn't want to waste unnecessary energy.

Not when he couldn't be certain he wouldn't need to protect Sophia.

Reaching the nearly half acre of parkland surrounding Sophia's house, he did a swift search of the grounds, including the pool house, before entering her home through the patio doors.

He'd checked through her living room, a guest bedroom, and the fully equipped gym before heading to the kitchen.

Not surprisingly, he found Sophia leaning against the marble counter, her arms folded across her chest. She would have sensed him the moment he entered her yard.

Halting in the center of the ceramic-tiled floor, Luc allowed his gaze to run over her slender body barely covered by a lacy red camisole and matching silk shorts.

He bit back a growl, his gaze lifting to the beautiful face framed by the pale golden hair.

The lust he didn't mind. What male wouldn't be hot and bothered by the sight of a gorgeous, half-naked female?

But the sense of recognition from his wolf, as if she . . . belonged to him, was unnerving.

Especially when the emerald eyes were glowing with a warning that was far from welcoming.

"Do your duties include breaking and entering?"

He deliberately glanced toward the door leading from the breakfast nook onto the patio. A dew fairy could break the flimsy-ass lock.

"No, but they include an inspection of your alarm system."

She snorted. "I'm a pure-blooded Were. That's all the alarm system I need."

Scowling at her nonchalant tone, he turned back with a glare of frustration.

Dios.

Did she know how her seeming lack of concern was challenging his wolf to do whatever necessary to protect her?

"Obviously not if some lunatic has managed to wander around your place without getting caught," he growled.

"The lunatic always trespassed when I was at the club." She allowed her gaze to drift down to his heavy boots and back to his narrowed eyes. "At least until tonight."

"You need an alarm system."

She heaved a purely feminine sigh of exasperation at his stubborn expression.

"Did you find anything at the office building?"

He moved past her to open the fridge and pulled out a bottle of perfectly chilled beer. Twisting off the cap, he downed half of it in one swallow.

"I found that the secretary from the insurance claims company is staying late to burn the midnight oil with the janitor."

"Midnight oil?"

He smiled. "And that the loan officer is sleeping on the couch in his office. No doubt his wife kicked him out."

Her gaze lingered a tantalizing moment on his lips before she was visibly squaring her shoulders.

"Fascinating."

"That was just the first floor."

"Did you find any clues that might lead us to my stalker?"

"Nothing." He polished off the beer and tossed the bottle into the recycle bin. "Which means they're very, very good. Or very, very lucky."

"So you basically have jack squat?"

He ignored her taunt, moving until he could grasp the counter on either side of her hips, effectively trapping her.

He was going to get answers.

One way or another.

"Actually, I have a question."

She stiffened, her power swirling through the air. Oddly, however, she made no move to shove him away.

"Let me get this straight," she mocked instead. "You break into my house at an ungodly hour. You help yourself to my private stash of imported beer. Now, having absolutely zero information for me, you expect me to play Twenty Questions." She tilted her chin. "And, for the true cherry topper, I'm supposed to pay you a weekly wage for the privilege?"

His gaze swept down to the delectable glimpse of her breasts beneath the red lace.

"Yeah, but I'll throw in the night of mind-blowing sex for free."

He heard her heart miss a beat, the scent of her ready response more enticing than any perfume.

Still she held herself rigid, clearly as wary as he was by the potent force of their attraction.

"What's your question?" she asked huskily.

"Tell me what you're hiding from me."

Her eyes widened before she was hastily smoothing her expression.

"Hiding?" She lifted her brow, trying to brazen her way past his question. "What the hell makes you think that I'm hiding something?"

"A pure-blooded Were doesn't hire a bodyguard just because she's being harassed."

The realization had struck him as he watched her flounce away from him in the stairwell. He'd started to halt her retreat then and there to demand an answer, but the rigid line of her spine had warned she wasn't in the mood to cooperate.

And in truth, he'd still been so cranked at being led around like a dunce by the mystery gunman that he knew he was bound to make matters worse if he tried to pry the truth from her.

Now he wasn't going to leave until he knew exactly what the hell was going on.

"My son-in-law made me promise I wouldn't kill any of my neighbors the day I moved in." She tried to hold her ground. "He didn't say I couldn't hire someone else to kill for me."

"Dammit, Sophia, I can't help you if you're not honest with me," he snapped. "Tell me."

They glared at one another, the air filled with a sizzling heat as they both fought a silent battle for dominance.

At last Sophia muttered a curse, sensing his grim determination.

"The harassment has been annoying, but I would have ignored it if I hadn't started feeling like I was being hunted," she grudgingly confessed.

"Hunted." He latched on to the revealing word. "Not followed?"

A shadow darkened her beautiful eyes. "It's been more than some pervert lurking in the bushes and peering in my window."

"Explain."

"I can't." Her sharp tone didn't entirely disguise her unease. "I just know that there's been someone shadowing my movements for the past week. And there have been"—she turned her head to glance out the window, as if hoping to hide her expression—"incidents."

"What incidents?"

"One day I was crossing the street and I was nearly run over by a car. The next day I was jogging through the park and I was attacked by a rabid pit bull. Then, two days ago, I was nearly brained by a stone urn that fell from the top of a building I was walking past."

Luc's fingers tightened on the granite counter, his wolf enraged by the mere thought of someone terrorizing this female.

His female.

When he finally got his hands on the stalker, he was going to make the coward very, very sorry.

"Why didn't you tell me this from the beginning?" he demanded, his voice thick.

She turned back to stab him with a glare. "In case you missed the memo, I've been trying to get rid of you, not give you a reason to stay."

No, he'd gotten the memo.

His brooding gaze slid down to the sensuous curve of her mouth before returning to the emerald fire burning in her eyes.

"And you thought if I discovered someone's been trying to kill you instead of just harassing you that I would be more likely to stay?"

"Of course," she said, regarding him as if he were being particularly dense. "You're an alpha."

"True."

"Which means you turn into a caveman when you think there's a damsel in distress that might need your protection." Her gaze warned him not to even try to deny the truth of her words. "I don't blame you. It's all that testosterone rotting your brain."

As if being drawn by a magnet, his gaze returned to her lips, all too easily imagining the havoc they could wreak as they moved down his body.

"It does more than rot my brain. Do you want me to demonstrate?"

CHAPTER 3

Hell, yeah.

She wanted him to demonstrate so badly she could barely breathe.

Which was exactly why she needed him gone.

Becoming involved with an alpha male was insanity under the best of circumstances.

Add in an unknown maniac trying to kill her, and her wolf's bizarre need to mark him so that every other female would know he was off-limits, and it became a recipe for disaster.

"See?" she accused as he stroked his lips over her cheek. "Caveman."

He shifted to nip the lobe of her ear. "There are benefits."

Oh . . . Christ.

She could already feel the benefits. They were melting through her body, making her knees weak and her hips press with restless need against the hard thrust of his growing erection.

In a minute she was going to rip off his clothes and push him onto the ceramic tiles.

Or maybe onto the breakfast table.

She wasn't particular so long as it was hot and sweaty and lasted until she was too sated to move.

Vivid images of straddling that bronzed, perfect body had her abruptly shoving him away so she could head for the door.

"It's late, go away," she muttered, ignoring her wolf, which snarled in frustration.

She didn't truly expect him to obey her order. Luc was a Were who would do what he wanted, when he wanted. But she hadn't expected him to actually sweep her off her feet, cradling her against his magnificent chest as he headed toward the nearby stairs.

"What the hell?" she rasped.

"You're right. It's late." He smiled down at her furious expression. "You should be in bed."

A jolt of white-hot excitement speared through her.

Dammit.

She narrowed her eyes. "Do you think I won't hurt you?"

"I'm your bodyguard." With astonishing ease he carried up the curved steps and down the hall to enter her bedroom. He never paused as he crossed the silver carpet that accented the black and white décor. At last reaching the ebony slipper bed, he laid her on the white and black striped comforter and straightened to study her with a hooded gaze. "It's my duty to tuck you in."

She pushed herself into a seated position, leaning against the pile of silver pillows.

"Your duty?"

The dark eyes ran a hungry survey down the length of her body, his own body tense as he struggled to leash the desire pulsing in the air.

"There might be a bit of pleasure mixed in."

She shivered. Not only from the rough edge in his voice that warned he was holding on by a thread, but by the possessive glow in those dark eyes.

"I'm not getting rid of you, am I?" she breathed.

"Do you want to?"

"I don't like Neanderthals."

"I can be as sensitive as the next guy." His gaze shifted to the expanse of pale skin exposed by her tiny camisole. "With the proper motivation."

She could physically feel the heat of his gaze, caressing over her with a searing pleasure.

Dammit, why couldn't he be just another stunningly hot guy whom she could use and abuse and toss aside when she was done?

"You're going to try to boss me around," she accused in frustration, "telling me what I can and can't do—"

"I'm going to keep you alive," he interrupted.

"I won't be caged." She shook her head. "Not again."

She regretted the words as soon as they slipped from her lips, abruptly turning to study the original Rembrandt etchings that hung on her wall.

"Sophia." She felt the mattress dip beneath Luc's considerable weight as he perched on the edge of the bed. When she refused to acknowledge his presence, he reached to cup her cheek in his hand and tugged her to meet his searching gaze. "Talk to me."

"You've done your duty, now leave me alone," she snapped.

His thumb brushed her lower lip. "Sophia."

"What do you want?"

"I want you to tell me why you think I would try to cage you."

She gave a restless lift of her shoulder. "It's just an expression."

"It's more than that," he stubbornly insisted. "Tell me."

"Luc."

"Please."

She stilled in surprise. She'd bet her favorite Hermès handbag that this man had never said the *P* word more than once or twice in his very long existence.

The fact he'd lowered his pride to use it now undermined any hope of resisting his soft plea.

"You know the history of our people," she hedged, feeling dangerously vulnerable.

"That covers a lot of ground."

"For far too long we have hovered on the edge of extinction."

"Yes, but that is all about to change now that Salvatore has destroyed the demon lord," he pointed out, referring to the King of Weres' recent battle with the demon who'd been draining them of their powers for centuries. "Already our strength is returning. Even those ancient powers that have been nearly forgotten." His lips twisted into a rueful grin. "Dangerous powers."

"I suppose you're referring to Salvatore discovering that Harley is his true mate?"

He nodded. "As I said . . . dangerous."

Sophia had to agree with him.

True matings between Weres had become nothing more than a distant legend until Salvatore's shocking bond with Harley. Now there were rumors of more and more purebloods becoming mated.

What would it feel like to know she was irrevocably tied to a mate?

That never again would she desire another in her bed?

She told herself that it was a horrifying thought.

And she almost believed it.

"Salvatore seems disgustingly pleased with himself, and I have to admit Harley is content."

His fingers traced the line of her jaw. "But you're still haunted by our past?"

Haunted?

It sounded dramatic, but Sophia couldn't deny it captured the memories that refused to leave her in peace.

"I was one of less than a dozen females capable of becoming pregnant," she abruptly admitted.

He stilled. "A breeder."

"Nice," she muttered, oddly offended by the term used for those rare fertile females.

"Sorry." He grimaced. "I never considered the burden you must have carried."

It had been more than a burden. Without their usual powers, the Were females had not only become increasingly infertile, but they'd lost the ability to control their shifts during their pregnancies.

It had nearly been the end of purebloods.

"When a race is trying to survive, we must all do our part," she said, doing her best to keep the lingering pain hidden.

Typically, Luc wasn't fooled.

"And we all must bear the scars," he said softly, something in his voice suggesting that he had a few unwelcome memories of his own.

"Yes."

He studied her in silence, his fingers continuing to wreak havoc with her senses as they stroked along her cheek and then tenderly tucked her hair behind her ear.

"How many children did you lose?"

She flinched at the low question. "Hundreds."

"Oh . . . *cara.*"

Her eyes lowered, unable to bear the sympathy gleaming in the dark eyes.

"I swore I was done when Salvatore convinced me to try one more time." Her gut knotted. She wanted to forget those days of being nothing more than a breeding machine, expected to try and carry a litter year after endless year. "He wanted to alter the DNA of my babies so they couldn't shift and would be more likely to carry a child to full-term."

"And spare them the pain you endured."

Her lips twisted. "That was the plan."

"And it worked." There was an unmistakable pride in his voice. "The entire Were nation celebrated your four miraculous daughters."

"Who were promptly stolen from the nursery," she reminded him, unwilling to reveal her confusion of emotions when she'd manage to produce her daughters, only to have them disappear. The anger, the dread, the overriding fear that made her emotionally distance herself from the children whom she'd never been allowed to hold in her arms. "I spent the past thirty years searching for my daughters."

"And now?"

"Now it's 'me time.'" She met his steady gaze with a stubborn tilt of her chin. "No responsibilities, no one depending on me, no one trying to control me. Got it?"

Luc got it.

He really did.

This female had spent her entire life with the fate of her people resting on her shoulders.

Was it any wonder she was so skeevy to maintain her independence?

Unfortunately she was in danger.

And even if he wasn't plagued by an ever-increasing need to protect her, he would be bound by his duty to keep her safe.

Regardless if it meant forcing her to accept his help.

And making an enemy of her in the bargain.

He hissed at the strangely painful thought, his hand shifting to trace the line of her slender throat.

"I got it, *cara*," he gently assured her, "but it doesn't change the fact that someone's trying to hurt you."

She made a sound of annoyance. "Which is why I hired a bodyguard."

He smiled, his wolf smug as she allowed his fingers to savor the satin skin of her neck.

It was an intimate touch that spoke of trust. And to his wolf . . . possession.

"So at least you agree that I'm hired?"

"I suppose," she muttered. "God only knows what Troy would come up with next."

"Good." He ignored her blatant lack of enthusiasm. Once he was certain she was safe, he would concentrate on teaching her the pleasure of having him as her personal bodyguard. "Then tomorrow you pack a bag."

He felt her heart leap beneath his fingers. "I beg your pardon?"

"I'm taking you to Miami."

She swore, batting away his hand as her eyes glowed with a dangerous power.

"No way in hell."

He swallowed his growl at her direct challenge. It was time for reasoning with the female, not . . . what had she said? Going caveman on her?

"Once I know you're out of the line of fire, I can concentrate on locating your homicidal neighbor."

"No."

"Sophia."

"No," she repeated, an edge of finality in her voice. "I just moved into this house and started my business. I'm not going to run and hide like a gutless mist sprite."

"It would only be for a few days."

"You can't know that." She held his gaze, silently warning him she wouldn't be screwed with. "It could take you weeks or even months."

His teeth clenched. "Then stay with one of your daughters until I've cleared up this mess."

"And put them in even more danger?" She shook her head. "No way."

His fingers encircled her neck, not in a threat, just an expression of frustration.

"You are . . ."

"The boss."

Their gazes clashed and Luc swiftly shifted through his limited options.

He could physically force her to go to Miami. He had the brute strength and the training necessary to manhandle all but the king.

But even as the thought raced through his mind, he was dismissing it.

He knew without a doubt that turning her into his virtual prisoner, even if it was for her own good, would break something fragile inside her.

"*Obstinada,*" he breathed, leaning down to yank off his boots.

Then, ignoring her sudden scowl, he rose from the bed to

strip off his T-shirt. He had tugged off his belt and was unzipping his pants when she found her voice.

"If you're auditioning for a position at my club, I have to warn you we only take experienced dancers," she rasped.

He shrugged, pulling down his pants and kicking them aside to stand in nothing but his black satin boxers.

"If the mountain won't come to Mohammed . . ."

"Then he gets kicked in his nuts?"

He stretched out on the mattress beside her, hiding a smile as he caught her covert gaze ogling his thickly muscled legs before lifting to linger on the broad expanse of his chest.

She might want him gone, but that didn't keep her from lusting after his body.

And frankly he was good with that.

For now.

"I can't protect you if I'm not close to you."

"That doesn't include sharing my bed."

"As a matter of fact it does." Lying on his back, he tucked his hands behind his head. "At least until I get a security system set up."

She bent over him, her expression hard even if she couldn't disguise the scent of her smoldering arousal.

"If you have to stay, then you can sleep in another room."

"Too far."

"Then use the chair." She pointed toward the charcoal-gray chair set next to the window. "There's an extra blanket in the closet."

"What's wrong, Sophia?" he teased. "Afraid you can't keep yourself from jumping me in my sleep?"

Unexpectedly the emerald eyes darkened, as if he'd injured her.

"Despite the rumors you claim to have heard about me, I don't spread my legs for every man who crosses my path," she said stiffly.

Dios.

Regretting his thoughtless words, he lifted himself onto his elbows, regarding her with a somber gaze.

"That was never a rumor I heard, and I wouldn't believe it if I did."

"Yeah, right."

"Sophia, I'm here to protect you." Her lips parted and he hastily pressed a finger to halt her angry words. "Hold on. I'm not going to insult your intelligence by denying that I want you." He allowed his hunger to simmer in the air, the heat stirring the satin strands of her hair. "Desperately. Or that I'm going to say 'no' when you finally accept that I'm irresistible." With an effort he leashed his aching desire, needing her to realize that she would always be safe in his care. Physically and emotionally. "But until that moment, I don't expect anything from you but your cooperation in keeping you alive."

Her expression remained suspicious. "You intend to spend the night with me and not have sex?"

Both wolf and man groaned at the mere thought of the long hours ahead, but his smile never wavered.

"I can keep our relationship platonic if you can."

It was a direct challenge.

One no wolf could back down from.

Her jaw clenched. "The boxers stay on."

His smile widened. "You're the boss."

Turning her back to him, she reached to switch off the Tiffany lamp.

"Christ, I must be out of my mind."

CHAPTER 4

It was late afternoon when Sophia woke. Considering that dawn had already crested when she'd at last fallen asleep, it was no surprise she'd slept late.

It was, however, a surprise to realize that she was not only wrapped in Luc's strong arms, but that she'd molded herself so tightly to his body that she might as well have been a damned barnacle on the bottom of a ship.

Her head was tucked beneath his chin, her ear pressed over the steady beat of his heart, and she had one leg thrown over his hip.

Pathetic.

Sensing he was awake and well aware of her embarrassment, she tilted back her head, intending to slay him with a heated glare.

Instead she forgot how to breathe.

Holy . . . shit, but he was beautiful.

Achingly, shatteringly beautiful.

Helplessly her gaze wandered over the chiseled male features that were only emphasized by his heavy morning beard and his tousled hair. The high cheekbones, the wide brow, the near-black eyes that could make a woman melt at a hundred paces.

It wasn't until his lips parted to reveal the teeth that were shockingly white against his bronzed skin that she was reminded that she wanted to punch him in his perfect nose, not . . .

Other things.

Wicked, delicious other things.

"If you intended to use this side of the bed you should have said so last night," she informed him, shifting her hands from his back to press them against his chest.

He smiled at her with a lazy satisfaction. "You were the one who wanted me to be more sensitive."

"I said I didn't want you acting like a caveman," she corrected. "Besides there's nothing sensitive in groping me while I'm asleep."

His hands drifted over her hips, touching her with a familiarity that should have been offensive, not exciting.

"You were whimpering and tossing around until I at last took you in my arms," he claimed. "Once I had you tucked against me you slept like a baby."

Her lips parted to deny his ridiculous claim, only to snap shut as a vague memory flashed through her mind—a nightmare in which she was being chased through a dark forest by an unseen enemy.

Muttering her opinion of arrogant Weres who should be neutered, she shoved her way out of his arms and headed toward her bathroom.

"I need a shower."

"What about breakfast?"

"Do I look like Julia Child?" she demanded, pausing to send him a warning scowl. "Don't even think about opening this door."

He grinned, looking edible as he tucked his hands behind his head, the satin sheet falling down to reveal his wide chest and washboard abs.

"I could scrub your back."

Fiercely refusing to allow the tempting image to form in her mind, Sophia slammed the door shut and turned the lock.

Not that she thought Luc would intrude into her privacy. He might be overbearing when it came to protecting her, but he would never force himself on an unwilling woman.

Why would he?

He no doubt had an entire harem waiting for him back in Miami.

Refusing to consider why that thought made her wolf snarl, Sophia yanked off her camisole and shorts before entering her shower and turning the cold water on full blast.

A half an hour later she was dressed in a tiny yellow bikini with a matching sarong that fell to her knees tied around her slender waist. Her hair was pulled into a high ponytail and her expression was defiant.

She hadn't chosen her favorite swimsuit to make Luc forget those females she was now convinced he must have left behind. That would be downright childish, she told herself as she made her way toward the delicious aroma of frying onions, garlic, peppers, and fresh tomatoes.

It was just that she always spent a few hours by the pool before heading to her club.

Of course, if it did make his jaw drop, then she wouldn't complain.

Her cocky smile lasted until she stepped into the kitchen to catch sight of Luc standing beside the stove still dressed in nothing more than his silk boxers.

Instinctively her hand lifted to make sure no drool was dribbling down her chin.

Holy crap.

Most women would sell their souls to walk in and find this bronzed god fixing them breakfast.

Including her, she abruptly realized.

For a crazed moment she considered the pleasure of walking across the floor and wrapping her arms around his narrow waist to press herself against his back.

Then abruptly she recalled he wasn't here because he'd been mesmerized by her charm. Or even because he thought she was hot.

He was here because her life was in danger. And while she didn't doubt for a minute he would be more than happy to fulfill a few of her deepest fantasies, she would be a fool to think she would be anything but a convenient female body he was willing to use until it was time to move on.

She didn't know why the thought should make her suddenly so grumpy, but she did know her fingers itched to toss a few of her Baccarat crystal glasses.

Instead she forced a casual smile to her lips as she crossed to the breakfast nook where the table was already set, complete with fresh roses from the garden.

"Making yourself at home?" she drawled, settling on a padded wicker chair.

Efficiently plating a mound of golden scrambled eggs that he covered with his chunky tomato sauce, he crossed to set it in the center of the table. Sophia breathed deeply, catching the spicy aroma of chilies and cumin and chopped oregano.

"You should be thanking me," he murmured, taking a seat across the small table, his grin distinctly wicked. "I've had women begging on their knees for a taste of my *huevos rancheros.*"

That wasn't the only thing they begged for, she silently acknowledged, piling her plate high with scrambled eggs before taking a sip of her freshly squeezed orange juice.

Heaven.

She glanced up to catch him watching her with an unreadable expression.

"Shouldn't you be rigging up my alarm system or something?"

"We need to talk first." He nodded toward her plate. "Eat."

She rolled her eyes at his commanding tone. "Are you going to give me a treat if I roll over and play dead?"

His lips twitched. "What do you want from me?"

"Ask me, don't order me."

"Do I get credit for not throwing you over my shoulder and hauling you back to bed?" Heat blazed in his eyes as they skimmed down her nearly naked body. "That's what my inner caveman is urging me to do. And my wolf agrees."

So did her wolf.

It didn't mind a bit of caveman.

Not when the end result was some raw, spectacular sex.

She shoveled the eggs into her mouth, barely taking time to savor the bold flavor as she cleaned her plate. Anything to distract her from the aching void between her legs that was becoming nearly unbearable.

Once finished, she pushed away her plate. It really had been delicious and she crankily wondered if there was anything that wasn't perfect about this Were.

"What do you want to discuss?"

Having polished off his own plate, Luc settled back in his chair, his arms folded across his chest.

"A party."

"Excuse me?"

"I want you to host a party."

She slowly narrowed her gaze. "What kind of party?"

He gave a sudden laugh. "Not the kind you're thinking of."

"Now you can read my mind?" she muttered, pretending the maddening image of Luc floating in her hot tub with a covey of water sprites pleasuring his naked body hadn't just flared through her mind.

He leaned forward, his hand reaching to cover hers. "I told you I'm not into public displays. Especially not when it comes to sex," he assured her in a voice filled with husky promise. "I like it *mano y mano* with lots of privacy and lots of time." The dark eyes flashed with sinful amusement. "And occasionally handcuffs."

"Handcuffs?" She pretended his light touch wasn't sending molten need through her veins. "Do you need restraints to acquire your dates? Or to keep them from escaping?"

He lifted her fingers to his lips. "Someday very soon I'll show you exactly what I do with them."

With a low groan she snatched her hand away. In a minute she was going to be knocking aside the table and crawling over him like a sex-starved harpy.

"So why do you want me to host a party?"

He shrugged, the amusement lingering in his eyes. "It's the

most convenient way to gather all your neighbors at one time so I can question them."

"You think they'll confess to being a homicidal maniac over apple martinis?"

"It's easier to read people when they're in a group," he explained. "If I do door-to-door interviews they'll be on guard."

"No shit," she muttered, her gaze skimming over the heavy muscles of his chest.

Even dressed he would be the sort of unannounced visitor who would make her neighbors hide under their bed and call the cops.

His smile widened. "This way they'll feel more comfortable."

"And more likely to give something away?"

"That's the hope."

She had to admit it made sense, she acknowledged, rising to her feet.

As he said, her neighbors were more likely to let down their guard during the course of a party. Especially if she could score a bottle of nectar from Troy. A few drops in her guests' drinks and their inhibitions would be lowered. Perhaps not to the point of revealing their most intimate secrets, but they would be more inclined to "share."

"Fine." She cleared her throat as he straightened, his muscles rippling in the afternoon sunlight that slanted through the glass wall. "I'll send out the invitations."

"You aren't really going to serve apple martinis, are you?" he demanded, moving to stand way too close.

"How am I supposed to explain your presence?" she abruptly demanded.

"I'm your latest lover, of course."

She snorted at his ready suggestion. "You could be my brother. Or the pool boy."

His hand lifted to skim along her hairline, following the curve of her ear.

"I'm not nearly pretty enough to be the pool boy, and we don't want to shock the natives if I happen to do this in front of them."

A part of her knew a kiss was coming. She also knew she could halt it by taking a simple step backward. Instead she tilted back her head to meet his descending mouth, her lips parting in invitation to the deep, hungry kiss.

He groaned, his hands gripping her hips as their tongues tangled in a silent dance of mutual need.

An enthralling pleasure blasted through her, making her arch against his hardening cock as her hands ran a restless path over his powerful back.

He was so deliciously warm.

And male.

Starkly, unapologetically male.

The kiss deepened as she rubbed her aching breasts against his bare chest, her blood on fire with the need to feel him plunging deep inside her body.

As if sensing her desperate desire, his hands skimmed up the curve of her waist, cupping her breasts to tease her sensitive nipples with his thumbs.

She growled her approval, arching toward his insistent caresses as her hands slid beneath the satin boxers to cup the hard muscles of his perfect ass.

Laughing softly he nipped at her lower lip before whispering against her mouth.

"This isn't at all brotherly."

Busy thanking the gods that she wasn't related to this intensely sexy Were, Sophia was taken off guard as a brick was tossed through the window over the sink.

They both stiffened in shock, but Luc swiftly recovered and was immediately out of her arms and sprinting toward the French doors leading onto the back patio.

Sophia felt a brief flare of fear at the realization he was unarmed as he charged after the trespasser only to grimace as the backlash of his power sizzled through the air. Even without shifting there were few demons who could match his strength.

And if he went wolf . . .

Well, she pitied anyone stupid enough to stand in his path.

Of course, a silver bullet could bring down the mightiest Were, an anxious voice whispered in the back of her mind.

A voice she hastily squashed.

Luc could take care of himself. She refused to even consider the thought of him being hurt.

Clenching her hands, she turned her attention toward the shards of glass littered across her floor.

Dammit to hell.

What was it with people busting her windows lately?

They were not only a pain in the ass to replace, but they left a mess that she was in no mood to clean.

Picking her way over the glittering shards, Sophia reached to pluck the brick from the sink, not at all surprised to find a note scribbled on the back.

"Leave or die."

Predictable. Tacky. And downright cliché.

Tossing the brick onto the countertop, she moved to retrieve a broom, sweeping up the broken glass and dumping it in the trash.

She'd just finished when Luc returned, his eyes glowing with the fury of his wolf.

"Anything?" she demanded, although she already knew the answer.

"No," he growled, his frustration thickening the air until it was difficult to breathe. "Whoever threw the brick had already taken off, and there are too many scents to pick out a specific person." His jaw knotted as he struggled to leash his emotions. "I do know it wasn't a human."

"How?"

He moved to pick up the brick, testing its weight as his gaze skimmed the words of warning.

"Unlike a demon, they would have to be standing in your yard to pitch this through the window. There's no way they could have escaped before I could catch them."

She nodded in agreement. "Then that narrows down the options."

"Not far enough."

Sensing his self-disgust, Sophia frowned. "What is it?"

"There's something off," he growled.

"Off?"

"If someone genuinely wants you dead they don't warn you," he muttered, throwing the brick into the trash.

He was right. She was trained well enough to know that the best assassin was the one who moved through the shadows and struck before their prey ever sensed the danger.

"The gunshot was genuine enough," she pointed out, sharing his confusion.

"So was the bullet."

"Yeah, the bastard ruined my desk."

"I went back to dig it out." His expression was grim. "It was silver."

She shivered. "I suppose crazy doesn't always make sense."

He looked like he wanted to bite something.

Hard.

"What are your plans for the day?" he abruptly demanded.

She shrugged. "A few hours by the pool and then off to the club."

"I'm calling a security firm to install your alarm system." He prowled toward the door. "Don't leave without me."

Ignoring the crowd of drunken females who screeched in wild abandon at the male Were gyrating on the stage, Luc leaned against the carved oak bar and sipped his Cognac.

No one would blame him for being in a foul mood.

Not only was he no closer to discovering who was trying to harm Sophia, but he was so tormented by his raging lust he could barely think.

Mierda.

This was supposed to be a simple job.

Get in, fix the problem, and get out.

That's what he did.

He fixed problems.

But from the instant he'd caught sight of Sophia, the job had gone from simple to simply insane.

Proving his point, his gaze skimmed over the mingling crowd, landing with unerring accuracy on the golden-haired female who was responsible for his current discomfort.

She looked exquisitely elegant in a silky ivory pantsuit.

The jacket was perfectly tailored to her slender frame, the plunging vee neckline revealing the lush curve of her breasts. The pants clung to her long legs before flaring above a pair of three-inch heels.

Her pale hair was pulled into a smooth knot at the back of her head, the style perfectly designed to rouse his wolf into a near frenzy as he pictured his lips and teeth nuzzling down the length of her neck.

Wondering what she would do if he tossed her over his shoulder and headed for her office, Luc's pleasant imaginings were interrupted as he watched a red-haired imp move to stand beside Sophia.

The tall fey looked a bit like Troy, but his hair was cut short and his far more bulky frame was covered by a black Armani suit instead of spandex. A smile touched his handsome face as he bent down to whisper something in Sophia's ear.

A growl trickled from Luc's throat as his fingers clutched the glass he was holding until it shattered.

Ignoring the Cognac that spilled over his hand, Luc prowled forward, his gaze locked on the fey who appeared unaware he was toying with death.

The crowd parted before him, the females giving tiny gasps of nervous excitement as they avidly watched him cross the room. He was indifferent to the stir of interest caused by his tight T-shirt and black slacks and the fluid grace of his movements.

He had only one thought in his mind.

Halting directly behind Sophia, he reached around her just as the fey was intending to take her hand. He grabbed the fool's wrist, barely repressing his urge to crush the bones beneath his fingers.

"Touch her and I'll make certain you never use that hand again," he warned, his voice thick with his wolf.

"Shit." Pale green eyes widened as the imp regarded him with a startled alarm. "Who the hell are you?"

"Luc."

"You work here?"

Releasing his grip on the imp, Luc wrapped his arm possessively around Sophia's waist, his chin resting on the top of her head.

"My only job is pleasing Sophia."

Holding herself rigid, Sophia covered his hand with hers, covertly allowing her claws to dig into his flesh.

A tiny warning that she wasn't pleased by his public claim.

"We'll finish our discussion tomorrow, Andrew," she smoothly promised the wary imp. "My office?"

"Four o'clock," the fey murmured, cautiously waiting for Luc's tiny nod of agreement before backing away and disappearing into the crowd.

Smart imp.

He obviously had enough sense not to piss off a Were. Especially not one in heat.

Of course, a female Were was equally perilous.

Tugging out of his grasp, Sophia turned to stab him with a furious glare.

"Are you demented?" she hissed.

"Odd." His lips twisted. "That question has been running through my mind with growing frequency." He nodded toward the fleeing imp. "Who was that?"

"My liquor distributor, who was giving me a very sweet deal until you came stomping over here like Conan the Barbarian," she rasped. "What were you doing?"

Ah, now that was a loaded question.

For the past centuries Weres hadn't been jealous creatures. The overriding need to produce children had destroyed the instinct to find that one special companion.

Was it any wonder he was as baffled as Sophia by his urgent

desire to make certain that every male in Chicago understood this woman was his property?

"Have you considered the fact that you opened this club at the same time you moved into your new house?" he hastily improvised.

"So?"

He waved a hand toward the stage where yet another overly pretty Were was stripping off his clothes.

"So your mysterious stalker might be someone you met here."

Her lips tightened, but it was obvious that she was considering his words.

"And how does pounding your chest and publicly branding me as your latest bimbo help?"

His brows lifted. "Bimbo?"

"Don't push me."

He shrugged. "Now everyone knows they have to go through me to get to you."

"Great." She didn't appear particularly pleased by his logic. "What if they decide to lie low until you leave? Then I'm back to where I started."

"But I'm not leaving," he assured her, moving forward to trace the line of her stubborn jaw. "Not until I'm absolutely certain you're safe."

Perhaps sensing that nothing short of death was going to pry him from her side, she heaved a sigh, her gaze shifting to the horde of females who were studying him with a rapt attention that was intended to be reserved for the entertainment.

"So much for blending in," she gave in with a sour frown.

He smiled, his finger lowering to follow the plunging neckline of her silk jacket.

"You were right to begin with," he murmured, his voice thickening as she gave a small shiver of pleasure. "I don't blend."

CHAPTER 5

The human caterers had arrived precisely at eight to transform the back patio into the predictable cliché of an oriental paradise.

Paper lanterns were glowing near the pool. Black and red tablecloths covered the long buffet tables that were lined with platters of sushi. And cheesy silk fans had been placed on every chair to be given as party favors.

Not Sophia's usual style.

She preferred champagne and caviar.

But considering one of her guests was quite likely trying to kill her, this was as good as it was going to get.

She did, however, manage to get her hands on the nectar she needed, and liberally dousing the drinks of the nymph and her cur lover, as well the vampire, she'd done her best to ensure that the party wasn't a complete flop.

Not that it was necessary, she sourly acknowledged, watching the flock of women fluttering around Luc like bees to honey.

But then, why wouldn't they flutter?

He looked like a bronzed god stretched on a lounge chair beside the pool wearing nothing more than a black Speedo that left nothing to the imagination.

The half dozen female mortals were so enthralled by the sight they were actually kneeling next to the chaise, as if they were worshipping him, while the dark-haired vampire with brown eyes and pale, pale skin had planted her ass on the edge of the chair, leaning forward as if afraid that Luc had missed the pair of boobs she had barely covered in a scarlet bikini.

Whose stupid idea was it to make this a pool party? she wondered in disgust.

Oh yeah, hers.

And why?

Because of the damned Were who had spent the past four days practically ignoring her.

Standing near the French doors that led to her kitchen, Sophia heaved out a frustrated sigh.

She supposed she should be pleased.

Hadn't she made it clear she had no intention in sharing her bed? Or her body?

But after the alarm system had been professionally installed, and Luc had moved into the guest room down the hall, she hadn't been nearly so relieved as she should have been. And she'd been even less relieved when he began disappearing for hours on end, popping in and out without warning.

Was he hunting for her mysterious stalker? Or had the fact that there hadn't been any more attacks given him the excuse to find another woman to ease his lust?

She told herself she didn't give a damn even as she'd abruptly decided to hold the party by the pool. Why not show off her new hot pink Dolce and Gabbana bikini? But even as she sent out the invitations she'd suspected that her reasons were a lot less about vanity and a lot more about Luc.

Stupid werewolf.

Sipping her apple martini while she imagined the pleasure of shifting so she could more easily rip out the throats of the twits paying homage to the man driving her nuts, Sophia abruptly caught a whiff of an approaching nymph.

Turning her head, she watched the auburn-haired woman with smoke-gray eyes halt at her side.

Victoria was lushly curved like most nymphs and at the moment was displaying those curves to full advantage in a black strapless one-piece swimsuit that was cut down to her navel.

The female smiled as her gaze shifted toward Luc. "You never mentioned that you had a lover."

Sophia barely swallowed her snarl.

Get it together, Sophia, she silently chided herself.

The opportunity to question this female was precisely why she'd agreed to hold this stupid party.

"My private relations are just that. . . ." She pinned a cold smile to her lips. "Private."

"If you wanted privacy then you should never have moved into this neighborhood," the nymph drawled. "We are incurably curious and far more interested in one another's lives than our own."

"Isn't that a little pathetic?"

"Perhaps." A sly expression crossed the nymph's pretty face. "Of course, I do understand your reluctance to share. He's yummy."

"Obviously you're not the only one who thinks so," Sophia snapped as Kirsten ran a provocative finger down Luc's bare chest.

Victoria wrinkled her nose. "That vampire should be staked and left for the sun."

Sophia was thinking more along the lines of ripping off her head.

Quick and easy.

"Not a big Kirsten fan?" she instead forced herself to ask.

"She's a whore."

Sophia lifted a brow at the sharp edge in Victoria's voice. "Don't hold back. Tell me how you really feel."

"She pretends she has no interest in my Morton, but I've seen how she sniffs at him when he's near."

"She's still a foundling, no doubt she sniffs everything with warm blood."

"Really?" The nymph sent Sophia a mocking smile. "Then you don't mind that she's currently latched on to Luc?"

"Of course not." It was a miracle that the words didn't choke her. "I trust Luc."

Victoria snorted. "Don't lie. You want to toss the bitch into the barbeque pit and watch her go up in flames."

Sophia hastily squelched the delicious image.

Focus, Sophia. Focus.

"If I do decide I need to defend my territory, I'll confront her directly." She narrowed her gaze. "I have no tolerance for creatures who attack anonymously."

The nymph paled, hastily backing away. "I don't know what you mean."

Sophia rolled her eyes. The stupid female might as well have tattooed "guilty" across her forehead.

Grasping her upper arm, Sophia yanked her to a halt. "Don't run away, Victoria. We have so much to discuss."

"Please," the nymph pleaded. "Don't hurt me."

"That all depends on you," she growled. "Confess and I won't kill you here and now."

The silver eyes shimmered with terrified tears. "How did you know it was me?"

"I'm a pure-blooded Were."

Victoria frowned at Sophia's deliberately vague response. "The witch promised me that the amulet would disguise my scent completely."

A disguise amulet.

That's how the woman had waltzed into her yard without leaving a trail.

"Why?" Sophia demanded.

"You know why."

It was Sophia's turn to frown, her gaze moving toward the short, stocky male cur built like a fireplug. He had brown hair and pale eyes with unremarkable features.

"You can't possibly imagine I would be interested in Morton?"

Victoria sucked in an offended breath. "He's perfect. Why wouldn't you want him?"

Where to start?

Sophia picked the first one that came to mind. "He's a cur."

"So?"

"So Weres and curs don't mix," Sophia snapped. "Now tell me why you've been harassing me."

The nymph licked her lips. "I . . ."

"What?"

"I didn't like how Morton watched you when he thought I wasn't looking."

Sophia swore. "So you thought you could badger me into leaving?"

"It was worth a shot." The nymph shrugged. "I couldn't physically force you to leave."

"And when that didn't work?" Sophia pressed.

"I don't understand."

"Did you decide on a more permanent solution?"

There was a stunned silence before Victoria at last gave a slow shake of her head.

"Permanent?"

"Running me over in your car?" Sophia suggested sweetly. "Releasing a rabid pit bull to attack me?"

Victoria lost another layer of color. "I'm in love, not insane."

"Not much difference," Sophia muttered.

"Perhaps not, but I know that none of those things would actually kill you," Victoria said. "Only piss you off."

Her words teased at the edge of Sophia's mind, but for the moment she was too preoccupied to sort through the sensation that she should be disturbed by the comment.

"A silver bullet through the heart would be lethal," she pointed out.

The nymph held up pleading hands. "Look, I left a few notes, a dead rat, and slashed your tires."

"The brick through my window?"

"Yes, the brick," she admitted. "I'll pay for the damages if that's what you want."

Sophia gave the spiteful female a small shake before shoving her away in disgust.

"What I want is for you to leave me the hell alone."

"You got it." Victoria visibly struggled to regain her composure, smoothing her shaking hands over her hair as her gaze shifted to Luc. "I think it's obvious to everyone in the neighborhood that you're taken."

Sophia stiffened. "I'm not 'taken.' "

"No? I doubt the Were would agree. The way he looks at you . . ." She gave a tiny giggle. "It gives me the shivers."

Sophia followed the nymph's gaze, finding Luc staring at her with a heat that made the very air sizzle.

Shivers? Her entire body trembled.

"He's an alpha," she lamely retorted.

"It has nothing to do with him being an alpha and everything to do with him being a man." Victoria heaved a feminine sigh of pleasure. "And what a man he is."

Sophia's power made the nymph's hair stir in warning. "I thought you were desperately in love with your cur?"

"I am, but I'm not blind." Not entirely suicidal, the female returned her attention to Sophia. "Take my advice and lock him away before some tart tries to steal him."

Sophia clenched her hands, her gaze still locked with Luc as she absently considered the logistics of holding such a powerful beast captive.

Preferably in her bed.

Luc was a typical male Were.

Warm-blooded, fully functioning, and possessing a fine appreciation for the opposite sex.

Tonight, however, he had to clench his teeth against the soft female hands that took every opportunity to touch his exposed skin and the plethora of boobs waggled beneath his nose.

There was only one woman he wanted touching his body or offering him the temptation of her firm, delectable breasts.

The knowledge should have sent him howling into the night in terror.

But if the past few days had taught him nothing else, it was that it was far too late to avoid his obsessive need for Sophia.

Even when he was miles away from Chicago she consumed his thoughts, the overriding need to return to her side a nagging ache that couldn't be denied. And when she was near . . .

Dios.

Pretending indifference to disguise his acute awareness of the female Were, not to mention his savage need to haul her nearly naked body away from the gawking male guests, Luc covertly monitored her every movement.

Which was why he knew the second the nymph approached her.

Tensing, he battled back his instinct to rush to Sophia's side. He didn't have to overhear their words to know that Sophia was in charge of the heated exchange, or to suspect that she was managing to bully information from the nymph.

A fact confirmed when Victoria crossed the terrace to grasp her lover's arm and with nervous glances toward Sophia urged him across the lawn toward the side gate.

Clearly, Sophia was more than capable of holding her own. At least when the enemy was face-to-face.

But when she turned to enter the house through the French doors, without so much as a glance in his direction, he could no longer deny his primitive male urges.

Nothing like the sight of his prey attempting to escape to send a predator into a frenzy.

Nearly bowling down the gaggle of females leaning against his lounge chair, Luc was on his feet and following in Sophia's wake. He didn't give a damn about the cries of protest. The only thing that mattered was getting to the female who had him so twisted in knots he couldn't think straight.

He caught up with her as she crossed the shadowed kitchen, moving with a burst of speed to block her path.

"What did you discover?" he demanded.

She came to a grudging halt, her hands on her hips. "How do you know I discovered anything?"

"You were looking very chummy with the nymph. I doubt you were exchanging recipes."

Emerald fire sparked in her eyes. "Is that an insult of my cooking abilities?"

His lips twitched as he recalled coming home last evening to find Sophia waiting for him at the table, her expectant expression revealing her pride in the hideous creation steaming on his plate.

It was a testament to his devotion to her that he'd managed to choke down more than two spoonfuls.

"*Cara,* I've eaten raw slug demons that tasted better than your meat loaf."

Her power slammed into him, nearly sending him reeling backwards.

"It was salmon loaf, and since I never wanted to cook for you in the first place I hope it gives you food poisoning."

"I think it very nearly did." He did a hasty sidestep as she attempted to circle past him. "Where are you going?"

Her jaw tightened. "To bed."

He hissed, his body reacting with violent excitement to her simple statement.

It wasn't helping matters that he'd spent the past four hours imagining how easy it would be to slice through the strings holding together her tiny excuse for a swimsuit.

Suddenly his Speedo was painfully tight.

"At this hour?"

"I'm tired."

Tired? *Mierda.* He had never felt more juiced in his life. As if his entire body was buzzing with electric anticipation.

He stepped closer, his wolf relishing the warm scent of woman and power.

Until Sophia he'd never noticed whether a female could match his strength. So long as she was attractive and intelligent enough to hold his interest outside of bed he considered it a good relationship.

Now, he found his wolf preening at the knowledge this female was capable of holding her own.

Even against him.

His fingers lifted to grasp a strand of pale gold hair, savoring the feel of the silky softness.

"You still have guests."

"They aren't waiting around for my company," she said, the bite in her voice unmistakable. "Just try to keep the noise down. We don't want to be busted by the neighborhood watch."

A slow, wicked smile curved his lips. "Why, Sophia. Are you jealous?"

Holding herself rigid, she met his teasing gaze. "I'm a Were."

"And?"

"And we don't get jealous."

His humorless laugh echoed through the kitchen. "If that were true then I wouldn't have waited outside your club for that damned imp to show up just so I could make it clear he wasn't to so much as smile at you during your meeting."

She blinked in surprise at his blunt confession. As she should. He'd felt like a dork waiting for the imp to make his scheduled appointment with Sophia and then accosting him as if he were some lethal assassin instead of a harmless liquor distributor.

Of course that didn't stop him.

He'd been compelled to make sure the fey understood that Sophia belonged to him.

"I wondered why Andrew looked like he'd just swallowed his tongue," she muttered.

"He was lucky he still had a tongue after I watched him whispering sweet nothings in your ear," he said dryly.

She sniffed, folding her arms over her chest. "At least he wasn't groping me like an octopus."

Ah. She was jealous.

Thank God.

"Are you referring to Kirsten?" he asked in an overly innocent tone.

Her eyes narrowed. "I've never cared for cold-blooded leeches, but to each his own I guess."

"My thoughts exactly."

Not giving her time to react, Luc scooped Sophia off her feet and headed out of the kitchen.

"What are you doing?"

She frowned, but astonishingly she made no effort to struggle out of his grasp. Or even to rip out his throat.

Progress.

"We need to talk."

"Then talk," she muttered.

He crossed the foyer and easily jogged up the curved staircase, using the excuse to press her tight against his chest.

"In private."

"What about your groupies?"

"They'll eventually find easier game." He held her petulant gaze, not bothering to hide his smoldering desire. "This one's already been bagged and tagged."

She licked her lips as he stepped into her bedroom and kicked shut the door behind them.

"Luc."

Still holding her gaze, which was now wary, he gently set her on her feet in the middle of the room, his hands resting on her nicely rounded hips.

"We won't be interrupted here."

She arched a brow. "And that's the only reason you chose my bedroom?"

His grip tightened on her hips, his already hardened cock throbbing with an eager plea for attention, but with an effort he forced himself to concentrate on business before pleasure.

Later . . .

Oh, the things he intended to do.

"Tell me what you learned from the nymph."

Her lips thinned at his commanding tone, but she wasn't a fool. She had to sense he was hanging on by a thread.

As if his raging erection didn't give it away.

"She was the one harassing me."

"You're sure?"

"She's not the brightest bulb," she said dryly. "With a little prompting she confessed to writing the notes and leaving dead animals and slashing my tires. Oh, and throwing the brick through my window." She made a sound of disgust. "Bitch."

He nodded. He'd pegged the nymph for the childish pranks, but it was nice to have it confirmed.

"And the attempts on your life?"

"She was clueless."

"You believe her?"

"Yes." She nodded without hesitation. "She might be a flake, but she's not bloodthirsty enough to try to kill me."

"So there are two separate enemies." Luc felt a piece of the aggravating puzzle slide into place. It wasn't that the harassment was escalating. It was that they were traveling separate paths. "One mystery solved."

She tilted back her head to regard him with a lift of her brows.

"What about you?"

"Me?"

"You were the one who insisted that I host this ridiculous shindig," she tartly reminded him. "Did you learn anything besides Cindy's bust size?"

"Cindy?"

"The mortal who was worshipping at your feet."

"Ah." He allowed his fingers to trail over her lower back, male enough to enjoy her pique. "Was she the brunette or the redhead? They all start to look alike."

"You . . ."

He pressed a finger to her lips, halting her furious words. "I've started the process."

She shook off his hand, her eyes narrowing. "What the hell does that mean?"

He reached into the side of his Speedo to pull out a small key. "This."

She snorted, unimpressed. "A key?"

"I lifted it from Kirsten when she was trying to stick her tongue down my throat," he explained.

If looks could kill, he'd be dead on the spot.

"And why would you need her key?" she managed to ask between gritted teeth.

She was beautiful when she was jealous, he decided.

Eyes glowing with emerald fire. Her hands clenched. Her breasts heaving as she struggled against her wolf.

Of course, she would be even more beautiful stretched across the nearby bed, her body softened with pleasure and her legs spread in invitation, he acknowledged.

His hands brushed up and over her bare shoulders. "Once it's daylight I intend to search her lair."

"She couldn't have shot at me." Her voice became husky as his fingers followed the plunging neckline of her bikini top. "The sun was out."

"She could have an accomplice," he said, already having considered the fact that the vampire could be using a less-flammable partner to throw them off track.

"Hmmm."

She tried to sound skeptical, but he didn't miss her tiny gasp of pleasure as his fingers slipped beneath the fabric of her swimsuit to find her nipples already beaded in anticipation.

Subtly he nudged her backward, herding her toward the bed that had featured in a hundred fantasies over the past four nights.

"After that I have a date with Morton."

Her lips curled into a mocking smile. "Is there something you want to share with me?"

With an impatient motion, he yanked off the tiny top, cupping her swollen breasts with a gentle reverence.

"A golf date."

She groaned, her hands reaching to grasp his shoulders. As if she was having difficulty standing.

He knew the feeling.

"You play golf?"

"How hard can it be?" he muttered, distracted by the spectacular sight of her rosy nipples that quite literally begged for his kiss.

"Fine." She cleared her throat. "If that's all."

Grasping her by the waist, he lifted her just high enough to toss her into the middle of the vast bed.

"Not nearly."

CHAPTER 6

Sophia shuddered, lifting herself on her elbows to regard the man standing over her like an ancient conqueror.

She should be pissed.

How many times had she warned him not to act like a caveman?

And yet, she'd not only allowed him to drag her to her bedroom, but she hadn't made so much as a peep when he'd ripped off her top and tossed her onto the bed like she was some sort of spoils of war.

Perhaps it was because she was so damned consumed by her cravings she couldn't think of anything but getting that hard, bronzed body on top of her.

Sucking in a deep breath, she struggled to regain command of the encounter that was swiftly escalating out of control.

"Have you been sneaking into the nectar?" she husked.

The dark eyes shimmered like polished ebony in the moonlight, his hands not quite steady as they tugged off his tiny Speedos.

"I don't need nectar to be on fire for you," he growled, his massive erection growing even larger as she studied it with an avid gaze. "These past nights have been unbearable."

Her heart stopped beating as he sprawled on the bed next to her, the heat of his naked body like a furnace.

"This is a very bad idea."

"Not as bad as denying what we both want." His wolf

glowed in his eyes as he reached for her hand, pressing it against his arousal. "Feel what you do to me."

"Luc."

Unable to deny temptation, she wrapped her fingers around his shaft, exploring down to the heavy testicles before slowly skimming back up to find the broad tip that was already damp with his seed.

"*Dios.*" He shuddered, exposing a claw to slice through the string holding her swimsuit bottom together. She parted her lips to protest the destruction of her expensive clothing, only to have a groan escape as he spread his palm over her bare ass, his fingers squeezing her flesh in promise of pleasure to come. "Hour after hour I lay in my bed, hearing you pace the floor while the scent of your desire filled the air." He peered deep into her eyes. "Do you know what it cost me not to come to you? Not to ease your need?"

She knew the torment of having him so near and yet too frightened to admit her growing desperation for him.

"Then why didn't you?"

His hand stroked up her back, cupping the nape in a gesture of comfort.

"My first priority is keeping you safe," he reminded her, a thin layer of sweat forming on his brow as she gave his cock a slow pump. "I can't do that if you don't trust me."

"And that's why you haven't tried to seduce me?"

He gave a strangled chuckle. "That and I feared you might slice my balls off."

Smart, smart Were.

He knew precisely what to say.

And how to touch, she acknowledged as his fingers moved from her nape to trace the line of her throat.

"Why tonight?"

"I'd like to tell myself it's because you have come to accept I only want what's best for you, but the truth is that I'm not a saint," he confessed, the rasp of his breath filling the air. "I need you so badly I'm not sure I can survive another night without you."

Without warning his hands shifted to grasp her hips, rolling her until she was lodged on top of him. Pleasure jolted through her as her already damp flesh was pressed to his thick cock.

"Holy hell," she moaned.

"Tell me you want this, Sophia."

She glanced down at his impossibly handsome face that was hard with barely leashed passion.

She'd fought this moment for so long. Ever since he'd walked into Sophia's Menagerie.

Only now, however, did she realize that it wasn't her fear of being used to simply pass the time that had made her wary of allowing him into her bed.

But something much darker and far more dangerous.

Something that she couldn't fight any longer.

"I want this," she whispered.

His hands skimmed to cup her breasts, studying her with the measuring gaze of a wolf.

She didn't know what he was searching for, but she sensed that it was important.

"Tell me that you want me," he prodded, rolling her tender nipple between his thumb and finger.

Oh . . . God.

"I want you," she breathed.

"Luc." His voice was thick with need. "Say my name."

"Luc."

"Now let me taste you."

She planted her hands on either side of his head, lowering her body until he could plant an openmouthed kiss at the base of her shoulder. She shuddered, rubbing against his hard erection as his tongue ran a wet path along the line of her collarbone.

He clamped his hands on her hips, holding her tight against him while refusing her the relief of moving.

"You aren't going to regret this in the morning, are you?"

She gave a husky chuckle as she turned her head to stroke her lips along his jaw, delighting in the rough scrape of his whiskers. She didn't doubt he had to shave more than once a day to look civilized.

The thought was oddly erotic.

"Will you?"

He hissed in pleasure. "No, but I don't want to be kicked to the curb because you blame me for taking advantage."

"No one takes advantage of me." She nipped his bottom lip. "And I'm not a silly juvenile who doesn't know what she wants from one minute to the next. I'm a full-grown Were and I want you."

A moan was wrenched from his throat as his lips traveled over the curve of her breast, at last latching on to her aching nipple.

Her eyes squeezed shut as a raw, savage pleasure raced through her.

"Oh . . . God, yes."

"You like that?"

Like it?

Hell, she accused him of being a caveman, but her urges in this moment couldn't be more primitive.

Give her a club and she'd make sure this man never left her bed.

"It's perfect," she whispered.

"You're perfect."

"You wouldn't say that if you'd seen me during a full moon," she teased with a small sigh. "I earn my title of Queen of Bitches."

"I like that you're a bitch." His mouth tormented her nipple, lapping and nipping until her fingers dug into his shoulders. "And that you're not afraid to speak your mind. And that you'll kick ass when necessary."

She shuddered, his soft words as much an aphrodisiac as his skillful touch.

Gods, she was on fire.

After waiting for so long to ease this burning ache, she had planned to enjoy a slow, mind-numbing seduction, but the pagan need to have him buried deep inside her was rapidly reaching a critical level.

As if sensing she was tumbling out of control, Luc pulled

back to study her with a gaze that sent tiny tremors down her spine.

It was a gaze that spoke of need and yearning and . . . possession.

Lifting his hands, he framed her face in his hands, pulling her down to kiss her with an aching sweetness. Sophia sighed. She didn't know what she had done for fate to have dropped this delectable man into her arms, but she intended to savor every moment he remained with her.

Her hands smoothed over the corded muscles of his chest. His skin was a warm, silken temptation, and with a moan of need, she moved to trail her lips over his face and down the strong column of his throat. Her stomach clenched in fierce need, her wolf delighting in the clean scent of male skin.

"You taste of heat and sunshine," she whispered as she continued her provoking caresses.

"I'm supposed to be tasting you," he growled, his hands clutching her hips as he sought to regain command.

Such an alpha.

"Do you object?" she whispered, moving steadily lower.

"Oh, hell no."

"What about this?"

"Sophia," he rasped as she reached the rippling muscles of his lower stomach.

"Mmmm?"

"I'm a Were who has wanted you for a very long time," he ground out. "I need to be inside you when I come."

She gave a throaty chuckle, oddly pleased by his words. Not that she was done with her playing. Deliberately rubbing her body back up the length of his body, she savored the electric sparks set off by the friction of their naked skin.

It'd been so long since she'd felt such overwhelming desire. Hell, she wasn't sure she'd ever needed a man like she needed Luc. Her every nerve felt alive, sensitized to the point she thought she might combust.

"You can't have wanted me that long," she murmured. "We've only known each other a week."

Without warning he lifted her hips, stealing her breath as the fierce jut of his erection settled in the damp heat between her legs.

She arched, the persistent throb in her sex rejoicing as the wide tip of him slipped just inside her body. But instead of shoving himself home, he clutched her hips and regarded her with smoldering eyes.

"I met you a week ago," he said in thick tones. "I've waited for you all my life," he murmured.

Oh shit, she was in trouble.

"Luc."

"Now . . . my turn for some torture," he informed her, drawing her toward his waiting lips. "I want you begging before I'm done."

With a wicked smile, Luc branded her lips with a kiss of pure hunger. The taste of his wolf on her tongue sizzled through her, setting off small fireworks of pleasure.

Then moving his mouth over her face, he stroked down the length of her arched neck. Sophia's fingers dug into his shoulders as he tugged her upward, catching the pouting nipple between his teeth. She gave a soft growl as he licked and suckled her, her head tilted back at the insistent bliss pulsing through her. He turned his attention to the other breast, deliberately urging her desire to a fever pitch.

She needed to get him inside her.

She needed to be so deeply connected to him that they reached paradise together.

But even as she struggled to slide onto his waiting cock, he was ruthlessly hauling her up to her knees. With a strangled moan she glanced down to watch his mouth explore the clenched muscles of her stomach, his tongue darting out to send shivers of delight through her.

She moaned, her heavy lashes lowering as he stroked over the curve of her hip and down the inside of her thigh.

Okay, she could take a small detour before riding him like a cowboy.

Then his seeking lips found her moist cleft and any logical

thought was destroycd. Oh, this was good. This was fan-freaking-tastic.

Struggling not to topple backward as his tongue stroked the highly sensitive flesh, she speared her fingers in the thick satin of his hair.

There was something a bit naughty about straddling him as he expertly tongued her, although she intended to become a whole lot naughtier before the night was over.

She hadn't forgotten those handcuffs he'd mentioned. . . .

Still holding her hips, Luc found the core of her pleasure, gently sucking as the magical pressure began to build.

"Luc, I'm close," she gasped.

"Yes," he muttered, guiding her back so he could position her over his straining erection.

Then, slowly he penetrated her damp channel.

Sophia hissed as she pressed herself ever deeper. She had logically known he was large. All over. But as he stretched her to the limit, she had to admit she hadn't actually considered the sensation of being impaled by such a generously proportioned shaft.

Holy crap.

Bigger really was better.

And when a man knew what to do with such a fine, fine instrument, then it was nothing less than a gift to women.

Briefly savoring his deep, steady pace, Sophia at last placed her hands on his chest, rolling her hips to meet his upward thrust. She smiled with wicked satisfaction as his fingers convulsively clutched her hips.

He wasn't the only one with talent.

"*Dios*, you feel so good," he panted. "So good."

Sophia lifted until the tip of his cock was nearly at her entrance before plunging downward. His hips jerked off the mattress, his eyes glowing as his wolf strained to be released.

Sophia chuckled, loving the sensation of being the one in power even as she knew that it was an illusion that he was offering her.

Just as he was offering her the illusion that he was hers.

The one wolf meant to be hers for all eternity.

Abruptly crushing the disturbing thought, she concentrated on the sensation of Luc's deepening thrusts, her soft pants filling the air as her muscles tightened in preparation for the looming orgasm.

Luc tightened his grip, his face burying in the curve of her neck. Then, still pumping into her at a furious pace, he sank his teeth into her flesh, sending her into a shattering climax.

Sophia shuddered in bliss, convulsing around him as he gave one more thrust and cried out with the violent pleasure of his own release.

Luc rolled to the side, wrapping his arms tightly around Sophia's trembling body as he struggled to catch his breath. His mind reeled from the astounding pleasure that continued to shudder through him.

Not just the orgasm that had ripped through him with the force of a tsunami, but the feel of her flesh beneath his fangs as he had marked her with his bite.

A damned shame that the mark wouldn't last. He wouldn't be at all displeased to have her walking around with a blatant display of his ownership.

Unfortunately even now her skin was healing, returning to the perfect, unmarred silk that tempted him to lean down and sink his teeth in for another bite.

He groaned, his body hardening.

Now that he thought about it, he was tempted to start the whole thing over. This time he wouldn't let the bewitching Were provoke him into such a swift conclusion.

He intended to take hours pleasuring her.

To have her pleading for release.

And most importantly, to make certain that he had entrenched himself so deeply she would never, ever want another lover.

Snuggling against his chest, Sophia heaved a sigh of contentment.

"That was . . ."

"Sensational?" he offered, his lips teasing over her brow and down the slender length of her nose. "Life altering? The best you've ever had?"

"Adequate."

He snorted. The earth had just moved.

For both of them.

"Adequate?"

He lowered his head to deliberately tease the tender spot just below her ear, chuckling as she quivered in ready response.

"Okay, maybe it was above average," she whispered huskily.

"You're playing with fire, *cara*." Nipping the lobe of her ear, he planted hungry kisses down the length of her throat, pausing to nuzzle the tender flesh he intended to hold in his teeth as he brought them both to an explosive climax. "Shall I remind you of just how good it is between us?"

She groaned, her hands branding a path of heat over his chest and down his stomach.

"It's coming back," she assured him. "Slowly."

For all his brawn, Luc had always been surprisingly intuitive. In truth, it was his ability to read others that made him such a lethal killer.

Any Were could use his teeth and claws to battle his enemies. But a soldier who could predict what his opponent was going to do before he did it, priceless.

It wasn't intuition, however, that made him pull back to study his companion with a searching gaze. No, this was much deeper. Much more . . . intimate.

"Sophia?"

"Hmmm?" she murmured, her hands continuing the path of destruction toward his fully erect cock.

Mierda, he wanted to forget the concern that niggled at the edge of his mind. Surely whatever was bothering Sophia could wait?

At least for a few hours.

Then, as he caught the scent of wariness threaded through the rich spice of her desire, he heaved a small sigh, catching her hand a mere heartbeat before she captured his shaft and put an end to any coherent thought.

"There's something on your mind."

She flashed a deliberately wicked smile. The kind of smile intended to divert any red-blooded male.

"A sexy six-foot Were who thinks he's all that?"

Bringing her hand to his lips, he pressed a kiss to her knuckles, his gaze never wavering from her pale face.

"Nice try, but I know when a female is distracted." He smiled wryly. "Not a problem I usually have when I'm in bed with her."

She rolled her eyes. "You really need to work on your self-confidence."

"Sophia, tell me what's troubling you."

There was a long silence as she inwardly debated the odds of keeping her secrets. Then, clearly accepting that there wasn't a chance in hell, she heaved a resigned sigh.

"I'm not sure you actually want to know."

He hissed, his muscles rigid as he prepared for an unseen blow.

"Dammit," he rasped. "If you try to convince me you regret our—"

"No, it's not that."

"Just tell me."

She licked her lips, looking oddly vulnerable. "I was attracted to you from the moment we first met."

"I knew you had good taste." His voice remained tense even as he gently tucked a golden curl behind her ear.

"But I told myself that I would be an idiot to give in to that attraction."

"Why?"

She lowered her lashes, as if she could somehow hide from his searching gaze.

"Because I wasn't going to be a convenient lay that would be forgotten the moment you returned to Miami."

He froze, his brows snapping together. "That's what you thought of me? That I intended to use and abandon you?"

"I wasn't judging you," she said. "I've enjoyed more than my share of meaningless hookups."

Was that supposed to reassure him?

Dios.

Abruptly rolling onto his back, he threw an arm over his face. Why didn't she get a little salt to rub into the wound?

"You're right, I don't want to hear this," he muttered.

He felt her turn to press against his side, her hand lightly running over his chest in a gesture of apology.

"Luc, let me finish," she softly pleaded.

He refused to look at her. Maybe he was being childish. After all, he couldn't deny that he'd had a few one-night stands in his past. And while he had never intentionally used a woman, there might have been a few who had wanted more than he was willing to offer.

But the thought that Sophia could ever have dismissed their powerful connection as a meaningless bout of lust pissed him off.

Royally.

"Say it," he snarled.

"I was lying to myself."

"About what?"

There was the slightest hesitation before she heaved a deep sigh.

"About you and why I was terrified to let you into my bed."

He lowered his arm, grudgingly meeting her troubled gaze. "Then what was the reason?"

"I was afraid I would never let you out of it."

The blunt words hung in the air as Luc allowed them to slowly ease the sick ball of dread that had lodged in his gut.

At last he lifted a hand to lightly touch her pale cheek. "Sophia?"

"My wolf recognized you from the beginning," she admitted. "It understood. . . ."

"Don't stop now, *cara*," he coaxed, desperately needing to hear the words.

"It understood that you belong to me."

"Ah."

The emerald eyes flared at his noncommittal response. "I warned you that you wouldn't want to know."

His laughter was filled with pure joy as he rolled her beneath him, pinning her to the mattress with his much larger body.

"How could you possibly think I wouldn't want to know how you feel?" he growled, not certain if he wanted to shake her or kiss her senseless.

The damned female could make him feel as uncertain and awkward as a pup.

Her eyes widened as she felt the blunt tip of his erection settle at the moist entrance between her legs.

"You came here for a job, not to become mated."

He cupped her cheek, his thumb brushing the sensuous curve of her lips.

Just a few days ago the word *mate* would have made him break out in hives.

Now he couldn't imagine his life without this woman.

"It doesn't matter why I came, only that I never intend to leave."

Her arms wrapped around his neck, her emerald eyes glowing with an emotion that was echoed in his racing heart.

"Never?"

He didn't hesitate. "I belong to you now."

"Mine?"

A smile curved her lips, then before he could guess her intentions, she'd captured his thumb between her teeth, gently sucking on it.

He growled in pleasure, the sensation of her tongue rubbing his thumb making his cock ache for the same delicious attention.

"Just as you are mine," he swore, lowering his head to press restless kisses over her face.

White-hot need blazed through him, but somewhere in the back of his mind he felt a brief moment of disquiet.

It wasn't just his fear for her safety, although that was a constant, biting concern. Until he'd captured and killed the bastard trying to harm Sophia he would always be on edge.

No, this was more personal.

But equally worrisome, he realized with a pang of surprise.

It wasn't that he regretted his actions. He'd done what he was commanded. And more importantly, his actions had always been in an effort to protect this woman.

But something warned him that Sophia might not be pleased when she discovered that he hadn't yet been totally honest with her.

Briefly he considered the notion of confessing all. It was, no doubt, the right thing to do. But even as the thought drifted through his mind, Luc was abruptly distracted when her legs wrapped around his hips, her nails biting into his ass in a silent plea for release.

There would be time later, he assured himself, squashing the tiny voice of warning.

Much, much later.

CHAPTER 7

It was late morning when Sophia and Luc crept into Kirsten's home, both shifting into wolf form to make a swift sweep of her lavish lair.

Once it was obvious there was nothing suspicious beyond an obscenely massive collection of Manolo Blahnik shoes that Sophia fully intended to get her greedy hands on, Luc gave her rump a playful nip and they headed back to her house.

Following him up the stairs to her . . . their . . . bedroom, she had an opportunity to admire her wolf.

And he was well worth admiring.

A large beast with massive fangs and dark fur, he was the size of a pony with a broad chest and thickly muscled legs. His eyes glowed with the midnight fire of his wolf, but there was an unmistakable intelligence that was as dangerous as all the strength of his heavy body.

Oh yes, he was fine, fine, fine.

An opinion that was only emphasized as a shimmering light haloed his body as he shifted back to his human form.

He shuddered as his body hovered between wolf and man, the ancient magic pulsing through the air. Then the transformation was over and with a remarkable ability to recover, Luc was rising to his feet, his naked body all chiseled perfection wrapped in smooth bronze silk.

Yummmmmm.

Sophia concentrated on her own shift, relishing the painful

stretch of muscle and popping of bone. There was a primitive satisfaction in calling on her powers.

Not quite as swift as Luc in regaining her balance, Sophia slowly rose to her feet and pulled on the short, silk robe tossed on the bed. Across the room, Luc was already dressed in a pair of khaki shorts and polo shirt that might have made him look civilized if not for the shadow of whiskers already darkening his jaw and the feral glint in his eyes.

"Anything?" he asked, referring to their recent jaunt through the vampire's lair.

"No."

He moved to the full-length mirror attached to the back of the door, smoothing back his hair.

"Which would seem to leave the cur as the last of our suspects."

"Morton?" She snorted. "I can't imagine him as a homicidal maniac."

He turned to discover her eyeing his ass. A smug smile curved his lips.

"Looks are far too often deceiving."

Sophia grimaced, picturing the dull fire hydrant of a cur. "They would have to be excessively deceiving."

He shrugged. "I'll soon find out."

"Assuming he is guilty, I don't know how walking around a golf course whacking at a white ball is going to convince the cur to confess."

Luc crossed to stand directly in front of her. "He doesn't need to confess."

"No?"

He reached to grasp a lock of her hair, smoothing it between his fingers.

"Given enough time alone with him, I'll know if he's guilty."

"Hmmm." She studied the supreme confidence etched on his face. "You're not a mind reader, are you?"

"I have any number of talents, *cara*." His voice lowered to the husky drawl that made her shiver. "Not all of them involve a bed."

"Arrogant dog."

He paused, absently twirling her hair around one finger. "What are your plans for the rest of the day?"

She gave a vague wave of her hand, hoping he truly wasn't a mind reader.

"Oh, you know."

"Know what?"

"This and that."

His eyes narrowed. "Your 'this and that' wouldn't include a visit to Victoria, would it?"

Dammit. How had he known she was plotting something?

"Isn't that what golf widows do?" she demanded. "Keep each other company with a bottle of Chardonnay?"

"No."

She planted her fists on her hips. "Excuse me?"

"It's too dangerous."

Odd. She would have thought their mating would have given him some insight into her aversion to being given orders.

He might as well have waved a red flag before a bull.

"How the hell can it be too dangerous?" she said between clenched teeth. "The cur's going to be golfing with you, not lurking under the sofa."

His expression was hard, as unyielding as granite. "The nymph might be working with him."

"I already told you that she knew nothing about the attempts to kill me."

"She could be lying," he countered. "And even if she isn't responsible, she will do whatever necessary to protect her lover if she realizes we suspect him."

She stepped forward, poking her finger into the center of his chest.

"Let me get this straight," she growled. "You intend to spend the entire afternoon with a cur who might or might not be a bloodthirsty murderer, but I'm not allowed to have a glass of wine with a damned nymph?"

He didn't even flinch at her fierce accusation. "I'm not the one being hunted, Sophia."

Her teeth snapped together at the truth of his words.

She was stubborn, not stupid. And while it aggravated the hell out of her, she had to concede he had a point.

The reason she'd hired a bodyguard hadn't gone away just because she'd fallen in love with the man, had it? The only sensible thing to do was to let him do his job.

Even if the thought of twiddling her thumbs while Luc was searching for her enemy made her want to howl in frustration.

"Dammit." She glared at Luc, in this moment holding him entirely responsible. Hey, what were mates for? "I hate feeling helpless."

"You will never be helpless, *cara*, but just for now you need to take extra care," he murmured, smoothing her hair behind her ear. "Let me protect you."

Like he was giving her a choice?

She heaved a sigh. "Fine."

"Fine what?" he demanded, almost as if he didn't trust her. Imagine that.

"I won't visit the nymph," she clarified.

"You'll stay home?"

"No."

"Sophia."

She met his smoldering gaze with a stubborn frown. She'd agreed to give up her plan to search Morton's house for signs of his guilt, but she'd be damned if she would remain trapped in her house like a damsel in distress.

"I need to go to the club."

"It can survive one day without you."

"Not today," she insisted. "I have payroll checks to sign and a new dancer scheduled for an audition."

He stilled, the scent of his wolf filling the air. The beast didn't like the thought of her being close to another male.

Understandable. She'd slice off his nuts if she thought he was sniffing after another female.

"A new dancer?" he growled.

"Yes." Her slow smile assured him that he was the only man

she wanted. "He's a Were from China who supposedly does things with his nun-chucks that make women melt."

Without warning she was wrapped in possessive arms and hauled against Luc's broad chest.

"When I get back tonight I'll show you my nun-chucks," he promised, planting an openmouthed kiss at the base of her neck. "I bet they're bigger."

A sure bet, she silently acknowledged, wrapping her arms around his neck.

"Just make sure you make it back," she commanded, studying him with open concern.

He might be the biggest, baddest Were on the block, but there was a psychopath out there who had a gun with silver bullets and wasn't afraid to use them.

"I promise." His lips nibbled a path up the curve of her neck, halting just below her ear. "And, Sophia."

She shivered, her body instinctively arching against him. "Yes?"

"We need to talk."

Pulling back she regarded him with a wary frown.

The words were as good as a cold shower.

"Why don't I like the sound of that?"

"I just need you to know. . . ." He bit off his words, his expression impossible to read.

"What?"

There was a pause, as if he was considering his words. Then he gave a short shake of his head.

"Later."

Okay. Her vague unease became downright worry.

"Luc?"

"Sorry." He leaned down to steal a searing kiss that sent bolts of excitement through her before turning to head for the door. "Can't be late for our tee time."

She watched his departure with a jaundiced frown, knowing it would be a waste of time to try and force him to reveal what was troubling him.

He would confess when he was good and ready.

Throwing her hands in the air she headed to her shower. "Men."

The exclusive country club south of town was precisely what Luc had been expecting. A large clubhouse designed in a tudor-style with attached pool, tennis courts, and stables all impeccably maintained.

The surrounding golf course was equally well-manicured. The fairways were narrow with deep sand bunkers and a line of overhanging trees that might have posed a challenge for a human. Luc, however, possessed the strength to simply hit his ball over any obstacles to the distant green, more often than not ending up mere inches from the flag that fluttered in the summer breeze.

By the time they'd reached the back nine, his physical superiority had accomplished precisely what he desired.

Morton had gone from a casual companion to a furious cur who was fuming with a frustration that reddened his round cheeks and made his eyes flash with sparks of crimson as he tried to hold back his wolf.

Unlike pure-blooded Weres, the curs were at the mercy of their beast, and while Luc didn't want the man to shift, he did want him so preoccupied with controlling his temper that his defenses were lowered.

Who knew what he might reveal?

Putting away his club after holing out on a par five, Luc joined his companion in the golf cart, nearly being tumbled out as the cur stomped on the gas pedal.

"Nice shot," Morton gritted.

Luc sprawled back in the seat, smiling with a lazy arrogance custom-designed to infuriate his companion.

"Not bad."

"Not bad?" Morton scowled. "It was a hole in one."

"A little competitive there, champ?"

Looking remarkably like a marshmallow with his square, squishy body covered in a white shirt and matching pants,

Morton gripped the wheel of the golf cart and struggled not to do something stupid.

"My name is Morton, not champ," he snapped, "and when I do something, I like to do it well."

"Don't we all?"

The pale eyes glowed with a crimson fire. "Some more than others."

Luc chuckled, reaching over to slap the man on the back, hard enough to rattle his teeth.

"You know, Morty-boy, if I didn't know better I might think you didn't like me."

The cur clenched his teeth, no doubt counting to ten.

"How long are you planning to stay in Chicago?" he at last demanded.

"Hoping to get rid of me?"

"I would think the suburbs would be a bore."

Luc offered a taunting grin, covertly studying the tension emanating from the cur.

So far all he'd managed to pick up was Morton's natural aversion to an obnoxious companion. Time to up the ante.

"True, but there are benefits," he drawled. "Sophia is smoking hot between the sheets."

The male hissed. "Typical."

"Did you say something?"

Without warning the cur veered the cart off the path and headed into a thick patch of trees. Turning in his seat, he studied Luc with a revulsion he no longer tried to hide.

Luc hid a smile. Action at last.

"Sophia is revered among our people, but of course a man like you would only consider your own pleasures."

Luc paused at the fierce words.

There was an edge of crazy that he'd been looking for, but he didn't sound like a man intent on killing a female.

Of course, there were always those bastards who were willing to murder the object of their fantasy if they couldn't have them.

He slouched against the leather seat, pretending he didn't notice the cur was a breath away from shifting.

"She may be revered, but she needs a good banging like every other woman."

More crimson fire in the eyes. "Animal."

"You seem abnormally interested in my relationship with Sophia," Luc mocked. "Don't you have your own female to worry about?"

Morton belatedly attempted to hide his obsession with his beautiful neighbor.

"I merely believe Sophia deserves a more worthy male."

Luc lifted a brow. "A male like you?"

"I would certainly appreciate her fine qualities." The crimson gaze flicked over Luc with a dismissive annoyance. "Unlike you."

"If you think she's so fine, then why haven't you made your move on her?" Luc deliberately widened his eyes, as if struck by a sudden thought. "Or have you already tried and been shot down?"

"Certainly not."

"No doubt for the best." Luc gave the cur another slap on the back, barely resisting the urge to unleash his claws and rip out his throat. The mere thought that the creep had been secretly lusting after Sophia made his wolf ache for blood. "Just between us, I don't think she would ever be interested. I believe her exact words were that you were 'a sorry excuse for a cur.' "

Morton flinched at the insult, but there was a grim set to his jaw. As if he'd made his decision and nothing was going to sway him.

"That's only because she doesn't know me."

"You think you'll grow on her?" Luc chuckled. "Like fungus?"

"I think she's an intelligent female who can appreciate the needs of duty."

Luc stilled, thrown off guard by the unexpected words. "Duty?"

"Precisely."

All right, enough was enough.

He had no doubt that Morton was the stalker and he intended to get to the truth, one way or another.

He actually preferred the "another" option, since it included a lot of pain and carnage.

"Is it your duty to try and kill her?"

Morton looked like a deer in the headlights for a split second, then meeting Luc's ruthless gaze he seemed to accept that he was busted. With a shrug he allowed his act to drop, a cunning expression settling on his pudgy face.

"Ah, I feared you had guessed the truth."

Luc subtly scooted forward, not wanting to be in the position where he could be pinned against the roll-bar of the cart.

Not that he believed for a moment the cur could physically overpower him. Still, better safe than sorry.

"The only thing I've guessed is that you're responsible for stalking Sophia."

"Not stalking . . ." Morton corrected, "testing."

"What the hell does that mean?"

"Although I've held the greatest respect for Sophia since the birth of her daughters, I needed to be certain that she retained her strength and agility over the years."

A chill inched down Luc's spine. There was something far more disturbing about this calm, almost condescending Morton.

"Why?"

"To bear my children, of course."

Fury pulsed through Luc, his wolf savagely trying to break free of his restraint. It would kill before it allowed another man to steal his mate.

And the man in him was in full agreement.

Ironic he was the one in a rage considering he'd been trying to provoke the cur.

"Are you insane?"

With a smooth motion, Morton reached into the cooler set

on the seat between them and pulled out a small gun loaded with a cartridge.

Luc frowned. A tranq gun? The cur truly was insane if he thought a pure-blooded Were could be put down by a mere tranquilizer.

"Don't ever question my sanity," Morton warned, obviously a little sensitive on the subject of his mental state.

Luc carefully judged the distance between them as he sought to keep the cur distracted.

"If you want her as a breeder then why did you try to kill her?"

Morton regarded him as if he were particularly dense. "I didn't try to kill her. I'll admit that I devised a few obstacles to monitor her physical condition, but I would never permanently harm her."

"Bastard," Luc snarled, furious at the thought of Sophia being systematically terrorized by this psycho. "I know you were the one who shot at her. A silver bullet through the heart would have been very permanent."

"I wasn't shooting at her, you fool." Morton smirked, clearly thinking that his peashooter gave him the upper hand. A mistake that Luc was eager to demonstrate. "I was aiming at you."

Luc frowned, startled by the confession. "Me?"

"I had borrowed Victoria's disguise amulet to follow Sophia to her club when you arrived in Chicago." His expression hardened with disgust. "I knew from the way you were watching her that you were going to interfere with my plans."

"What plans?"

"To capture Sophia and impregnate her with my litter."

Any coherent thought was lost as a red mist descended over him, his beast beyond the point of no return.

"No way in hell," he growled, his words nearly unintelligible.

Looking almost bored as Luc began to shift, Morton pointed the gun at the center of his chest.

"I just knew you were going to be trouble."

Distantly Luc heard the pop of the gun and felt the dart plunge into his flesh, but, lost in his transformation, it was too late when he realized his muscles were slowly being paralyzed as the unknown substance began to flow through his blood.

Regarding the smug cur in horror, he realized he should have paid far more attention to his own warnings.

Looks truly were deceiving. . . .

CHAPTER 8

Sophia was running late.

After reviewing the payroll and dealing with the linen service that had forgotten to bring their laundered tablecloths and napkins, she had been forced to soothe one of the waiters who had been insulted by the bartender and locate the key to the back freezer that had been lost.

At last she was able to settle in a chair to audition the Were who had traveled thousands of miles just to perform at her club.

Unfortunately, she struggled to concentrate.

It wasn't that Jian wasn't spectacular. He nearly set the stage on fire with his lean, muscular body that moved with a fluid grace that was amazing even by Were standards.

But tapping a finger on the arm of her chair, she realized she felt . . . weird, unsettled.

She told herself that she was merely impatient to return home to Luc. He was bound to be finished with his golf match by now and waiting for her return.

Hopefully naked in her bed.

What woman wouldn't be anxious to be done with work?

Counting down the minutes until she could politely bring the audition to a close, Sophia was startled when she caught a familiar scent.

Turning her head, she watched the crimson-haired imp dressed in a silver mesh shirt and black spandex cross the room to take the chair beside her, setting a leather briefcase at his feet.

"Mmm," he moaned, his gaze drinking in the sight of the near-naked Were dancing on the stage. "Tasty."

"Troy." Sophia gave a lift of her brows. "Don't you have your own business to run?"

"Yes, but the view isn't nearly so nice."

She reached to grab his chin, turning his fascinated attention in her direction.

"If you want to ogle the talent, you're supposed to pay a cover charge."

He pouted. "Is that any way to treat your bestest friend?"

"The last time I came to your coffee shop you charged me an arm and a leg for a cappuccino the size of a thimble," she reminded him in dry tones.

"But I sprinkled it with my special fairy dust."

"Special fairy dust, my ass," she scoffed. "It was cinnamon."

A smile twitched at the edges of his mouth. "Maybe."

"I assume you have a reason for being here beyond trying to sneak a peek?"

The smile faded, leaving the handsome face unexpectedly somber.

"I think we should talk."

"Uh-oh." Sophia frowned. "I seem to be getting that a lot lately."

"A lot of what?"

"Nothing." Trying to shrug off her persistent unease and the sudden certainty she wasn't going to like what Troy had to say, Sophia rose to her feet. "Let's go to my office."

With a thumbs-up toward Jian, she led the towering imp into her office, closing the door behind them.

Troy strolled to inspect her enviable collection of Fabergé eggs.

"Nice."

Sophia moved to the wet bar behind her desk. "Something to drink? Water? Brandy?" She pointed toward the sleek silver cappuccino machine. "A ten-dollar cappuccino with fairy dust?"

"No need." Troy took the seat opposite her desk, opening his leather briefcase to pull out a small flask. "I always carry my own."

"You came prepared," she murmured, noting the stack of manila folders in the case. "Should I be worried?"

He took a swig from the flask. "I'm not sure."

Shit.

She sat in the chair behind her desk, her heart lodged in her throat.

"Troy?"

He replaced the flask, regarding her with a guarded gaze. "When you asked me to find you a bodyguard I went through my usual contacts to locate one."

"Is that a problem?"

"Not usually."

She tucked her hands beneath the desk, unwilling to let the imp see her clenching them.

"What's different this time?"

The imp paused, as if considering the wisdom of confessing whatever it was that had brought him to the club. Sophia forced herself to keep her mouth shut.

What not? If he tried to leave she was quite prepared to beat the truth out of him.

At last he squared his shoulders and took the plunge. "After it was obvious that you were enjoying more than just Luc's professional services, I decided to double-check the background information I was given."

"And?"

"And it's bogus."

A cold ball of dread lodged in the pit of her stomach. "What's bogus?"

"Everything."

"Be a little more specific, Troy."

He reached into his briefcase, pulling out the top file and tossed it onto her desk.

"The references he listed on his résumé," he said. "His address. His social security number. None of it's real."

Squashing the urge to toss the folder across the room, Sophia instead lifted her hand and flipped it open, scanning the documents inside.

"He lied," she said at last.

"Yes."

With a jerky motion, Sophia was on her feet, crossing to stare out the newly replaced window.

What the hell?

The documents that Troy had produced clearly revealed that the Miami addresses were fake, along with Luc's supposed references.

But why?

It wasn't as if she was freaking Katy Perry. Becoming her bodyguard wasn't some fantastic position that a man would lie to acquire.

"I'm sorry," Troy murmured softly.

"Not nearly as sorry as I am," she muttered, wrapping her arms around her waist. Why did she suddenly feel so cold? "What's that saying, 'There's no fool like an old fool'?"

She heard the imp cross to stand directly behind her, his hands landing lightly on her shoulders.

"You aren't a fool, Sophia," he assured her. "Luc managed to deceive us all."

"Yeah, but you're not sleeping with him."

"Only because he didn't ask."

Sophia started to smile when she was abruptly struck by a thought that made her heart clench in agony.

"Holy shit."

Giving her shoulders a tug, Troy turned her to meet his searching gaze.

"What?"

"He could be working with the maniac who has been stalking me," she breathed. "Hell, he could *be* the stalker."

Troy gave a firm shake of his head. "No, he's not the stalker. That's one thing I'm absolutely certain of."

So was she.

Her lips thinned as the thought whispered through the back of her mind.

She had proof that he had lied to her from the beginning of their relationship. Why did she find it impossible to accept he would ever do anything to hurt her?

"How can you know?"

With a grimace he moved back to the briefcase he'd left on her desk, pulling out yet another folder.

"Because he's one of Salvatore's most trusted lieutenants," he said, pressing the file into her hands. "Here."

She leaned against the window, her head dizzy as she tried to process yet another shock.

Damn the King of Weres.

She had known when Salvatore capitulated so easily to her refusal to join them in Styx's lair that he was up to something. Something devious.

He was a Were who always believed he knew best.

So the fact that he had somehow managed to discover she was seeking a bodyguard and had planted his own trusted soldier into her house to keep an eye on her wasn't at all a surprise.

But that didn't make Luc's deception any easier to bear.

He might not be her stalker, but he'd used her desire and all too vulnerable emotions to make sure he could remain close to her and fulfill his duty to his king.

The . . . jackass.

Her gaze dropped to the folder she was clutching in her hand. "What's this?"

"The information my private investigator managed to dig up. At considerable expense, I might add." Troy shook his head. "The man buried his identity deeper than Jimmy Hoffa."

"You have a private investigator?" she absently demanded, flicking through the various pages.

She paused to take in the photos of the large stucco mansion surrounded by palm trees that was Luc's true home and an unmistakable picture of Luc and Salvatore meeting in a park several miles west of Chicago.

Another shaft of pain sliced through her heart.

"It's a dangerous world these days," Troy explained. "You can't trust anyone."

"No shit." She threw the folder across the room, watching the papers fan across her carpet.

Troy nervously cleared his throat. "Are you going to be okay?"

Was she?

At the moment she wasn't entirely certain.

The pain and disappointment clawing through her felt lethal.

Then realizing that the imp was watching her with a sympathy she couldn't stomach, she gave a toss of her hair.

"I'm Sophia," she announced, her head held high. "No man's going to get me down. Even if he is a lying, mangy piece of shit."

Troy gave a snap of his fingers, a smile curving his lips. "You go, girl."

"Now, if you'll excuse me."

Sophia headed for the door, her need to find Luc an overwhelming compulsion.

"Uh, Sophia," Troy called out.

She glanced over her shoulder. "Yes?"

"If you decide to kill Luc you need to make sure you hide the body," he warned. "I doubt that your son-in-law would be happy to learn you offed his most trusted soldier."

A humorless smile curved her lips. "Actually I was thinking I could use a new fur rug in front of my fireplace."

Troy's eyes widened. "Yikes."

Leaving the office, Sophia headed out of the club, her fierce glare keeping the milling employees at bay.

She wasn't in the mood to deal with clogged drains and missing G-strings.

In fact, the only thing she was in the mood for was blood and mayhem.

Storming out a side door, she was halfway across the parking lot when she heard a faint click. She slowed her furious pace at the same minute she felt a prick in her upper chest. Looking down she realized there was a small dart sticking from her skin.

What the . . . ?

That was as far as her confused mind managed to get before

her muscles became paralyzed and she was tumbling toward the paved ground. Then her head was smacking face-first into the pavement and the entire world exploded into black.

Waking, Sophia cautiously held herself still as she took stock.

She hadn't gone to the great kennels in the sky, thank the gods.

She had a throbbing head, and she could feel an odd metal collar strapped around her neck, but the rest of her seemed to be back in working order.

Cautiously she allowed her senses to spread further.

She was in a basement, she realized with a stab of surprise. Or at least underground.

And night had fallen while she had been conked out.

Oh, and the stench of cur was thick in the air.

The same scent she'd caught mere seconds before she'd been shot by the dart.

A growl trickled from her throat as she wrenched open her eyes to discover Morton leaning over her, his face the nasty color of paste in the fluorescent light.

"You." She surged to a sitting position, barely noticing the narrow cot beneath her as Morton hastily backed away. "Bastard."

With a visible effort the cur halted his retreat, gathering his shaken courage as he sent her a chiding glare.

"Now, Sophia, I must insist that the mother of my children not use such foul language," he informed her. "It's indecent."

Still weak from whatever poison he'd pumped into her system, Sophia swayed on the edge of the cot, wondering which of them had lost their minds.

She was betting on the cur.

"Mother?" She shook her head, trying to clear the cobwebs. "Are you mental?"

Pinpricks of crimson flashed through the pale eyes. "Don't push me."

Oh, pushing him was going to be the last of the little prick's concern once she got her strength back, she assured herself, glancing around the six-by-six-foot cell that was paneled with sheets of silver.

"Where are we?"

"My private lair beneath Victoria's house." He regained command of his composure, one hand smoothing down his white polo shirt. His other hand held a small device that Sophia suspected was some sort of weapon. "Don't worry, she knows better than to come down here. We won't be interrupted."

Her lip curled in scorn. "Does she suspect that you're a psychopath?"

She had barely finished her taunt when Morton pressed a button on the device and the collar around her neck began to sizzle. The next thing she knew a massive jolt of electricity speared through her body, nearly toppling her off the cot onto the cement floor.

"Shit," she breathed.

"I did warn you."

She clenched her teeth, imagining the pleasure of gutting the pasty-faced cur over and over and over. . . .

"What do you want with me?"

"I told you," he scolded. "I've chosen you to be the mother of my children."

"No doubt in your demented mind you think I should be honored by the offer, but I'm afraid I'll have to take a pass." Her stomach heaved at the mere thought. "Thanks, but no thanks."

Even prepared for the bolt of electricity, Sophia couldn't halt her yip of pain, her legs trembling and sweat coating her skin.

"You will learn," Morton growled.

Her hand weakly lifted toward the metal wrapped around her neck.

"Christ, where the hell did you get this thing?"

"I invented it myself," the cur preened, as if expecting Sophia to admire his handiwork. "Just as I invented the serum that knocked you out. I'm a scientist."

"So was Dr. Frankenstein," she muttered. "You know how that turned out."

Zap.

She leaned down until her forehead touched her knees, fighting against the urge to vomit.

"You will learn to respect me," Morton abruptly shouted, clearly unhinged by her refusal to play the game by his rules.

Not surprising.

Morton-the-cur was a born victim who had no doubt been bullied and mocked by others his entire life.

"Why?" she demanded. "Because you can create torture devices?"

"That's merely my hobby." His smile was edged with a smug pride. "My true genius is chemistry. Which is why Caine hired me."

Her eyes widened in surprise.

Caine was currently missing along with her daughter Cassandra.

At one time he'd been under the sway of a demon lord who'd convinced him that he was destined to change curs into pure-blooded Weres.

A part of the prophecy had come true when the same demon lord had taken a path directly through Caine on his way back to hell, transforming him from a cur into a Were.

"You worked with Caine?"

The cur shrugged. "Yes, although we disagreed on how to accomplish our goal to turn curs into pure-blooded Weres."

"And how did you hope to accomplish such a miracle?"

She expected him to refuse to answer. Weren't mad scientists usually secretive about their strange experiments?

Instead he answered without hesitation.

"In the same way your king did."

"I beg your pardon?"

"I intend to alter the DNA of our children while they are still in your womb."

"You . . ."

Words failed her, her mind refusing to return to those long days in Salvatore's clinic. She'd been a willing participant and it had still been near unbearable. With an effort she squashed the rising panic. She would die before she allowed this freak to impregnate her. First, however, she would try to reason with him.

"Even supposing that you do manage to change our children into Weres, how does that help the other curs?" she asked.

His eyes lit with the gleam of a true fanatic. "I can use their blood to help create a vaccine that will transform all of us."

She shook her head, not about to try and point out to Dr. Evil that the magic that created a pure-blooded Were couldn't be found in a test tube. It was always futile to argue with a true believer.

"Why me?" she instead asked.

"You've already proven yourself to be a fertile breeder."

She rolled her eyes. "Gee, thanks."

He seemed caught off guard by her response. "I mean that with the greatest respect."

Said the psycho to his electrified prisoner.

"And?" she prompted, knowing there had to be more.

"And when you moved into the neighborhood I realized that fate had at last smiled upon me," he admitted. "Why else would you be here if not to fulfill my destiny?"

Great. Of all the neighborhoods she could have chosen, she had to pick the one with Morton-the-crazy-ass-cur.

"Have you considered the fact that I might not be willing to become your lab rat?"

"I'll admit that it's been a concern," he said. "I hated the thought of holding you prisoner down here for months, perhaps even years. I'm not a monster, after all."

She choked back a laugh at his seeming sincerity. "You could have fooled me."

He ignored her response, moving toward the small stool in the corner of the barren cell to pick up a heavy leather glove.

"Then a solution literally dropped in my lap."

Sophia's wolf was on full alert although the serum still pumping through her bloodstream refused to allow her to shift.

"What solution?"

Using his gloved hand, the cur reached for the small handle on the wall, pulling back the silver panel to reveal that the cell was divided in two.

Sophia hissed in sudden horror as she caught sight of the dark Were lying unconscious on the floor, a silver collar around his neck that was attached to the heavy chain bolted to the wall.

Luc.

Stupidly she'd assumed that he was waiting for her at her home. Perhaps even now wondering why she was so late.

For a moment panic threatened to consume her.

He might be a deceitful bastard who had broken her heart, but the thought that he might be dead was enough to send a crippling agony through her.

Then through her pain, she detected the unmistakable beat of his heart.

Oh . . . thank the gods.

He was alive.

She turned her head to stab the cur with a fierce glare. "What have you done to him?"

"I gave him the same drug I used on you, although in a considerably larger dose." He gave a dismissive wave of his hand. "He'll eventually wake up."

Sophia sensed the sudden increase in Luc's heartbeat.

He was awake, she abruptly realized, but feigning unconsciousness. A task made possible by Morton's inferior senses.

She smoothed her expression, inwardly gathering her strength. Although she was still weak, she knew she would have to strike swiftly. The amount of silver in the room would drain what little power she had remaining in a matter of hours.

"What's the point of holding him prisoner?" she demanded. "I'm fairly certain he can't carry your litter."

"My first thought was to kill him," he admitted, his voice revealing his deep regret in being denied the pleasure. "Not only because I knew that he'd be a threat to my plans, but because he's a genuine pain in the ass." He heaved a sigh. "Then I realized he could be my assurance for your good behavior."

Shit.

With an effort, she forced herself to pretend confusion as she shakily rose to her feet. She needed to distract him just long enough to get that damned device out of his hand.

"I don't know what you mean."

"I'm not blind." His lips thinned in revulsion. "I saw how you watched him during your party."

"He's gorgeous." She shrugged. "How could I not watch him?"

"You care for him," he insisted, the crimson flickering in his eyes. "Which means you'll do whatever I ask to make sure he eventually gets out of this basement alive."

"You're right." She gave a wave of her hand to distract from her covert step forward.

He sniffed. "Of course I am."

"You're right that I *did* care for him." Another wave, another step. "Past tense."

"I don't believe you."

"Then call Troy."

He frowned. "The imp?"

"Yep." She turned to glare at the unmoving Were, not having to feign her simmering anger. "Right before you went all *Man vs. Wild* on me in the parking lot, he revealed that Luc had lied to me."

Watching him with an eagle eye, she easily caught the faint twitch of his ears.

Guilty conscience?

Or annoyance at having been busted?

"What was the lie?" Morton wanted to know.

She pointed a finger toward Luc, again taking a step forward. Just a few more feet and she would be close enough to knock his ass to the ground.

She didn't have a plan after that, but she was willing to play it by ear.

"He's not a bodyguard like he told me," she revealed. "He's a right-hand man to Salvatore and he was sent to Chicago to spy on me."

Morton scowled, obviously reluctant to believe her. Her outrage at Luc's betrayal did, after all, ruin his diabolical plans. But even a stupid cur could sense the sincerity of her angry words.

"Why would the king wish to spy on you?"

"He obviously believes I'm too stupid to make my own decisions," she snapped. "An opinion shared by that Were lying on the floor." She moved toward the cur, keeping her steps slow and unsteady, as if she was having trouble with her balance. "So if you hope to use him as a bargaining chip then you're shit out of luck, because as far as I'm concerned you can dig his grave and toss him in."

"No." Morton pressed his gloved hand to his forehead. "You're trying to confuse me."

"What's confusing?" With another step she was able to reach out and grab his white polo shirt, giving him a small shake. "Where's your gun? I'll shoot him myself."

"Stop. . . ." He regarded her in puzzlement, unaware of his danger. "Don't do this. . . ."

Knowing she'd only have one shot at escape, Sophia pulled back her arm and smashed her fist into his face with enough force to make him fly across the cell and smack into the far wall.

If she'd been at full strength, the bastard would have been dead.

As it was, he was only knocked loopy.

With her heart lodged in her throat, Sophia darted toward Luc, who was on his feet, regarding her with a burning black gaze.

She didn't need to be able to read his mind to know he was furious she was trying to rescue him rather than escaping.

Ignoring the massive fangs he bared as she knelt beside him, she clamped her hands around the silver collar. The silver seared into her skin, burning away the flesh, but there was no time to search for a key.

Already she could feel Morton stirring.

Luc growled, using his large head to try and push her away, but she held on. She could feel the silver stretching and weakening beneath her powerful tugs. Just a few more seconds and she'd be able to snap it in half.

The prickle on her neck was the only warning before a bolt of electricity shot through her body. She screamed, her back bowing beneath the impact, but grimly ignoring the brutal pain she continued to pull at the collar.

Distantly she was aware of Luc's furious growls and yet more lightning dancing down her spine. Christ. She was about to black out.

Again.

Out of time, Sophia gave one more massive tug, not certain if she actually felt the collar snap beneath her grip, but there was no mistaking the sensation of Luc's massive body brushing past her as he launched himself forward or the shrill screams of Morton.

Death screams.

CHAPTER 9

Once again Sophia was struggling out of a blanket of darkness.

This time it took only moments to realize she was lying on her own bed wearing a clean camisole and silk shorts. And that she wasn't alone.

Luc filled the room with his presence.

The rich, male scent. The restless power of his wolf.

And above all, the prickling awareness that set her blood on fire.

For a crazed moment she felt an overwhelming surge of relief at the knowledge that they had both survived the basement from hell and that they were seemingly safe from Morton the crazy-ass cur.

Then she abruptly remembered that Luc was a total creep who'd played her for a fool.

And that she wanted to kick him in the nuts, not shiver in pleasure as he settled on the mattress beside her reclined body and gently tucked a curl behind her ear.

"Sophia?" he murmured softly. "I know you're awake."

She kept her eyes squeezed shut. Maturity was highly overrated.

"Go away."

"No."

She heaved an aggravated sigh. "I hate you."

He trailed his fingers down the stubborn line of her jaw. "Sophia, open your eyes."

"Will you go away if I do?"

"No."

"What if I get a gun and shoot you?"

He chuckled, his fingers shifting to outline the curve of her lower lip.

"You won't shoot me."

Her eyes snapped open. How else could she glare into his handsome face?

Unfortunately, she also managed to catch a glimpse of his broad shoulders and the chiseled muscles of his chest that were perfectly outlined by his tight black T-shirt.

Dear gods, but he was gorgeous.

Edible.

Treacherous, unwelcome heat curled through the pit of her stomach.

"Why won't I?" she asked between clenched teeth.

A smile teased at his lips, but the dark eyes remained watchful. Wary.

"Because you love me."

She stiffened at the accusation. "Arrogant ass."

"Maybe, but I'm *your* arrogant ass."

With a curse, Sophia scooted until she was leaning against the pile of pillows at the head of the bed, pleased to discover that her wounds were completely healed.

She could feel Luc's gaze skim down her half-naked body with a tangible hunger, but she resisted the urge to crawl beneath the covers.

She wasn't going to give him the satisfaction of knowing he could still disturb her.

"Do you really think that I'm going to forgive and forget that you came to me under false pretenses?" she rasped. "That you climbed into my bed with lies? And that even after we . . ."

"We what?" he prompted as her words broke off.

"Supposedly mated."

His jaw clenched, his power thickening the air. "There's no 'supposed' about it, Sophia. We are most definitely mated."

She ignored his interruption, despite the voice in the back of her mind that warned he was right.

Mating wasn't marriage. It couldn't be ended by a couple of lawyers and a restraining order.

At the moment she wasn't in any mood to admit they were still bonded.

"Even then you continued to deceive me."

Something flared through the dark eyes. "I know."

She blinked. "That's it? That's all you have to say for yourself?" She lowered her voice, mimicking his less-than-impressive explanation. " '*I know.*' "

"I was scared," he clarified.

Her brows snapped together. "If you're trying to be funny . . ."

"I'm not."

"Mr. Neanderthal was scared?" She allowed her gaze to trail down the hard, toned perfection of his body. "Of what?"

"I didn't know at the time." He studied her with blatant regret. "I only knew that whenever I told myself I had to confess the truth, I found some reason to put off the inevitable."

Her heart gave a renegade flutter. "And now?"

"Now I know that I was terrified that when you learned the truth you would never be able to forgive me. If I lost you . . ." He abruptly reached to grasp her hand in a near painful grip, a haunting fear briefly flaring through his eyes. "I wouldn't be able to survive."

A portion of her fury faded. There was no doubting the sincerity of his words.

She could *feel* the fierce emotions that pulsed through his body. They echoed in her own heart.

"What exactly is the truth?" she asked, her voice thick.

"I think you know most of it." His thumb caressed her inner wrist, the light caress sending jolts of pleasure shooting through her. "I was contacted by Salvatore two weeks ago. He said that his mother-in-law was in danger, but that she was too stubborn to accept his help." He grimaced. "To be honest, I wasn't happy about his request. I'm a soldier, not a babysitter."

Her eyes narrowed. "And I'm not an aging, feebleminded female who needs her hand held by a big, bad male," she snapped.

"Aging?" He seemed baffled by her outrage. "You're an exquisite female who is just reaching her prime."

A secret part of her preened at his words—she was, after all, about to become a grandmother, she had every right to be sensitive. But she was still angered by the thought she'd been treated as if she was incapable of making her own decisions.

"And feebleminded?" she pressed.

Frustration tightened his expression. "Of course you aren't feebleminded. Hell, you're clever enough to ensure my life is going to be a constant battle to keep up with you. But I won't apologize for trying to keep you safe, *cara*," he rasped. "It's what I was born to do."

Okay.

That was exactly the right thing to say, she wryly acknowledged.

Not that she was ready to concede defeat. There were still a few bones to pick.

"If Salvatore realized I was searching for a bodyguard, why did he send you?" One day she would discover exactly how her son-in-law had known she was in danger and that she was looking for a hired thug. "It was obvious I was taking steps to protect myself."

"Because I'm the best."

She snorted. "Even if you do say so yourself?"

His dark gaze never wavered. "It's not a boast, Sophia, it's the simple truth."

She believed him.

There was a vast difference between arrogance and confidence.

But she didn't accept that it was just his talent in providing security that had prompted Salvatore to choose him.

"And because you would report to him?"

"Yes," he admitted without hesitation. "Your daughters were anxious to know you were safe." Abruptly his grip on her hand tightened, his wolf glowing in his eyes. "Of course, in the end I failed you."

Sophia sucked in a sharp breath as she felt the guilt that was festering deep inside Luc.

Christ, she'd never thought he would be blaming himself for her being kidnapped by Morton. The cur was raving mad. Who could possibly have predicted what he would do?

She leaned forward to frame his face in her hands, glaring into his wounded eyes.

"Don't say that."

"It's true. *Mierda*." He shuddered, his hands lifting to lightly grasp her wrists. As if he needed to reassure himself that she was alive and unharmed. "I was so worried you would be lured into a trap and I walked straight into one. And then, when Morton was torturing you with that damned collar . . ."

Without thought she leaned forward to halt his pained words with a fierce kiss. She couldn't bear for him to be burdened with regret when he'd done everything possible to keep her safe. But as soon as their mouths connected, the gesture of comfort combusted into something far more intense.

Dangerous.

Hurriedly she jerked back, licking her tingling lips.

"I'm assuming he's dead?"

His brooding gaze remained locked on her mouth. "Yes."

"Good."

There was a short silence as they both savored the thought of Morton dead.

Sophia hoped the bastard was rotting in hell.

At last, Luc slowly smiled. "Of course, there was one good thing about being locked in that basement."

A good thing?

She scowled. "Did you take a blow to the head? That place was a nightmare."

"You risked your life to rescue me," he pointed out softly. "You wouldn't have done that if you didn't still love me."

"I was too weakened to shift," she lamely tried to argue. "I knew I would need you to kill Morton and get us out of there."

"Liar."

"Luc . . ."

Tugging on her wrists, which he still held in a loose grip, he kissed her with an aching tenderness.

"I'm sorry, *cara*," he whispered against her mouth. "I regret ever deceiving you, and if I could go back in time I would change everything. But all we can do is go forward."

She pulled back to study his somber expression. Deep inside she knew that he hadn't meant to hurt her. At least not intentionally.

He'd come to Chicago as a soldier obeying orders. And like her he'd been knocked off guard by the power of their mating.

Could she truly blame him for being reluctant to confess the truth?

Not that she didn't intend to keep his blunder as ammunition to pull out whenever she screwed up. It was almost like having a Get Out of Jail Free card, she decided.

"You swear never to lie to me again?"

She could feel the tension drain from him at her question, a small smile curving his lips.

"I swear I will never ever give you a reason to regret trusting in me," he hedged, knowing better than to make a promise he could never keep.

A Were who could be trained.

A good sign.

"And you won't interfere when I kick Salvatore's furry ass?"

"He is my king, but you . . ." The dark gaze seared over her face, his steadfast love burning like a beacon. "You are my mate."

"Smart Were," she whispered, a delicious warmth spilling through her as she wrapped her arms around his neck. "Maybe you should remind me why that's a good thing."

"With pleasure." He pressed her back against the pillows, his lips tracing a path of erotic fire down the curve of her neck. "For both of us."`

MURDER ON MYSTERIA LANE

ANGIE FOX

CHAPTER 1

Last time I got stuck in a graveyard after dark, I missed the final episode of *Lost*. This time, an immense werewolf leveled a shotgun at my nose.

I could smell the sharp tang of gun oil in the dry desert air.

"Heather McPhee"—he cocked his weapon—"I order you to halt!"

"You and what army?" I came up short, less than an inch from the double barrel. You really could poke an eye out with that thing. My gray cargo pants clanked with handcuffs, a stun gun, mace, two fixed-blade daggers, and of course my lucky boot knife.

A desert wind blew in from the west, pelting the aged tombstones with rocks and debris. Two more werewolves emerged from the darkness. They took positions on either side of the scraggily, bad-breathed Goliath.

Great, just great.

"What's the password?" he growled.

Like I knew. "Out of my way you, hairy oaf." I started to move around him until his hand closed around my arm in a vise grip. "Ow!"

"Don't play with me, girl. I'm not afraid of your kind."

Too bad everybody else was.

"Listen, brainiac," I said, fighting the urge to stomp his foot, "I'm here on the Alpha's orders, so unless you want to take it up with Finnegan—"

The guard growled low in his throat, his face a mix of shadows. "Finnegan should have told you—"

"Well, he didn't." Not that he wouldn't be on my shit list for that. But to be fair, the guy had a pack to run. And an emergency it seemed.

I craned my neck around the wall of weres to see if I could catch anybody peeking out from the crypt.

There was no little stone house-like structure or stone angels to guard it. The Topanga Pack buried their alphas bunker-style. The shadow of the hole gaped low and menacing in the canyon bedrock. Thirty stone steps surrounded by sandstone walls ended in a solid oak door.

Lovely. No help in sight. Whoever was there to meet me was already inside—waiting.

"He's not answering his phone," barked the bodyguard to my right.

"I'm thinking he might be busy," I snapped. I would be, too, if I could get past these clowns.

The top dog didn't just open up the Crypt of the Alphas for his health, or an all-night kegger. It was unsealed maybe once or twice a year for matters of pack justice. I was his only interrogator, a position I rather liked. So when Finnegan ordered me to get my ass down there, I'd bailed on my dinner date with a bucket of KFC's original recipe and made a beeline for my boss.

Until I'd run smack-dab into a boulder.

"You know I'm not a threat," I said. For heaven's sake, it's not like the overgrown Chewbacca and I weren't on a first-name basis. We'd played together as kids—Mary Poppins to be exact. And I wasn't the one dressing up as the flying babysitter.

Just because he'd avoided me for the past twenty years didn't mean I'd forgotten. The bodyguard had other secrets, too. Everyone did. That's why my bugged-out powers came in so handy.

I'd been born with the Truth gene, an obnoxiously rare and recessive trait that showed up about once every seven hundred years. Lucky me. I could ask a question and literally make a person tell the truth.

Within limits. But I wasn't about to start broadcasting that little tidbit.

"Want me to start asking *you* questions?" I asked.

"Can it, McPhee," he said with a snarl, casting a glance at the wolves on either side of him. His eyes had widened a touch. I recognized the fear.

Good.

I reached into my back pocket for a rubber band and proceeded to pull my long red hair into a ponytail. Lucky for him I wouldn't be unleashing my powers in the middle of the Wolf's Lair flats. First off, it would be downright mean, even if my old buddy was being an ass. Second, using my powers gave me a massive hangover.

This joker wasn't worth it.

"What's it going to be, meathead?"

He scowled.

"I can stand here until Finnegan comes out looking for me. No sweat off my back. Though it may mean the skin off yours."

He growled low in his throat as I started whistling the *Jeopardy* theme song.

"I don't have time for this bullshit," he grumbled, standing aside.

"Thank you."

I nudged him with my elbow as I brushed past.

He growled low in his throat. "Freak."

Oh goody. Things were back to normal.

I descended the thick stone stairs into the darkness of the tomb. I might not win Miss Popular 2011, but my pack was stronger because of me.

Frankly, I'd rather be needed than accepted.

The coarse walls were broken every so often by burial carvings and caked with canyon dust.

"Where were you?" Finnegan's voice boomed before I'd even reached the bottom of the stairs. "Never mind," he added. "Just get your ass down here."

It was cooler underground, the air stale. I could smell the

pack leader's agitation even before I came upon him pacing in the center of a small, circular room.

A turquoise and orange pack crest spread across the ceiling. In the flickering light, I could read the inscription: *Riamh daingnithe i gcúinne.*

Never backed into a corner.

Damned straight.

It didn't look like our pack leader was doing so hot tonight. Finnegan jammed his hands into his copious red hair. His bulbous nose had gone red and his beard twisted sideways where he'd been yanking on it.

Behind him, a shirtless human sat lashed to a wooden chair etched with runes and death spells.

"We need you to question this . . . gardener," the Alpha said, as if he wasn't quite sure what a gardener even did. "He's from Eternal Life Estates."

I wrinkled my nose. "In Vampire County?"

The humans called it Malibu.

It was where trophy wives went to die.

Or not die . . . as the case may be.

Finnegan gave a tight smile. "I'll remind you of my littermate who moved to Eternal Life Estates."

I nodded. Sunshine McCarty, the bleached blonde, boob-enhanced darling of the pack. Growing up, she liked to tease me by pretending I was a boy.

As far as insults went, it was pathetic.

Let her yank out her eyebrows and wobble around on stiletto heels that, let's face it, would make it impossible to knee anyone in the balls. I liked to keep my options open.

I studied the olive-skinned gardener. I didn't get why any were—or this human for that matter—would move in with the vampires. Sure, it beat Botox. Once you married a vampire, you stopped aging. Trophy wives for centuries.

Ridiculous.

I blew a few strands of hair out of my mouth. No matter what I did, my hair always ended up in my face. "What do you want to know?"

Finnegan folded his arms over his chest. "Sunshine was killed three nights ago."

I shook my head, not sure what to say. Comforting words weren't exactly in my nature. Not that the Alpha would want to hear them anyway.

He gave me a long look, the candles flickering shadows over his burly features. "She was murdered."

Now that surprised me. If Sunshine had been willing to chip a nail, she could have gone up against any were. Unless she'd come face-to-fang with her vampire husband.

"How did it happen?" I asked.

"Crushed to death."

Ouch.

Finnegan tugged on his beard. "We've kept it out of the papers. The pack won't know until we get justice." He stood behind the visibly shaking man. "It happened yesterday afternoon."

That ruled out a vampire, at least directly.

"This is our witness," Finnegan continued. "His name is Marcos."

I studied the man, glad to be back in familiar territory. "Let me guess. He's not talking." We'd change that.

Poor sap.

I tilted my head, my boots grinding grave dirt into the stones as I approached. "What did you see, friend?"

The man shook his head, a thin sheen of sweat slicking his forehead. "N-nothing. I was trimming the hedges."

"Her hedges?"

"The hedges! I heard a loud noise. I ran. Upstairs." His eyes darted away. "That's where I found her." His lower lip trembled. "Under her bathroom chandelier."

I resisted the urge to ponder the idea of a chandelier in the bathroom. I swallowed hard, locking eyes with the man in the chair as I unleashed a magnetic power from low in my chest. "What did you hear?" I felt the buzzing in my head, the dry tightness in the back of my throat. Marcos and I were connected, as if by a thin wire.

"A woman's voice," he said, clearly surprised to hear the words come out of his mouth. "I could barely understand her. She said that Sunny deserved what she got. And then she got even angrier. She said, 'and I hate your lawn.' "

Finnegan rushed to the bound man's side. "Who was it? Did you see her?"

My mind reeled as if he'd smacked me upside the head.

"Finnegan." I cringed. He knew better.

He halted, but he didn't apologize. Being an Alpha meant never saying you were sorry.

Head clanging, I asked the question. "Did you see who was in the bathroom?"

"No." He winced. "I was tied to the bed."

"Of course you were," I said, throwing up a warning finger at my leader. If he jarred my mind again, I was going to lose our witness. And because Finnegan knew the stakes, I got away with it.

I turned back to the gardener. "How often did you have sex with the victim?"

"Mondays, Wednesdays, and Fridays. Whenever I worked."

"Son of a bitch!" Finnegan swore behind me.

"Did her husband find out about your sex-capades?" I asked.

Vampires tended to be intensely sexual, and not particularly good at sharing. Then again, if the husband knew, he probably would have just eaten poor Marcos.

The gardener trembled, his eyes wild. "Her husband was too busy with his own mistress."

"Who was?" I prodded deeper.

He was sweating heavily. "Sunny wasn't sure," he said on an exhale. "She only knew it was one of the other Predators."

My head was pounding now, but I had to hold on. "Who are the Predators?

"Five shifters." He caught himself. "Well, now there are four: Francine, Nina, Bliss and their whipping girl, Tia."

"Gotcha." I glanced up at Finnegan. "We'll start there."

My vision swam and I felt my hold loosening. I broke our contact. "I'm done."

My record was five minutes. This? Well, this was the best I could do tonight. My head throbbed. It would only get worse. Tapping minds gave me a hangover like I'd downed a fifth of SoCo. Not that I'd ever voluntarily do that to myself.

"Nice work."

Shaking, I folded my hands behind my back and lowered my chin to the Alpha.

"Very nice indeed," said a man's voice, smooth as glass.

I whipped a dagger out of the back of my pants as a vampire emerged from the shadows behind me.

Panic shot through me. Why hadn't I smelled him? Why hadn't I seen him? My blood ran hot.

Finnegan must have blocked him from me. I didn't understand.

He was taller than I would have liked. Leaner. His shoulders were wide, his stance confident. This one was going to be a bitch to take down.

Finnegan raised his hand. "Hold back, McPhee."

"He's a vampire." I might be able to get hold of him by the hair. It was clipped short and blond.

"McPhee—" Finnegan's tone was a direct order. "This is Lucien Mead. My guest." He put an emphasis on that last word.

The vampire bowed at my pack leader's introduction. A hint of a grin gave him an almost boyish charm. A swirl of desire wound through me. Leftover adrenaline, no doubt.

Get it together. Hot or not, he was still a vampire. A fucking bloodsucker! I wasn't going to be seduced and bitten.

Even mosquitoes had more integrity than that.

The Alpha was not amused. "Lose the knife and say hello."

I gritted my teeth. If Finnegan was okay with the vampire, he must be working with the pack.

"Hello, Lucien."

I couldn't quite bring myself to put away the knife. Not yet. He was easy on the eyes. In fact, he reminded me of Iceman from *Top Gun.* He had that look, and that cool confidence.

"How did you do it?" he asked, his eyes raking over me.

"McPhee's power is a pack secret," Finnegan said, as if he knew how I did what I did. Hell, I didn't even know. Finnegan stood his ground in front of the vampire, who was a full foot taller than the Alpha. "Do you want us or not?"

Lucien gave a long, slow grin. "All right. I'll take her."

My head hurt for a whole new reason. "Take me?" He couldn't take me. I had a pack. I had a home.

Sensing my urge to bolt, Finnegan laid a hand on my shoulder. "It's only temporary. We need someone to go undercover."

I'd never been undercover.

Lucien drew too close for comfort. "I need a were to pose as my wife."

"Hell, no."

Finnegan continued as if I hadn't said a word. "You two will be the newest couple to move into Eternal Life Estates."

"I'd rather eat glass."

Finnegan's hand tightened on my shoulder. "You'll be going to Malibu, McPhee. Haven't you always wanted to see Malibu?"

"No." I had everything I needed right here in the canyon.

"Nevertheless, your skills are required," Lucien said. "We have a window of opportunity. A new couple was set to move into Eternal Life Estates. We've commandeered the house for the investigation. However, it will be tight. Mr. and Mrs. Duke are scheduled to arrive tomorrow evening."

"You and Detective Mead will pose as the Dukes," Finnegan said.

"Detective?" I stared at the vampire. "What are you, some sort of undead Columbo?"

Lucien grinned. "You could say that. I report to the Vampire Council."

Lovely. Even if the man was some kind of an eternal cop, he couldn't just drag me into this. "Aren't there protocols? Rules?"

"Yes," Finnegan growled. "Obey your pack master."

Had he lost his mind? "In case you two haven't noticed, I'm not the trophy wife type."

"Lower the dagger," Finnegan snapped.

Oh yeah. I hadn't noticed I'd been waving my knife. I pulled it back and used it to clean a wedge of dirt out from under my ring fingernail.

This was ridiculous. How was I supposed to be a Sunny clone? He'd better not make me wear a girdle.

"You're going to help Detective Mead sniff out Sunny's murderer," Finnegan said, by way of a rah-rah speech.

Fuck a duck.

"You'll get the truth out of the were wives of Vampire County."

As if I wanted to know.

"You'll blend," he insisted.

I snarfed out loud. Had he taken a look at me lately?

"We'll get to the truth," Finnegan continued, nodding to Lucien, "or else the pack has no choice. . . ."

"Wait," I didn't like the sound of that. "No choice in what?"

"We need closure by the full moon," Finnegan said.

"Or?" There had to be an alternative. That was only three nights away.

"Or," Lucien said, as if it were obvious, "your pack will avenge the death."

Of course. We'd declare war on a county full of vampires. And if the rest of them were like this solid blond wall, we didn't have a chance. It'd be suicide for pack pride. And I really didn't want to die. Not for Sunny anyway.

"Okay." I threw up my hands, remembered I was holding the knife, and sheathed it before Finnegan yelled at me again.

As if I was the one causing the problem.

"I'll do it. I'll be the good wife." Ick. It even hurt to say the word. "We'll start with Sunny's old crowd. The Predators. We'll learn the truth."

"Good," Finnegan said, a victorious glint in his beady little eyes.

"But I'm not wearing heels," I added.

Lucien leaned in from behind, his breath tickling my ear. "You'll have to do a lot more than that."

CHAPTER 2

I stared out the tinted glass of the Lincoln Town Car at the even darker night outside and wondered how on earth I was going to pull this off.

No. Don't think that way.

My newly manicured fingers fiddled with the obnoxiously large diamond on my left ring finger. God. I didn't even recognize my own hands. "I can do this," I murmured to myself.

I didn't have a choice.

A green road sign announced we were *Entering Malibu.* I smoothed the yellow baby doll dress over my knees. I had everything I needed to play the part.

Six coats of mascara? Check.

Bright red lipstick and matching strappy sandals? Check.

Model-worthy hair? I swear I used an entire bottle of Aqua Net.

We'd had only last night and today to prepare, but I'd been on tougher missions than this. I'd wrangled the truth from a bullheaded minotaur, I'd warned the pack about the Berserker Charge of 2010, and I'd scared the feathers off a flock of angry harpies.

Surely I could face a pack of trophy wives with names like Francine and Tia.

Lucien lounged comfortably opposite me, one arm stretched out over the seat back between us. He wore an Armani suit and seemed like a natural for this job and this neighborhood.

I didn't know if that made me feel better or worse.

We had less than seventy-two hours to pull this off.

Just breathe.

Yeah, well maybe I could breathe if I didn't have a girdle mashing my rib cage into my liver. I scrunched my shoulders and leaned forward, hoping for a measure of relief, but that only made me notice the reinforced toe of my panty hose peeking out from my red shoe. I'd tried to stuff the dark brown part under my toes, but it kept inching back.

Oh well, what kind of woman notices another woman's shoes?

Lucien regarded me with a mixture of interest and distrust. From his piercing blue eyes to the blunt tips of his fingers, a cool power seemed to radiate from him. More than that, he was unapologetically male. A lick of desire slipped down my spine.

"Do you want to go over the plan again?" he asked.

"No." We'd been over it a half dozen times. I knew my role. And I was willing to do anything, even wear panty hose, to do the job right. It was a matter of pride—for me and for the pack.

His smile was pure sin. "Then stop fidgeting."

I shot him a dirty look. Oh please. "Let's wrap you in a sausage casing and see how you fidget."

The car bounced over a series of speed bumps at the entrance to Eternal Life Estates. We wound through streets lined with palm trees, past the kind of houses you saw on the cover of magazines at the grocery checkout. The landscaping was impeccable, the façades ornate, and the front lawns trimmed down to the last blade of grass.

At least the place looked deserted, except for, "What is that?" I thrust my head between the two front seats. A mass of shape shifters and vampires gathered in the road. As we neared, I could see that they had completely taken over a circle drive lit by torches in the ground.

Like an old-fashioned werewolf hunt.

I double-checked the twin knife holders I'd strapped to my thighs.

Lucien hissed. "I told them we did not want a welcome party on the first night."

No kidding. "They might have figured out the truth about us." I twisted around to face him. "Someone probably knows the Dukes."

Lucien was oddly focused on my thighs.

"We'll keep our cover." His steely gaze met mine. "As long as you don't blow it."

"Thanks a lot. Nothing like a supportive partner to get the job done right." This was why I liked working alone. "And stop staring at me like you want to bite me."

Sure he looked like sex on wheels, but that didn't mean I was going to serve myself up with a sprig of parsley between my teeth.

His lips parted. "I do want to bite you."

"Do it and I stake you."

Why hadn't I brought a stake?

"Don't worry, little werewolf," he said, sending a shiver down my spine. "I'm always in control." He held my gaze a second longer than he needed. "As for tonight, follow my lead. Remember, the less contact you have, the better."

Maybe I could find a nice tree branch.

I nudged the hem of my dress to make sure I wasn't giving any more free shows. "Anything else, your brood-i-ness?"

He cocked a grin. "You said you knew the plan."

Oh sure. The plan: Keep quiet. Look pretty. *I need you until I don't need you.*

I leveled a perfectly glossed fingernail at him. "Keep in mind that you picked me. I'm the best interrogator you have."

He seemed amused at that. "Interrogator? Yes. Investigator? No." His voice lowered a notch. "You do not handle the case. I do. You get them alone later and you question them. But for now, you don't talk."

"You're an ass."

He didn't react. Stone-cold Luke this one was.

At least he knew what he was doing. According to what Finnegan had told me this afternoon, Lucien Mead was one of the Vampire Council's top guys. They brought him in to handle tough cases like this—at least ones that could result in war. I had no problem following his lead—as long as he didn't force it.

I wrangled halfway through the space between the two front seats to get a better look at the doom that lay straight ahead. Oh my God, they had mint tins.

"You are here to be pretty. You are here to be vapid."

I slammed back into the seat next to him. "Oh yes. Like the time I was too busy painting my nails to wrestle down a banshee and force him to give up the rest of the murdering horde."

"Heather—" Lucien leveled an icy gaze at me.

"Lay off the tall, blond, and frigid act. I've got enough problems." I rubbed at my eyes, leaving a sparkly blue eye shadow streak on the back of my hand. Great, just great. I wiped it on the back of my dress where no one would see.

"Think before you act." He planted a hand on the seat back behind me. "You are the only one who can learn the truth and prevent this war."

Oh yeah. No pressure there.

He had this whole calm and collected investigator persona down pat. But I was an interrogator. And I was good at my job precisely because I was willing to do whatever it took.

Like pretend to sleep with a vampire.

"Drive casually," Lucien said to the driver as we drew near the crowd.

"No problem, boss." The ponytailed driver eased us between two party rental trucks.

"He's staying in the car, right?" The guy looked like he should be working as a bouncer at a nightclub instead of driving a pair of pretend socialites. He also needed a shave.

The driver cocked his head toward me, silver rings piercing his right eyebrow and a black spike earring dangling from his left lobe. "*His* name is Vinny," he drawled with an unmistakable New Jersey twang, "and you bet your ass I'm getting out."

"Vinny is my daytime eyes and ears," Lucien explained.

"Vinny would never even make it through a metal detector."

"Oh yeah? Fine." Vinny turned around and I about fell over

as his hair shimmered from jet-black to white. Not only that, it shortened into a close-clipped haircut.

The scent of wood and grass filled the car. "What the—" I watched Vinny's hands on the wheel age right in front of my eyes. His black T-shirt morphed into a silver suit jacket. His scraggly near-beard faded. By the time we parked, he looked like Jeeves the butler.

"Satisfied?" Vinny asked, with the same rough Jersey accent.

Hardly. "What are you?"

The old butler grinned back at me. "I'm special."

No kidding.

"Stop showing off," Lucien said, as Vinny got out of the car to come open our door.

I didn't know what to think—about Vinny or Lucien or this entire situation.

"One question," I said, as we watched Vinny circle around the front.

I knew all about my role in this—and I had the lipstick on my teeth to prove it. But I sure as hell didn't know what Lucien the super cop was up to—or what he wanted. What did the council care if the vampires slaughtered a pack of wolves?

Lucien closed his hand over mine as Vinny made a great show of standing by the door, preparing to open it. "Why are you two doing this?"

Lucien gave me a quick squeeze. "Because you'll never set foot outside if you see the karaoke machine."

"Call the guard, the vampire made a joke."

"Heather"—he looked at me, really looked at me, for the first time—"I'm here because I want to know the truth," he said, a determined slant to his jaw, "just like you."

Vinny opened the door. Jazz piano music flooded in. From the middle of the street at ten o'clock at night. This was weirder than that coven of narcoleptic werebats we busted a while back.

Lucien stood outside the car, his hand extended to help me. His grip was firm and left no room to wrangle.

Deep breath. This was a special assignment, an important one that only I could do. I didn't want to let my Alpha down.

Lucien took my hand once more, his grip cool and strong. "Relax. You'll do great."

"I know," I said. I'd never been so plucked, sprayed, and manicured in my life. I'd fit in. We'd find the Predators. We'd get to the bottom of this.

A brunette with a heart-shaped face and a sleek red sundress sauntered toward us on ice pick heels. "Mitzy, Luke!" she exclaimed. "Look everybody, the Dukes have arrived!"

I turned to him. "Luke Duke? You've got to be kidding."

He squeezed my hand. "Don't talk."

The waif-like woman stopped in front of us and smirked. "Nice earrings."

My stomach lurched. There was nothing wrong with my red hoop earrings. I'd matched them to my shoes.

"I'm Francine Sharp," she continued, as if she hadn't just insulted me, "head of the welcoming committee."

And a Predator. This was shaping up nicely.

Francine was also a werevulture from the smell of it. She fingered the gold locket at her neck, openly eyeing my fake husband.

"A pleasure," Lucien said, kissing her delicate hand.

I waited for her reaction. Was she sleeping with dear departed Sunny's husband? Or would she be open to Lucien's attentions? I couldn't wait to get her alone to ask.

Only she'd stopped eyeing him and had turned her sharp gaze on me.

A warm flush began in my stomach and heated me all the way up to my cheeks. Yes, I was being scrutinized. I'd prepared for that. But I didn't like standing here being submissive.

I wanted to jump, holler, scream. Anything.

Instead I said, "That's a pretty necklace."

"It's Bvlgari."

"What?" I asked.

She pursed her lips together. "Exactly."

I had the distinct impression I'd done something wrong, but I had no clue what. I mean, who names a necklace?

Lucien leaned close enough to whisper loving encouragement into my ear. "Keep your mouth shut."

Too late.

I fought the urge to snarl.

The werevulture tilted her head. "Where are you from?"

I tried to think of somewhere both exotic and cosmopolitan. "East of here," I said, mimicking Francine's head tilt. "Las Vegas," my mouth supplied before my brain could say *what?*

I wanted to wince, sink into the ground, walk away, and make these people forget they'd ever met me. The entire crowd had stopped talking. For the first time, I noticed everyone surrounding us, staring at me.

I struggled to think of something both vapid and agreeable that would satisfy these trophy wives and their husbands. "I moved to Las Vegas to better myself. You know, to meet guys."

Lucien groaned under his breath.

Oh, the poor vampire was suffering? Well, he could help me out here.

I'd been judged quite enough for one evening.

The air felt heavy as the wall of shifters closed us in. I wanted to bolt. I didn't like crowds, or attention, not to mention being hemmed in on all sides. But I stood my ground. I was a wolf on a mission, even if that meant I was alone in a crowd, teetering on shoes no woman should be forced to wear, holding a purse that could fit a gumdrop.

He'd asked for inane. What else did he expect from a werewolf who'd just had half of her eyebrows yanked out of her head?

He gripped me. Tight. "Now Mitzy, that's not exactly how we met."

"Yeah?" I asked, heart speeding up. "Why don't you tell the story?" Or why didn't he just let me out of here?

This was going bad in a hurry. Every second I spent around these people was making it worse.

It didn't even make sense to talk to the Predators tonight. I needed to question these werewives individually, not in the middle of a game of This Is Your (Undead) Life.

I was about two seconds away from telling this vulture where she could go.

Deep breaths.

She twirled her necklace on one finger, daring me.

That was it. "Why don't you take your Blvgari—"

Lucien hoisted me by one arm. "We're leaving."

"And shove it up your ass." The vampire oofed as my stiletto met his knee. "And you—" I spun toward Lucien the grabby. "Do you *want* me to tackle you?"

Boy, he looked pissed. "We're leaving," he hissed.

"Why? I can take her." The vulture would never screw with me again.

"Now." He grabbed me around the waist.

"Let me down, you cretin!" I seethed, as he carried me like a sack of rice away from the welcoming committee.

CHAPTER 3

Lucien opened the four paneled door with a snarl. "After you, dear," he said, dumping me into our new home.

"Bite me, bloodsucker."

A wave of cold air slapped me upside the head. The foyer was the size of my entire apartment back home. And I could barely believe it, but there was actual furniture inside the door—a couch and a chair, a statue of a woman with half her clothes falling off, and a large potted palm.

He slammed the door behind us. "What the hell was that?"

As if he didn't know. I scrambled to my feet. "I thought I was being vapid," I said sweetly.

"Try again."

"Pretty?"

His eyes raked over me from head to bare toes. "You are something."

"The vulture provoked me." He'd seen it.

Lucien towered over me, glowering. His dress shirt was disheveled, a vein pulsed at his neck, and a lock of blond hair had fallen straight over his left eye. "It doesn't matter. She doesn't matter. You can't let her get you riled up."

"Oh, believe me, you haven't even seen riled." I stood up to him. Eye to chest. "When I can approach her on my terms," on an even playing field, "her ass is mine. I'll learn the truth." He'd seen me in an interrogation room. "Trust me."

"No."

"I don't see that you have a choice."

"Touché," he said dryly.

"Stop it. I don't speak French."

I kicked off my shoes. This was going to be a long three days. Still, I had to keep my wits about me. I didn't want to let my pack down.

Next came the knives. I stacked them on the hall table. I didn't choose to be different. I stripped off my panty hose and tossed them over the potted palm.

The whole situation felt so suffocatingly wrong.

I shucked off my yellow baby doll dress and hooked my thumbs under the top of my bra and girdle combination. The cool air hit my overheated skin as I peeled the garment away. I whimpered in relief as it dropped to my feet. Heaven.

I used my toe to flick it away.

In a few seconds I'd be blissfully free. I stopped when I caught sight of my partner.

"What?" I demanded. He had a funny look on his face. Like he'd swallowed a bug. "Lay it on me. What else did I do wrong?"

"Nothing," he choked.

So much for honesty. How long had that lasted—five minutes?

He cleared his throat, his gaze positively feral.

Holy heck. Was he going to sink his fangs into me?

My pulse quickened and I took a careful step toward the door. "There'd better be some law against biting your partner."

"I will not bite you," he said, his voice rough.

"Then why are you looking at me like I'm the main course?"

"A thousand pardons," he said, breathy. He'd even taken on a slight Spanish accent. "Your decision to disrobe was most unexpected."

What did the guy want? I'd kept my red thong. God, I couldn't wait to get back to the pack where I could run around naked in peace.

I planted my hands on my hips. "Do you really want me to put that crap back on again?"

The front door burst open and I lunged for my knives. I had them at the intruder's neck before he'd taken two steps inside.

"Whoa! Whoa!" He gurgled. "It's me. Vinny."

"How do I know?" I demanded.

This guy looked like a waiter or something. Then I smelled him. "Hey, it is Vinny."

"And yet you're still holding a knife to his throat," Lucien pointed out.

Vinny's eyes flicked down to my breasts, which were smashed up against his chest. "You know, I don't mind so much."

"Pervert." I let him go. What was it with non-weres and nudity?

Lucien flung off his tie and unbuttoned his crisp white dress shirt, his fingers impatient. Just when I thought he'd seen the light, he shoved his shirt at me. "Put this on."

As far as chests went, he had a nice one. Smooth and firm. Ripped without looking like he tried.

I took the shirt. "So you can relax, but I can't."

"I'm not relaxed."

"Oh fine." I slipped the cotton monstrosity over my shoulders.

Vinny shook his head. "I gotta tell you, 'Mitzy' sure stirred things up out there."

The back of my neck prickled. "How do you know?"

"Waiters hear all. They're wondering if Mr. Duke here has a Las Vegas hooker fetish."

Lucien groaned.

"Come on, gorgeous. Blue eye shadow?"

"I like blue," I protested.

Lucien sighed. "Vinny, maybe you can give her some pointers?"

"Are you kidding? I'd make it worse. I even liked her shoes."

"What was wrong with my shoes?"

"Damn it." Lucien pulled out his phone. "We need some more backup."

Another creature in the mix? "I don't like it," I said to Vinny.

He threw the bolt on the door. "You didn't like what happened out there, either."

I crossed my arms over my chest as Lucien left a message for someone named Tia.

Wait. "Not *the* Tia?" Otherwise known as a Predator?

"She's trustworthy," he said, slipping his phone back into his pocket.

"Oh yeah?" I bristled. "When were you even going to tell me you knew her?"

"Right now."

Well, la-dee-dah. "Anything else you'd like to share?" I demanded.

"This is how I work," he said, closing the distance between us. "I'm an investigator. I have a network. I have contacts. I focus on the facts, the details, the minutiae others miss."

"I don't care if you're the Sherlock Holmes of the undead. I want you to level with me. How do you know Tia?"

He backed off. "I've known her husband for nearly a century."

"What? Were you drinking buddies?"

He ignored me. "His pharmacy was on my beat. Many years ago."

"Oh goody." I broke away to inspect the first floor, giving in to the urge to roam.

Naturally Lucien followed. The man needed a lesson on werewolves.

Of course, I could also use a guide to all things posh and annoying. "What aren't you telling me about Tia the Predator?" I didn't need my powers to know he was holding back. He'd held himself wrong. Everyone did it when they lied. One shoulder down, spine bent slightly crooked. I'd learned to recognize the signs.

"She lives on this block. On Mysteria Lane."

"I figured that."

"Tia is"—he paused, searching for the words—"she's a survivor. And she's trustworthy," he insisted. I could tell he believed it.

"Okay." My day couldn't get any worse. Might as well partner with a predatory werewife. I'd mojo her with my truth powers and see for myself whether I should trust her—or truss her up in the basement.

"That's it?" he asked.

"So it seems." What you see is what you get.

I don't know why he was so surprised.

Lucien trailed behind me as I began to inspect our headquarters. It was a security nightmare—windows everywhere. There was a door leading out to a sunroom, a door to the garage, a door out the back of the kitchen. We'd have to invest in some good locks. I didn't look forward to sleeping here without them.

"So have you spent a lot of time on Mysteria Lane?" I asked.

"Hardly," he said behind me. "I try to avoid eternal life-digging weres."

"It would cramp the bloodsucking playboy routine a bit, wouldn't it?" I asked, moving on to the sunken living room.

He shrugged, not bothering to deny it.

Why would a vampire even get married?

Mmm . . . I wriggled my toes. The thick plush carpeting felt amazing.

He stopped at the edge of the sunken living room. Everything was done up in shades of white—the couch, the woven rugs, even the mantel decorations.

"So what do we tell the vulture the next time?" I asked, inspecting a white pointy piece of marble. "Why did you marry me?" It was an element of our story we hadn't worked out.

"It was love at first sight," he said tartly. "I couldn't help myself."

I laughed out loud. "No one's going to buy that." I wasn't sure which was funnier—this broody vamp falling in love or me being the object of anybody's affections.

I tried a light switch and the fireplace roared to life. Sweet.

"No offense," I said, "but you don't impress me as the lovey-dovey type." In fact, he had the brooding down pat.

"I can be affectionate," he said, in that pounce-y way of his.

Oh no. "When was the last time you ate?" I fought the urge to run, feeling his shirt swirl along my thighs.

"That's a little personal," he said, his eyes roaming my body.

No, it wasn't. But what he wanted to do to me sure was. "I don't care how sexy you are. I'm not dinner."

"I didn't ask."

"You implied."

He gave me a heated look. "I can't help what I am."

"What? A ravenous vampire?"

"No. Male."

I felt my cheeks flush. "Let's get one thing straight, buddy. We are a pretend married couple. Fake!"

He arched a brow. "Yes, but we might as well enjoy our roles."

He had to be kidding. "What is that? Part of your method of deduction?"

"Actually, yes."

"Well, quit it. I'm off-limits."

"Pity," he said, as if he meant it.

For a moment, I felt like more than a meal. It was as if he noticed me. He wanted me.

But it was impossible. I'd always be on the outside. I'd learned that back with my pack.

"You said all weres were eternal life-diggers."

"I didn't ask you to marry me."

A flicker of warmth caught my stomach. "Then what exactly are you asking?"

A long beat passed between us.

"Forget it." I rushed to say something—anything—before he did. "I don't want to know."

He didn't want me anyway. He couldn't.

I retreated through the kitchen, my bare feet slapping against the chilly ceramic floor. "Where's the luggage? I'm going to bed."

I could hear his easy strides behind me. "Clothing and personal items were delivered to our bedroom this afternoon."

Our bedroom? I halted at the foot of the stairs. "Listen, fang breath, I sleep alone."

"Shocking." He trailed me up the stairs.

"Isn't it, though?"

We arrived at a master bedroom suite, large enough to house a family of eight. It was done up in gold and burgundy, with antique furniture and ornate lamps scattering warm yellow light.

"That is the biggest bed I've seen in my life."

"You won't even notice I'm there," he said behind me.

"Of course not because you're sleeping in there." I turned and pointed to a well-appointed room across the hall.

He didn't even bother to look. "Vinny is sleeping across the hall."

"Then take one of the other five bedrooms." I didn't care.

It was a shame, though. I was used to being both respected and shunned by the pack. Nobody had ever wanted me. Now the one man who might, also happened to want to eat me.

I couldn't win.

Lucien braced his hands on the door frame, filling it completely, and I had the horrible sensation of wanting to close the distance between us.

He gave a sexy smile, as if he knew. "We need to feel comfortable around each other if we're going to maintain our charade."

Luckily I was not vapid or stupid, even if Lucien would prefer it. "Kissing you was not in the contract."

He moved his mouth dangerously close to mine. I felt strangely vulnerable as he brushed his fingers along the edge of my jaw. His thumb found the curve of my chin. "You could use a good kiss."

I didn't doubt that. But I didn't need it from him.

He broke the contact and I nearly slithered to the ground with relief. If he'd tried to kiss me at that very moment, I wasn't sure what I would have done.

He brushed past me, toward the bed, which gave me time to press my legs together tightly and try to forget I'd ever met a vampire named Lucien.

He stretched out over the bloodred bedcovers, his back against the antique headboard. God, he was a solid piece of man. And I'd seen a lot of well-built weres.

I couldn't let Lucien get to me. "What do you really want?" I demanded. But I was already in trouble. I'd never been so aware of my body—or tempted to learn the god-awful truth.

Darned if the vampire didn't know what I was thinking. "You're not about to use your power on me."

"Of course not," I snapped.

"Then why are you tilting your chin down?"

"My chin?"

"Back in the crypt, you lowered your chin a fraction right before you began the interrogation."

Interesting. I'd never been aware I did that. I tried to imagine interrogating someone and realized he was right.

Lucien went cold. "Don't you ever interrogate me."

"There's no need," I said. "Is there?" I ignored his scowl. "It might not even work on your kind." Although I believed it would.

"Nevertheless," he said, "I'll question the vamps. You question the wives."

I crossed my arms over my chest. "Fine."

I had a feeling I was going to be doing the heavy lifting.

His phone beeped. Lucien eased it out from his back pocket and checked the screen. "After you speak with Tia, I think you should question the vulture. She seems a likely suspect."

"Agreed. Where will you be tomorrow?" He certainly couldn't sleep in the bedroom. It had three bay windows.

His expression didn't give anything away. "The Vampire Council has made certain provisions for me."

"But you won't tell me what or where?"

His pointed look said it all.

"Way to go, partner." I should have known. "You'll hop into bed with me just so long as I don't know where you sleep."

He patted the mattress next to him. "Must you make things difficult?"

"Actually, refusing to sleep with you will make things a lot simpler. And while we're at it, let's lay down some ground rules. Number one: no bed sharing."

Lucien scowled.

"Number two: no kissing."

"I think you'd like it."

"That's beside the point," I snapped, reddening when I realized what I'd said. "Number three," I said a little louder, ignoring his smug expression. "No bloodsucking."

"Those are not very good rules."

I didn't ask for his approval, just as he hadn't asked for mine. "They're my rules."

"Agreed," he said. "Now I have one more."

"Lay it on me."

He gave me a long look. "Never use your truth powers on me."

"Where's the fun in that?" I asked just to tick him off.

He didn't even have the courtesy to take the bait. "Agreed?" he asked.

"Agreed," I said, slipping out of the room.

This was going to be a long three days.

CHAPTER 4

I smelled Vinny before I heard him. "Wake up, cupcake." He still had that odd mix of old wood and grass going for him. Only now, he had the body of a French maid from the Playboy Mansion.

"You like?" he asked, as I stared at the boobs practically popping out from under the lacy front of the dress. His voice was as gravelly as ever, only now he had cover model features, big doe eyes, and legs that wouldn't quit. "I'm your house-keeper, Helga."

"The garters are a bit much," I remarked, climbing out of bed.

"Right-o. This coming from the fashion queen."

"Don't you start."

He leaned up against the edge of the dresser. "Lucien has it so you're gonna go over to that gal Tia's house. Nine o'clock sharp."

I checked the bedside clock. "Okay. I have a half hour." Plenty of time.

"I paid her a visit last night."

No wonder Lucien never went anywhere without Vinny. He was handy to have around. "Let me guess," I said, "pizza delivery guy?"

"Nah." He scratched at his ear. "These women don't eat. Besides, I had to get on the inside."

"Stranded motorist?"

He grinned. "She has a thing for hurt bunnies."

Somehow I couldn't picture Vinny as a fuzzy bunny.

"Anyhow, I checked her out good. She don't seem to be working for anybody else. You might want to do your woo-woo thing"—he twirled a finger on the side of his head—"just in case."

"Thanks," I said. I fully intended to use everything I could on her—and the rest of the werewives.

A half hour later, I rang the doorbell at 12 Mysteria Lane. Tia Lovelace lived in a pink two-story flanked by climbing white roses and a generous front porch.

I was wearing a lovely orange pantsuit, perfect for concealing weapons. The pockets were big enough for my stun gun, I had my fixed-blade daggers tucked in the back and two pairs of handcuffs—one in each bra cup.

A dazzling auburn-haired were opened the door. She had the same pouty lips and impeccable skin as the rest, yet she seemed a little fresher than the others, more real.

"You must be Heather," she said, treating me to an uneven smile.

"That's Mitzy to you."

"I didn't get a chance to say hi last night," she said shyly.

No kidding. "Lucien said you could help." I didn't need to elaborate. We both knew.

"Come in," she said, standing behind the door while she opened it, as if she could disappear.

"Nice spread," I said, if you liked peach and white. She led me into the most un-vampirish living room in the universe. It was sleek and clean. In fact, it would be very hard to hide a weapon in this place.

Still, as soon as my butt hit the couch, I leaned forward and drew my power up into my chest. "Tia," I said as I felt it move through me, "why are you helping me?"

My head throbbed and my ears began to buzz. Her glossed lips parted and I could feel the taut pull of my powers, binding her to me.

"Have you seen yourself in the mirror?" she asked. "That vulture is going to tear you apart."

"Okay, so I had a few problems last night," I admitted. We'd work on that later. I needed to know her connection to Lucien.

Tia furrowed her brow. "A few problems? Red stilettos with a yellow peasant dress?"

Oh come on. "Red shoes are sassy."

"You looked like an eighth-grade hooker."

My temples ached. "Tell me what you really think," I said, resenting my power for the first time.

But Tia was on a roll. "Francine is openly asking why a status-seeking vampire would marry you. It's only a matter of time before you're discovered."

I focused on her, ignoring the pounding behind my eyes. "Why are you helping us?"

She pursed her lips. "I started this. I led the council to Marcos the gardener."

I sat back. Well, that was news.

"Why?" I asked slowly.

"Sunny was my friend. She had her faults, but she was a good person." She sighed. "I knew I could go to Detective Mead." She crossed her long legs. "My husband trusts him."

"Is he going to be able to work with Lucien as well?" It would be nice for Lucien to have an ally among the vampires.

"No." Tia chewed at her lip. "My husband is asleep."

"Well, sure," I said. "It's daytime."

"No"—she wrung her hands—"Thomas has been asleep for the last six years."

"In the ground?" I'd heard of vampires who did that.

"Here at home," she said. "He's very tired."

"Obviously." I didn't know what else to say.

Tia gave a small smile. "Thomas would approve of my going to Lucien. He's a good man."

"Maybe." I was the one asking the questions, and fighting a massive headache. It still didn't explain why she'd called someone like Lucien in. "Do you know anyone who wanted to hurt Sunny?"

"No."

"Did she have any enemies?"

"No."

Damn. I couldn't hold on much longer.

"How well did you know her again?"

"We saw them often. Sunny's husband, Gaston, is business partners with my Thomas."

She glanced over at a series of framed photographs crowding the top of a white baby grand piano. "Sunny was part of Francine's circle. There were four of them. Now there are three."

I tried to examine the photographs, but couldn't without breaking contact with Tia. So instead, I asked, "Aren't you part of the group?"

She folded her hands in her lap. "I don't know."

"How can you not know?"

"I'm the omega."

I sat back and tried not to imagine what kind of hell it was to be Tia. Omegas were the lowest of the low. They were the ones who ate last, groveled most, and acted as the general whipping boys, and girls. And that was in what shifter society considered a normal functioning pack. I couldn't imagine what it would be like to be an omega under a vulture like Francine.

Even though my head was pounding, I held the connection. "You don't have to be the omega." Or anywhere near Francine. "You can break out of this."

She shook her head. "Have you ever tried to break rank in a pack?"

I rubbed at my temples, willing the pain away. I had and I'd failed. I broke contact. She was telling the truth.

"Thank you, Tia," I said, meaning every word. "I know you can help me."

"Yes." She brought a trembling hand to her forehead. "I'm sorry. I feel a little dizzy."

Join the club. I rooted around in my teeny yellow purse for Advil. My fingers clutched the small bottle and I stopped. "You know, Tia. I'd like to help you, too."

She flashed an indulgent smile. "First things first."

"No kidding." I popped two Advil.

She went to the kitchen and returned with a glass of mineral water. "Here," she said, handing it to me.

Well, that was nice.

"Heather," she began, "I think perhaps you may want to look at new eye makeup."

"I just bought some." Too bad I didn't have it with me. I tossed my purse onto the ground. It would never fit. "I have a whole kit full of sparkly blue and red and yellow. . . ." Her eyes widened as I ticked them off, one by one. "What? No good?"

She faltered for a moment, deciding what to say. I already missed the truthful Tia, but frankly, my head couldn't take any more. "You may want to consider a more subtle color palette."

I looked around her living room. "What? Like white?"

She almost cringed. I could tell she wanted to. Good. Maybe I could bring this girl out of her shell. "Look, why don't you show me? We'll take a field trip."

Tia broke out into a shy smile. "Yes." She lowered her eyes. "If you really want to go with me."

"Do you have a car?" I asked, because I didn't. Well, unless I wanted to share this part of the journey with Vinny the chauffeur/ bunny/cross-dressing housekeeper.

"I do," Tia said, reaching for an immense pink bag that could have easily fit a bowling ball or three.

"That's in style?" I asked, imagining all the weapons I could stuff into that puppy.

"Sure," she said, "this is the new Christian Louboutin Sylvia Large Softy Calf Hobo bag." A flicker of doubt crossed her delicate features before she pressed ahead. "See how it matches my yellow and black round-toe T-strap shoes?"

"No." I honestly didn't.

Confidence crept into her tone. "You will."

"Then lead the way, Kemo Sabe," I said, whisking her to the door, Finnegan's American Express card burning a hole in my pocket, "I can be the Eliza Doolittle to your Henry Higgins."

She opened the passenger door of her white Mercedes convertible before she rushed around to open her own. "If you want, I could even coordinate some outfits for you."

I popped two more Advil as I slid into the car. "You could match them for me and tell me what to wear: outfits A, B, C. . . ."

"You don't need that much help," Tia protested, settling in next to me.

"Stop lying," I told her, slamming my own door shut. "You don't have to do that with me."

CHAPTER 5

I stood alone in my room late that afternoon and made two twirls in front of the mirror. And then—just because I had the momentum going—I made a third spin.

Unbelievable. Tia's stylist had tamed my out-of-control hair into sleek copper layers. I ran it through my fingers. The kicker was I could still tie it away from my face. Only now I didn't need to.

Tia showed me how to wear makeup without looking like I was wearing makeup. You'd think that would defeat the point, but I stopped debating her on it after she almost jammed a mascara wand up my nose.

Tia was easily flustered.

I rubbed my lips together, tasting a hint of cherry gloss. I looked like me, only better.

Yes, she'd forced me into white pants, which are a really bad idea if you want to wrestle a murderer to the ground. And don't even get me started on the flimsy emerald top. Tia said it matched my eyes. I wasn't sure why that was important, but I figured she knew style just like I knew how to slap a pair of handcuffs on a drunken werepoodle.

Speaking of cuffs, I had both pairs in my what-cha-ma-call-it Softy Calf Hobo bag. The silly purse cost more than a case of those fancy cigars Finnegan liked to smoke, but I figured he owed it to me for making me wear mascara.

Tonight would be my big chance. The vulture herself was

throwing a luau, complete with a roasted hog, in honor of me and Lucien. Of course, if Francine had her way, I'd be the one tied to the spit.

Let her try. The deep pockets allowed enough room for my mace. I'd sliced a stun gun holder into the lining of my fancy new purse. The cut of the pants was generous enough for my two fixed-blade daggers, and I had my lucky boot knife in my bra.

Gorgeous.

The silk against my skin made me feel almost naked. Sleek. I placed my hands on my hips and studied the image in the mirror. I looked like I could pull this off.

Tia had even suggested a bottle of the vulture's favorite French perfume as a hostess gift. The contents of the tiny gold bottle smelled like half-dead rabbit. I had to admit it wasn't bad.

My heels caught every crack in the sidewalk as I hobbled over to Francine's hacienda-style home. The scent of roast pig lingered in the air, and I could hear voices and laughter coming from the back of the house. A plant-filled courtyard dominated her front lawn, featuring terra-cotta birdbaths, lush floral arrangements, and tasteful sitting areas. I took the stone path through the garden and straight to the looming stucco house, painted in burnt orange. Before I could even knock on the heavy wood door, it opened.

"Hola, missus," a uniformed housekeeper in her midfifties answered. She led me though the foyer and into a boldly decorated room that led to I didn't even want to know how many more. This place could have fit half our pack.

A bank of glass at the back of the house opened out to a patio.

"Mitzy!" a voice called from the kitchen as we passed.

I stopped short as an impossibly skinny woman with a broad-brimmed hat poured herself a glass of white wine laced with fruit. She had a helmet of straight black hair that ended stylishly at her prominent collarbone.

"Care for some dinner?" she asked.

"Where?" I asked, not sure what to make of her.

"Here." She jiggled the pitcher.

"I think I'll wait," I said. I wasn't really into drinking, especially now, when I needed to keep my wits.

"Suit yourself," she said, leaving the pitcher behind for the maid. "I'm Nina, by the way."

One of the Predators.

And a wereleopard from the way she smelled. She was impossibly bony, yet sleek, and she moved with a fluid grace.

"Tia told me about your little shopping trip," she said, a conspiratorial smile tipping her lips.

It was then I noticed she was wearing a silver bikini under an elaborate white silk wrap.

"Don't worry. It's not real silver," she said, as if that's why I was staring.

A ribbon of dread wound its way through me. "This is a pool party," I said, stating the obvious.

And I was in pants.

I could have sworn I knew how these things worked. I'd watched *Dynasty*. Alexis Carrington and her pack wore skimpy gowns and jewels to outdoor parties. They even had shoulder pads. I was not overdressed for a society party. I couldn't be.

"Don't worry about it," Nina said, as if she could read my mind. "Nobody swims anyway."

I was just about to think of a way to escape when one of the glass doors at the back of the house slid open. "Nina!" Francine breezed in wearing a getup that reminded me more of a 1940s pinup outfit than swimwear. "Stop drinking your dinner and get your ass out here."

"I need to fortify myself before Samuel arrives," she said, fishing out a cherry and biting it.

"You knew he was a Puritan when you married him."

"Yeah, but I thought in four hundred years, he would have grown out of it." Nina glanced at me. "He's going through a relapse. You know how it is."

I nodded, not even wanting to think about how these women could marry vampires.

"What are you wearing?" Francine asked, walking a slow circle around me.

"I don't swim," I said through gritted teeth.

"Obviously."

My fingers squeezed the crinkly wrapping of my hostess gift as I endured her scrutiny. At that moment, I wished I'd been holding my lucky boot knife, and it took everything I had not to reach down in my bra and pull it out.

At least then I'd feel capable of defending myself.

Nina breezed past. "Let's get out to the party."

The entire patio was filled with women in swimsuits and wraps that were never designed to touch water. In fact, I'd be willing to bet that everything out here was dry-clean only. They clustered around mosaic tables and on padded chaise lounges. A band had set up in the back, playing island-themed music.

My skin crawled with the need to escape. It wasn't only the fact that a twelve-foot wall surrounded the entire pool area, it was the keen knowledge that I did not belong here—even if I was a guest of honor.

Ha.

More like the main course.

Okay, well, the sooner I questioned Francine, the faster I could make my escape. I knew she was involved in Sunny's murder the same way I knew she'd taped her boobs into that gravity-defying pinup swimsuit.

"Francine," I said, as she attempted to glide toward a cluster of polished women. "I have a gift for you." I dangled Tia's perfectly wrapped bottle of eau de dead chipmunk.

The vulture assessed me. "Not now, werewolf."

I gripped her on the arm, knowing her kind didn't like touch. "I need to talk to you."

Her eyes were dark with fury as she attempted to shake me off.

I held on tighter. "Don't think I won't make a scene."

"Tsk! You think I care if you make a scene? Hell. It would be the highlight. They'd be talking about my party for the next year."

"Don't you want to know why Lucien married me?" I asked, tempting her with information.

"Sure thing, hon. I'm dying to know what you had on him," she said, shrugging out of my grip, while at the same time smiling to a group of guests. "Over here."

She led me to the edge of the pool area, where plants spilled from terra-cotta pots and part of the stone wall gave way to a rocky waterfall.

"Now let's get one thing straight," she began, as I locked eyes with her and released a surge of power from low in my chest.

She made me jumpy, nervous. I channeled that anxiety and more as I flung my power out at her.

Shadows fell over her face as she backed farther into the palms, wet with water.

That's it. Back away. Run. There's nowhere to hide.

My head buzzed with energy and a dry tightness seized the back of my throat. My mind locked with hers. As soon as I felt the connection, I asked, "Did you kill Sunny McCarty?"

"Ouch!" she said a second before my power whipped back and smacked me between the eyes.

"Son of a—" I stamped one well-heeled foot on the pavement so hard I was sure I heard a crack.

I knew better than to jump too far, too fast. I'd let her get to me. I so wanted this to be over.

Francine cringed like I'd raked my nails over a chalkboard.

Join the club. My head was ringing, too. The goal was to slip into someone's mind, not zap her with a thousand volts.

"Let's start over," I croaked, trying to act as if my skull wasn't ringing.

This time, I eased into her mind. I let the power connect naturally. We'd start with simpler questions.

Francine's fingers shook as she checked her diamond earrings and smoothed her hair behind her ears.

I could feel the magnetic pull of the connection as I drew closer to her.

"Why are you such a bitch?"

She laughed. "Because I can be."

Of course. I'd forgotten how straightforward it was for bullies like her.

"What do you know about me?" I asked.

"I know you don't belong here." She fixed on me then, as if she could see straight into me. "I don't think you belong anywhere."

The truth stung.

"Tell me a secret about Sunny."

She considered the question. "Nina hated her."

That surprised me. "Nina?" Sure, I'd only known her for about two minutes, but she didn't seem like the hateful type. Or maybe she was just drunk.

"Why?" I prodded.

"Sunny was blackmailing her."

Some friend.

Francine stared out past me, toward her party. "You'd think Bliss would have been the blackmailer. She's had money problems ever since her dead husband left his money to the dog."

"What?" I hadn't met Bliss yet.

Francine glanced at me. "And by dog I don't mean someone like you. He left their fortune to Chi-Chi the Chihuahua."

"Poor Bliss." I didn't even know her and I felt sorry for her.

Francine shrugged. "She gets by."

And, if I was reading between the lines right, it also meant Bliss would never eclipse Francine, which seemed to be a requirement for being a Predator.

"Introduce me to Bliss," I said, scanning the designer crowd, as if I could somehow pick her out.

"No problem. I've been dying to show her what a train wreck you are," Francine said, making me instantly regret my truth powers.

My head throbbed, the pain moving down my neck and into my shoulders and back as I pushed deeper into Francine's mind.

I didn't need the vulture's approval. At least she didn't know I was investigating.

She smirked down at me and I braced myself. Hopefully my

initial questions had gotten me into her head enough, because I needed to know. "Did you kill Sunny McCarty?"

Francine tossed a lock of gleaming hair over her shoulder. "A massive Gothic chandelier killed Sunny."

She was resisting. It seemed she'd dish out anyone else's dirt, but there were barriers up when I aimed directly at her.

I regrouped and hit her again. "Were you behind the falling chandelier?"

"That would be impossible." She pursed her lips. "The chandelier fell from the ceiling."

Just shoot me now. I was running out of juice and she was playing semantics.

My head pounded. Dang. Most of my subjects would at least elaborate a little. Francine was going to torture me for every sliver she gave me. "Did you rip down the chandelier?" I pressed.

"According to the rumor mill, the chandelier was cut," she said, her voice breathy with meaning, or perhaps the strain of avoiding my questions. "I'd say it was a planned job. You cut all but one wire and then . . . Snip, snap."

Oh geez. My temples rang and the patio began to spin.

"Did you have *any*thing to do with Sunny's death?" I shrieked.

She blinked. "No."

Finally. I wanted to curl up and sleep on the patio. "Then why?" Why had she made this so difficult? "Are you holding anything back?"

She leveled a predatory smile. "Yes."

"What?" I grimaced. I couldn't hold the link any longer. I let her go and with a crack, I felt our connection break.

My power shot back into me like a rubber band snapping. "Ow." I clutched my head and fought a wave of nausea.

I was going to have a massive hangover from this one.

Francine felt it, too. She stared at me, rubbing at the spot above her ear. "What did you do?" she asked, the words coming slowly.

She squared her shoulders, regaining her trademark control. "Never mind." She brushed past me and back to her party.

I could barely walk straight as I made my way through the partygoers, who were at this point almost giddy with anticipation. The vampires would be arriving soon. I could tell we had some werewife hopefuls in the house tonight.

Run, I wanted to tell them. Run and never look back.

"Nina," I nearly ran into her.

"Whoa, girl," she said, steadying me. "I see you had some of the sangria."

"I'm looking for Bliss," I said.

I didn't know how I was going to question her. The pain in my head was growing worse and worse. I'd pushed myself too hard back there with Francine. But I couldn't help it. The woman's mind was a brick wall.

"Bliss had to cancel," Nina said. "Oh yeah—excuse you," she added sarcastically as a bimbo nearly trampled her on the way to go see a vampire.

"Why did Bliss cancel?" I asked. "I really wanted to meet her." And her little dog, too.

Nina shrugged. "Why does Bliss do anything?"

I'd like to find out.

"Wait." I needed to talk to Nina, too. My brain felt like cotton.

"Why are you cringing?" Nina asked, as I prepared to draw my powers out once again.

My head felt like it was going to split in half. I rubbed at my temples as I used all of my strength to draw a line between us.

"Mmm," she said, bringing the fruity wine to her lips. "That tickles."

At least her mind was open. It felt like walking through a soap bubble.

Even so, I knew I wouldn't last long. I hadn't even found a private place to question her. "Francine said Sunny was blackmailing you."

"I'll say. She was taking me for five thousand dollars a month."

No way would I get deep enough to ask if she was the killer. I was surprised I'd gotten into her mind in the first place.

"Why was Sunny blackmailing you?"

Nina took a sip of wine, holding her glass to the side with two fingers. "She caught me giving my personal chef a bonus."

"That doesn't seem so bad."

"On the dining room table."

My brain was fuzzy, yet another side effect. "Well, he is a chef."

"We weren't eating, babe."

Oy. I didn't need that mental picture.

She noticed my discomfort and answered it with a sultry smile. "Oh, don't be a prude. My husband doesn't eat. I don't eat. Our personal chef has to do *something*."

"Just shoot me now." These people were all nuts.

She tilted her head and studied me. "No. If I was going to kill you, I'd maul you." She grinned. "Or just smack you with a chandelier, right?"

"What?" I demanded. But it was no use. The connection fizzled out. I had nothing left. Nina didn't even notice.

She bent closer. "You don't look so good." She shook her wine goblet, the half-melted ice at the bottom sloshing from side to side. "You'd better lay off the hooch."

I stumbled backward. I'd never questioned two people in one night and now I knew why. There wouldn't be a third, that much was certain.

"I gotta go," I said to no one in particular as I made my way back toward the house. The cool slap of air-conditioning hit me as I slid the glass door open. It felt good in a way, like laying my head on the cool porcelain of a toilet seat after I got sick questioning that Harley-riding witch back in Las Vegas.

She'd been a stubborn cuss.

But at least the biker witch wasn't evil. I had a feeling there was more to Sunny's murder than one desperate werewife gone off the deep end.

Francine and her dodgy answers.

Nina and her talk about chandeliers.

A large hand closed around my shoulder and I shouted.

"Heather," he hissed in my ear.

"Lucien." I about fell over with relief.

He wore no shirt, which was a total waste because at that moment I knew I wasn't fully appreciating his fine vampire self. I also liked the concern I saw in his eyes. Sue me. It felt kind of good that someone cared whether or not I passed out next to the fake tiki hut.

"It's done," I murmured as he wrapped his arms around me. "I'm wiped."

Wait. I thought about resisting as he pulled me close against his chest, but then again—I wasn't crazy.

I supposed I should have been trying to keep my distance from him, but at that moment, I didn't give a rip.

My cheek rested against Lucien's chest and something warm pooled inside me.

"Okay, let's get you out of here," he said as he drew away and helped me down the hall.

He didn't ask me any questions. He didn't push me. He just walked with me. And as soon as we'd cleared the threshold of Francine's house, he picked me up and carried me home.

"I can stand," I insisted as Lucien kicked our front door closed.

"Leave it to me," he said, as we headed for the stairs.

You're not listening, I protested, or maybe I just thought it as he carried me up the steps like a child, all the way to his room.

His bed was an ornate cherry wood antique with bloodred sheets. "I'm not sleeping in your bed," I groaned.

"Of course not," he said, easing me into the soft mattress and stretching out next to me. "Advil?"

My head hurt too much to argue. "Better make it a double."

He fetched me four pills and a chaser of water. I swallowed them down and wished he could just knock me out. "I feel like I got hit by a garbage truck."

The bed dipped as he sat down next to me. "Is it always this bad?"

"No." I'd pushed myself hard tonight. "Go away." That's what my pack did at this point. They cleared out and left me to my pain.

He stood. The lights dimmed and I thought that would be the end of him, but Lucien came back. "Where does it hurt?" he asked, the bed creaking under his weight.

"My head."

His cool hands slid across my cheeks as if he were preparing to play a delicate instrument. His fingertips found my aching temples and lingered, rubbing hypnotic circles until I felt the tension loosen.

He kept on. Every thought I had focused on the way his hands soothed me. I shouldn't have let him touch me like that. No one else did. Why should he be any different? He was vampire. Not pack.

He was dead. He was a Predator.

I swallowed and let him touch. To hell with it. I needed this.

His hands moved through my hair, over my aching head, sending tiny chills down my body.

"Not my neck," I murmured.

"No worries." I heard him grin as the palm of his hand slid down the back of my head to rest at the aching spot at the top of my spine.

He wasn't going to bite me. I knew that somehow. And as soon as I decided, I tried to shove it out of my mind. I didn't want to think of him any other way. I needed him to be a Predator. I was good at having enemies. The rest was too hard to figure out, especially right now.

His hands found my shoulders.

I rolled onto my stomach and let him dig his strong fingers into my aching muscles. Good lord, I hadn't been petted in a long time. Ever, really. Damn, it felt good.

His hands found the edges of my silk top and I let him strip it off. The air felt wonderfully cool against my skin, his fingers soothing.

I floated above the pain, focusing only on Lucien's touch. He worked the muscles along my spine, easing away the tension.

He found the back of my bra. "Take it off," I ordered. My voice betrayed none of the shakiness I felt.

It was no big deal to be naked around pack. But it was different with Lucien. I knew that now.

Still, I needed his skin against mine. It was a werewolf thing. It had nothing to do with the way he was touching me.

The pain had eased somewhat, replaced by . . . what—comfort? No, it was more than that.

I had the sudden, maddening urge to touch him back.

Gah. I shoved both hands under my pillow. "Take it off," I said, voice muffled by the pillow. I wanted to feel his hands and nothing else.

"Heather," he said, his voice husky.

"Please," I said, before I could change my mind.

I closed my eyes as his hands slid up either side of my chest, skimming the outer edges of my breasts. Awareness pricked me as his fingertips lingered above my nipples. It was everything I could do not to press forward against his hands.

He wanted to touch me. I knew he did.

I wanted it, too. But it would change everything.

Lucien was too much of a gentleman to press me. Damn it. I let him slip my bra off.

I didn't even care about my lucky boot knife.

Right now that didn't matter. Nothing did.

I was facedown, half-naked under a vampire and I didn't care.

Scratch that.

I wanted him.

It would be so easy to roll over and let him run his hands over my breasts, my stomach, and every other part of me that ached for him.

"Lucien." I felt the weight of him on the backs of my thighs as I turned over on the bed.

I couldn't help smiling at his hunger.

"Watch it, werewolf." He stroked a finger down my cheek, over the pulse of my neck and down to my breast. My breath caught as he found my nipple.

Our eyes met.

His faltered.

"Not like this," he whispered, pulling the covers over my body.

The crisp white sheets felt smothering. "What do you mean?" I started to sit up until the pounding in my head returned, or maybe it had never stopped and I just hadn't noticed.

"You're hurt," he said, as if that would keep me from wanting to see him naked.

"I'm going to be more hurt in a minute." My body was screaming with frustration.

He made it worse by pressing a kiss to my forehead, and then to the soft spot in front of my ear.

I sighed. "You like to torture me, don't you?"

"More than you'll ever know." He settled in next to me. "Sleep." He pressed against my back until he was spooning me in the most delicious way. It was warm, protective. It felt like the pack I'd never had.

"Lucien, I—"

"You need to rest, Heather." He nuzzled his chin on my shoulder. "You did too much."

"But—" He was so close.

"Shhh . . ." His steadying weight blanketed me. "We'll talk later."

I snuggled into the pillow, almost content. It did feel good. "You're bossy."

"I know."

He held me like that until we drifted off to sleep.

CHAPTER 6

A curtain creaked open and sunlight flooded my face. "Wake up. You going to sleep all day?"

I cracked an eye open. Sweet heaven above. An Alexander Skarsgard look-alike stood next to my bed, shirtless, wearing battered Levi's and a smile.

He cocked a grin. "Don't get too excited. It's me."

Vinny.

Of course. I'd recognize that New Jersey accent anywhere.

I squinched my eyes closed and burrowed into the pillow. My head pounded and my stomach churned. I'd hoped the hangover would be gone by now.

"Yo, sleeping beauty." Even his voice made my head hurt.

"If you want to investigate Bliss's house, you'd better hurry."

Of course Lucien had updated Vinny. Worse, Vinny didn't seem to be surprised to find me in his master's bed. I was the worst werewolf ever. Sleeping with a bloodsucker.

Damned vampire.

I shoved a pillow over my face. Naturally, it smelled like him.

The pillow went sailing across the room.

Oh, who was I kidding? It wasn't Vinny's fault. Lucien had touched me and rubbed me and comforted me through my pain like no one else had, or probably ever would. I didn't even know I needed that until I had it.

I'd better not get used to it.

I groaned and rolled over, certain traitorous parts still wishing they'd had their way with Lucien last night. Of course it would have been amazing. Damned vampire. I sure hoped he didn't tell Vinny everything.

"Come on." Vinny shook the bed. "Lucien said you might want to do some investigating that didn't involve thwacking your brain against a mental wall, so to speak." He yanked back the covers. "Up and at 'em." My shirt thwomped me on the head. "The lady just left for her weekly massage and seaweed wrap."

"Who?"

"Bliss," he said, losing patience.

"Oh yeah." I rolled over, tugging on my shirt. "And how do you know that?"

"I flirted," he said, as if it were obvious. "She's leaving the alarm off for me. It's a one-time opportunity, babe."

He tossed a key at my head.

"Cripes, Vinny," I mumbled as I caught the key, almost jealous of the fact that he'd allowed himself to flirt without feeling guilty about it. "What are you supposed to be anyway?"

"I'm your gardener," he said, relishing the role. "I mow things. I chop down trees. I flirt with the neighbors."

"I don't think you're supposed to chop down trees."

"Oops."

"Okay, scram," I said, forcing myself out of bed. I needed to get started.

Knowing these women, a beauty treatment would give me several hours alone in the house. I'd like to find a bankbook and check into her money situation, maybe uncover anything else that I could ask her about. I needed to keep my conversations with these women useful and targeted—or else my head was going to explode.

Besides that, we were on a deadline here. I had less than two days to figure out who'd killed Sunny or this would all be for nothing. My pack would be at war.

A shower and four Advil helped perk me up. Then I grabbed a cream and blue sundress with straw sandals that Tia had picked out. She'd labeled them with matching florescent yellow dots, which she'd found demeaning and I'd found extremely helpful. I tossed the dots into the trash and committed the outfit to memory.

I waved to Vinny on my way out the door and couldn't help grinning when he accidentally sliced a chunk off the front rose-bushes. I had to think that was for me. And I enjoyed it immensely. Maybe it wasn't so bad being a girly girl—at least while I was undercover.

Of course, it would have been wiser to wear black while breaking into a house, but somehow, I fit in better in this neighborhood as I was. And it wasn't like there'd be anyone home.

According to Vinny, Bliss lived in the chocolate brown house on the corner. It was accented by large dark timbers and leafy palm trees. I was pleased to see that plants, rather than a fence, formed the barrier to the backyard. I'd rather not be seen entering through the front door.

I ducked between two bougainvillea bushes. Dark-green leaves slapped at my face and thorns clawed at my skin and my dress, but I didn't care. Once I made it past, I'd have plenty of cover to enter through the back.

A finger nudged me on the shoulder.

"Gah!" I stood straight up and banged my head on a heavy branch. "Ow!" I turned, trying to think of just what excuse I could give for slogging through Bliss Leeson's bougainvilleas.

Tia stood directly behind me. "Hi," she whispered.

I craned my neck to see who else might be watching. "What are you doing here?" The wind crackled the trees around us.

She pulled a strand of auburn hair away from her face. "I stopped by your house. Vinny said you were investigating."

Vinny needed to keep his mouth closed. "What else did he say?" He'd better not have mentioned my powers.

"Nothing," she said, her expression earnest. "I figured you could use some help."

That surprised me. "What? You want to break into Bliss's house?"

Tia reared back like I'd struck her. "No!" She gathered herself. "Of course not." She wet her lips. "It's just that you might need a lookout." She pointed a pink nail toward her immaculate front lawn across the street. "I can pretend to do yard work," she said, way too excited.

Aye yae yae. "Fine. Go." We couldn't be seen chatting in the bushes.

She gave a shy smile. "You look good, by the way."

"You picked it out," I said, parting the branches again.

"Take credit, okay?" She turned and headed back.

Right. I had bigger things on my mind. Like breaking and entering.

I pushed my way through the foliage and into a heavily wooded backyard. Of course, what else could I expect from a weretiger? It was like a jungle back here. Tree branches wove overhead as clusters of jasmine and tall grass filled in underneath. Insects buzzed all around, and I could swear it was hard-packed mud and not sandy California soil under my feet. I picked my way through tangles of plants as they grabbed at my skin and clothes.

At last I made it to a heavy oak door at the back of the house. Long gashes marred the wood. Someone had been playing—or using it as a scratching post. I hoped Bliss wasn't an angry tiger. I mentally crossed my fingers as I inserted the key into the lock.

Yip-yip-yip! A dog blustered on the other side. No doubt it was Chi-Chi, who was technically the owner of this place.

Yip-yip-yip!

Fierce.

Yip-yip-yip!

Luckily I had a way with dogs.

I pushed open the door and stepped into the cool, dark interior of the house. "How goes it, Chi-Chi?"

The little tan dog couldn't have weighed more than two pounds wet. She had bulging eyes and a tail that wouldn't stop. Yip-yip-yip! Every time she barked, the backfire sent her an inch off the hardwood.

I bent down and let her sniff my hand before she nudged underneath and forced me to pet her between the ears. Well, at least I tried to give her a nice rub. Chi-Chi was having a hard time standing still.

"You gotta stop barking, okay? Auntie Heather has a hangover."

She licked my hand and I took that as agreement.

Chi-Chi followed me through the mudroom and into the kitchen, collar jingling and nails clacking on the floor.

It was lighter in here, although Bliss kept plants clustered around the narrow windows.

I opened the fridge and found a few bottles of white wine and a package of steaks.

Chi-Chi whined.

"Hey, I'd give you one, except nobody can know we're hanging out."

Chi-Chi had to sit and think about that one.

I moved on down a side hallway and found Bliss's office. Rich Indian fabric covered the walls. The desk itself was painted with images of four-armed women and colorful elephants. Mirrored tiles studded the corners.

I started on the drawers at the upper right and worked my way down. "You know where Mama keeps her financial files?"

The dog growled.

"Fair enough. I won't call her that."

I rifled through years of household documents, plastic surgery records—who injects themselves with neurotoxins in the name of beauty? Finally, I found her bank records shoved in a heap in the bottom drawer.

The gossip was wrong. Her finances looked great—better than great. Bliss was getting large influxes of cash. She was spending it, too. I couldn't tell where the payments were coming from. They were merely noted as transfers. Still, they couldn't be blackmail, unless she was blackmailing Donald Trump.

After the office, I searched her bathroom. You could tell a lot about someone by her bathroom. What I learned about Bliss was that she was a slob, and if there was ever a shampoo shortage, I knew where to go. The woman had at least a dozen different bottles.

"We need, more, Chi-Chi," I said, moving to her bedroom.

The Chihuahua jumped up on the bed and gave a big yawn. Yeah, I knew it wasn't her problem.

I checked my watch. I'd been in here for an hour. We had to pick up the pace. "Okay, Chi-Chi, where would I hide something I didn't want anyone to find?"

My eyes settled on the walk-in bedroom closet, with its door hanging open and clothes littering the floor. I ignored them, and the endless shelves and teak wood racks. Instead, I walked to the very back of the closet. It was stacked with shoeboxes. They were perfectly dusted, but older. I could tell by their slightly caved-in lids. And so I went through boxes. I saw blue heels and gold heels and enough heels to make my own feet ache. Until I opened a box and found row upon row of pill bottles.

Excitement zinged through me. This was what I'd been looking for. I knew it before I even knew what it was.

None of the bottles had prescription labels. Instead, they were marked with expiration dates written in black Sharpie and tiny brand labels—Slimprol.

I popped open a bottle and discovered sparkly blue tablets about the size of aspirin.

Slimprol. I'd never heard of it. Of course that didn't mean anything. I kept myself fit without this junk. Still, if this was legal, it wouldn't be stuffed in the back of a closet.

It killed me not to take a sample, but I didn't want to rouse suspicions—not until I knew what we were dealing with.

Instead, I found a pen and began a complete inventory of the box, including expiration dates and pill volume. Well, until Chi-Chi shot off the bed barking.

Yip-yip-yip!

Her barks grew fainter as I heard the front door open.

Bliss was home!

Yip-yip-yip!

I was trapped!

Yip-yip-yip!

Hands shaking, I made sure there was no trace of my presence, then dashed for the window. I threw open the curtains and found an ornate wooden grate.

"What the—?"

I tried to shove it back, but it wouldn't budge.

Yip-yip-yip! Chi-Chi's barking grew closer. Bliss could probably smell me. She was tracking me!

Calm down. I had to think.

At least she didn't know who I was—yet.

I attacked the grate and felt it start to give. I'd rip it off the hinges before I got trapped in here with a tiger.

"Bliss!" Tia called from the front of the house. "I'm so glad you're back. I need to talk to you."

I heard a low growl from the hallway.

"Bliss." Tia was inside the house. "It's important."

"Not now, Tia," Bliss said, her voice throaty.

"But"—Tia's voice cracked—"you put me in charge of planning the midnight golf scramble and I know we're having it at the country club, but we never did decide if the men were going to take golf carts. I know that vampire you're dating likes to levitate."

"Don't you dare talk about who I'm dating," Bliss roared.

"I won't," Tia squeaked. "I can't. You never told me. Anyhow, we really need to decide on the carts or else we might not get enough or even the ones we want and . . ."

I could feel Bliss losing patience as I renewed my struggle with the grate.

Forget it. It wasn't budging. I hoped Tia had drawn Bliss far enough away from the back hallway. I had one shot at escaping.

I darted out into the hall, ready to be bowled over. But it was empty. Hallelujah! I dashed out the way I'd come in—down the hall, through the kitchen. I thought I spotted a glimpse of yellow as I darted past an area exposed to the front door, but I didn't hesitate. In fact, I didn't stop until I was back home with the door locked behind me.

CHAPTER 7

I tossed a ThighMaster out of my closet, followed by a pair of wedge sandals and a paraffin wax hand-dipping kit.

"Ow!" Vinny protested behind me, rubbing his forehead.

Oh, come on. I couldn't have hit him that hard. Besides, we had bigger problems. "Where are my heels?" I groused. "The ones with the green stickers?"

Tia's dress-to-shoes color-coding system was no good if I couldn't keep my new wardrobe straight.

Vinny massaged his head in a clearly dramatic attempt to make me feel like a crazy woman. "I don't care where your green stickers are. I came up here to tell you Lucien is making a call. After that, he needs you downstairs."

"Help me look." The closet was a mess. I'd never had this much junk before. "Turn yourself into Martha Stewart or something."

"Not for all the tea in China, babe."

Oh yeah, now he gets picky.

We were due at Nina's dinner party and I'd underestimated the time it took to get tweezed and sprayed and polished for the evening.

It had never taken me more than five minutes in the past.

Truth be told, I'd had a hard time tearing myself from the computer. I'd been online, investigating Slimprol. Not that it did any good. I couldn't find any mention of the drug, much less what it did—or why Bliss would hide it.

Lucien said he'd put the Vampire Council research department on the job. I'd try to question Bliss at the party. Although I'd rather use my resources to ask questions about Sunny's murder.

Finding the killer was my main priority. We had tonight. Tomorrow at dusk would be the full moon, which would be the end of our investigation, and the beginning of a war.

Vinny shoved the ThighMaster back into the closet and right in my way.

Say . . . I turned to him. "You have an 'in' with Bliss."

I tossed the ThighMaster out of the closet before I tripped over the thing.

Vinny simply stared at me.

Honestly, the man was causing more problems than he solved.

Did I have to spell it out?

"Think you can romance me the 411 on Slimprol?" I asked.

"You're the one who gets them to spill the truth, sweetheart," he said, shoving the ThighMaster onto an upper shelf. "I'm just your eyes and ears."

"Oh, so now you stick to your job." Men. I'd never understand them. I stared up at the hinged contraption that was now threatening to smack me on the head. "What's that thing doing in here anyway? I didn't buy it."

"Don't worry about it," he said, deliberately avoiding the subject.

Vinny began digging through my pile of shoes. "Wear these." He held out a pair of brown flats that most certainly did not go with my slinky black dress.

See? I was getting better.

Granted, Tia had forced me to buy a lot of beauty gadgets, but, "if I didn't buy it and you didn't buy it and—"

"I can't keep it in my closet, okay?" he said, tossing the flats and shoving a pair of gold strappy sandals at me.

"Hey, green stickers. Thanks." Then it occurred to me. "Why do you have a ThighMaster?"

"It doesn't matter," he grumbled, retreating from the closet. "Just leave it in here."

I perked up. "You don't want Lucien to know you have a ThighMaster."

Hidden in plain sight.

Vinny didn't share my amusement. He rubbed at the stubble on his chin. "I told you to can it."

I gave him the once-over. Okay, so maybe Vinny in his natural state had a few jiggly spots, but it wasn't like he needed to "squeeze his way to fitness."

His nostrils flared and I swear his eyebrow ring even jingled a bit.

"I'll take it to the grave," I said, carrying my heels to the bed so I could sit and fasten them. "It might happen soon, too, considering Bliss is about to tear me apart."

She had to have smelled me in her house. Once she locked on to my scent tonight, I'd be toast.

A part of me was actually relieved. I liked confrontations. I'd rather know where I stood than sneak around waiting for the other shoe to drop.

"I've got your back," he assured me.

"What? Are you a waiter tonight?"

"Better. That's another reason I came up to talk to you." He'd propped an elaborate curved sword against my nightstand. "Lucien thought you'd enjoy seeing this. It's from his private collection."

"Lucien likes knives?" I loved blades.

"You two have a lot more in common than you think."

"I don't want to hear it from you."

"It needed to be said," he stated. "Anyhow, I'm acting like scenery tonight. Sadly, this isn't the first time I've had to be live sculpture art during a vampire party."

"That is so pretentious."

He shrugged. "I meet a lot of people in my line of work. Some act like God's gift because they can put on a show." There was that meaningful look again. "Others are full of themselves because they don't."

But Vinny didn't dwell on it. "Nina has an Arabian Nights theme going." He grinned. "Meet the burly harem guard." He took a swoop at thin air. "You have a problem, look for the sword."

Got it. "Much better than you with a chain saw." We'd lost three trees during his stint as a gardener.

We headed downstairs to find Lucien waiting. He looked fantastic in an understated black suit and a blue tie that set off his eyes.

I felt his gaze touch me and it was all I could do not to trip down the last three steps.

"Is the research department working on Slimprol?" I asked, just to have something to say.

"They are," he said slowly.

I couldn't help remembering the way he'd touched me the night before. Clearly, he was thinking of it, too.

He ate me up with his eyes. "You look amazing."

I snorted. "You're only saying that."

"No, I'm not."

I moved close enough for him to smell my honeysuckle perfume. "You just want to bite me," I said, my voice huskier than I would have liked.

He took my hand as I tried to breeze past.

"Maybe," he said, drawing me back, his hand cupping my chin, his thumb grazing my lower lip. "I also want this."

His mouth brushed mine once, twice. The thrill of it slapped through me. I grabbed his head and deepened the kiss.

My body collided flush with his. And those parts that had ached in frustration roared back to life.

God, I'd waited so long for something like this. I deserved it.

Lucien wanted me. It was a heady feeling.

If I should have been kissing him.

I broke away, trying to keep my breath even and failing miserably. "We said no kissing."

A brief flash of stark emotion crossed his features. Good. "*You* said no kissing," he said, with his infernal logic. He nipped short kisses along my jaw, as if he couldn't quite help himself. "Do you like it?"

Too much. My breasts felt heavy as he nuzzled my earlobe. "That's beside the point." One of us had to be sensible.

It probably should be me. I ran my hands down his shoulders and arms, feeling the heavy weight of his suit jacket. Then again, maybe the whole sensible thing was overrated.

He pressed tight against me.

Oy vey. What was I getting myself into?

Yes, I found I enjoyed touching and being touched. But we were pretending here, playing roles. I'd forgotten that last night. When this was over, he'd be sent on another job for the Vampire Council and I'd be returning to my pack. Alone.

He lowered his mouth to mine again and I let him. I let him kiss me into a heart-pounding fury until I forgot all about what I'd said I was going to do.

He slid his hands down to the small of my back, tempting me closer, but I didn't need any help. I rubbed against Lucien like a cat, savoring every rock-hard inch of him.

"You like it," he said, drawing back just long enough to grin at me with boyish pleasure before he devoured me again.

Damn the man. He was good at making me forget just why I said I'd never kiss him in the first place.

"I like it, too," he whispered against my lips.

"I can tell," I said, wriggling against him, a victorious twinge lancing through me when I felt just how much I affected him.

Lucien wasn't the jaded creature I'd first imagined. He was a man. Admittedly an immortal one, but a flesh-and-blood man all the same.

His expression softened as he saw the change come over me. "What are you thinking?" He tucked a lock of hair behind my ear.

"Hmm . . ." I mused, enjoying the sexual power I held over him. "I'm thinking you need to kiss me again."

I beat him to it. I took the lead this time as I tasted him, savored him. Our kiss deepened as he pushed back. He wanted me. We drove into each other. He wanted me so bad.

I'd never had this with a man. Sure, maybe I'd had a few meaningless flings, but no one like Lucien.

To the males of my pack, I was a dare, an experiment. But this affair with Lucien went much deeper. It was both alarming and exhilarating.

"Okay, come on. Break it up." The front door creaked open with Vinny behind it. "I got the car started, for all you noticed."

Lucien drew back a fraction. His lower lip glistened. God I wanted to kiss him again.

"We'll walk," he said, turning his back on Vinny.

Vinny stood on the front stoop, arms crossed. "What? You think I'm nuts? You two will never make it."

Lucien raised his hand and the door slammed shut.

"Real nice!" Vinny hollered from the other side.

"Ohh . . . telekinesis!" I said, impressed.

"I have all kinds of things I'd like to show you," Lucien said, moving in to seal the deal.

I hated to think Vinny might be right, but, "We might actually have to go."

"Damn."

I nuzzled him. "Yeah."

Lucien's amusement faded, replaced by something primal. "One more kiss." He took me with such force it was a wonder I held on. I was aware of every touch, every caress of his mouth as my senses came vibrantly alive. The hot glide of his tongue sent heat washing through me. It was all I could do not to climb the man as he deepened the kiss even more.

He groaned as I cupped his butt and pressed him tighter against me.

Lucien wanted me. He wasn't afraid to admit it—or slam the door on Vinny. That part had actually been kind of fun.

But could I really have an affair with him?

I hated weres who paired with vampires. Well, maybe not Tia. But I couldn't stand the type. I didn't want to be the kind of woman who needed a man, much less a vampire.

Heck, I didn't even need my pack. I was fine on my own.

Wasn't I?

I arrived at Nina's house with a satisfied Vinny and a frustrated Lucien. I knew how the vampire felt. My body was screaming for five minutes, okay four—okay, one minute alone with him.

Maybe after the party, I reasoned, trying to get a choke hold on my raging libido. As it stood, Tia had worked hard in order to secure us an invite. She'd probably agreed to paint Nina's toes for the next year. It burned me to see how the Predators treated her.

Vinny watched us walk in the door, promising to "arrive" shortly after.

Nina lived in a modern-style home with lots of clean lines. The front room was done in black and white, with zebra and gazelle fur accents. Charming. Low pillows and flowing fabric accents gave a nod to the Arabian Nights theme.

A stoic vampire with bowl-cut hair and a long black salt-and-pepper beard greeted us.

"Samuel." Lucien nodded to him, holding my hand. His thumb caressed the soft skin below my wrist. "This is my wife, Mitzy."

"The women are in the living room," he said to Lucien, as if I wasn't there.

Fair enough. It was Lucien's job to question the vampires. At the moment, I didn't envy him. Samuel seemed like a cold fish.

Strange that Nina would ally herself with an unusually grim vampire. Then again, my job here wasn't to question lifestyle choices, just potential murderers.

My shoes were already digging into the sides of my feet. It would be nice to take a load off.

A mouthwatering scent filtered in from the kitchen.

I found the wives perched on Nina's impossibly white couches and chairs. Tia in white. Francine staring daggers at me in red. And an Indian woman in a gorgeous blue dress who literally growled. Bliss.

The coffee table in front of us was covered with plates of caviar and crackers, pine nut puffs, and all kinds of tiny appetizers that looked like they each took about an hour to make.

"Help yourself." Nina, who wore a black dress at least two sizes smaller than mine, waved a hand toward the display, as if daring me.

None of the wives had so much as touched a plate.

"I'll wait until dinner," I said, my stomach protesting. Now that my body wasn't pulsing after Lucien, I remembered that I hadn't eaten lunch. "You have a fantastic home." I took a seat, ignoring the way my dress shifted sideways.

"You want a tour?" Bliss asked, wasting no time.

Her smile didn't reach her eyes. She knew.

"Sure," I said, "why not?"

Let's get it over with. She could try to tear me apart, but I was all wolf.

I stood. I gave myself decent odds, especially if Lucien jumped in.

Tia cast a worried glance my way. I could see the indecision eating at her.

"Mitzy—" The were rushed after me as I was about to leave the room with the tiger. Once she made it to me, she scrambled for what came next. "You have a smidge of something on your dress." She scrubbed with bare fingers at the area next to my back zipper. "I'm scared," she whispered in a rush.

Me too.

"Thanks for saving my hide this afternoon," I murmured under my breath.

"I didn't," she said, growing desperate.

"You did." I turned to her, keeping my voice low. "You're strong, Tia. You have to be. You're on my team."

She chewed at her lip.

"You need to stand up for yourself."

I did, too.

"But—"

I left her with the Predators and followed Bliss.

Tia couldn't help me right now. I needed to do this on my own. If I was smart—and lucky—I might be able to pull this off.

I just needed to grab her mind, preferably before she took me by the throat.

The weretiger turned on me the minute we were out of the room. "What were you doing in my house?" she demanded, nostrils flaring. "And don't bother to deny it." She leaned in close, her face inches from mine. "I smelled you."

"Funny thing, Bliss," I said, trying to buy precious seconds, grasping with my mind.

Steady.

I couldn't afford a backlash. I channeled the power from deep inside of me. It flowed between us and I felt the invisible cord tighten. I tested the connection and sighed with relief when it held. "Okay, tiger. I have a few questions I'd like to ask you."

Her face went slack. "I'm in charge of this conversation," she said, but it was only a line. I had her now.

We'd start with something easy.

"Are you aware that Sunny was blackmailing Nina?"

"No," she said, eyes widening.

Fair enough. "Were you sleeping with Sunny's husband?"

She grinned. "He's fantastic in bed."

"I'll take that as a yes," I said, my head beginning to pound. "Do you know where Sunny's husband is now?" I asked.

Bliss tilted her perfectly oval face. "Overseas," she said, repeating what I already knew. "On business."

I'd never got around to asking, "What does he do?"

"Pharmaceuticals."

No kidding. "Like the Slimprol you have in your closet?"

"Yes," she said, almost in a trance.

"What does Slimprol do, Bliss?"

She blinked once. Twice. "It makes you sleepy. You go to sleep and you lose weight."

Great. An unapproved drug for extreme weight loss. I could already tell Sunny's husband was a real piece of work.

Pain lanced through my head. I was losing the connection. I knew I'd laid it on thick, but dang, when somebody wants to kill you, it's a good idea to crank up the happy current. "What else can the drug do, Bliss?" I pressed. "Can it kill people?"

She snarled at me. "I hope so."

Our connection unraveled.

Bliss bared her teeth.

Oh come on. I was offended she'd think I'd break into her house. Even if I did break into her house.

I threw up a hand. "I was in your house trying to find *my* gardener. I don't care who you are. What's mine is mine."

She should know wolves are territorial.

"Bitch," she snarled, unsure for the first time. She narrowed her eyes. "I don't like wolves who sniff around my business."

"Bliss!" Nina called. "Mitzy!"

"In here," I gave a ready answer.

She found us with no trouble. "Dinner is served."

The tiger growled low in her throat. "This isn't over, werewolf," she said, stalking past me.

I never said it was.

Lucien and I were seated near the head of the table for dinner. Samuel sat at the head. Lucien at his right side. I sat next to Lucien, with Nina across from me. Luckily, Bliss was at the far end with poor Tia in a werewives version of the singles' section. That meant I got to chat with Francine and her husband, Olaf.

Worse, I couldn't help picturing what else Nina had served up on the sleek black dining room table.

Vinny the Arab warrior offered us each a small bowl of rose water with a fingertip towel.

Despite the fact that I'd come one mind-reading trick from being consumed by a tiger, my stomach growled as I anticipated dinner. I needed to eat. Food helped me think. It helped me heal.

And just when I'd worked myself up into a frenzy of anticipation, my plate arrived.

The waiter served up one tiny chicken wing with grated cucumber on top. A date cut into a flower served as garnish. I supposed it was gourmet, but it made me want to cry.

I couldn't take it.

These people could threaten me. They could lie to me and demean me and make me wear god-awful heels with pointy tips. But they couldn't starve me. It wasn't right. My head hurt and my dress was still kind of sideways and I just needed one thing tonight to go the way it was supposed to go.

I needed crackers. I needed anything but a puny chicken wing with a garnish.

The vampires sat drinking their wine. The weres picked at their cucumber as if touching it would make them gain weight. What was wrong with these people?

I needed to eat.

And so I did.

I ate my chicken wing clean. I devoured the cucumber. And the cut-up date. Then I marched out to the living room and loaded up on appetizers—caviar, lamb with goat cheese, fancy fruity tarts. I ate it all. And when I was done with that plate, I went and got another.

Bliss growled. Francine sneered. Tia stared, openmouthed.

Nina couldn't care less. "More wine?" she asked the table.

She shrugged off her Puritan husband's glare. "What? I'm just being a good hostess."

Everyone agreed to refills, except for me. I hadn't touched my glass. I'd never been one for alcohol. And now that I had my third plate of lamb thingies and a raging psychic hangover, forget it.

The waiter started pouring at the other end of the table and the bottle of white was long gone by the time it reached our end. Nina cracked open another and gave me a healthy pour.

"Thanks," I said, "but I've gotta save room for the ham puffs."

Bliss stared at me as I slid my glass over to Lucien.

He winked at me and drank.

CHAPTER 8

I cleared away the rest of the lamb, all of the puff pastries, and a good portion of the caviar. I'd never been huge on fish, much less their eggs, but it was there. And the crackers weren't half-bad, either.

"Bet you never even heard of a saltine," I said to Nina.

"I'll drink to that," she said, either half-soused or highly amused, probably both.

"Here, here," I said, toasting her with the last of the caviar.

I had plenty to celebrate. Topping the list was the fact that I had not been eaten by a tiger tonight.

The vampires had lost interest by this time and were busy trying to one-up each other on who had endured the most annoying minions. Points were given for base groveling, years served, and most obnoxious way they died. And it seemed they always died.

Big surprise there.

Yet another reason why no self-respecting weregirl should bind herself to a guy like that.

I licked a bit of caviar off my fingers.

Of course I did notice Lucien hadn't joined in on the minion talk. In fact, he looked a little green. Good for him. Using people was just plain wrong.

I nudged him. "You feeling okay?"

He nodded. "Slightly put off by the conversation."

Lucien used a napkin to wipe his forehead and a trickle of perspiration glinted near his ear.

I'd never seen him sweat before. I'd never even seen him warm.

His chin dipped and he braced his hands on the edge of the table. If I didn't know better, I'd say he was struggling to remain upright.

I covered his hand with mine. "Cripes." Something was definitely wrong. "You're burning up."

I flagged down the waiter. "Can we get him some water?"

He was abnormally pale.

Everyone at the table was watching now—except Bliss. She'd become quite interested in her gold bracelets.

Then it hit me with a sickening thud. "You drugged him, didn't you?"

Her eyes locked with mine. "No."

She'd answered too fast, and without a hint of surprise.

Bliss had been after me. I'd given my wine to Lucien right before he got sick.

I ran a finger along the inside of his glass and found traces of glitter. Slimprol.

Of all the . . . Fury welled up inside me as I stalked toward the tiger. "Now would be a really good time to tell me what's in Slimprol."

She stood, her chair toppling over. "I don't know what you're talking about."

I resisted the urge to grab her by the braid and shake her. Barely.

"Get him into the car," I said, refusing to turn my back on the tiger.

Vinny hoisted Lucien out of his chair.

"Is he okay?" Tia stammered, bobbing in her chair, clearly afraid to stand.

"No, Tia," I bristled. "He's not okay."

But he would be. I'd see to it myself.

I snarled at Bliss and a blaze of triumph shot through me when she backed up a step.

She'd messed with the wrong werewife.

"I'm not through with you," I said, as Francine led her away. *That's it. Run, tiger.*

It took all I had not to chase her.

Soon. Right now, I had to take care of my own.

Lucien was getting sleepier and sleepier. His head dipped and Vinny had to readjust his grip as he took on more of Lucien's weight. I helped make way for them as they rounded the table.

Lucien's breathing grew shallower with each breath. "I don't understand," he gasped as we led him out the door. "Alcohol doesn't affect me."

"You've been drugged," I said, helping him navigate the front step, hoping he was aware enough to understand. "You have to stay awake."

"Drugs don't work on me," he said, voice slurred.

I glanced back at Nina's house. "This one does."

We sped off in Vinny's car, not even caring about breaking cover. Lucien lay across me in the backseat. He wasn't moving. I smoothed his hair back, just to have something to fuss over.

This was bad. We had no idea how to reverse whatever Bliss had given him.

"Contact the Vampire Council," I told Vinny. "See if they've learned anything about Slimprol."

Lucien was dead weight as we pulled him out of the car. His skin was clammy, and his face had gone deathly pale.

"Drag harder," Vinny said. He took Lucien's head and shoulders while I took his feet. "He's not helping us at all."

"Stay with me." I planted Lucien's feet on the ground, then slipped underneath and helped lift him out. "You hear me?"

Tia came running up the driveway. She'd lost her shoes and had the wide-eyed look that told me she'd be no help to us.

"Go home, Tia."

"But, Heather, I—"

"Not now."

We could be fighting for Lucien's life here. He was immortal, but he wasn't un-kill-able and I still didn't trust Bliss not to make a lethal move. She was desperate, vicious, and out for blood.

Vinny was thinking the same thing. "Lock the door," he said when we'd made it inside.

I threw the dead bolt and the chain. Then I set the security alarm.

There was no way we could drag Lucien up the stairs. In fact, we made it as far as the couch in the living room.

"Easy does it," Vinny said, out of breath as we laid Lucien on the white couch facing the fireplace.

"How could Bliss even think she'd get away with this?"

Vinny pulled out his cell phone. "I doubt she was thinking that far." He hurried toward the kitchen. "Rodger? Get me Milosh." He took the rest of the conversation in the garage.

Lucien struggled just to keep his eyes open. His pupils were fixed and dilated. His breathing had slowed as if he were asleep.

"Stay with me." I ran my fingers through his short blond hair and touched my lips to his forehead. "Come on. You can do it." I kissed his eyelids and his cheeks.

God, he had impossibly long eyelashes.

I was anxious. Terrified, really. It was as if a big hole had opened up in my chest, waiting to be filled, or crushed.

His eyes fluttered.

"That's it," I said. "You don't want to miss this."

I brushed a kiss over his lips, and then another. A tear splashed down on his cheek and I wiped it away, glad that no one saw.

"See?" I asked, wiping my eyes. "You're fine."

What was wrong with me? Getting blubbery over a job.

I'd seen death more than I cared to admit. It was part of being a pack enforcer.

But this was Lucien and he was different and he didn't deserve this.

The garage door burst open. "No information on Slimprol, but they're sending a medic."

"How long?"

Vinny shoved his phone in his pocket. "A half hour."

"Damn it, Vinny."

"What?"

"I don't think he has a half hour." My voice caught in my throat.

His breathing had all but stopped. He wasn't keeping his eyes open and he'd gone deathly pale.

Vinny stood frozen. "Shit."

"Get on the phone," I ordered. "Figure it out."

"Yeah," he said, fishing in his pocket.

Vinny retreated back to the kitchen or the garage or wherever the hell he went. Damn the Vampire Council for being so slow. Damn Vinny for not figuring this out. I wanted to scream. I wanted to beat something because Lucien was dying right in front of us and there was nothing I could do.

I couldn't cure a vampire.

I couldn't make this better.

I—

"Wake up." I tapped at his cheek until I was full-fledged slapping him. "Wake up!"

His eyes cracked open.

"You're going to have to drink from me," I said, breathless. I couldn't believe I was saying it, much less thinking it, but there was no other way.

Lucien was a vampire. He needed blood to heal and I would give it to him.

"Lucien!"

He groaned.

"Damn it, Lucien. Wake up. You have to drink from me."

I rubbed at my wrist, trying to figure out where there'd be an artery. I'd heard there was one in there somewhere.

To hell with it. No time.

I climbed on top of him and lowered my neck to his mouth. "Drink!"

He didn't move.

"Oh well, this is just great!" I hollered. First he could barely keep his fangs to himself, and now when I had to save his miserable life, he wanted to go to sleep. Well, not on my watch.

"You are not going to die," I growled. "In fact, I'm going to seduce the hell out of you."

I got an eyelid flutter for that.

Ha!

"That's right," I said, wrestling with the back zipper of my dress. "I know you've been dying for this."

I dropped my bra. Damned vampire.

My mouth skimmed his jaw and nibbled at the soft spot behind his ear. One by one, I freed the buttons on his white dress shirt until I could press my hands against his deathly cold flesh.

Don't think of that. I focused instead on the hardness of his muscles, the wisp of hair that trailed from his chest and disappeared into the front of his dress slacks. I flicked a nipple and he groaned. I took it between my teeth and he groaned harder.

That a boy.

I pressed my breasts flush against him and let his coolness seep over me. He'd begun to breathe harder. So had I. I paused for a moment to breathe in his spicy, masculine scent.

I almost forgot this was a rescue mission instead of a mutual pleasuring. He felt so good. I brought my body flush with his, toying with his belt buckle, nibbling my way up his chest as I reached lower.

He inhaled sharply. "Heather."

"Um-hum," I said, nuzzling his ear. God, he was hard.

"Help me get undressed."

"You have to drink," I said, lips crushed against his ear.

"I want to be inside you."

"Drink." I tilted my neck toward him. His fangs pricked the tender skin of my neck, sending a jolt of panic through me.

"Heather?" he whispered against my neck.

I wet my lips. "It's okay."

His fangs sank into my neck and my fear vanished. I squirmed, rubbing myself against him as I experienced the most explosive connection I'd ever felt.

Lust swamped me. I shivered with the intensity as he pressed me against his hard body and drank. My body stretched like a bow with sheer pleasure, held in place by Lucien's steady hands.

He was with me, alive. And he felt amazing.

I was wet, shaking, and on the verge of climax when Lucien sank back from me, dazed. "Is this a dream?" he asked, rolling me under him.

"No," I said, blinking back to reality. He was alive, and strong. I didn't know whether to laugh or cry. "Not a dream."

There was stark, sexual hunger in his eyes. "Good."

I was naked before I knew what had happened.

"Lucien—" His fingers found the core of me and I stopped complaining.

He drew me into the most erotic kiss of my life, his fingers exploring me until I thought I was about to scream from the intensity of it. A second later, I came.

"May I?" he asked.

I threw my head back against the couch. "God, you're polite."

"Hardly," he said, pressing the tip of himself against me. His radiant blue eyes fastened on me. "Tell me you want it."

My breathing hitched. "I do."

He drove into me, setting off another wave of pleasure. Sweet heaven, how could anything feel so good? I thought I'd had men before but I'd never had anyone like Lucien.

He pushed me. He filled me. He drove me to heights I hadn't even let myself imagine before.

I nipped at his shoulder, his neck, anything I could reach.

Lucien let his head drop. His face pressed against my shoulder as his fangs slid along my neck.

"Do it," I gasped as he bit me again.

Yes! I slammed hard against him as he drove into me. We took from each other and gave to each other until it was impossible to separate our two selves.

This time, I screamed as I came.

Lucien gasped and cried out as he stiffened above me. It was the most beautiful thing I'd ever seen.

Afterward, we lay in a boneless puddle, Lucien on his back with one arm behind his head and me using his chest for a pillow.

It was safe to say I'd cured him.

I couldn't help grinning. "How do you feel?"

"My head hurts."

I felt myself giggle. "Join the club."

He was kissing my hair, my forehead, my nose, pretty much any place he could reach. "I haven't had a headache since 1908."

"Then you're due."

He found my lips again. The man could not keep his mouth to himself.

"1908, huh?" I said, when I managed to extricate myself from yet another deep, hungry kiss (admittedly, I hadn't been trying very hard).

He scooted back on the couch and cradled me in next to him. "I could tell you stories," he said, toying absently with my hair, "if you'd let me."

"That might be nice." I'd have to think on it.

He propped himself over me. "Heather, not that I'm complaining"—he caressed the stretch of skin between my ear and my chin—"but what happened tonight?"

I was almost afraid to tell him. "What do you remember?"

He looked somewhat embarrassed. "I was at Nina's party, and then nothing."

"You were drugged."

"Me?" He seemed surprised. "Amazing."

"Slimprol."

His expression darkened. "Bliss."

"Exactly."

He nodded to himself, calculating. "Where is she now?"

Just like that, I knew our alone time was over.

Lucky for me, I liked a good fight.

CHAPTER 9

I strapped on my fixed-blade daggers, holstered my Glock 22 with silver bullets, added handcuffs, a stun gun, mace, and of course, my lucky boot knife.

It felt good to look like me again, with certain improvements. I wore a pair of black leather pants Tia had picked out, with a matching tank top that let me move.

Lucien watched me with obvious hunger, which I enjoyed thoroughly.

Probably because I knew he was going to do something about it later.

When I'd double-checked my gun and finished with my daggers, he tucked a stray lock of hair behind my ear. "Thanks for saving my life."

"My pleasure." Parts of me went gooey just thinking about it.

Vinny clomped through the kitchen, carrying a shotgun in each hand. "Never mind the fact that I was stuck in the garage for the last two hours."

I checked the clock on the mantel. Two hours? I ran a palm up Lucien's arm, admiring his tight black T-shirt. "I'm impressed." The man had stamina.

"And I had to send away the medic," Vinny grumbled. "Good thing you weren't exactly subtle. I don't like surprises."

"Why does he think this is about him?" I asked Lucien.

He kissed me on the nose. "I have no idea."

Vinny headed for the front door. "Can you knock it off? We have a tiger to cage."

It was about the only thing he could have said to move me from that spot.

"Later," Lucien whispered, his breath hot against my ear.

God, I hoped so.

I admired his ass on the way to the front door. He wore jeans and combat boots, which was a very nice look for him. I was about to tell him so when we opened the door and found a visitor on the front stoop.

"Tia," I said, surprised. I remembered her following us earlier tonight, but I had no idea she'd still be here.

She stood as soon as she saw us. Tia wore her dress from the dinner party, although it was torn on one shoulder and bore grass stains up the side. She'd also lost her shoes.

Guilt pricked at me. I'd been inside, having my way with Lucien, while she'd been, well, what had she been doing?

"What happened to you?" Vinny asked.

She ignored the question, eyes trained on me. "I told you I needed to talk to you," she said, voice shaky.

"That you did." But I really didn't think she'd camp out.

Vinny took her by the arm. "Did someone attack you?"

"Excuse me?" She seemed surprised. "Um. No. I, well, it's hard to run in a dress."

Funny. That had been my point all along.

Tia being here was all fine and good, but we had to get moving. I'd say we had barely an hour of darkness left.

I led her down the front walk while Lucien started up the car and Vinny loaded the trunk with shotguns. "Okay, well what did you need to talk about? We're on our way to kick some tiger ass."

"That drug you found in your drink," she said. "It was sparkly."

"Yes." I didn't want to rush her, but as soon as Vinny went back for a few extra cases of silver bullets, we were leaving.

Tia touched my arm. "Sunny had been giving me vitamin

supplements, for my husband. They were supposed to help him get extra nutrients, because, well, I'm anemic and"—a blush crept up her cheeks—"he only wanted to drink from me."

"How romantic," I said, stunned that I almost understood.

"It is," she said dreamily. "Anyway, it seemed he needed more. Or at least we thought he needed something. Thomas was getting more and more tired, until one day he decided to sleep."

Then it hit me. "Sunny was mixed up in Slimprol."

It made sense, and it didn't. Sunny and Bliss were friends, but Bliss didn't seem all that eager to share her pills—or her secrets.

"How can we be sure?" Lucien asked.

"I'm sure." She gripped my arm. "The vitamin supplements are blue and sparkly, about the size of an aspirin."

"Holy hell."

Vinny slammed the trunk. "All set."

"Get in the car," I told her.

I took a seat next to Lucien and yanked the door closed. "Sunny was giving Slimprol to Tia's husband, Thomas."

His expression hardened. "How can you know?"

Tears welled in her eyes. "I put one on his tongue every morning." She ended in a wail. "I thought I was helping him. I love him! Why would Sunny want him to go to sleep?"

"She wouldn't," Lucien said, pulling out of the drive. "But her husband, Gaston, is Thomas's business partner, correct?"

Tia gave a sniffling nod.

"Pharmaceuticals," Lucien added.

"What do you want to bet they're the makers of Slimprol?" Vinny asked.

"About a hundred billion percent." I wondered just what Sunny had gotten herself mixed up in. Tia, too.

"Is he—" Tia sobbed, "is he going to be okay?"

Vinny patted Tia on the leg, clearly uncomfortable with the grieving woman next to him. "How long has your husband been taking it?"

She gazed at him through red-rimmed eyes. "Six years."

"Oy," Vinny said.

"Vinny!" If I could have flicked him on the head, I would

have. We all knew it was bad. She didn't need to hear it from him.

What I wanted to know was, "What's Sunny's husband been doing for the last six years?"

Tia shook her head. "I don't know, but I saw him tonight."

"Here?" Lucien asked. "In Eternal Life Estates?"

She nodded. "While I was waiting on the porch. But he didn't go home."

"Where'd he go?" I asked, as we pulled up to Bliss's house, ready to spring into action. By the expression on Tia's face, I already knew.

"I love when a plan comes together," Vinny said, cocking his shotguns like a Wild West cowboy.

"You call this a plan?" I asked, on Lucien's heels.

Oh sure, we had Bliss and Gaston in one spot. "It also means we're about to barge in on a pissed-off weretiger *and* a blood-sucking vampire—no offense, sweetie."

"None taken," he said, as we stalked to the front door, using the dense foliage as coverage. "I think our biggest consideration is that I'm still weak."

"And I can't shift," I said, "not so soon after interrogating."

Lucien gave me a long, concerned look as we waited for Vinny and Tia.

I held up my hands. "Hey, I can't change my nature."

He should know that by now.

"Here, babe," Vinny said, handing Tia a shotgun.

Oh yeah. That was a good idea.

"Ready?" Lucien murmured, right before he rushed the door and kicked it in.

I sprinted after him with Vinny on my heels.

By the time I got there, Lucien was locked in combat with a white-haired vampire. In the split second it took for me to assess the situation, Bliss tackled me from behind.

My head smacked the ceramic floor and my vision swam.

Yip-yip-yip!

I turned over to see Chi-Chi launch herself at Bliss's neck.

The tiger slapped the dog away. She yelped as she slammed against the wall, but it was enough time for me to unsheathe my dagger. It sliced Bliss across the chest and she roared.

Bliss shifted, lowering her head as tiger fur raced down her back.

Vinny fired his shotgun, blowing Gaston off of Lucien. I stood, wiping blood out of my eyes.

Gaston hissed, fangs bared. Lucien was pale and bloody. He launched himself at the white-haired vampire, but Gaston dodged, tossing Vinny through the front window. His body smashed through the glass.

"Heather!" Tia screamed as Bliss readied to pounce.

I fired my pistol once. Twice. My silver bullets didn't even slow her down. The wounded tiger kept coming. She was after blood now and there was nothing I could do.

Vinny was out. Lucien was locked in his own life-or-death battle. Tia crouched in the corner.

"Tia!" I screamed as Bliss landed on me like a two-ton brick. I pulled out my lucky boot knife, sinking it into her chest as she hit me. She kept coming. I hit the floor, rolling with her to keep her from taking out my neck, but it was just a matter of time. Only seconds.

My fingers gripped her coarse fur. It felt like time slowed as her sinewy muscles moved under my hands. She was a killing machine.

I waited for the end as blood spurted across my face. At first, I thought it was mine and I marveled at how I didn't even feel any pain.

The tiger roared and fell backward. A large brown wolf had it by the neck.

I shot Bliss with my stun gun and reached for the last thing I had—mace—for all the good it would do us.

But Tia had the tiger in a death bite. Blood poured from the animal's neck.

"E-yah!" I turned just in time to see a bloody Vinny move up behind Gaston and stake the vampire in the back with a broken windowpane.

I stood for a moment, in shock, as Vinny helped Lucien pick his way through the pulpy mess formerly known as Gaston. Meanwhile Tia was using the tiger for a chew toy. I wiped my dagger on the curtains and resheathed it.

Yip-yip-yip!

"You okay, Sparky?" I scooped up Chi-Chi and together we surveyed the damage. Someone was going to need the services of about a dozen Vinnys in French maid costumes to clean up this place.

Gaston was clearly no more, which was a shame. I would have liked some answers. Then I saw a hairy tiger paw twitch.

"Tia, hold back."

The werewolf growled.

"Oh yeah, now you get pushy."

"What is it?" Lucien asked behind me.

"I think Bliss is alive."

Between Lucien, Vinny, and me, we managed to tempt Tia away from her prey. Actually, it was Chi-Chi's idea. We used the steaks from the refrigerator, on a white plate for presentation. Tia was a sucker for white.

Bliss shifted back to human faster than any of us expected, but she was still weak enough that we managed to handcuff her to a pole in her garage.

I leaned against a silver Bentley while we waited for the Vampire Council police to arrive.

Bliss was blubbering by this time, although more for her vampire lover, it seemed, than for herself.

"He was the only man who ever loved me," she sobbed, clutching the housedress we'd thrown around her.

I almost felt sorry for her.

Almost.

Gaston was not only a drug dealer, he was also a cheat.

"He had a wife," I reminded her.

"He didn't love them!" she wailed. "He was impulsive. He didn't mean to marry them!"

Say what? "Exactly how many wives are we talking about?"

"Only eight"—she sniffled—"mostly in Europe."

"Busy guy," Vinny said, feeding Chi-Chi yet another slice of steak.

She stared off dreamily. "He was supposed to take me to Italy next month."

I snorted. "Watch out for blue pills."

"You might not be too far off," Lucien mused. "What if he put them to sleep while he was gone?"

"That's sick," I said.

"Makes cheating easier if wifey doesn't know you're gone. We'll have to investigate further, but I'll bet some of these women are literally sleeping their lives away."

"You'd think they'd know." I'd know if I was married to a seven-time bigamist. I hoped. I felt my gaze harden as Tia strolled up to the weeping tiger.

Blood streaked her arms and she wore a pale pink dressing gown Vinny had found in one of the closets. "My Thomas found out about the drug, didn't he?"

"He was high and mighty about it. He wanted to spill the whole thing to shareholders. Gaston didn't kill him," she said, as if that made a difference.

"No, he just put him to sleep," I said.

"What are the side effects?" Tia demanded. "How do I bring him back?"

"I don't know. You could ask Gaston but you killed him!" Bliss collapsed into another round of sobbing.

That's when I knew. "Sunny figured it out, didn't she?"

Bliss sniffled. "The bitch. She couldn't just be happy being one of his wives. She had to be his only wife."

"Did she know you were sleeping with him?" Wild guess, but I wasn't about to try to enter her mind right now.

"No," she gulped, "but Sunny was going to tell about his other wives. She was going to bring in her wolf pack. She told me and Francine all about it." Her eyes were wild. "She was going to take him from me!"

"So you killed her," Lucien said.

She nodded, gulping. "You don't understand. I need a man. I have nothing. The damned dog has more than I do!"

Chi-Chi growled.

Damned straight.

"The only money I had came from Nina," she said.

Right. "You mean from blackmailing Nina."

Who *wasn't* blackmailing Nina?

Bliss shrugged. "She had the money. And she's a slut."

Err . . . pot calling kettle?

"Sunny's husband, Gaston. He was giving you money, wasn't he?" asked Lucien.

Bliss stiffened. "He could afford it."

Maybe. Still, "You didn't love him. You just needed a sugar daddy."

"I loved him!" she wailed. "And I hated Sunny."

"How'd you kill her?" Lucien demanded.

She cowered, trapped.

"You already told us you did it, Bliss," I reminded her. I could see how getting clocked with an ornate medieval chandelier would kill Sunny. But how had Bliss nailed her with it?

I could see her making her decision. Finally she relented. "I snuck in while she was out mooning over that damned gardener. It didn't take long to cut the links on the chandelier." She gave a sullen look. "I only had to knock it enough to spin free of the broken link for it to fall. I hated that god-awful piece of junk. *He* gave it to her. She didn't deserve anything from him. She didn't even see it coming." Tears welled in her eyes. "Now he's never coming back."

I just hoped Tia's husband could.

CHAPTER 10

The werewolves arrived that morning. The war was off, which was great because my pack seemed more interested in raiding our kitchen than fighting. The vampires would arrive tonight.

Bliss was taken into custody by her own people, which I thought was horse pucky until Finnegan told me what they'd probably do to her. It wasn't pretty, but at least she'd live. Unlike Sunny.

That left Chi-Chi the Chihuahua at loose ends. I offered to take her in if she was willing to give up life on Mysteria Lane. From her enthusiastic wriggling, I figured she was up for the challenge.

We retreated back to the Duke house to wait for representatives from the Vampire Council. Nina sent her chef over to help out, which was pretty nice of her, all things considered.

He'd loaded the granite countertops with meat pies, steak tartar and roasted venison. I slipped a bite to Chi-Chi and wondered if I should break it to the cook that we did eat other things besides meat. You know what, though? The guy looked happy. He was actually getting to cook for once, so I left him to it.

Tia had skipped her husband's pill that morning and had reported no results yet. She planned to sit with him all day, to see if she could detect a change.

I'd spent as much time as I could that morning interrogating Francine and Nina, just to make sure there wasn't anything we'd missed. Nina had been telling the truth all along. Good for her. And it turned out Francine was bald as a bat under that expensive brunette wig.

I insisted she remove it for the remainder of our questioning.

None of the residents of Mysteria Lane would be any wiser. But I'd sure enjoyed it.

I managed a quick "hello" with Lucien when he woke up for the evening. I made sure to show him exactly why I was so glad we'd survived the night before. He returned the favor.

Twice.

I love it when the Vampire Council runs late.

But they eventually arrived. More's the pity. And went into closed meetings with Finnegan and our pack elders.

The pack used it as an excuse to enjoy an eighteenth course, courtesy of Nina's chef. I swear if he ever wanted to leave her, he'd have his choice of about thirty slavering Topanga Pack members, ready to bow at his command.

Good food could do that to a wolf.

Vinny plucked a beef skewer off a silver tray and leaned up against the counter next to me. "Tia's husband woke up."

I smiled. "Fantastic. When?"

"About ten minutes ago. She skipped his evening meds. I helped her prop him up enough for a drink."

"Good for her."

"I'll say. They're even louder than you two."

"Oh, shut up."

"I ran like a girl."

I smacked him on the arm, not really meaning it. I wished Lucien would get back soon. No telling how much time we'd have before he had to be on to his next assignment.

The mere thought of it made my stomach hollow.

Suck it up, McPhee.

I'd known this moment would come. I couldn't have Lucien forever, even if I wanted it.

And boy, did I want it.

The Vampire Council and the wolf elders made it back to the house alive, which was a good sign.

Finnegan slapped me on the back so hard he almost knocked the wind out of me. "The war is off," he announced to the crowd at large. "Thanks to your hard work," he added under his breath.

Sure. Nothing like accolades for a job well done.

Oh, who was I kidding? I didn't need praise. I had a happy ending.

At least until, "Hi, Lucien." The corners of my mouth turned up as he wrapped his arms around me and kissed me on the head.

We ignored the catcalls from my pack mates.

Yeah, yeah.

McPhee was smiling. McPhee was smitten.

McPhee was in love.

Damn it all.

I vowed to keep my pride. I'd let him go when the time came. I just hoped it wouldn't be tonight.

"Heather," he said into my hair, "we need to talk."

Damn.

I felt my smile falter. "Sure. Whatever you say."

He led me out of the packed kitchen and upstairs to his room.

Hoo-boy. To be dumped in the same spot where we'd made love this evening. I could hardly wait. Then again, maybe this was for the best. I'd know it was over. We'd make a clean break. I could do this.

I let out a hard breath.

This was worse than preparing for a fight.

"Heather." Lucien held my hand, his expression earnest. Curse him and his amazing body and his gorgeous lips and the way he made me feel hot even now when I knew he was about to hightail it out of town.

"Look," I said, unable to stand it. "I know you have to leave. You said it before we ever got involved."

It wasn't his fault.

It was mine for being stupid enough to fall for him.

"I do have to leave," he said, in that same infuriatingly calm tone.

I was so tempted to use my truth powers on him. My chin lowered and I stopped myself. What was the point? I already knew he was heading out for the next assignment.

Damn the man. Would it kill him to be a little upset about this? Meanwhile my insides felt like they'd turned to glue.

"I'm heading down to New Orleans," he said, oblivious. "We're looking into a coven of voodoo mambos turned vampire."

"Sounds lovely," I said, just trying to make it through the conversation with my pride intact. In a second, I was going to cry.

He caressed my cheek, which made it worse.

Could we just get to the dumping part?

"It will be amazing," he said.

"I'm sure," I agreed.

"If you join me," he added.

"What?"

He looked vulnerable all of a sudden. "I could use a were who can make people tell the truth."

Was he actually saying what I thought he was saying? "I'm not even sure it works on vampires."

"Ask me if I care."

I couldn't leave with him. I didn't quite know why, but I knew there was a reason it had never occurred to me. "You can do this on your own," I said, making complete sense.

"It wouldn't be half as much fun," he said playfully.

Maybe so, but, "My pack needs me."

"You can fly back home if they do."

I tangled my hands in my lap. "Finnegan would never let me go."

He untangled them. "I made it part of our negotiations this evening."

"So you knew—"

"I think I've known all along." He brushed his lips over mine. "Go with me, Heather. Let's see where this leads."

I pulled back, but not so far as to unwrap my hands from his. "It can't be this easy," I said, trying to reason with him.

Nothing in my life had ever been this easy.

It could be amazing.

"Heather?" he asked, waiting for my answer.

He wasn't going to beg. I liked that in a vampire. Oh my God, was I actually considering this?

"Voodoo vampires, huh?" I asked. It could be interesting. And I'd never been to New Orleans.

"If I go"—I ran a finger down his chest—"will I get to sleep next to you?"

He pulled me closer. "Yes."

A smile tickled the edges of my lips. "Kiss you?"

His voice grew husky. "I hope."

"Would I have to let you bite me?" I hoped.

He nibbled kisses along the soft spot in front of my ear. "If you're lucky."

I tilted his chin my way for a long, lingering kiss.

"Okay," I said, before I lost all control and jumped headlong into bed with him. "I'll go to New Orleans."

"Ha!" He let out a very unvampirish whoop before tackling me back onto the bed.

"But I have a few rules," I said, wriggling against him. Anticipating what was to come.

"I can't wait," he said, propped above me.

"I will not wear high heels."

"Done."

"I absolutely refuse to do any more breaking and entering."

"Prude."

He kissed his way down my neck until I almost forgot rule number three. "And," I said, running my fingers through his thick, blond hair, "I will not fall in love with you."

I could feel him smile against my neck. "We'll see."

WEREWOLVES IN CHIC CLOTHING

TAMI DANE

Michelle Stewart waited her whole life for something exciting to happen. As an eight-year-old, she dreamed of learning she was actually a princess, inheriting a crown and massive fortune.

Didn't happen.

As a teenager, she hoped to be discovered by an Elite Modeling agent in the mall.

Didn't happen.

As an adult, she fantasized about being swept off her feet by her Prince Charming and living a storybook happily-ever-after.

To everyone—but Michelle—it appeared she was living that last fantasy. In reality, Michelle wouldn't live to see any of her dreams come true. . . .

CHAPTER 1

I think I might have just moved into Stepford. If you've seen the movie, you know what I'm talking about. If you haven't . . . what are you waiting for? *The Stepford Wives* (I'm talking about the original film) is a classic.

Back to Stepford. Why do I think I've moved there? Let me paint a visual picture for you. I was driving a rusty U-Haul, twenty-five years' worth of personal possessions, including my collection of vintage purses, packed into beat-up cardboard boxes. I was rolling past one perfectly kept home after another. The flower gardens were weed-free, grass freshly mowed. And everyone I saw was smiling.

It was damned creepy.

Maybe I'd lived in the city too long. I wanted to hear someone yell, "Fuck you!" I ached for the reassuring sound of a horn blaring in anger. Instead, I was getting happy birdsong and the distant rumble of a lawn mower.

Why did this bother me so much? Because if this suburban nirvana was anything like Stepford, there was absolutely no way I was going to fit in. I hate cooking. I kill plants. I've never been crafty.

And . . . what the hell was I doing?

You'd better be worth it, Jonathan Stewart.

One look at Jonathan Stewart, and almost every niggling doubt in my mind immediately evaporated.

Hellooooo, handsome.

FYI, Jonathan Stewart, my soon-to-be fiancé, is traffic-stopping gorgeous. He's also powerful, successful, generous, kind—downright perfect . . . and he was standing in his driveway, wearing the world's biggest smile.

I am the luckiest woman alive.

Now, back to my story.

Jonathan was at my door, yanking it open before I'd even gotten the truck shifted into PARK. "Hello, beautiful," he said, pulling me out of the vehicle.

"Hello back," I said, sliding my arms around his waist. We kissed, and I saw stars. I heard angels singing, too. Then again, that might've been the robins. My knees were a little wobbly by the time the kiss ended.

Jon brushed my windblown hair out of my face. "How was your drive? I wish you would have let me handle the move for you."

"My drive was fine, thank you. And there was no point in hiring movers to load a few cardboard boxes." I motioned toward the house, which was huge and immaculate. "So, this is where you live?"

"*We*. This is where we live." Jon stepped to the side, one arm still curled around my waist. He motioned to his picture-perfect brick house. "Christine Price—soon to be Christine Stewart—welcome home."

"Home," I echoed, letting him guide me inside. "Oh . . . wow." I couldn't believe this . . . showroom . . . was going to be my home. First, it was huge, but I'd already said that. And beautifully decorated, and . . . there was absolutely no way the particleboard and laminate "furniture" I'd just hauled across three states was going to fit in here. We meandered through the foyer, past the sweeping staircase leading to the second floor, down a hallway that led to the rear of the house. On our way, we strolled past a formal living room that looked like it had never been used, past a formal dining room that also looked unused, and finally an office-slash-library. The hall ended at an open space housing the family room and eat-in kitchen.

In the family room my eyes jumped from one thing to another. The sectional sofa screamed, *Sit on me!* The ginormous flat panel TV on a wall gleamed in the sunlight. A pair of comfy-looking leather club chairs created a cozy nook that inspired me to grab a book and cuddle up to read. The floor-to-ceiling windows lining the back wall beckoned me, the lush green landscape beyond framed in drapes (were they . . . happy sigh! . . . *silk?*).

The whole place whispered expensive. Tasteful. Classy.

Jon looked proud. "I want this place to feel like home. If there's anything you'd like to change—and I'm hoping there is—I want you to do it. Just tell me what you want, what you need, and I'll make it happen."

I tested one of the chairs. Heaven. "Thanks," I said, beaming as I ran my hand over the arm. I pulled in a deep breath, drawing in the scrumptious scent of the leather and the equally intoxicating aroma of the man standing next to me. Whatever cologne he was wearing, it was pure aphrodisiac. "But everything looks so new. I don't see why we'd need to change a thing."

"Doesn't matter. Do whatever you want." He grabbed my hands, eyes twinkling, and pulled me to my feet. "Don't get too comfortable yet. I still need to show you the rest of the house."

He escorted me into the kitchen, which sported all the essentials of fine suburban living. Stainless steel appliances, natural stone countertops, beautiful wood cabinets and floor. There were two ovens. Two. I rarely put one to use. How would I ever find a reason to use two? Jon informed me the stove was a chef's stove, whatever that meant. It was big and looked dangerous. I decided I'd stick with microwaving for now. The fridge, on the other hand, was also enormous but not at all scary. It was well stocked with all my favorite foods. There was even a month's worth of my fave ice cream in the freezer.

This man deserved a kiss. I gave him one. And a second. And a third.

He growled like a man-bear—how I adore the way he growls—scooped me up into his arms, and turned a one-eighty, heading back toward the front of the house.

With one arm looped around his neck, I swallowed a girly giggle. Would this be my life from now on? Filled with toe-curling kisses, manly growls, and a never-ending supply of German chocolate ice cream? I didn't dare hope so. A past full of heartache, hardship, and frustration had shattered the lenses in my rose-colored glasses a long time ago.

That didn't mean I couldn't enjoy this moment.

"Now, to show you *our* room." Upstairs, Jon turned into the first room on the right, and I literally gasped.

"No way. Is this really our bedroom?" I asked, gaping like a kid who'd just stepped into the world's largest toy store. I was beginning to see a trend here. The bed, just like the stove and refrigerator and television downstairs, was gigantic. Who would need so much space to sleep? Then again, I wondered if that space was intended for something else, something besides sleep. As a few possibilities played through my mind, I licked my lips.

Jon said, "I just had this room redesigned. But if you don't like it—"

"I love it."

"Good." Jon dropped me on the bed. It was like landing on a cloud. He palmed my cheeks and stared into my eyes, his expression dark and manly and one hundred percent sexy. "I want you to be happy."

"I have a feeling I'll be very happy."

"You can bet I'll do everything in my power to make sure of that." He tipped his head, and I closed my eyes, bracing for another mind-blowing kiss. But a knock on the door had me snapping them open and Jon jerking back.

"Dad." Joshua, Jon's twelve-year-old son, was standing just inside the door, his cell phone in his hand. He had the world's worst timing. But I'd heard that was true for all kids. "Can I go to Ethan's house?"

I scrambled to my feet and tried to pretend my face wasn't about to combust into flames. I was slightly aware of Jon pushing to his feet beside me.

I stuttered, "Josh, it's good seeing you again."

Josh gave me one of those looks, the kind that said, "yeah, whatever."

Jon said, "Josh, I told you, I need your help today. Christine's moving in."

Josh's expression darkened. "But Dad, it's Labor Day weekend. School starts Tuesday. It's my last weekend of summer vacation—"

"Jon," I whispered, turning to face my hot, sexy almost-fiancé. "If you're making Josh stay home for my sake, it's okay. I'd rather he go play with his friends, have fun."

Josh adopted a convincing sad puppy expression.

Jon thought about it.

"Please," Josh said, his voice doing that preteen-boy cracking thing. Ugh. I was about to become a stepmom to a teenager. Good times were coming my way. I could see it already. "I'll be back by seven. That'll still give you plenty of time to make me work."

"Fine. By seven. Not a minute later."

Josh roared out of the house as fast as his twelve-year-old legs could take him. When the deep thump of the front door slamming echoed through the house, Jon strolled to the bedroom door and closed it. Turning, he gave me a look hot enough to melt lead. "Now, where were we?"

I fell onto the mattress, batting my eyelashes at him. "I think you were about to make me very happy—" I gave a little shriek as he pounced on me like an overgrown jungle cat.

Angled over me, Jon gave me a Cheshire grin. "Ah, yes. And so I was."

Okay, so there was at least one thing about this Stepford setup I'd like. . . .

Jon nibbled on my earlobe.

The doorbell rang.

"Urk," I said.

"Damn," Jon said. He scowled. "The hell with it. They'll go away." He went back to nibbling, and I went back to melting.

The freaking doorbell rang a second time. Jon kept on nipping my neck, but I wasn't into it anymore. I was distracted. When the bell rang a third time, I shoved him. "Okay, Dracula"—it's a silly pet name, but the man has a thing for necks—"we're going to have to take a timeout. I can't get into the mood with all that ding-donging."

Jon sighed. It was his turn to give a sad puppy look. It was clear where Joshua had learned it.

"Won't work." I pushed on his chest until he was upright.

"But it worked for Josh." *Ding dong.* "Ignore it." He grabbed my hand, flipped it over, and scattered tickly little kisses over the inside of my wrist.

Ding dong.

"I can't ignore it."

Ding dong.

Sheesh, whoever that was, they were persistent.

Jon motioned to me. "Stay put. I'll be back in a minute."

I decided I was okay with that plan . . . until I heard a woman's voice downstairs. Laughing.

I'd just left the best job of my life, said *sayonara* to every friend I had in the world, and hauled everything I owned three hundred miles. I didn't do that to sit upstairs and listen to my soon-to-be husband flirt with another woman.

After a quick mirror check—a girl needs to make a good first impression—I headed downstairs to see why my not-quite fiancé hadn't returned to me yet.

I wasn't happy with what I saw when I reached the foyer. The world's most perfect woman—Stepford, I'm telling you—was standing a little too close to Jon for my comfort. She was holding a covered Pyrex pan with something red in it. As I stepped onto the stone tile, the visitor's attention snapped to me. So did Jon's.

"Hi," I said to them both.

Jon and the Stepford wife began chattering at the same time. Jon stopped.

Mrs. Perfect beamed at me. Perfect blond hair. Perfect makeup. Her dress was very well-maintained vintage. 1950s. Silk. I was guessing Harvey Berin. She was wearing a wedding ring. "Hello, Christine, I'm Samantha Phillips. I live next door. So good to meet you at last." She shoved the hot dish into my hands, cherry pot holders keeping them from blistering. "I made a pan of lasagna, thinking you'd probably be too busy to cook tonight."

The scents of tomato sauce and garlic and cheese tickled my nose. "How thoughtful. Thank you." I took the pan to the kitchen and set it on the stove. I heard Jon and Samantha following me.

"Thank you," Jon echoed.

When I turned around, I found Samantha standing with her hands clasped in front of her A-line skirt. I shoved the pot holders into her empty hands. "Thanks again."

She jammed one hand into a skirt pocket, produced a business card. "I guess I should get going. Don't want to keep you from your work." She extended her arm, offering the card. "If you need help with anything, please don't hesitate to call. I'm home all day. I can be here in a blink. Michelle and I used to—" She cut herself off. "Forgive me. Michelle was a good friend."

"It's okay. I understand." I accepted the card and set it on the counter. "Thanks again. I'll keep your offer in mind."

"Okay, then. I can see myself out." Samantha threw a cute little wave at Jon and hustled toward the door. I watched Jon watch her leave. When he finally glanced my way, I probably wasn't looking too happy.

"I'm sorry about that. Samantha and my first wife were close. She had a very hard time after Michelle died. But I'd rather not talk about that right now." He hauled me into his arms. "Michelle was my past. You are my future. And if you're worried about Samantha, don't be," he said. "She's very happily married. And I'm very happily almost-married."

The man knew just what to say.

He also knew just what to do. He kissed me until I couldn't breathe and I'd forgotten all about whatshername and her lasagna and her stupid cherry pot holders.

Oh yes, I was definitely feeling better now. Warm. Tingly. Happy.

"Shall we head back upstairs?" I asked, dragging my finger-nails down his chest. I hadn't seen that chest in three weeks. Long-distance dating sucked. It was so good to be done with that now.

"Yes, let's go." Jon tossed me over his shoulder like a cave-man. I gave a little shriek of surprise, flopping over to give his cute butt a smack. He gave me one in return as he headed toward the staircase.

Then the doorbell rang again.

"Ohmygod," I said to his back. "Are you kidding me?"

"Ignore it."

Ding dong.

Still atop Jon's shoulder, I wriggled. "I just want to have sex. Who would've thought that would be such a problem?"

"It isn't a problem. Let's go have sex."

Ding dong.

"No. Set me down."

Jon grunted.

Down I slid. On the way, I happened to notice he was sport-ing a somewhat obvious hard-on. I motioned to his crotch. "You might want to cover that up."

He glanced down, looked up, and gave me a crooked grin. "Maybe it'll chase whoever it is away so we can get back to what we were doing." He yanked open the door, and another attractive woman stepped into my new home.

The woman either didn't see me or didn't care. Tall. Brunette. Slim. And also well dressed—her clothes weren't designer, but they looked like they'd been tailored to fit her perfectly. She blurted, "Jon, I need to talk to you right now about Carson. He's—"

"Lindsay Baker," Jon interrupted, motioning toward me. "This is Christine. Christine's moving in today."

Lindsay finally realized I was standing there. "Oh! Hello." She shook my hand. "So good to meet you. Welcome to the neighborhood." She thumbed over her shoulder, toward the open door behind her. "I live across the street." Looking slightly wilted, she frowned. "I'm sorry I forgot you were moving in today. Jon told me last week. He's been very excited." She glanced at Jon. "I'm guessing Samantha's already been by to welcome Christine?"

"Yep," I said. "She brought lasagna." That was slightly bitchy of me to rub it in, I'll admit. I'll probably pay for it, one way or another.

Lindsay's smile was only slightly forced. "Of course she brought lasagna. Enjoy. The woman is the best cook on the block, now that Michelle—I mean, Samantha makes everything from scratch. Me, I'm lucky if I don't burn a frozen pizza."

"Yeah, me too," I admitted. Two neighbors. Two welcomes. And both had mentioned Michelle, Jon's deceased wife. I was beginning to worry I had some insanely perfect shoes to fill.

We exchanged a smile. For some reason, regardless of her mention of Michelle, I had a feeling I might get along with this neighbor. The jury was still out on Samantha.

"Anyway, I guess I'll head out now. I'm sure you're both very"—Lindsay's gaze paused on Jon's crotch before jerking away—"busy."

"Thanks for coming by." Jon grabbed the doorknob, ready to close the door behind her.

"Oh!" On the porch now, Lindsay spun around to face him. She opened her mouth to say something but then shut it. "Yes." She waved at me. "Again, welcome. If there's anything you need, please don't hesitate to ask."

"Thanks." I waved back.

Jon shut the door. He gave me a look that made my heart flutter. "Now, let's get back to welcoming you home—"

Ding dong.

I sighed. "We might as well forget it. It's not happening. I didn't know you were so popular." We'd met on an online dating site. Jon had flown out to meet me exactly one month after we'd started chatting online. And he'd made the trip every other weekend after that, for the next five months. I mentioned, once or twice, coming out to see him instead, but he'd insisted it was better for him to do the traveling. He could write it off as a business expense. I couldn't. And once I got over the suspicion that he was actually married and trying to keep me from finding out, I couldn't argue with that logic. All that to say, this was the first time I'd seen him in his hometown.

"I'm not 'popular,' " he said. "My neighbors are all just extremely nosy. You're the first woman who's been in my house since . . . since Michelle died."

While our two visitors had already mentioned his wife, today was the first time Jon had actually said her name in my presence. I saw that as a sign. "Speaking of Michelle, you promised to tell me what happened when I moved in. So I knew how to handle Josh. Here I am."

He started to respond, but the doorbell cut him off. He lifted an index finger.

Ding dong.

He opened the door to reveal yet another attractive woman. Stepford Wife Number Three was suited up tight in Hugo Boss, her hair coiled on the back of her head. Her makeup was flawless but understated.

"I'm sorry if this is a bad time. . . ." The woman, who was still standing on the front porch peered in at me. ". . . but I saw Samantha and Lindsay—"

"No, of course it's not a bad time." Jon motioned her inside. "This is Christine. Christine, this is Erica Ross. She lives next door—on the other side." He motioned toward the opposite side of our home.

"Good to meet you," I said.

"Welcome to the neighborhood," Erica said, shaking my hand. She produced a card. "If you need anything, feel free to call. I work quite a bit, but my husband's home with the kids during the day. Adam's pretty handy—unlike Jon here." Erica and Jon exchanged a smile.

"That's true," Jon admitted. "I won't even try to argue with that. Which is why I have a list of trusted contractors on file."

Erica continued, "Michelle used to call Adam whenever she had a minor emergency. Plugged sink, that kind of thing. He doesn't mind at all. Gives him something to do."

"Okay. Thanks." I put the card in my pocket.

"Thank you," Jon echoed, looking like he might shove the woman out if she didn't leave on her own.

"I can't stay," Erica said, turning toward the exit. "I'm on my way to meet a client. But I didn't want to go without at least saying hello."

"That was very thoughtful. Thanks." I gave her a wave as she hurried out the door.

Jon closed and locked the door behind her. "Okay, now that's enough of the neighbors. I don't give a damn if the mayor rings my doorbell to give you the keys to the city. I'm not answering. We're going to our room." He grabbed my hand and took the stairs two at a time. "I'm going to have sex with you if it kills me."

Kills him? I wasn't sure how to respond to that statement.

The truth of the matter was, the moment was over. Between worrying about being interrupted again, and curiosity about the wife Jon hadn't talked about before today, I was more interested in getting back to the discussion we'd started before Erica's entry.

Once we were inside the bedroom, Jon, true to form, went for my neck.

I held him off with outstretched hands. "Hang on, there, Dracula. I want to talk about Michelle first. How did she die?"

CHAPTER 2

"Okay," Jon said, sitting on the bed. What do you want to know about my first wife?"

Standing next to the door, I said, "Well, how she died, for starters."

Jon nodded. Looking solemn, he patted the bed, inviting me to sit beside him. I did. "Michelle had a lot of issues. Emotional problems. Not many people knew. Not her friends. Not her parents. Not even Josh. Only her doctors and me. It started almost immediately after we were married. She seemed happy for a little while, maybe six months or so, but then my crazy work schedule got to her. She became lonely. Depressed. I suggested we start trying to have a child, and her mood picked up again." His smile was wistful, sweet. "I thought we were going to be okay. But when she didn't get pregnant right away, her depression came back. And it was worse. I suggested we give up, think about adopting to take the pressure off. She insisted we keep trying. So we saw a specialist. Had some tests run. Turns out she had some kind of hormonal imbalance. She was given some pills and a few months later, she was pregnant."

He hadn't gotten to the part about her dying, but I was willing to be patient. This was, by far, the most words I'd heard Jon speak consecutively since meeting him. He wasn't the chit-chatty kind.

"After Joshua came home, things were good. Perfect. She was

busy. Happy. She poured her energy into taking care of our son. She volunteered at his school. She made cupcakes for his bake sales. She helped him with his homework and hauled him to soccer practice and baseball games. Her world revolved around our boy for ten years. She was a wonderful mother. A wonderful wife. But when he started to become more independent—as is normal for boys that age—she told me she was ready to have another child. And I was glad to try for another, especially if it meant she'd be happy. Unfortunately, it wasn't so easy. She took hormone treatments. But they didn't help. We even tried IVF. Nothing worked. One day, two years ago, I came home from work to find she'd killed herself." Jon blinked. His eyes reddened. He sniffled. "I never thought. . . ."

"I'm sorry." I set my hand over Jon's. His was trembling. Made me wonder, was he over his wife's death? "Two years isn't a very long time."

"I'm okay. I even went to a counselor for a while." He didn't exactly sound okay. "If you're worried that I'll be comparing you to Michelle all the time, please don't be. I told you she was my past, and I meant it. She's gone. I'm ready to move on. I'm looking back now only because you asked me to. From this point forward, we'll be looking to the future. Our future."

"I hope so." I wasn't one hundred percent convinced. "I quit my job for you. I gave up my apartment. I don't have a safety net, if this doesn't work out—"

"You don't need one, Christine. Trust me. Please."

I wanted to trust him. I was almost afraid not to.

Shifting to face me, he took my hands in his. "Look, I told you things won't be perfect. And it won't be easy. My hours are crazy. I'm not home much. Josh will need time to adjust to having another woman in the house. But I will be here for you, just like I was for Michelle."

Feeling slightly chilled, I crossed my arms over my chest. "I'm a little scared. I'd be lying if I said I wasn't."

"I understand. I would be, too." He pulled me into a hug. I relaxed in his embrace. He was warm and strong and I wanted to believe he was the man of my dreams. Easing back, he brushed my hair out of my face and gave me a sweet, gentle kiss. "I want you to always feel you can be honest with me."

I nodded. "You too."

"Now, there's one room I haven't had a chance to show you yet. I think now's the time." He stood, offering his hand. I accepted it. Down we went, to the main floor of the house, through the kitchen, and down a second, steeper set of stairs to the finished basement.

I stopped at the bottom of the steps, clapped my hands over my mouth. "What is this?" I said through my fingers, my eyes sweeping over the bright, cheery space. I saw three long counters, dotted with various sewing machines. Three dress forms stood along one wall, in front of floor-to-ceiling shelves. And sitting on a stand was a very special machine.

"It's your sewing studio," Jon said.

"You're kidding." I made a beeline for the commercial grade embroidery machine. That one alone cost anywhere from ten to fifteen thousand dollars. I'd been dreaming of getting one for ages. Gaping, I glanced around the room again. "I can't believe this."

"I wanted you to have everything you'd need to make your dream come true. I couldn't expect you to launch your clothing line with that rusty old Singer of yours."

"Are you for real?" I asked, throwing my arms around his neck. I kissed him all over his face. "Ohmygod, thank you."

"You're welcome." His eyes twinkled. How I adored those twinkles. I adored a lot more than his twinkles. *Just tell me this man is everything he seems to be.* "Now that you've seen your surprise, how about we get that truck unpacked?"

I could care less about all the crap I'd hauled here now. Outside of my clothes and a few personal items, none of it was worth anything. None of it would fit in this glorious house. But I had to return the truck to U-Haul in the morning. "Okay."

Jon gave my butt a little tap as he led me toward the garage. "And maybe when we're done, you'd like to take a nice, long bath. . . ." A bath? My apartment had only had a tiny shower stall. I couldn't remember the last time I'd taken a bath. ". . . together."

A hot man. A gorgeous house. A dream studio. Could my life get any better than this?

"And tomorrow, you can go shopping for material," he added. Shopping?

I wasn't in Stepford. I was in heaven.

The next morning, I was sorting through my sewing pattern collection when the doorbell rang. Jon was upstairs sleeping. So was Joshua. That meant it was up to me to answer. Looking glorious (not) in a ratty pair of sweats, a T-shirt that said, NY LOVES ME, and a ponytail, no makeup, I checked the clock as I padded barefoot to the front door.

The bell rang two more times before I finally answered.

What a surprise (not). It was Samantha, Lindsay, and Erica. Samantha was holding a plate covered in foil. Lindsay had a steaming carafe of something that smelled incredible, and Erica was holding a white bakery box.

"Good morning." I stepped aside to invite them in. "What a surprise. At nine o'clock in the morning. On Labor Day weekend."

Lindsay, donning a semi-scowl, gave me a quick up-and-down inspection. "We didn't wake you, I hope." She lifted the carafe. "I brought caffeine."

"No, you didn't wake me, and thanks." I had to admit, nobody had ever gone to such lengths to make me feel welcome before. In the city, it was a big deal if my neighbors gave me a little nod in the stairwell. I wasn't sure how I felt about this. Was it a suburbia thing?

"I made muffins this morning. They just came out of the oven," Samantha said as she click-clacked past me.

"I brought bagels." Erica, following on Samantha's heels, lifted the box. "I hope you like Einstein's Everything bagels."

I motioned them all into the kitchen. "I do, thanks." After

four tries, I found the cupboard with the cups. I grabbed four and set them on the island-slash-breakfast bar. Then I went in search of plates.

"I just love Everything bagels," Lindsay said, pulling out a stool and sitting.

"Me too. The saltier and garlickier the better," Erica said, sitting beside Lindsay.

"I prefer plain," Samantha said, taking the third stool.

Standing on the opposite side of the bar, I placed a plate in front of each of them.

Meanwhile, Lindsay poured a steaming cup of coffee and handed it to me. I took a whiff. My mouth watered. "What kind of coffee is this?" I sipped. Delicious. But hot. I set down the cup to look for knives.

"My own blend. I may not bake." Lindsay put a bagel on her plate. "And I'm not much of a cook. But when it comes to coffee, I know a thing or two. Erica, tell me you didn't forget cream cheese?"

"Of course not." Erica spread a handful of little packets on the counter.

We all settled in, nibbling on the world's best muffins and munching on bagels for a few minutes.

It was Lindsay who eventually broke the silence. "We thought we owed you an apology for yesterday," she explained.

"Oh? Why's that?" I asked around a mouthful of muffin.

"Because we all just met you, and right off the bat we were talking about Michelle," Erica said. "Talk about insensitive."

"It's okay. I understand." I spread some more cream cheese on my bagel. "Jon told me you were close friends."

"Yes, we were. For ten years. Since the day they moved in." Lindsay gave me a charming smile. "But that doesn't mean we can't be friends with you, too."

"I'm glad." At least, I thought I was glad. A part of me was unsure about this whole thing. These three women, The Pack, seemed a little too eager to be my friends. It was odd.

"Jon told us you were living in New York," Erica said. "I imagine you think we're strange."

"Oh no, of course I don't." I felt my face warming.

Erica laughed. She tucked her hair behind her ear, revealing a simple, but pretty, diamond earring. "Liar. I lived in New York for two years before I married Adam." She glanced down at the enormous diamond ring on her finger. "This has got to be a culture shock for you."

"Okay, maybe it's a little strange," I admitted.

The three friends exchanged nods.

Samantha, looking as perfect and perky as ever, smiled. "We're not as desperate for friendship as you probably think."

"I don't think you're desperate—"

"We're just trying to be friendly." Samantha leaned closer. "You see, you don't know it yet, but you're going to need all the friends you can get."

Now, that was a weird thing to say.

"Why?" I asked.

"Because that man upstairs—the one you're about to marry—he's not exactly what he appears to be."

"We think he killed his wife," Lindsay whispered.

Holy shit.

"She committed suicide," I said, wondering why they would think such a thing.

I don't know these women. They could be lying to make me leave. Maybe they're all in love with Jon.

"Suicide? That's what he told you?" Giving me a pitying look, Erica shook her head. "That's a lie. If you don't believe us—and really, why would you?—check it out for yourself." She motioned for a pen with her hand. I found one in a drawer, along with a little spiral notebook. She pulled a sheet out and wrote a website on it, folded it, and handed it to me. "I hate to be the one to tell you this, but Jonathan Stewart was investigated for murder. He hasn't been brought up on charges . . . yet. They couldn't find enough evidence. But the case is still open. Here's the write-up in our local paper."

Lindsay reached for my hand. "Be careful."

I was dumbfounded. Speechless. What the hell was this? "Jon said she was depressed," I stuttered. "She couldn't get pregnant."

"Depressed?" Samantha pulled a cell phone out of her pocket, hit some buttons, and handed it to me. "Depressed people isolate themselves from friends, from family. They don't go to parties. They don't laugh with friends. This picture was taken the day before Michelle died. At our neighborhood block party. Does she look like she was isolating herself?"

I looked.

First, Michelle could pass for my doppelganger. That was freaky enough. But second, she looked like she was having a great time at the party. And when I say *great,* that might be a slight understatement.

A shiver swept up my spine.

"There are more pictures," Samantha said. "Hit the button."

"I don't need to see more." I handed Samantha the phone and glanced down at my plate. My appetite was gone. Had I made the mistake of a lifetime? Had I left my job, my life, to move in with a murderer? "The pictures don't prove anything."

"You're right. They don't," Erica said. "But we're hoping the police will find some solid proof soon. You could help."

"You want me to dig for clues while I'm living with a man you believe killed his *wife?*" This was crazy. Insane. Unbelievable.

I needed to find out more. About Jon, yes. But also about these women. I was having some doubts about Jon. Any girl would. After all, I'd learned a long time ago that something—or someone—who seemed too good to be true generally was. But I was also having some suspicions about my three neighbors. What were their stories? Why were they so hell-bent on convincing me Jon killed his wife?

"You don't trust us. I can appreciate that," Erica said. "At this point, all you have is what we've told you. But once you do a little digging, you'll realize who has been telling you the truth and who has been lying." She stood, motioning to the other two. "Ladies, I think we've taken up enough of Christine's time." She gave me a smile that seemed genuine. "Our offers still stand. If you need anything, from any of us, we're here for you." She was the first to head for the door. Samantha was second. Lindsay was the last.

At the door, Lindsay leaned over and whispered, "I really like you already. Please be careful."

CHAPTER 3

I couldn't push the freaking button. I was too afraid of what I'd see.

After The Pack cleared out, I returned to my girl-cave and tried to get back to work. As I moved things from one place to another, I kept telling myself they'd been lying to me. Jon's wife had killed herself just like he told me. When I could no longer believe that, I switched to the theory that they weren't lying—they really believed Jon might be a killer—but the police were wrong. Jon was innocent.

Eventually, after several hours, I hadn't completely convinced myself of that explanation, either. So I'd done what any normal girl would do. I powered up my laptop, jumped a few hoops to get it connected to the house's Wi-Fi, and typed in the URL Erica had written out for me.

It was there now, on my browser's search line. But I couldn't hit the button, calling up the page.

Hit the button, dammit. You need to know the truth.

Hand on the mouse. Cursor sitting on top of the SEND button, I closed my eyes. The muscles of my hand tightened. My heart constricted. My lungs slowly deflated.

I clicked.

I swear, my heart stopped completely.

After waiting a handful of seconds, I forced my eyes open.

The newspaper article was open. Oh God. I was about to learn whether I'd just made the mistake of a lifetime.

The first thing I saw was a photograph of a smiling, pretty Michelle Stewart. The sight of that image felt like a sock in the gut. The headline was even worse.

Husband Suspected in Wife's Mysterious Death.

Shit!

Footsteps pounded overhead. They came closer. Someone was coming down the stairs. I clicked the red X, closing the page.

"Chrissy? Are you down here?" Jon called from the stairs as he stomp, stomp, stomped down them.

My hands were shaking as I grabbed the box of patterns I'd been sorting and pretended to be working. "Yep, I'm here."

Jon turned the corner.

There he was. So handsome. Strikingly handsome. Was that the face of a killer? Were those dark brown eyes the eyes of a murderer? He smiled at me. The expression looked genuine. He looked happy, as glad to see me as I had been to see him only yesterday. "Hello there. Settling in okay?"

"Yes, I sure am."

He came closer, too close. I felt my body stiffening, even though I knew that one newspaper article did not mean he was definitely a killer. I hadn't even had a chance to read the article. Perhaps the headline had been misleading. Perhaps the article's author had taken liberties with the facts in the case.

Perhaps I was hoping for a miracle.

He bent to kiss me but stopped short. "Is something wrong?" Clearly, the man knew how to read body language.

How to respond to that question?

"I'm just feeling a little . . . overwhelmed, I guess."

He straightened up. His expression was puzzled, not at all hostile or suspicious. "Overwhelmed about what?"

Of course, he had to ask that.

"About . . . being a stepmother. About facing this huge change. We don't know each other as well as we probably should, so there's that, too." It was a partial truth, as close as I dared get.

He glanced at the box at my feet then up into my eyes. "I

understand." He motioned to the box. "Can I help you un-
pack?"

"That's very sweet, but I think I can handle this. Are you
hungry?" I asked, thinking it might be wise to deflect his attention. "Do you want me to make you something to eat?"

"No, that's okay. I didn't bring you here to become my live-in
waitress. Go ahead and keep working. I can find something."

"Your neighbors stopped by. They brought muffins and
bagels. They're on the counter."

Now his expression turned tense. "They did?" Underlying
the tension, I sensed a little hint of hostility. I hadn't seen any of
that yesterday. Okay, maybe I had. But I'd assumed that was because they'd interrupted us. "They were here this morning?"

"Yes. Is that a problem? Do you dislike them? I didn't get
that impression yesterday."

"No, I don't 'dislike' them. Not at all." As if a switch had
been thrown, his expression brightened again. His stop-your-
heart smile was back in place and the twinkles I'd always found
so charming began twinkling. That shift had alarms ringing in
my head. Back in college I'd dated a guy who'd had a bad temper. His moods shifted like that. Hot. Cold. Happy. Furious.
Not a good sign. "If I can't help you, I guess I'll go upstairs,
drag my lazy son out of bed, and get us something to eat."

"Sounds like a good plan."

He gave me a friendly, chaste kiss on the mouth then stared
into my eyes for a handful of heartbeats. I wasn't the first to
look away. I didn't want him thinking I was hiding something. I
didn't want him knowing I was afraid, or suspicious, or having
second and third doubts about the move. More than anything, I
didn't want him suspecting I knew about that newspaper article.

He straightened up. "Shout if you need anything."

"Will do." I waited until he had closed the door at the top of
the stairs before I turned back to the computer. This time, I was
determined to read the whole article. I needed to find out the
truth, ugly or not.

The article was dated September 22nd, 2008.

Michelle Stewart, 28, was rushed to University of Michigan

Hospital on Saturday, September 20th, 2008. It was thought at the time she had attempted suicide, although that wouldn't explain all the evidence found at the scene.

Stewart died at the hospital within hours of being admitted and mystery surrounds her death. On September 23rd, less than forty-eight hours after her death, Stewart's husband, Jonathan Stewart, was brought in for questioning. At this time, no formal charges have been filed.

Authorities admit this case is shrouded in mystery. The Ann Arbor PD is not willing to provide many details in the case. However an informant has come forward to tell me Michelle Stewart had notified Jonathan that she wanted a divorce shortly before her death. At this time, that cannot be confirmed.

An autopsy has been performed but police are not releasing Michelle Stewart's cause of death. Items removed from the home paint a gruesome picture. Until more details are released, we're left to wonder and speculate on what happened on Saturday, September 20th. It's possible we may never know.

I took a long, deep breath. It was far from condemning, much too vague to tell me if I had anything to worry about or not. I decided I needed to do a search, see if the reporter had written any follow-up articles on the case. Or see if the case had been reported by any other newspapers.

An hour later I had nothing else. Strangely, that article was the only one I could locate on the Internet. A search under both Michelle's and Jon's names had turned up nothing. Not even the expected online phone directory. It was as if, outside of that newspaper article, they didn't exist in cyberspace. Just for kicks, I Googled my own name. Sure enough, there were pages of links, though many of them weren't for me. My name wasn't exactly unique. I shared a name with a famous handbag designer, for one. I was going to have to assume a new identity when I (hopefully) released my clothing line.

I decided to Google my new neighbors next. But I found nada, nothing, not one single blog entry, Facebook page, or Classmates profile. Like Jon and Michelle, Samantha Phillips, Lindsay Baker, and Erica Ross did not exist.

Feeling a little twitchy after having accomplished so little, I went back to sorting my sewing stuff, organizing it in the nifty boxes tucked into the floor-to-ceiling wall of built-in storage cubicles. I played episodes of *Project Runway* on my computer as I worked. The noise kept my mind somewhat occupied until, a little after six, Jon came down to check on me.

"Hey, baby. You've been down here all day. How's it going?" he asked, looking all tall and dark and mysterious as he leaned against the door frame.

"I'm almost done. This room is amazing. So many places to store things."

"I'm glad you like it." Pushing away from the door, he prowled nearer, stopping so close I could easily reach out and run my hand down his broad chest. Despite what I'd been told about him, the familiar butterflies started fluttering in my belly. I was still wildly attracted to him. And, more than that, I wanted to believe he was being wrongfully accused of a non-existent crime. "Are you hungry?"

My stomach growled. I'd been so busy, I'd forgotten to take a break for lunch. "Starved."

"Come on up. I grilled us some steaks."

My mouth watered. "Steaks? I haven't had a steak since the last time you came to visit."

He offered a hand and I accepted it, and together we clomped up the stairs. The moment we stepped into the kitchen, the aroma of grilled meat hit me.

"Oh wow, does that smell amazing."

He escorted me to a chair at the dining room table. Josh was waiting, in his chair, his thumbs flying over the keyboard of his cell phone.

Jon's eyes narrowed. "Josh. Phone."

"Sure, Dad. Just a minute." He punched a few buttons then slid the phone's display over the keyboard and put it in his pocket. After giving me a weak "hey" he grabbed a foil-wrapped potato out of the bowl sitting in the table's center and started unwrapping it.

I did the same. And, in silence, we ate our first dinner as a family. It was all very ordinary. Josh shoveled his food into his mouth like he hadn't eaten in weeks while Jon was more well-mannered, cutting small pieces of meat and chewing. I wasn't more than halfway finished when Josh asked to be excused. At his father's nod, he bounded from the table.

"I'm going to Ethan's," Josh announced.

"Be home by nine," Jon called after him.

"I wonder if he tasted the food," I said, chuckling as I listened to the distant thud of the front door.

"I doubt it." Jon motioned to my plate. "What about you?"

"It's delicious. I'm just taking my time, enjoying each bite."

"Good. After dinner, how about we settle down to watch a movie? I have to head in to work for a few hours tonight—"

"Tonight? On a Sunday?" Was I really feeling so let down?

"I told you my hours would be rough. I need to take care of a few things so that there won't be any snags tomorrow morning. And I'd rather do it now than at three A.M." His look was apologetic as he stood with his empty plate.

Deciding I was full, I followed him into the kitchen, wrapping up the rest for tomorrow's lunch. We headed into the family room and he turned on the ginormous TV while we made ourselves comfy on the couch. He pulled me into the crook of his arm as he channel-surfed. "What are you in the mood for?" he asked, blazing through the hundreds of channels in his satellite TV lineup.

"Actually, I'd like to talk."

Click. The TV went black.

"Okay." He set the remote down. "About what?"

"Your neighbors."

His brows rose to the top of his forehead. "What happened this morning? Did they say something to you?"

"Something about what?" I asked.

"About Michelle."

Truth? Or lie?

I didn't move three hundred miles to live with a man I couldn't trust. I had to hear his side of the story. I owed him that much . . . didn't I?

"Yes. They told me. . . ." Shit, this was rough. "They said. . . ."

"I killed Michelle," he finished for me. "Is that what they said?"

I nodded.

His lips thinned. "What else did they tell you?"

"They said the case is still open."

He shoved his fingers through his hair. He stared down at the floor. He sighed. He did all the things a man who is furious, but who doesn't want to look angry, does. His jaw tensed. "That's not true. I have an alibi. The case was closed." He looked at me. "But you don't know what to believe, do you? You're scared."

I hated feeling this way, I really did. "A little."

"I'll set up a meeting with the detective tomorrow. He'll answer all your questions. Until you know where you stand"—he stood, turned stiffly away—"I'll keep my distance. I can stay at the office."

Oh shit. "Jon, I'm sorry. Please don't—"

"Don't be sorry. This isn't your fault." His jaw was clenched so tightly, the column of his neck protruded. "A word of advice. You might want to check out those new *friends* of yours, too, before you believe everything they tell you. They might not be killers, but they aren't perfect. Nobody is."

He left.

with me like this, at the drop of a
Did he owe Jon a favor? Were th
strumental in getting Jon
around kick up a hornet's
There was reason to s
"Such as?"
"Sorry, I can'
"Is the ca
"It is.
Cle

"Hello, Miss
with me?"
wearing a uniform
Police Department
guess, I'd say he wa   was built like a guy
twenty years younger. "Detective Foster." He motioned through
a doorway. "How about we go somewhere quiet?"

"That would be nice." I followed Detective Foster down a
white-walled corridor and into a small room furnished with a
table and a couple of chairs. It was small. Cramped. Smelled like
stale smoke and sweat. The overhead fluorescent light fixture
flickered. At the detective's invitation, I sat in one of the metal
and plastic chairs.

He took the chair opposite me, leaned forward, resting his elbows on the tabletop. "Now, what can I do for you?"

"First, I appreciate your taking the time to talk to me."

"Sure. Not a problem." He glanced at his watch. "It's a holiday. I'm off the clock. Just dropped in to take care of a few
things."

"It's about Michelle Stewart's death."

"Yeah. Stewart said you had some questions."

"I read an old article in a newspaper that suggested her death
might not have been a suicide."

The detective didn't respond right away, which made me
wonder whether he'd tell me the truth or not. To agree to meet

…at, had to mean something.
…ey old friends? Had he been in-
…ff the hook? Would my poking
…nest? "That article was partially right.
…spect her death wasn't a suicide."

…t give you that information."
…e still open, then?"
…ut Jon's been cleared. He had a rock-solid alibi."
…ared.

…was almost afraid to believe what the detective was saying. I heard myself make a little squeaking noise. "You're sure he's innocent?"

"Absolutely. He was seen in a public place by several people, including a very reliable witness, at the time of her death. There is absolutely no way he could have killed his wife."

A nervous chuckle bubbled up my throat. I couldn't hold it back. "You have no idea how worried I was."

"I understand." He glanced at his watch again. "Any other questions?"

I bolted from my chair. "I've taken enough of your time. I'm sure you have more important things to do than to reassure me that I wasn't about to marry a murderer."

Foster's smile was genuine. "No problem." He stood, opened the door.

On the way out, Jon's warning played through my head. "I'm sorry. Can I ask you one more question?"

"Sure," he said, looking a little stiff. "Shoot."

"Are any of the neighbors suspects?"

The detective's smile was coy. He took a moment to answer. "Let's just say there are a few people who haven't been cleared yet."

"Thank you." I wanted to kiss the man but I didn't. For one thing, he was wearing a wedding ring. Instead, I practically danced out of the police station. My heart felt light. My over-wound nerves were unknotting with each deep breath I took.

Ah, the joy of breathing easy. I hadn't even realized how freaked out I'd been.

I sang to Lady Gaga's "Telephone" as I drove home. At the top of my lungs. I collected a few stares as I waited for the traffic light to change. But I didn't care. I was too happy to worry about what anyone thought. Jon's wife might have been killed. That was a terrible tragedy, one I shouldn't take lightly—not for Josh, not for Jon—but at least I didn't need to worry that I was living with a killer.

After checking the house, and finding I was alone—Jon had said he was going to work and Josh was at a local fair with a friend—I headed down to my girl-cave and pulled out my sketchbook. It had been weeks since I'd had time to work on my collection, with the move and everything. I flipped through my drawings.

Flat.

Boring.

Blech.

Yuck.

What in the world had made me think these designs were any good? Sheesh.

I flipped to a fresh page and gathered a handful of freshly sharpened pencils.

Hours flew by.

I took the occasional break to stretch and eat. Before I knew it, the world outside my window was dark. I took a look at the day's work—hoping I wouldn't open my sketchbook tomorrow and think it all sucked—before shutting everything down and going upstairs.

The house was dark. Über quiet. Empty.

I padded into the kitchen for a snack before heading into the family room. I channel-surfed for about two minutes. Cut off the TV. Nothing worth watching. I glanced outside at the deck, the nicely wooded backyard, the silvery moon.

What the heck? I headed outside and flopped onto one of the chaise lounges on the deck.

The air smelled great, like freshly mown grass and damp earth. It was so quiet I could hear the insects, the birds, the skittering of an animal somewhere—I hoped that was just a squirrel. Finding one of Josh's baseball bats sitting propped up against the house, I moved it next to my chair. Just in case.

I glanced up. There were a couple of floodlights pointed down at me. They weren't lit, so they weren't activated by a motion sensor. Must be a switch inside somewhere.

The distant sound of someone shouting echoed through the neighborhood. It was coming from . . . I turned my head . . . *that* way.

Hmmm . . .

I'll admit, I'm nosy by nature. Add in the possibility that one of my neighbors might be a suspected murderer, and I couldn't resist the impulse to snoop. I followed the sound of the voices. They were coming from Erica's house. She was the one who was yelling. Interesting. Miss Cool, Calm, and Collected was having a moment.

There was no fence between our yards. Convenient.

The visibly furious Erica was in the family room, which, like ours, opened onto a wide deck in the backyard. Her back was to the door wall, arms flailing. Thanks to the fact that the wide glass doors were open, I could catch bits and pieces of what she was saying. None of it was nice. Her poor husband. She didn't have a shred of respect for the bastard. Not an ounce.

But hey, she'd said he was handy with power tools. That had to count for something.

After throwing one last insult about his lack of skills in the bedroom—low blow, if you asked me—she stormed out of the room. The show was over. Just as I was about to head back home, something lunged out from behind a low shrub and sank its fangs into my ankle.

I screamed like a girl. Couldn't help myself. Then I did what anyone else would do. I kicked my foot like a wild woman while running as fast as I could with some ferocious beast tearing at my flesh. It was agony. I mean, seeing-stars painful. Stomach-clenching painful. Tears-welling painful. I slammed my ankle against everything I could. A tree trunk. The deck post. The house.

The damned thing wouldn't let go.

Every cuss word I knew flew from my mouth as I clawed at the furry beast, trying to tear it off. From the weak light leaking out through the glass door, I could see the animal was brown. The coat was smooth, like a dog's.

Maybe it's a rat.

Gag.

Desperate now, I grabbed the baseball bat, swung.

Crunch.

Another gag.

I shook my leg. The crunched animal flopped lifeless onto the deck. I stooped down to get a look at it, wondering if I should put it in a box, in case rabies was suspected.

Big ears. A little pointy nose. Long, skinny legs. And a rat tail.

What the hell is that?

Creeped out, my ankle throbbing, I set the bat down and went inside to check my leg and look for a box. After cleaning my wound and a ten-minute search that got me nowhere, I opted to sacrifice one of my designer shoe boxes. I went for my least favorite—apologies to Lauren Jones. Box in hand, I headed back to the family room. Before heading out, I searched the wall for the light switch. Found it. Didn't find the ratdogwhatever.

Gone?

Something caught my eye. A flash of gold. I squinted into the darkness about thirty feet from the deck. Were those . . . eyes? Glowing? Big eyes. Was it a big dog? Coyote? Did they have mountain lions in Michigan?

I dove back inside the house and slammed the French doors, throwing the lock. Evidently, the ratdogwhatever had just become something else's dinner.

I didn't want to be dessert.

"You're hurt."

It was dark. I was in bed. The lights were out. And my bandaged ankle was under a sheet and a blanket. I squinted at the clock. It was three in the morning. I blinked up at Jon, who was standing next to the bed. "How do you know I'm hurt?"

"I saw the bandages and bloody towel in the bathroom." He sat. The bed sank, and I sort of rolled downhill, closer to him.

"Oh yeah. Of course you did. Sorry. I guess I forgot to clean up."

"It's okay. What happened?"

"I was outside in the backyard, enjoying the nice evening, when something jumped out of nowhere and bit me."

"Hmmm. Let me see."

"Now? Can't it wait until morning? I mean, I cleaned it up real good, and it doesn't look as bad as I thought."

"I . . . suppose." He stood. "How did your meeting with Detective Foster go?"

"He explained everything. And I feel so bad that I doubted you. I mean, we haven't known each other long, and we dated long distance, so we're still kind of strangers. But I should have trusted my instincts."

"And your instincts tell you I'm . . . ?"

"A good man, though flawed. At least, that's what you tell me."

His chuckle reverberated through every cell in my body. It was a very pleasant sensation.

I slid a hand over his thigh, gave it a little squeeze. "You'll forgive me, won't you?"

"I'll think about it." He stripped off his shirt. The dim light leaking through the open drapes skimmed over the swell of his shoulders, highlighting them while keeping his face masked in darkness. "That happens to be one of my faults, you know."

"What is?"

"I hold grudges. For a long time."

I figuratively stepped into his shoes. They weren't very comfortable. "I guess I can't blame you in this case. I don't know how I'd react if you thought I'd killed someone."

The sound of a zipper being opened—*ziiiip*—cut through the silence. The sloughing of material followed. And after that, a heavy male sigh. "Okay. I forgive you." He dove onto the bed, landing next to me, the force of his landing sending me bouncing up into the air. A shrill little squeak burst from my mouth just as he caught me midair and wrestled me onto my back.

"That wasn't such a long time," I said, running my hands down the sides of his torso. His body was to-die-for beautiful. I couldn't keep my hands off.

"I guess the definition of 'long' is relative. Now, how about we start over? You've just moved in and we're both insanely happy . . . and horny."

"Oh yes, we are." I wrapped my legs around his waist, my arms around his neck, and kissed him.

CHAPTER 5

The rolled-up flier, printed on neon green paper, was rubber-banded to our front door the next morning. I found it when I went out to check the mailbox.

Figuring it was an advertisement for lawn cutting, I shoved it in my pocket and continued my trek to the end of the driveway. Lindsay came stomping outside just as I was yanking open the mailbox. She let the huge cardboard box she was carrying fall to the ground. It landed with a dull rattle.

Intrigued, I waved, donned a cheery smile—which wasn't such a hard thing to do after last night—and said, "Having a yard sale?"

It was Tuesday. The day after a holiday. The first day of school. Seemed like the most unlikely day to have a yard sale, but whatever.

"No. I'm not selling this stuff. I'm giving it away." She nudged the box with her foot. "I've got some good things in here. Come on over and take a look." She thumbed over her shoulder. "There's more inside, too."

In my book, *free* was another word for junk. But I was curious. "Okay." I headed across the street and peered into the box while Lindsay headed into the house.

The carton was full of electronics. A Nikon digital camera and an Apple iPad were on top. They couldn't work. Right? Nobody would give away something that nice. When Lindsay came staggering out with the second box, I held up the two items that had caught my eye. "What's wrong with these?"

She grunted. "Not a thing." She dropped the second box next to the first.

"Nothing? They work?"

"They're practically new. Both have a factory warranty. I think we've had the camera for only three months."

"Really?" My bullshit meter was screaming at full volume, but what did I have to lose by taking them? I tucked my new treasures into the crook of my arm and dug back into the box, in search of more goodies. "If they work, why are you giving them away?"

"Because I just found out the bastard is cheating on me."

"Ohhhh." Now, things were starting to make sense. I gently set the items back in the box. I wasn't about to take something that wasn't Lindsay's to give away. "Sorry."

"Don't be." She planted her hands on her hips and glared out at the street. "It's better I found out now, rather than later. Sure wish I'd had the guts to do this sooner. The bastard's been cheating on me for over two fucking years. Two years." She dug the camera out and shoved it into my hands. "Take it. Please. He won't give a damn. It'll give him an excuse to go buy the latest and greatest model. After all, that's what he likes to do best— trade up." Then, to my surprise she snatched it back, set it in the box, and hauled the whole carton into her arms. Before I realized what she was doing, she shoved it into *my* arms. "As a matter of fact, take all this stuff. The camera's cords and lenses and manual are in there. Same with the iPad's accessories."

"I can't—"

"Sure you can." She gave me a little push.

"No, really. I have a camera. And I don't read much. I doubt I'll have any use for the iPad. . . ." My voice trailed off.

Lindsay clapped her hands over her face.

While I stood there holding the box, trying to think of what to say, she was slowly sinking. Not because she was standing in quicksand or anything, but because she'd gone semi-boneless and was crumpling to the ground. Some strange sound—a . . . burble?—came from behind her hands.

Shit, she was crying.

If there was anything I couldn't handle, it was the sight of a grown adult crying.

"Okay," I said, "if it means that much to you, I'll take the stuff."

She didn't stop crying.

I bent over her. "I said, I'll take the box."

She cried harder.

"Isn't that what you want?" I asked.

"Take it all," she said between sobs. "Everything."

"Okay. I'll take everything. But only if you stop crying."

She stopped.

Great.

Wonderful.

Just nifty.

Now, I was stuck with two boxes of stuff that belonged to someone else. I wondered if I might find a way to get it all back to him, whoever he was.

She blinked red, watery eyes up at me. "Thanks." She snuffled, dragged her hand across her face.

"You're . . . welcome?" I motioned to Jon's house—my house. "I guess I'll take this box over and come back for the second one."

Making a full recovery, Lindsay scrambled to her feet. "I'll help. There are about ten more boxes in the house."

Ten? Did I actually agree to take more than two?

Stomping across the lawn, she said over her shoulder, "I want it all out before my kids get home from school. They're not going to take this well." Turning to face me, she blinked a few more times. "They liked the bastard. They loved him. He's the only father they've known." Jerking around, she ran into her house and slammed the door.

We had all fifteen—she'd underestimated—loaded into the garage within an hour. Right about the time Lindsay was stacking the last box in place, Joshua came racing into the garage.

He skidded to a stop. "What's all this?"

"Just some old things Lindsay wanted to get rid of," I said. Hoping to distract him, I asked, "Shouldn't you be in school?"

"We had a half day."

"I better get home," Lindsay said. "Carson and Avery will be home soon. Thanks, Christine. I owe you one."

"No problem," I said to her back.

Josh flipped open the top box. "Oh cool! An iPad! Can I keep it?"

I slapped the flap down. "No. It's not ours."

"But—"

"I'm giving all this stuff back to its rightful owner. As soon as I can figure out how to do that. I don't even know who it belongs to."

"Maybe I can help." He dug deeper into the box. "I recognize this camera. It's Matt's stuff. He took pictures at our block party with it."

"Did you know Matt?" I asked, marveling at the number of words Josh had actually spoken today. To me. It was an all-time record. Could he be getting used to me already?

"Sure. Everyone knows Matt. He's okay." Josh dropped the camera back into the box. "If you want to know how to find him, I bet Mrs. Ross could tell you." He motioned toward Erica's house. "I saw her talking to him sometimes."

"Thanks for the tip." Remembering I'd forgotten to get the mail, I headed back down the driveway. The mailbox was packed full. Most of it was advertising. I dumped it all, and the rolled-up flier, on the table in the foyer.

"Anything for me?" Josh asked, coming in through the garage.

I hadn't sorted the mail yet. "I don't know. Are you expecting something?"

"You never know." He shrugged, grabbing the flier and unrolling it. "Oh, look at this, Mrs. Wahlen's dog is missing again."

"Mrs. Wahlen's *dog*?" I echoed, peering at the printed flier. The photo was black-and-white and grainy, but there was no question. That was the thing that had bitten me last night. "That's what that was? A dog?"

"Skippy's creepy-looking. And mean," Josh said. "Everyone in the neighborhood hates him."

"That's not very nice." Now I was feeling bad, knowing I'd killed some lady's beloved pet. Kind of. After all, he was mean. Josh said so. Hopefully hiding the guilty look on my face, I went back to sorting the mail.

"Okay, I kind of feel bad for Mrs. Wahlen. She loves that creepy dog. Buys it ugly little sweaters and boots to wear in the winter. Mr. Wahlen died a few months ago. The dog is all she has now."

Oh God. I'd killed an elderly woman's only family member. Now I really felt like crap.

Finished sorting the mail, I gave Josh a shrug. "Nothing for you today."

"Maybe I'll go out and look for Skippy," he said.

"That's a very nice thing to do."

I think his cheeks pinked up a little. He shuffled his feet. "I'm not trying to be nice. I want to buy a game for my DS. Maybe she'll pay a reward." He rolled the flier back up.

I didn't believe that was the only reason why he was going in search of the so-called lost pet. But I figured I'd let him save face. "Ah, okay." Of course, I knew he wasn't going to find the dog—at least, I was pretty sure he wouldn't. That meant he wasn't going to collect any reward. "What game do you want to buy?"

"Ghost Trick. My dad won't buy it for me. He says I can wait 'til my birthday. But that's months from now."

I mentally filed away the game's name, thinking I might pick it up for him just because.

He headed for the door. "I'll be around." He waved. "Do you want me to ask Mrs. Ross if she has Matt's phone number?"

"No, that's okay. I can ask her myself. Later. Thanks."

He stepped onto the porch, his body half-in, half-out of the house. "She's outside now. I'll send her over." A second later, before I could stop him, he hollered, "Hey, Mrs. Ross, Christine needs to talk to you!"

Two minutes later, Erica was at my door.

Decked out head to toe in clothes that made me green with envy, she raised one perfectly plucked eyebrow. I made a mental note to tame my own overgrown eyebrows pronto. "Joshua said you needed to speak with me?"

"Yes." Reluctantly, I pulled her inside, away from the door. I didn't want Lindsay to catch wind of what I was trying to do. But I couldn't stomach the thought of keeping someone else's belongings. "I need to get in touch with Lindsay's . . . er, ex-boyfriend, I guess it would be. Josh said his name is Matt?"

"And you need me to do what?"

"Do you have a phone number? An address?"

"No."

"Oh. Darn. I was hoping."

She crossed her arms over her chest. "What made you think I would know how to contact him? He was Lindsay's boyfriend, not mine."

"Joshua said you talked to him sometimes." At the sight of something dark, something a little creepy, glittering in her eyes, I quickly redirected the conversation. "What about a last name? Did Lindsay ever tell you his last name?"

"No. I'm sorry. Well, she probably did, when she first intro-duced him to all of us. But I don't recall what it was."

"Okay, then. I guess that's it."

"Why?" Erica asked, not budging from my porch.

"Well . . . I have his things." I thumbed over my shoulder. "Lindsay sort of insisted. She wanted everything gone before her kids got home from school. I'd like to return his belongings to him."

Erica looked genuinely confused. "Why would she do that?"

"I get the impression she's angry with him. She said some-thing about him cheating."

"Oh." She blinked. Swallowed. Then smiled. Leaning close,

she whispered, "While I'm here, did you have a chance to read that article?"

"I did."

"And . . . ?"

"And I think you believe what you believe for a reason, but I don't see anything in that article to make me believe it, too." I shifted back a little, giving myself more space. "It was all very vague. There was a mention of evidence, but nothing specific. And, after talking to a detective at the police department, I'm pretty confident I have nothing to worry about." I left out the part about the police investigating the neighbors. For all I knew, I could be talking to Michelle's murderer right now. There was something very unsettling about Erica Ross. She gave me an odd feeling, one I didn't care for. Keeping her at arm's length was probably a good idea.

Her smile faded. "Keep digging. There's a lot you don't know about Jonathan Stewart. He told you she was depressed, correct?"

"Yes. They were trying to have a child, and she couldn't conceive. And that led to her committing suicide. I guess they even tried IVF. Nothing worked."

"I don't believe that." Erica planted one manicured hand on her hip. "First, she loved Joshua too much to kill herself and leave him motherless. Second, we were very close and never once did she mention any of this."

"Well, it is an extremely personal issue."

She waved off my comment with the flip of a hand. "We go to the same OB-GYN. We talked about everything. *Everything.*" She tapped her chin with an index finger. "You know, there might be a way for me to find out if she'd been referred to a specialist."

"I don't know. . . ." The fact that Erica was encouraging me to dig deeper into this mystery made me want to believe she wasn't the killer. I mean, surely the killer, or anyone who knew who the killer was, would want me to keep believing Michelle Stewart had killed herself. Right? But Erica wasn't doing that.

She was pushing me to find out more. "Okay. See what you can do."

"I'll get back to you tonight." Erica glanced at her watch. It was a Rolex. A real one. "Gotta go. I need to meet a client in a half hour." She waved over her shoulder.

"Okay. 'Bye." Standing at the door, I watched Erica hustle past a hunched-over lady with wispy white hair waddling down the street, pushing a walker. The wheels bump, bump, bumped every time they hit a crack. The woman saw me at the door and turned her walker toward our front walk.

"Have you seen my Skippy?" she asked.

CHAPTER 6

I was looking into the gray-blue eyes of a distraught woman. How could I lie to her?

That's just it. I couldn't.

"Yes, I did see your dog," I answered.

The woman's weathered features brightened instantly. "You did? You saw my Skippy? Where? When?"

"Last night." I thumbed over my shoulder. "On my back deck."

"Show me."

"I'm sure he's not there now." How was I going to tell this sweet old lady that her beloved pet had been eaten by some huge dog . . . or cat . . . or whatever? I couldn't do that. Then again, how cruel would it be to let her keep thinking he might be alive?

"Show me now, dammit," Mrs. Wahlen snapped, "or I'll call the police."

Maybe *sweet* wasn't the right adjective.

"Okay." I offered a hand to her as Mrs. Wahlen stepped up onto the porch. She waved it away. "I can do it myself."

"Sorry, ma'am. Didn't mean to offend."

She grumbled as she stomped over the threshold. I followed. "Why didn't you call?"

"I didn't know who the dog belonged to," I answered, pushing the door open wider to accommodate her walker. "It was *last night*."

"But I put fliers on everyone's door. On your door. You could have at least called to tell me you'd seen him."

"I didn't get a flier."

The lady, whose mind was definitely still razor-sharp, made a point to look at the rolled-up flier, sitting on top of the mail.

Busted.

"I . . . erm, that's your flier? I didn't read it yet." I snapped the rubber band still circling it. "See? It's still rolled up." After dropping the rubber-banded tube back on the table, I directed Mrs. Wahlen through the house to the French doors. She sniffed as she glanced around. "Where is he?"

"I don't know." I opened a door for her. "But he *was* outside here *last night.*"

Mrs. Wahlen slid four fingers into her mouth and produced an eardrum-piercing whistle. "Skippyyyyyy!"

That dog wasn't going to respond, no matter how loud she whistled.

"Where was my baby when you saw him?" Mrs. Wahlen asked, squinting against the sunlight.

"Right there, on the deck." I pointed at the spot where I'd left him. I noticed the dark stain on the wood too late.

Leaving her walker behind, Mrs. Wahlen hobbled outside and bent down. She poked at the spot with an arthritic finger. "Is that . . . blood?"

"I don't know." My heart started thumping loudly in my ears.

Mrs. Wahlen looked at the bat, which was lying next to the stain. "Did someone hurt my Skippy?"

"No."

"Where is he?" she snapped.

"I didn't hurt him." At her glare, I amended my answer. "Well, maybe I hurt him *a little.* I didn't know he was a dog."

Her face turned the shade of a tomato. "How could you not know that? The ears? The tail?"

"It was dark outside. I didn't see a collar or leash. I thought he was a wild animal." I pulled up my pant leg. "He bit me."

"Of course he bit you," Mrs. Wahlen scoffed. "You were hurting him."

"No, he bit me first. Then I . . . sort of . . . accidentally . . . erm . . ."

"My Skippy wouldn't attack anyone unprovoked. Now, where is he? Did you take him to a vet?"

"Um, well. I don't know where he is. When I came inside to find a box or something to put him in—so I could take him to a vet, of course—another animal, a bigger one, grabbed him . . ."

The woman's eyes widened. Her tomato-red face went instantly white. Afraid she was about to pass out, I grabbed her arm, but she yanked it away. "Don't touch me, you murderer!" Mrs. Wahlen stomped—as hard as a hundred-year-old woman could—back inside, reclaimed her walker, and headed out the front door. Once she was safely down the porch steps, she turned and shook an arthritic finger at me. "You'll be hearing from my lawyer."

Nifty. I was being sued. For killing a dog that had attacked me. With any luck, the attorney would tell her to drop it and that would be the end of that. But still, even if there was no lawsuit, my conscience was going to nag me for years about this one. I donate money to the Humane Society every year. Animal cruelty is my thing. My cause.

"I'll look for his call then," I said, thinking I might offer to pay a settlement if I was contacted by a lawyer. I didn't have a lot of money in the bank, and I didn't have a full-time job, but I had sold my apartment for a tidy profit. I would sleep better at night if I donated some of that cash to Mrs. Wahlen's pet replacement fund. "One question, though. Was Skippy up-to-date on all his shots?"

The woman leered at me then stormed away.

"I'll take that as a no?"

Someone was screaming. Outside. The sound was shrill. Eardrum-splitting. I thought someone might be dying. I pictured severed limbs, spurting blood. So, of course, I went racing outside to see.

It wasn't what I imagined.

There were no severed limbs. No spurting blood. Just two little people—imagine Thing One and Thing Two from *The Cat in the Hat,* sans the red suits—racing up and down the front sidewalk, screeching at the top of their lungs like stuck pigs. Oh, and they were smiling. It would seem they were making that noise for the hell of it.

Immediately, I unchecked the *Have Kids* box on my mental *Ultimate Things to Do* list. With my luck, my kids would possess supersized lungs like these two lovely angels. And the energy of a pack of hyenas.

As I was about to go back inside, a serene-looking Samantha strolled onto her porch. Seeing me, she smiled and waved.

Before I could ask her whom the little monsters belonged to—thank God, that could've been a bad thing—they started trotting toward her, yelling, "Mama!"

Poor woman.

As I watched them bounce around her like jumping beans, knocking flowerpots over and trampling the petunias, I concluded she was either an angel or on Valium. There could be no other explanation for how she maintained her cool while chaos erupted all around her.

I returned her wave when she glanced my way, and in she went, following on the heels of Things One and Two. The blissful silence returned.

There wasn't anything interesting to watch now, so back in I went. I headed down to my girl-cave and got to work. Roughly an hour later, I heard the doorbell. Being a girl who had lived in the city for years, I was starting to have some serious people-withdrawal. All this quiet, the solitude, the peace, it was getting to me.

I opened the door. Samantha. Smiling. As usual, she was wearing pristine vintage clothing—Chanel today—and her hair and makeup were flawless. If I was going to start spending a lot of time with this woman—which was still very much in question—I was going to have to do better than sloppy sweats and a ponytail. After all, I was a clothing designer. "Hello, are you busy?"

"Nope. Come in." I ushered her inside, to the kitchen. "Something to drink?"

"No thanks." She settled on a bar stool and watched as I poured myself a diet cola. She waved away a second offer at a glass.

I sat beside her. "Your children are very . . . energetic. Very cute." I wondered where they were now.

"Thank you. They're napping."

"Ah." I sipped my cola, wondering if Samantha had come over for some adult time or if she wanted to talk about something specific.

"Have you had any luck with your little investigation?" she asked.

Aha, so there was an ulterior motive. "I have. I learned Jon has an airtight alibi. But that's as far as I've gotten. I don't even know what sort of evidence was found when the police arrived."

"I do," she said. "I came to return Michelle's Cuisinart. She'd loaned it to me a few days before. I was the one who found her."

Hadn't Jon said he was the one who discovered her? Had he lied? Or forgotten?

"Okay, so tell me. What did you see? Blood? Signs of a struggle?"

"No, none of those." Samantha spun the swiveling stool around, so her back was facing the counter. "She was right there, lying on the floor, a wire dog cable hanging around her neck."

"And . . . ?" When Samantha didn't add any more details, I asked, looking up, at the ceiling, wondering how the former Mrs. Stewart had hung herself. "Is that all?"

"Yes, that's all."

"Am I missing something? A broken window? Signs of a struggle?"

"No. There was none of that."

"Then what makes you think it wasn't suicide?"

"First, the cable wasn't attached to anything. It was just looped around her neck. Did she strangle herself by holding it there? Can you do that? Second, can you think of anyone who has killed herself in the middle of her kitchen? It's such an odd place to pick. Could you imagine her strolling around her house, that cable knotted around her neck, and her stopping right there saying, 'I think I'll die right here,' and pulling the chain? And third, Michelle would never do anything so . . . dirty . . . in her kitchen. She was a germ-aphobe, especially when it came to Joshua. He'd been sick a lot that summer. She was bleaching and Lysoling everything. If she ever thought to kill herself, she'd do it someplace safe, somewhere easy to clean, like her bathroom. And I told the detective that."

"Strangled?" I stared at the floor, almost able to picture Michelle Stewart lying there, her sightless eyes staring back at me. I shivered.

"Yes." Samantha spun back around. "Wouldn't you think that the instant she passed out, the cable would loosen and she'd start breathing again?"

"I would." My throat was dry. I gulped half my glass of cola.

"But you said Jon has an alibi?"

"He does." I emptied the glass. "Why do you suspect him?"

"Well, everyone knows that the spouse is usually the killer. Plus, I'd heard them arguing that week. More than once."

"That doesn't necessarily mean anything. Married people fight," I pointed out. "It doesn't always lead to someone dying."

"True." She crossed her arms over her chest. "But I've watched enough episodes of *CSI* to know that a strangling is a more intimate way of killing someone. The killer has to get close to the victim, within reach."

"Stands to reason."

"Which is generally why they're someone the victim knows."

Little did Samantha realize, that statement put her, and her friends, on my short list of suspects.

"It was in her house. The kitchen. There was no sign of a break-in," Samantha continued. "Yet another reason to believe it was someone she knew well. Like Jon."

"So tell me, who else would Michelle let into the house?"

"Besides her husband? And me, of course . . ." Samantha's eyes widened. "You don't think . . . Do the police suspect me?"

I shrugged, doing my best to hide the truth. "I wouldn't know."

"But you said you talked to the detective."

"I didn't tell you that. How did you know?"

She blanched. "Lindsay told me. Was she lying?"

"Hmmm. I see good news travels fast around here," I said to nobody in particular. "I did talk to the detective. But he wouldn't even tell me as much as you did."

Samantha shifted in her seat, checked her watch. "Oh darn. I need to get back. Need to take the bread out of the oven." She slid from the stool. "Do you believe what the detective said about Jon?"

"I do. It sounded like there was absolutely no question of his innocence."

"Well, I guess that's good news for you? I imagine you weren't too thrilled to learn you'd just moved in with a suspected murderer."

"I imagine nobody would be thrilled to learn that."

"True." Samantha strolled to the front door, seeming to be in no hurry to get to her baking bread. "I guess I must believe it, too, then."

"I think you'll believe whatever you want," I said as she stepped outside. As soon as I closed the door, I went down to the girl-cave to take some notes. What Samantha said made a lot of sense. At least, the part about the untied cable and the notion that Michelle might have known her killer.

At this point, I was ninety-nine percent sure Michelle Stewart had been murdered. I made a list of suspects. It was short. Very short. And I had serious doubts about all of the people on it. There was Jon, whom I couldn't remove yet because of that inconsistency in his story versus Samantha's. But I was pretty sure it wasn't him. Samantha was on there, too. And Lindsay. Erica was the last name on the list. Because Lindsay, Erica, and Samantha were pushing me so hard to investigate, I was having a difficult time believing any of them were the killer. Jon had an alibi.

That left . . . who else?

I needed to find out who else might have been close enough to Michelle to be invited inside the house. I was missing something. Something big. The puzzle pieces just weren't fitting. Who would kill Michelle Stewart? And why?

The more I learned, the more I needed to know.

CHAPTER 7

There was a dead cat on the front porch. Make that, a *mangled* dead cat. Creepy eyes wide open. Mouth agape in an eternal hiss, teeth bared. It was dead for sure. I'd nudged it with a toe. It was stiff.

I slammed the door and locked it.

Jon, why aren't you home yet?

I checked the clock. It was after midnight. I'd been so sure the sound I'd heard outside was him, I hadn't thought twice about throwing the door open to greet him. But instead of getting a nice, warm hug, I'd received the shock of the night.

This whole dead animal thing was getting much too common.

Inching open the door, I checked to see if it was still there.

Yep.

Damn.

I went to the girl-cave and retrieved the shoe box that had originally been intended for Skippy. Then I collected a pair of thick rubber gloves and a set of salad tongs. There was no way in hell I was touching that . . . thing. Out I went, back onto the porch, yellow gloves gleaming, metal tongs reflecting the overhead porch light. I gingerly grabbed a leg with the tongs, lifted. The foot slipped loose, and the animal hit the porch with a stomach-turning smack. Swallowing bile, I made a second attempt, this time grabbing the base of the tail.

Success. I slammed the box top on and, leaving my tool on

the porch, hurried the makeshift coffin into the attached garage, trying hard not to inhale through my nose. As disgusting as the animal had looked, I was sure it smelled even worse. Into a black trash bag it went. And the bag—tied, knotted, triple-knotted—went into a trash can. Lid on. Hopefully the garage wouldn't stink like dead cat by tomorrow.

That unpleasant task completed, I spun around.

"Gak!" I screamed as I smacked right into a man's wide chest. I jerked my head back and let out an audible exhale. "Ohmygod, you scared me. I didn't hear you."

Jon was holding the tongs. He gave my rubber-covered hands a pointed look. "What are you doing?"

"Um." I snatched the tongs out of his hand and threw them into the nearest garbage can. "We can't use those anymore. They're dirty."

"We can wash them."

A very reasonable suggestion. Unfortunately, in this case, it wouldn't work. Those tongs could be sterilized, sanitized, boiled in bleach, and I wasn't going to touch them. "Sure. But they have dead cat germs on them."

His eyebrows scrunched together. "Huh?"

"There was a dead cat on our porch. I didn't want to touch it."

"I see. Where'd you put the cat?"

I pointed at the can. "It's boxed, bagged, and tied." I snapped off the rubber gloves and they joined the tongs. "It's not going anywhere."

"Hmmm. I guess I'll dispose of it tomorrow." He looped an arm around my waist, leading me back into the house. "Anything else exciting happen today?"

"Well, let's see," I said, walking arm-in-arm with Jon up the stairs. "This morning, Lindsay forced me to take her exboyfriend's stuff because she's mad at him. And Mrs. Wahlen is suing me for killing her dog, Skippy. By the way, I'm still unclear whether I need to go get a rabies shot since she wouldn't tell me if Skippy was up-to-date on his shots. Oh, and Skippy was eaten by some big animal last night. At least, I think he was. I saw something. Some eyes. Big, glowing eyes. And then Samantha came over to talk about . . . to visit. And Josh had a half day at school. He took off with his friends for a few hours then came home and went straight to his room. Didn't say a word to me. And finally, well, I already told you about the dead cat."

"Sounds like you had an interesting day."

"A strange, bizarre day is more like it. And here I thought living in the 'burbs would be boring."

He stripped off his shirt and gave me a hungry man leer, and I knew my day was going to end on a much higher note. He pulled down his pants, and all thoughts of dead cats and ex-boyfriends flew from my mind. "Come here." He took my hands and led me to the bed. "Let me show you why living in the 'burbs will never be boring."

"Hmmm," I said, as I slid between the sheets and into his arms. "I like the sound of that."

"I'm having a dinner party and you're invited. Six o'clock. Tonight."

That was the greeting I received when I answered the front door the next morning. The party holder was Erica. She was dressed for work, knotted up in a chic black suit and a killer pair of Manolos. Someday I would just love to raid her closet. "Thanks for the invite. Shall I bring something?"

"Maybe a notebook. Something small that you can conceal easily."

"Wouldn't a casserole be more appropriate?"

"Not in this case. I've invited everyone I could think of who knew Michelle." Her purse started buzzing. She dug inside, checked her phone, then hit a button, ending the noise. "I'd like you to come over at five. I've asked Lindsay and Samantha to come early, too, so we can make plans."

"Plans for what?"

She shrugged. I've never seen a more elegant shrug in my life. "Our interrogations."

"Interesting."

Erica's purse buzzed again. Scowling, she checked her phone. "Dammit." Hit the button. "Gotta go. See you at five."

"Okay."

"Oh, and if you happen to see a cat running around, please let me know. Ramzes got out last night and he hasn't come back. The kids are a mess."

"Cat?" I echoed.

"Yes, he's rare breed, Ural Rex. It was a nightmare getting him into the States. We bought him from a breeder in Russia during a family vacation. I'd hate to think I might have to go to all that trouble again. At any rate. He's brown with a wavy coat and a mostly black head."

And he's now an occupant of our garbage can. I forced a smile. "I'll let you know if I see him."

"Great. Thanks." When her purse buzzed yet again, she sighed and hurried toward the door, throwing a wave over her shoulder. "Work calls. See you at five."

"See you then."

Ural Rex. From Russia. Great.

I closed the door and headed upstairs to wake Josh. He didn't have a lot of time to get ready for school. Only about twenty minutes. His door was open. I could see some hair poking out from under the covers. I flipped on the light. "Rise and shine. The bus'll be here in twenty." Stepmotherly duty done, I trotted back downstairs to start the coffee. Josh came dragging down just as the first drops were hitting the carafe. His eyes were bloodshot, deep black smudges staining the skin under them. His clothes were rumpled, as if he'd slept in them—he probably had. And his unzipped, bulging-with-books backpack was dragging on the floor behind him. But more importantly, he was sporting the worst bed head I'd ever seen. He substituted an empty mug for the glass coffeepot for a few seconds, replacing it when his cup was full.

"I've heard caffeine stunts your growth," I told him.

"Uhn," was his response. He blinked slowly.

I pointed at his head. "Hair."

He grabbed a baseball cap off a nearby table and smacked it on his head. After downing a few gulps of coffee, he lumbered toward the front door.

"Have a nice day," I called, exaggerating the cheerfulness in my voice. Smiling at his back, I said to myself, "I think I could get used to this. If the whole dead animal thing would just stop."

I headed into the shower, spying a sleeping Jon as I tiptoed through our bedroom and into the attached bath. I was tempted to crawl back under the covers and snuggle up to him, but I re-sisted the temptation and went for a shower instead. When I came back out, he was gone. And I was home alone, again.

After dressing, I killed some time down in the girl-cave, working on some sketches and scouring the web for inspiration. At noon, I headed out to check the mailbox. Thing One and Thing Two were racing tricycles down the sidewalk. Thing Two clipped the back of my leg with a pedal as she was roaring by.

Samantha, whom I hadn't realized was sitting on the front porch, called out an apology. Finding the mailbox empty, I cut across our yards, joining her on her porch.

She was dumping a few pills out of a prescription bottle as I climbed the steps. Recognizing the fact that I'd seen her, she lifted the bottle, saying, "Anxiety," before tossing the tablets into her mouth. She washed them down with a gulp of vitamin water. "What do you think about Erica's dinner party. Brilliant, isn't it?"

"I guess."

"You don't sound convinced."

"Do you really think the killer will slip up and say something self-incriminating—assuming, that is, the killer is one of the guests?"

"Well . . . I have a little secret weapon. . . ." Samantha waved me into the house. She dug a small bottle of pills out of her handbag, sitting on the console table just inside the door.

Stunned, I asked, "You're going to dose everyone?"

"Sure. This stuff won't hurt anyone."

"What is it?"

"Just sleeping pills. I have insomnia." She dropped the bottle back in her bag. "I read online that they work like truth serum."

"But sleeping pills will just put people to sleep."

"Not if I only give them a light dose."

"This is a bad idea."

"Wouldn't you like to find out what really happened to your fiancé's first wife?"

"Sure, but giving innocent people drugs is taking things too far."

Samantha sighed. "Okay. You're right." She headed back outside.

Following her, I said, "I'm glad you think so. I mean, if someone had a reaction, you could put someone in the hospital. Or worse."

"Yes. That would be terrible." She returned to her chair.

I leaned against one of the vertical porch posts. "We can get people talking other ways. Less dangerous ways."

She shrugged. "Sure."

"Like a strong punch. Alcohol makes people talk more, be more impulsive, more honest."

"Absolutely. I can whip up a killer punch—no pun intended." She waved at Things One and Two. "Time for lunch, kids."

I straightened up, prepared to scamper down off the porch before the two wild things came up. "I'll see you later."

"Yes, later."

I wondered if I'd talked her out of spiking the punch. As much as I hoped I had, I figured it was maybe fifty-fifty I hadn't.

CHAPTER 8

At exactly five fifty-nine the last guest arrived at Erica's dinner party. All totaled, including Erica, Lindsay, Lindsay's "date," Nicole, Samantha, and me, there were ten people at the party. None of them were kids. Erica had shipped hers off with her husband before I'd arrived, and Lindsay and Samantha had opted to leave theirs at home, too.

Upon the arrival of the last person—a nurse working with Michelle's former OB/GYN—the girls set their plans into motion. The first goal was to serve light hors d'oeuvres so that the effects of the punch would be exaggerated. Dinner would be served later.

Within a half hour, it was obvious their scheme had worked.

"That dress is butt ugly," one guest said, her perky little nose scrunched up in disgust. Pointing at another guest, she said, much too loudly, "I would never, ever put that shape of skirt on a curvy client."

"At least my dress fits," the recipient of her verbal assault tossed back. "Yours is so tight, I can see every lump of cottage cheese on your thighs. I'm guessing you spent a hell of a lot of money on your nose, your lips, and your boobs. Why wouldn't you get lipo?"

"My husband's leaving me for another man," the third guest sobbed.

"I hate my job. My boss is an ass," said another.

"I paid ten grand for new boobs and they are hideous," wailed the first. "And that bitch is so right. I should've gotten the lipo. What the hell was I thinking?"

"This punch is delicious," said the woman with the cheating husband as she poured herself another glass.

We exchanged grins. Samantha shrugged. "I told you, I have a killer punch recipe."

If nothing else, this was going to be one very interesting evening.

"Just tell me there's nothing but alcohol in it," I said, watching as things started heating up.

Samantha nodded. "I promise, I didn't even bring the pills."

We huddled in the kitchen, planning our strategy. Erica gave us a rundown of each guest, why they were invited, and why they were suspects. The fashion critic, Rachel, was Michelle's former personal shopper. She regularly spent hours in the Stewart home, helping Michelle plan outfits for the many charity events she attended. There was a rumor that she was in debt and desperate for cash. The fashion victim, Theresa, was the nurse at Michelle's former OB. She wasn't a suspect per se, but Erica had hoped to get some information about Michelle's alleged fertility problems. The dumped wife, Kelly, was the mother of one of Joshua's friends. She visited Michelle occasionally, enough that Michelle would have let her into the house without thinking about it. And even two years ago, there'd been rumors about her marriage being on the rocks. There'd also been rumors that Kelly had a thing for Jon. The last guest was Heather, also someone who'd met Michelle through Josh. Michelle had told Erica only a few days before she'd died that she'd had a huge blow-up-drag-down fight with Heather over something that happened between her son and Josh.

"Time to get to work." Feeling like a football coach, I pointed at Erica. "Why don't you start with the nurse? You know her best, since she works for your doctor." Erica agreed with a nod. Next I pointed at Kelly. "Lindsay, why don't you take the friend with the gay husband? She's in I-hate-my-husband mode. You just broke up with a boyfriend—" Lindsay blanched then gave Nicole a guilty look. "Sorry. Didn't mean to bring up a touchy subject."

"It's okay. We're on a mission. I get it." To Nicole, Lindsay said, "Long story. I'll tell you later." Lindsay glanced over her shoulder, at her target. "If she knows anything about Michelle's death, I'll get it outta her."

"Good!" I motioned to Samantha next. "Samantha, why don't you take Heather the boss-hater? I'll take the one that's left, Rachel, the personal shopper." I checked my watch. "How about we reconvene in a half hour and see what we need to do next? And let's keep that punch flowing."

Off we went, to question our so-called persons of interest.

I headed for my target, who was standing next to Heather, pointing out all the flaws in everyone's fashion statement. According to Erica, Rachel worked as a personal shopper-slash-stylist and had reportedly made a lot of deliveries to the Stewart household in the past. Since fashion was my thing, I figured I stood as good a chance as any of getting her to talk.

"Hi there, I see you have an interest in fashion," I said as I approached her with a full glass of punch. I motioned to her empty glass, trading it for the full one in my hand.

After nodding a thanks, she said, "I'm a stylist and personal shopper." She gave me an up-and-down look. I was wearing one of my own dresses. "Who are you wearing?"

"Actually, it's my own. I'm a designer."

"Really?" She gave my dress a closer look. "Nice. Have you had samples made? I'd love to show this piece to a few of my clients."

"Not yet. I'm working on it."

She dug into her purse, produced a card. "When you do, I hope you'll keep me in mind."

"I will. Thanks. I understand you worked for Michelle Stewart."

"Michelle was one of my best clients."

"Really?"

"Yes." Rachel gave me a sad look. "Actually, she was my best client. My business has taken a nosedive since she died, and—don't tell anybody—I had to take a part-time job, working at JCPenney to make ends meet. You won't tell anyone, will you?"

"Absolutely not."

"Good. I'd hate for them to know." She plucked a nonexistent piece of fuzz from her skirt. "My business is all about appearances, you know."

"That, I know."

She smoothed her sleeve. "I mean, who would want to pay top dollar to a part-time sales clerk to be their stylist?"

"I'm sorry your business has suffered. Has it been a long time since you've shopped for a client?"

She didn't answer right away. "Yes, it has been a long time, since the week before Michelle died."

"That long ago? That's terrible."

"I'd met with Michelle the week before she . . . you know. She had a few events coming up, and she wanted me to come by. In fact, we had an appointment for that very day. But I didn't get the chance. I was . . . well, detained." Her face turned red. "Parking tickets. I was in jail."

"Oh." I patted her shoulder. "Sorry for dredging up unhappy memories. Hopefully you'll pick up some new clients soon. I'd better move on to the other guests." Feeling a little guilty for pretty much dumping her after that confession, I explained, "I'm new in town. Would hate for anyone to feel slighted. Say, maybe you can come back another day, and I'll take you down to my studio, let you get a firsthand glimpse of my collection."

Her eyes actually sparkled. "I would love that."

After making the rounds, filling punch glasses, I was the first to return to our predetermined meeting spot. The other ladies soon joined me. "I'm pretty sure we can cross Rachel off the list," I said. "Her business has tanked since Michelle died. She has no motivation to kill her best client. She was anticipating more business from her in the upcoming weeks. So if her motivation was money, it doesn't make a whole lot of sense. Plus, she has an alibi that should be pretty easy to verify." I glanced at the other ladies. "Anybody get something good?"

"Got nothing from Kelly," Lindsay said, "other than she was very sad to learn about Michelle. Evidently, she called her often to talk about her troubles with her husband."

"Heather seems to be a dead end, too," Samantha said, frowning. "That big so-called fight was just about Joshua borrowing a pair of her son's gym shoes. The shoes were ruined, and there'd been conflicting stories about who was responsible. I don't know. Even if they were Alexander McQueens, a pair of shoes is hardly worth killing over."

All of us shared a heavy sigh.

"But wait. All's not lost," Erica said. "I had Theresa, Dr. Orenstein's nurse. I'm thinking we need to follow up on the doctor. Evidently, he had a secret thing for Michelle."

"Thing?" I echoed.

"Obsession," Erica clarified.

"A secret obsession," Lindsay repeated. "That could be a motivation for murder."

"Maybe," I agreed.

Erica continued, leaning in, "Evidently, Jon's story about her going to a fertility specialist was partially true. Michelle did ask for a referral. But Dr. O insisted she didn't need one and persisted in treating her himself. It's possible Michelle didn't tell Jon the truth, letting him think she was going to someone else. Jon wasn't fond of Dr. O and had told her to change doctors."

Lindsay's eyes widened. "Now, that is interesting—"

"You bitch!" someone shouted from the living room.

I jerked around, catching Heather tossing a glass of punch into Rachel's face.

"How dare . . ." Eyelashes dripping, mouth agape, Rachel grabbed the first thing she touched—a potted plant—and threw it. Heather ducked. The pot hit the wall and shattered. Dirt flew everywhere. The plant landed on Kelly's head.

"What the hell?" Kelly screeched, untangling philodendron leaves from her hair. "I just paid two hundred dollars to get my hair done."

"Uh-oh," I mumbled, watching Kelly lurch to her feet. "This is getting ugly. Fast."

"Ladies," Erica shouted over the mounting wave of expletives filling the room. She waved her arms. The cuss words just kept flowing.

"If you paid that, you were robbed," Rachel sneered. "I've seen better dye jobs walking out of Fantasic Sams."

Kelly charged at Rachel like a bull, nostrils flaring, fury burning in her eyes. She tackled Rachel to the ground, and a catfight ensued. There was hair flying, clothes tearing, fingernails clawing. A couple of the other guests jumped into the fray before we could get it broken up, and before we knew it, we were ducked behind the kitchen island while things crashed and shattered all around us.

"Samantha, what the hell did you put in that punch?" Erica snapped.

Crack.

Samantha shrugged.

"Just alcohol," I said. "Right, Samantha? You only put alcohol, like you said."

"Well . . ."

Crash.

"Dammit, I think that was the plasma TV." Erica poked her head up. "Yes, that was the plasma." She glared at Samantha.

"You'll pay for that, whore!" Kelly screeched.

"What did you put in the punch?" I repeated.

"No drugs." Samantha raised her hands. "I swear."

"Then what is in that punch?" I eyeballed the bowl, not sure whether I should empty it to keep them all from drinking more or just put it away, in case someone had a bad reaction. "It can't be just fruit juice and ginger ale."

"No, it's not." Samantha sighed. "I got a truth potion from someone I know. She promised it was safe, made from all organic ingredients. I've used her potions before. Never had a problem."

"A potion?" I echoed.

Ka-blam.

Erica sank to the floor. "Samantha, do you have a Valium on you?"

"Sure." Samantha produced a bottle from her skirt pocket, dumped a handful out, and handed them to Erica. "Take a few."

"Thanks." Erica dry-swallowed half of them. "I can't believe this."

Smash.

"Hey," Samantha said, sounding a touch defensive. "If it wasn't for the punch, do you think we'd have what we do on Dr. O?"

Erica shrugged. And sighed. "Point taken."

"Thank you."

Crack.

Lindsay giggled.

We all looked at her. She was batting her eyelashes at her new *friend*, Nicole.

"Do you really think she's turning lesbian?" I whispered to Erica.

"She's no more a lesbian than I am. But I'm not going to tell her that. She'll figure it out. But I will say one thing—she has great taste in women. Nicole's very attractive." That statement had me second-guessing both their sexual orientations. To Samantha, Erica said, "Okay, that's enough. My living room is destroyed. My dining room table is covered with broken glass. I'd like to preserve at least some of my furniture. How about making it stop?"

"Very well." After straightening her hair, Samantha stood up. "Excuse me, but . . . dinner is served."

Silence.

It was a freaking miracle.

CHAPTER 9

An hour later, Lindsay, Erica, Samantha, Nicole, and I were sitting in the middle of a war zone. The police had just left, toting away Rachel for assaulting Kelly with a fireplace poker. We hadn't known it, but she had a record for felony assault. If not for her alibi, she would have moved to the top of our Persons of Interest list.

As it was now, we had only one name on that list—Dr. O, the OB. And at this point, we didn't have any substantial proof he belonged there.

"What now?" Lindsay asked, glancing at her watch, then at Nicole. "It's almost eight. I need to get home and relieve the sitter soon."

"It's okay," I told her. "I think we've accomplished all we can tonight. I'll take what we found out to the police tomorrow. Maybe they can do something with it."

Erica and Samantha agreed that was a good idea.

Lindsay looked unsure as she stood. "All right. I'll go. Do we want to meet tomorrow sometime?"

Erica shook her head. "Tomorrow's bad for me. I have meetings all day. What about Saturday?"

Everyone checked their calendars. Saturday it was. Lunch at Samantha's.

Nicole gave us all a handshake. "This was the most interesting dinner party I've ever attended." She left with Lindsay.

Erica headed into the great room to look at her smashed television. I joined her.

"That is a sad, sad sight," I said.

Erica shrugged. "I was thinking about getting something bigger. I work my ass off. What the hell?" She circled around the far end and stooped down to pick it up. I took the other end, and together we hauled the broken TV out to the garage. When we went back inside, Samantha was hard at work, cleaning up the kitchen. Erica found some trash bags, handed me one, and together we picked our way through the great room, broken glass crunching under our feet. A little while later, Erica went back to the kitchen, her bag full.

She dunked a glass into the punch bowl.

I waved my hands. "Um, Erica . . ."

Too late. She'd downed the punch faster than a thirsty sailor. Smiling, she smacked her lips. "That punch is good."

"It's lethal," I reminded her.

"It is not. It's just punch. And a few organically grown herbs." That was yet to be proven. "I'm not going to get violent, and I have nothing to hide." She refilled her glass and emptied it. "Samantha, this is some damned good punch."

Samantha beamed. "Thanks."

"Maybe you should ease up on the punch." I tried to take the glass from her. She didn't let me. "You took those Valiums earlier."

"Yeah, yeah. I'll be fine." Erica chugged a third glass then crunched across the room to the couch. She plopped down, flung a leg over her knee.

She patted the seat and crooked a finger at me. "Come here. Let's talk."

I lifted an empty flowerpot. "But don't you think we should get things cleaned up? I'm happy to help."

"Fuck that. The kids and that ass I'm married to will be home in a few minutes anyway. But the hell if I care. The lazy bum has nothing better to do. He can clean it up tomorrow."

I exchanged looks with Samantha.

Samantha glanced at her watch. "I need to get the twins into bed."

"Yes," I agreed. "It's getting late—"

"Fuck that. Joshua can get his own ass in bed. He's not two. I need someone to talk to."

Samantha made a hasty exit, leaving me with Erica, who was in the mood to talk.

Erica let her head flop back. Her eyelids fluttered closed. "Did you know that dumb bastard hasn't even tried to get a job? It's been five years. Five long years. He knew I wanted to have another baby before Paris started school. But now . . ." Rocking her head to the side, she looked at me. "It's too late."

"Oh, Erica. Are you sure it's too late? You're not even thirty-five yet, are you? I've heard of women in their forties—"

"I can't stand him. Can't stand his voice. Can't stand looking at him. And most definitely can't stand him touching me." Crossing her arms over her chest, she gripped her upper arms. "Can you blame me for taking a lover?"

"Um . . ."

"Okay, maybe some people would. But I didn't plan on cheating. It just sort of happened. We were both there. Lindsay had to leave, and the next thing I knew, we were making out in her living room."

Was Erica telling me . . . was she sleeping with Lindsay's ex-boyfriend? Was Erica the other woman?

"Who?" I asked.

"Matt. I thought you figured it out already. That's why you asked me about him, right?" Erica got up, sauntered into the kitchen, helped herself to another glass of punch, and drank it without taking a break to breathe.

In the interest of preserving her marriage—which was probably on its way to hell, anyway—I took the liberty of emptying the punch bowl down the drain. "Actually, no. I asked because I wanted to return his stuff. It's still in my garage."

"Here." She scribbled a phone number on a napkin. "His

phone number." She slid the napkin across the granite counter. "The best time to reach him is early afternoon."

"Thanks." I tucked it into my pocket just as the echo of voices signaled the return of Erica's family. "Well, I'd better be going."

Erica threw her arms around me. "I'm so glad you're here. We're going to be good friends. I can tell already."

I wasn't sure about that, not after she found out about her cat. Speaking of which ... "Um, Erica, I need to talk to you about your missing cat."

"What the hell happened here?" Erica's husband bellowed.

"Later," Erica said, shooing me toward the door. "Paris, up-stairs." She pointed and a pretty little girl of about ten stomped toward the staircase. Then Erica turned an angry glare at her husband. "Listen up, asshole. I've had one hell of a day. Don't you dare take that tone with me."

I made a beeline for the front door.

The sounds of their argument followed me through the house and even outside. As I scuttled across the front lawn, heading home, someone grabbed my arm, giving it a tug.

I gave a little *yipe!* and spun around, half-expecting something to fly at my head.

Jon chuckled. Sneaky bastard.

"Ohmygod, where did you come from?" I asked him, clapping a hand over my racing heart.

"I was just heading to the party."

"You're a little late."

"I'm sorry. I had some things to handle at work. They couldn't wait."

"Yeah, well. You missed the whole thing."

"Tell me." Looking all tall and dark and mysterious—the moonlight did amazing things for the man's face—he gathered my hair over one shoulder. Then—no surprise here—he started nibbling on my neck. Outside. In the middle of the front lawn.

"Jon ..." I said, tipping my head to give him better access. Little tingles were quaking through my body. They felt mighty good. I decided I didn't need to tell him about the party right now. It could wait. "Where's Josh?"

"Up in his room. Why?" He nibbled on my earlobe.

"Because I don't think he should see us."

"See us doing what? We're not having sex . . . yet. I'm just having a little snack." He nipped at my neck.

"But I don't think he likes me as it is. I don't want him to dislike me even more."

"What makes you say that?" He dragged his tongue down the column of my neck and I shivered.

"Because he hasn't spoken to me in days."

"It's just stress. Tests. That kind of thing. Don't worry. He likes you just fine. Now, since you're so concerned about people seeing us, why don't we go inside?" Before I could respond, he scooped me off my feet.

Grinning at nobody in particular, I tossed an arm around his neck. As he climbed the stairs, I squinted at a dark shadow sitting smack-dab in front of the door. My blood, which had warmed up nicely, chilled. "What is that?"

"What?" He halted at the door. "Can you grab the doorknob for me?"

"What's under your feet?"

"Nothing."

"It looks like something."

"I don't see anything." In he went. He set me on my feet before pushing on the door to shut it.

I caught it just before it slammed, snapped on the porch light.

"Oh shit! What is that?" I stabbed a finger at the little pile of brown fur lying in front of the door. "See? I told you I saw something."

"It's probably a dead rabbit or cat," he reasoned, acting as if it was no big deal to find dead animals lying on the welcome mat. "I'll take care of it later."

"But, Jon, there was a dead cat there last night. That's two nights in a row. Whoever heard of such a coincidence?"

"It's hardly a coincidence. There are a lot of stray animals around here. I used to leave food out for them. Some of them keep coming back, looking for more."

Was I buying that explanation?

He licked the spot on my neck, the one that sent tingly shivers down my spine, and I decided I didn't care. If it was still there in the morning, I'd worry about it then.

Laughter. In my dreams. Women laughing. Talking. A party?

My eyes opened.

The laughter continued.

I wasn't dreaming.

Driven by overwhelming curiosity, I checked the clock. It was a little after midnight. I carefully extricated myself from Jon's embrace—yes, he was a cuddler when he slept—and went to the window.

More laughter. Shadows moving. There. It was coming from Samantha's yard.

I had to know what was going on. Having slept in a T-shirt and sweats, all I had to do was grab a pair of flip flops and quietly head downstairs. I bypassed the front door, opting for the French doors opening onto the back deck. Out I went into the cool, cloudless night. Yet another round of laughter beckoned to me, coaxing me to wander farther away from the house. My shoes smack-smacked under my feet, but nobody would hear. The laughter and lively chattering would drown out the sound.

Creeping closer, almost at the far side of Samantha's house, I kept to the shadows. For some reason, I didn't want Samantha, or whoever it was, to know I was spying.

But just as I rounded the far corner, everything went silent. No laughing. No chattering. Not even any insect buzzing. A strange chill raced up my spine.

I turned to go home. Stopped.

Were those . . . ? Glowing eyes. Two. No, four. No . . . six.

Three pairs of eyes were staring at me from the shadows between the houses. I had no idea what they belonged to. Dogs maybe. Big dogs. Instantly, the vision of that little scraggly

Skippy came to mind. One of these . . . dogs . . . had snatched him. I knew it. What would they do to me?

Nothing if I could help it.

I backed up, moving as slowly, as quietly as possible.

Avoid eye contact, I told myself, remembering the first rule of Aggressive Dogs 101.

Protect your head and neck.

Remaining standing, but turning sideways, I inched along the back wall of the house. My foot landed on something soft. Rubber.

Squeak.

Damn.

One of the animals stepped out of the shadow. It was big, muscular, a dog of some kind, with a long pointed snout and a thick, dark coat. For some reason, my gaze snapped to its eyes. Blue? A clear, ice blue. The dog's ears twitched, and I yanked my gaze away, hoping it wouldn't attack.

I lifted my foot off the toy and another loud squeak cut through the thick silence as the hollow rubber inflated again. I held my breath when a second dog cleared the shadows. It stopped a few inches behind the first, flanking it on the right.

Watching me.

Still. Silent. Tracking my movements.

The third stepped forward. It was holding something in its mouth. Small. Brown. Furry.

Now I had an idea where all the dead cats were coming from.

The dog with the dead animal slowly crept forward, ears back, tail low. I smooshed my back against the house and held my breath as it moved close, closer, too close. It stopped a couple of feet away, lowered its head, and dropped its prize onto the dewy grass. Then, moving just as cautiously as it had when it approached, it backed away. When it met up with the other two, the pack turned around and raced into the still, dark shadows.

Finally, I was able to breathe again.

Afraid the dogs would be back at any moment, I hightailed it out of there, dashing around the side of the house. Something jumped out of the shadows just as I was about to turn the front corner. I slammed into it, bounced backward and landed on my ass. The air left my lungs with an audible "oof."

Jerking my head, I looked up.

Jon.

"Why do you keep doing that?" I said, not hiding my exasperation.

"What do you mean, *me?* I was just looking for you. You're the one who keeps slamming into people. You need to watch where you're going."

"I do watch where I'm going. You're so freaking quiet and sneaky, I don't see or hear you coming." I started to push to my feet. I got a little help from Jon.

He dusted my ass, then gave it a pat. "I'm not sneaking up on you on purpose. When I didn't see you in the house, I got worried."

"Okay. Fine. Thanks for coming after me. As it turns out, you had good reason to be worried." I started toward the house, Jon falling into step beside me.

"What happened?"

"I ran into a pack of dogs. Big ones."

"Were you hurt?"

"No. Not at all. They didn't seem aggressive. Although there was something really weird about them." At the front of the house now, I glanced back.

"Weird? Like what?"

"I don't know. Just . . . something." I wrapped my arms around myself as a little shiver shot up my spine. "One of them had a dead animal in its mouth. It brought it to me, dropped it at my feet. Like it was some kind of gift." I stepped up onto the porch and checked the welcome mat. Dead animal–free.

"I'll call animal control tomorrow." Jon reached around my side and opened the door. "I think it would be better if you stayed inside after dark until those animals are caught. It's after midnight. What made you go outside in the first place?"

"I heard voices."

"Voices?" he echoed, stepping into the foyer.

"Yeah. Women's voices. I thought it might be Erica. And maybe Samantha. So I came outside to check."

As Jon reached for the door to close it, the soft sound of a woman's laughter carried through the still night.

"There it goes again! Did you hear that?" Pushing past Jon, I rushed back out onto the porch, following the direction of the sound with my eyes.

Not far away, I caught sight of a tall shadow. Thin. "Samantha?" I called as I skipped down the front porch steps. I halted in the middle of the front yard, realizing there were shadows bouncing around the taller one. Big, dog-shaped shadows. Taking a step backward, I bumped into a walking brick wall. "I think those might be the dogs I saw before. Is that Samantha? She's not afraid. Are they her dogs?"

"Uh, you might say that." Jon looped an arm around my waist, hauling me up to him.

"But . . . I didn't know she had dogs. I've never heard barking, never seen them outside doing their doody—"

"We shouldn't disturb them. Let's go inside."

I took one last look at the strange scene—straight out of *Dances with Wolves*—then let Jon lead me back into the house. This time, he shut and locked the door as soon as we were inside.

Feeling even more shivery than before, I asked, "Is it just me, or do you think it's a little strange that Samantha is outside after midnight playing with her dogs?"

"Some people might think a lot of what goes on in this neighborhood is strange."

That statement got my attention. "Like what?" I asked.

Jon shrugged and, taking my hand, headed toward the stairs.

I yanked my hand away, planted my feet, and refused to budge. "Jon, what did you mean by that? Ever since I arrived, I've been feeling like things around here are a little . . . off. Is there more going on than a few dead stray cats?"

"I don't know what you mean." He swept my hair over one shoulder. There was no doubt what he was about to do next.

I shrugged away before he got his first nibble. "Jon."

"Chrissy." He cupped the back of my head, pulling me into a kiss.

Just as his mouth settled over mine, I shoved him. "It's not going to work. You're not going to distract me. What aren't you telling me?"

"I don't know what you're talking about. I'm not keeping anything from you." Undeterred, he lunged forward, tackling me, looping his arms around my knees. I flopped over his shoulder like a big bag of . . . something . . . as he stood up.

I smacked him on the back, once for each step he ascended, the sound of each strike punctuating my words. "Jon." *Smack.* "You can." *Smack.* "Get all caveman." *Smack.* "On me." *Smack.* "But I'm not giving up." *Smack.* "Tell me."

He set me on my feet at the top of the stairs and gave me some seriously hungry eyes. "Have I told you how sexy you are when you're annoyed?"

Argh! I shoved past him, slamming the door behind me and locking it.

Jon knocked. "Baby, let me in."

"Not until you tell me what's going on. You're hiding something. What is it?"

He audibly sighed. "You're going to have to ask them. I can't say."

"I left my job, my home, to come here. You should be able to tell me anything."

"I'm sorry."

"Fine," I said, giving the door my best mean eyes. "You can sleep in the guest room." Frustrated, I flopped onto the bed and stared up at the ceiling.

Six hours later, I gave up. There was absolutely no chance I was going to fall asleep. Feeling groggy, confused, foggy headed, and slightly depressed, I jumped into the shower, hoping some scalding hot water would wake me up a little. It helped. Figuring a half of pot of coffee would help even more, I staggered down to turn on the coffeemaker.

When I rounded the corner, lumbering into the kitchen, I stopped dead in my tracks.

There was a wire dog cable lying on the kitchen floor.

Right where Michelle had died.

Was this some kind of warning? A joke?

Telling myself it was nothing, absolutely nothing, a weird, terrible coincidence, I dashed outside, down to Samantha's house, and up her front porch steps. She answered my knock dressed in yet another adorable vintage dress, her hair and makeup picture-perfect. Like always. "Good morning, Christine. What a surprise." She looked me up and down. I knew I wasn't looking my best, but who would in my shoes?

"Good morning," I snapped, trying to peer around her. I didn't hear any barking. Surely there'd be barking from those huge dogs.

What the hell was going on?

"I need to talk," I said.

"Sure." She escorted me into the kitchen.

No sign of dogs.

She invited me to sit at her breakfast bar and poured a cup of coffee.

No sign of dogs. Or kids, for that matter. The kids, I might guess were still sleeping. But the dogs . . . ?

She asked, "What do you want to talk about?"

"What I saw last night, for starters. And then what I found this morning."

Her lip twitched, but otherwise she remained as cool and collected as usual. "What did you see last night?"

"You. Outside. At roughly midnight. Playing with some . . . dogs?"

"That couldn't have been me. I was sleeping. And I don't have any dogs. After I came home from the party, I took a Xanax and had some wine. . . ." She slumped onto the stool next to me. "Okay, I'll admit, I don't remember anything about last night. All I recall is going to bed and waking up this morning." Staring down at the counter, Samantha clasped her hands in her lap. "My feet were a little muddy."

"Did you black out?"

Samantha nodded. "I guess so, if you're sure it was me you saw."

I wasn't one hundred percent certain. "Are you taking more than Xanax? And Valium?"

"Sometimes."

"Do you have a drug problem?"

She shot to her feet, hurried to the sink, and began scrubbing an empty, presumably dirty, pot.

I didn't like what I was seeing. Not one bit. Maybe Samantha had seemed a little too perfect at first. And maybe I hadn't trusted her because of that. But seeing her like this, the perfect, flawless veneer cracking wide open, I wanted to help her. If she'd let me. "Do you need help?"

"No, I'm fine." Her lips curled up. As if a wilted smile would convince me she was telling the truth.

"Samantha—"

"I don't want to be rude, but I have a lot to do before the twins get up. Was there something else you needed to talk about? You mentioned something about this morning."

"Yes. You'll never guess what I found this morning, lying on my kitchen floor. Right where Michelle died."

"No clue."

"A dog cable." Weighing Samantha's nonresponse, I added, "Do you think it's a coincidence?"

"I don't know. Did you ask Jonathan about it?"

"Not yet."

"Why not?"

"I didn't have a chance." I wasn't going to tell her we slept in separate rooms.

"I don't think it's anything to—" A crash upstairs cut Samantha off. She gave me another semi-wilted smile. "The monsters have risen."

Taking the hint, I stood. "I'll head home." I reluctantly left.

CHAPTER 10

I scuttled back home and cautiously entered the house, listening for sounds of a would-be killer. Silence. Feeling slightly tense, I went into the kitchen. The cable was gone. I wasn't sure if that was a good thing or a bad thing. Or maybe neither.

I headed upstairs.

Josh was gone—hopefully at school.

The bed in the guest room was made. I guessed Jon had gone to work. No good-bye. As usual. After checking every room in the house for an unwanted visitor, I showered, dressed, then headed down to the girl-cave. Flipped on the lights. As I headed toward my drawing desk, there was a loud buzz and a zap and then everything went black.

Standing in the middle of the room, I blinked, frozen in place, instantly terrified. Was this a trap? Or merely a short circuit? My heart thumped against my breastbone. My ears strained, listening. Nothing. Just silence.

One second passed. Another. Nobody grabbed me. Nobody clobbered me over the head.

A short circuit. That was all it was.

Slowly, gradually, I started breathing again. My heart rate settled into a more normal pace. Already becoming disorientated in the blackness—I couldn't see my hand in front of my face, literally—I turned around, extended my arms, and took one, two, three baby steps. I hoped I was heading in the right direction! I took a few more, expecting to feel the wall enclosing the side of the staircase any time now . . . any time . . .

Crack.

Crash.

Instinctively I dove forward, away from the earsplitting noise. Something had fallen. Something huge. Finally, my hands smacked into a wall. I flattened my body against it and caught my breath again.

Dust choked me.

I was feeling closed in, suffocated, trapped. Using the wall to support me, I sidestepped five, ten paces. Hit another wall. I groped. It was the cubbie wall. Damn, I'd gone the wrong way! I was cowering in the far back corner of the room. Which meant the thing that crashed was probably blocking the exit. This was not going to be fun.

I reversed directions, walking carefully until I couldn't go any farther. Something big and wooden was lying in a heap on the floor, directly in front of the staircase. Fortunately I discovered—after feeling my way around like a blind woman—I could climb over it. When I stepped foot on the staircase, I gave a little shout of victory.

I threw the door open and squinted against the bright light. All it took was one quick glance in the kitchen to see the power hadn't gone out in the whole house. Just the basement. Lucky me. I looked down the steep staircase. The light spilling from the floor above illuminated part of the rubble at the bottom. Looked like one whole section of the cubbie wall had fallen. I was damned lucky I hadn't been standing there when it had given way. I might have. . . . I could have been. . . .

If I'd been standing just a few feet over, I very well would have been the second woman to die in this house.

Another coincidence?

Feeling a little sick, I flopped onto a bar stool and let my head fall. It landed on the cool granite countertop.

I'd almost died.

Was it an accident? Or not?

I sat there, stunned, staring at the back of my eyelids for who knew how long. A knock at the front door brought me out of my stupor.

I opened my front door to discover I was having guests for an early lunch. Samantha, Lindsay, and Erica were standing on my porch, each of them holding a covered dish.

"I brought a salad," Lindsay said. "That's one thing that not even I can burn."

"Pasta from Juliano's Restaurant," Erica said.

"And I brought dessert," said Samantha, following the other two ladies into the house. "I hope you don't mind our little surprise visit."

"No, I don't mind at all." I shut the door and followed them in the kitchen.

Finally, one of them clued in on my dazed condition. "Christine, are you okay?"

"Um, I'm not sure. Something just happened. Downstairs." I pointed and all three of them looked toward the basement.

"What happened?" Lindsay asked, plunking the salad bowl on the counter. "You look absolutely petrified."

"I think I almost died."

"What?" Lindsay rushed to me, eyes flying over me, probably looking for injuries.

"I went downstairs to work and the light went out. It's freaking dark down there when there are no lights. And then I was trying to get back upstairs but there was a crash, and, and . . ." I swallowed but my mouth and throat were stone-dry. Lindsay rushed to the refrigerator, grabbed a water bottle, and handed it to me. After thanking her, I continued, "The built-in shelf fell, right in front of the stairs. If I'd gone the right way, instead of back—I got a little turned around—it would have landed on me."

All three women gaped at me. Then two of them looked at Erica.

Quietly, she said, "Adam built those shelves."

"We didn't think about him," Lindsay said.

"Michelle would let him into the house without a second thought," Samantha said, softly.

We all looked at Erica.

Erica shook her head. "No, it couldn't be Adam."

"Were you home with him that day?" Samantha asked.

"No, I wasn't." Erica fiddled with her hair.

"Then you can't know that for sure. Right?" Lindsay asked.

"I know he wasn't home," Erica repeated, sounding absolutely certain. We all waited for her to tell us why she was so sure. She sighed. "I came home early that day. His car was gone."

"Maybe he drove it around the block and parked it?" Lindsay reasoned.

"No, he didn't do that."

Everyone, including me, gave Erica a pitying look.

"Dammit, don't look at me like that. I'm not fooling myself. I know for a fact that Adam wasn't home because I sent him and the kids to my parents for a long weekend. I wanted some time to myself."

Okay, that made sense. But why had it seemed so difficult for Erica to spit it out? She was acting guilty, like she was hiding something.

"That was the weekend I found out Matt was cheating on me for the first time. . . ." Lindsay said softly. She seemed to be talking to herself, not to anyone in particular.

Now I understood why Erica had tried to avoid telling us she'd been home alone.

Lindsay lifted her gaze to Erica but didn't say a word. I think she understood, too.

"We should eat before everything gets cold." I jumped to my feet. After setting out all the essentials and pouring drinks, I sat down at the dining table with my three friends. Over heaping plates of pasta, we talked about the case. Turned out the doctor was a dead end. Erica had been able to sweet-talk Theresa into checking his schedule that day. He'd delivered not one, not two, but three healthy baby boys that day. He didn't leave the hospital until after five P.M. And that could be confirmed.

The doctor wasn't the killer.

Which left . . . the three women sitting around me and . . . ?

Josh skulked into the kitchen just as I was about to say something. He looked . . . strange. Tense. His eyes snapped to mine. They were dark. Cold. Empty.

That was one person we'd never considered.

"Josh . . . ?" I said.

He knew the victim.

He had access to the victim.

But two years ago he would have been just a child. Much too young to do anything so horrid.

A sick feeling swept through me.

"No school?" I asked.

"I'm sick." Josh jerked his gaze away and left the room. A chill skittered through my body.

Could it be Josh?

"I don't know what the problem is with Josh lately," I grumbled, not really expecting anyone to respond. "I thought we were getting along okay, but the last few days, he's been so . . . tense."

"What if it was Joshua?" Lindsay whispered as if she'd read my mind.

"Why would he kill his own mother?" I asked, afraid to hear the answer. Lately it seemed he'd gone out of his way to stay away from me. But that was expected, normal. After all, he was a preteen. They were prone to mood swings. And getting adjusted to having a new adult in the house took time. There'd been no sign of instability, no sign of hostility. At least nothing out of the ordinary. Every teenager got cranky sometimes.

Could a ten-year-old child really kill his mother? Could a child live with that kind of guilt for years? Would a child who had killed his mother even feel guilt? How would he hide what he'd done from everyone?

"Erica, I started to tell you something the night of the party," I said, intentionally shifting the conversation. I wasn't comfortable with the direction my thoughts had drifted.

Erica nodded. "Of course, Josh," she said, ignoring me. "We should've thought of that possibility sooner."

"Your cat's dead," I said.

Erica didn't respond. Didn't blink an eye. "Christine, have you noticed anything unusual around here?"

"Like what?" I asked.

"Anything. Anything at all."

"I've noticed . . . neighbors getting wasted and dancing around their front yards in the middle of the night. Having affairs because they hate their husbands. Becoming lesbians because they've been heartbroken one too many times. But I'm thinking that's pretty normal stuff."

"No, you're right. That is pretty normal stuff, compared to—" Erica cut herself off. "I'm thinking more like finding dead animals at your doorstep?"

"Yes. Why?"

"That's it." Erica slapped her flattened hands on the table. "They're gifts. For Jon. A plea for forgiveness. It makes perfect sense, and it explains why we suspected Jon in the first place."

"Huh?" I said, not following.

Lindsay agreed with a nod. "He knows the truth. We smelled the deceit."

"What are you saying?" I asked.

"He's protecting his son," Samantha explained, her pretty ice-blue eyes full of understanding. "Jon has been protecting Joshua all this time."

"But why? Why would Josh kill his mother?"

"I'm guessing it was The Change," Samantha said, shaking her head. "He probably couldn't help himself."

"What change?" I was so fricking lost. Would somebody explain it in simple terms? "What about the shelves falling? The dog cable?"

"An accident, I'm guessing," Lindsay said.

"Adam built some shelves in our house, too. They fell," Erica admitted. "The cable was probably left by Jon. He might've been trying to secure Josh."

"Secure Josh?" I echoed.

Samantha pulled a pill bottle out of her purse, studied it, then dropped it back in. "How terrible for Jon. To lose his wife and then face the stigma of a police investigation. Not to mention,

I'm sure he was terribly worried about what would happen to Josh if anyone discovered the truth. And here, I thought *I* had a lot of stress to deal with."

"What are you talking about?" I said.

Samantha, Lindsay, and Erica exchanged glances. Finally Erica spoke, "There's something you don't know about us. All of us. You see, we're not exactly what you think we are."

"I don't understand."

"You were right." Samantha emptied her purse onto the table. I counted five prescription bottles. "I am addicted to prescription drugs. Lindsay is sexually confused. And Erica hates her husband and is sleeping with a younger man. But that's not the worst of it. Not by a long shot."

I held my breath, knowing I was finally going to have the answers I'd been searching for.

Samantha folded her napkin and, after dry-swallowing a handful of pills, clasped her hands in her lap. "I started taking Xanax years ago. For anxiety. Then I added Valium to my daily diet. And sleeping pills. I couldn't handle it anymore. The stress. My husband is a demon, and I do mean that in the most literal sense. If you have any doubt, just look at my children."

Demon spawn? They were a little loud, slightly wild, but hardly the offspring of the devil.

"And I have my reasons for resenting my worthless husband," Erica said. "He's a dragon. Because of his hair-trigger temper, he hasn't been able to keep a job for more than a month. And he won't try anger management therapy."

"My run-around, cheating ex-boyfriend was a fae. I'm telling you, they cannot be monogamous. It's simply not in their blood. I know that now. And we"—Lindsay motioned to Samantha, and Erica—"are werewolves. So was Michelle. You saw us. With Samantha."

My gaze snapped back to Samantha's eyes. Ice-blue. "There's no such thing as werewolves," I said.

"Oh yes, there is," Lindsay said. "You're not only sitting at the table with three, but you're living with one, too."

This was crazy. Insane. Silly.

A joke. Had to be.

I stood. I sat back down. I stammered. Finally, I was able to speak. "First you tried to convince me that Jon killed his wife. Now you're telling me he's a werewolf?"

"No," Erica said. "Jon's not the werewolf, although he isn't what you'd call human, either. Josh is a werewolf."

"What are we going to do about Josh?" Lindsay asked, genuine concern pulling at her brows. "We can't take this to the police. You know what will happen."

"No, we can't. You're right about that." Erica's gaze swept around the table. "We have to keep it to ourselves. We know the truth at last, and we can let it rest. It's the best thing for everyone. It's what Michelle would want. He's made it through his first Change. He isn't dangerous anymore."

Was I buying this?

Hell, no.

Not at all.

Were these people all crazy?

I just wanted them to leave. Now. My skin was feeling creepy-crawly. My insides were twisted into knots.

"Christine, you're looking a little pale," Lindsay pointed out.

I stood, bracing my hands on the tabletop. My knees were soft, my head a little swimmy. "I think I need to go lie down."

They all stood at the same time and filed toward the door.

Lindsay was the last to leave. She touched my arm, and I twitched, some instinct inside of me jumping at the contact. "If you want proof, come outside tonight. Midnight. It's a full moon. You'll see for yourself."

"Sure. Thanks."

I shut the door and vowed I wouldn't get anywhere near a door or window after eleven tonight.

Of course, I broke that vow.

At exactly midnight, I stepped out onto the deck. And I watched the three women who were slowly becoming my friends change into wolves.

After swallowing the contents of my stomach a few times, I

staggered back inside and stumbled right into Jon's arms. I flung myself as far from him as I could, then turned to face him.

"Did Josh kill his mother?" I blurted.

Jon didn't answer right away. He looked torn, guilty, conflicted.

I saw red.

"Jon, you know I've sensed something wasn't right about this place since I arrived. I'm telling you right here, right now, that you owe me the truth." Folding my arms, I took another step backward, afraid I might do something impulsive if I didn't put some space between us. I couldn't ever remember being so angry, so hurt. "If you can't trust *me* with all your secrets, every last one, I have to leave. That's all there is to it."

His jaw clenched. "Please, sit down."

Reluctantly, I followed him into the family room and sat.

He sat opposite me, on the ottoman, elbows resting on his knees, body angled forward. "I take it you know about Lindsay, Samantha, and Erica?"

I nodded. Couldn't say the words yet. It was all too freakish to speak aloud.

"Then you know werewolves exist."

"But what does that have to do with Josh?"

"What I told you about Michelle having trouble getting pregnant was true. After trying for years, we adopted Joshua, knowing he would become a werewolf someday. I thought we could handle his first turning without help. I was wrong." He gritted his teeth and stared down at the floor. "I'll regret that mistake for the rest of my life."

Werewolves. Changing. What the hell? Was I having a nightmare? Was this all a big joke? I felt like I'd fallen down the rabbit's hole and landed in some kind of freakish Wonderland that not even Lewis Carroll could have cooked up.

"What happened?" I asked as I struggled to sort through what I was hearing, thinking, feeling.

"During a werewolf's first turning, the wolf instinct can be very strong. Too strong. Joshua was young. He couldn't control it." A tear slipped from Jon's eye. "My wife." He dropped his face into his cupped hands. Didn't speak for a long time. I didn't know what to say. "She wouldn't have wanted me to turn Josh in, knowing what would happen to him. I knew, too. We couldn't. . . . I couldn't. . . ."

"He's a werewolf."

Jon nodded.

"You, too?"

"No." Jon's eyes found mine. "You've always called me Dracula—"

"It was a joke."

"Maybe to you, but it was closer to the truth than you realized."

I staggered to my feet. Stunned. Too overwhelmed and shocked to think straight. But I knew one thing. I was hurt. Deeply. Jon hadn't trusted me enough to tell me the truth. About himself. His son. His wife. Not even his neighbors.

"Are you leaving?" he asked as I headed toward the foyer.

"I don't know yet. I need some time to think."

"If it makes any difference, I do trust you, Chrissy. That's why I told you the truth."

A tear dribbled down my cheek. I sniffled, dragged my hand across my face. "It sure took you a long time, though."

He rose to his feet and slowly walked toward me. "You're right. But am I the only one who was afraid to trust, Chrissy? Or were you putting up a few walls, too?"

"What are you talking about?"

He gave me a pointed look.

Shoot, he was right.

I fell right into defense mode. "But if you hadn't given me a reason to be distrustful—"

"Chrissy, the first day you were talking about safety nets."

I was. I had. Shit. How could I have been so insensitive?

"Jon, I'm sorry—"

"I love you," he said, interrupting me. "I want you to be a part of every aspect of my life. The dark and the light." Closing the distance between us, he clasped my upper arms in his fists and searched my eyes. I don't know what he saw, but it couldn't have been what he'd been hoping for. "You have to be willing to trust me. Do you want to? Are you capable of trusting anyone? Or do you need to jump off the high wire now and let your safety net catch you?"

I didn't know how to answer him.

He released my arms and I breathed easier. And yet I felt worse. Cut off from him. As if I'd lost him already, despite his words. And, oh God, how awful that hurt. Like a red-hot blade plunged into my gut.

This man had grieved the death of a wife and still fiercely protected the child who'd killed her.

This man had gone out of his way to make me feel at home, welcomed.

This man had silently endured my distrust since the day I'd moved in, waiting patiently for me to decide whether or not I could trust him.

What the hell was I doing? How could I even think to leave this man?

Eyes burning, I flung myself at him. He caught me, just like I knew he would, and pulled me into a bone-crushing embrace. "I'm so sorry," I said to his chest. "You're right. I was basically sabotaging our relationship from the minute I stepped out of that truck. It's a wonder you didn't throw me out then."

"I couldn't do that. I need you too much. You're *my* safety net." He stroked my hair, cupped my chin, and lifted it until our gazes met. "Tell me you love me." His eyes were pleading.

"You're my safety net, too. I love you, Dracula."

"Oh yes. Chrissy." He kissed me and I kissed him back. He would never again doubt how I felt about him. Never. Vampire or just a guy who works some crazy hours, this man was my dream man. Mr. Perfect. I was going to do everything in my power to be his Mrs. Perfect.

On Halloween, I received a very special gift—the ring, and the proposal that I'd been waiting for. Of course, I very happily accepted both. I'd found a home, a future, a family. Here. In Jonathan Stewart's arms. In his house. In his town.

Not to mention, a very dedicated, well-dressed, wonderfully goofy Pack of friends to dance with in the moonlight.

As the old saying goes, the grass is always greener on the other side of the fence. That was never more true than on Lancaster Street. Samantha Phillips was jealous of Lindsay Baker's freedom. Lindsay Baker envied Erica Ross's lifestyle—the cars, the clothes, the vacations. And Erica Ross begrudged Samantha's job as full-time mother.

But they all envied Michelle Stewart. Because everyone knew a vampire—who perhaps was a little too undead to be fairy-tale Prince Charming material—was still a better catch than a hot-headed dragon, a runaround fae, or a demon with an attitude.

WHAT'S YOURS IS MINE

JESS HAINES

CHAPTER 1

Fashion fades, only style remains the same.
—Coco Chanel

"That is a darling color! Very flattering with your skin tone."

Cassandra, who had been busily staring into space while her nails were being painted, blinked and turned her attention to the woman in the chair next to her. A "city bitch," Vera would have called her. The woman's hair was chemically blond and straight, her tan spray-on, and her face painted with colors that gleamed and glittered like the jewelry on her wrists and throat.

Cassandra couldn't help but smile. "Thank you. I like that shirt. Gucci?"

"Close. Dolce," the woman admitted, flexing her toes in a way that had the lady working on her pedicure scowling. She fluttered her already painted fingernails in greeting. Rhinestones flashed. "I'm Tiffany. Tiffany Winters."

"Cassandra Sachs. Nice to meet you."

The intricate dance of Who Has More Money had only just begun. Cassandra surreptitiously eyed the purse at the foot of the woman's cushy chair; she couldn't see the brand name, but the Prada sunglasses hanging off a strap were a clue.

Tiffany smiled, revealing blindingly white teeth. "Say, I'm new to town. I just moved into the Still Waters community." Another hint, this one as subtle as a solid gold brick to the face. Still Waters was one of the most exclusive—and expensive—gated communities in town. "I don't suppose you know of any places closer than Manhattan that have some *real* nightlife, do you?"

"Oh, absolutely!" Cassandra ignored Ling's gasp when she shifted to ensure the huge rock on her finger caught the light, figuring her nail stylist would fix the smeared polish without a fuss. Ling made a small sound in her throat that might have been a curse, but she was paid too much money to scold one of her best customers. "As a matter of fact, we're neighbors. I live in Still Waters, too. A few of us get together and go to the Smoke & Whiskey downtown for drinks a couple nights a week. You're welcome to join us."

The two women chatted for a while, their despairing nail technicians doing their best to ensure no more polish was smeared as the ladies moved *just so* to ensure their skin, jewelry, and clothing was displayed to best advantage, preferably with brand names visible at all times. Cassandra finally felt she had the upper hand when Tiffany's blue eyes (contacts, she was sure) widened perceptibly at the sight of the pink diamond on her ring finger. It caught the light as no imitation would, practically crackling with sparkles.

Tiffany did as any woman would when confronted by such an eye-catching stone. She cooed over the diamond, clearly lusting after one of her own.

"My goodness, you must have found yourself quite a catch to get a rock like that!"

Cassandra's lips curled, practically purring with pleasure. "Oh, he is, no doubt of that. Gabriel's great-great-grandfather was a partner in the original Kimberley diamond mine excursion. He could have lived on the trust his father set up, but he opened his own architectural firm instead."

Tiffany's eyes widened, suitably impressed. Cassandra, for her part, was not about to let an opportunity to pry slip by.

"What about you? What does your husband do?"

"Oh," Tiffany said, airy tones dripping with indifference, "I'm not married. Not anymore, as far as I'm concerned. My husband dealt in security and built custom firearms. We had our differences and separated last year. The divorce is nearly finalized, and I'm not in any rush to replace him. The alimony and sales of my artwork keep me comfortable."

Cassandra clicked her tongue, making sympathetic sounds, eyes bright as she studied Tiffany more closely. "That's a shame things didn't work out."

"We didn't have any kids and we discovered late in the relationship that we both wanted different things out of life. The separation was amiable, and the divorce was relatively painless. Truthfully, it's better this way for both of us."

"Well, I'm glad you've got such a bright outlook on things. You really should meet the other ladies. I think a girls night out would be just the thing. Meet us at the Smoke & Whiskey tonight at ten. I'll introduce you to everyone."

Tiffany's plush lips curved in a wicked smile as she leaned back in her salon chair, closing her eyes.

"I can't wait."

"Oh, you'll like this one," Cassandra said, stirring her martini with a thin crystal swizzle stick. "New to town, no kids, no husband, and positively *desperate* to fit in."

"Desperation should suit our needs quite nicely," Vera replied before she sipped her lemon drop, crossing her slender legs primly at her ankles. "When's the last time we took in new blood? If we don't work to expand our ranks as much as we have our fortunes, we'll never have the kind of influence over the Were communities that Gabriel keeps going on about. If he wants to be the next Rohrik Donovan, he needs to *work* for it."

"Oh please," Alexis scoffed, waggling fingers wrapped in jewels in airy dismissal. "Our husbands would have done something about it already if they knew how. Their little yacht club meetings and golfing excursions are just excuses to avoid facing facts—that scouting their usual haunts isn't going to get us any new wolves. It just goes to show that, as always, it's the women behind the men in power who really make history."

Heather shifted uncomfortably, twining her fingers in her long auburn hair as her attention shifted back and forth between the other ladies. She opened her mouth to add her thoughts to the conversation, but Cassandra smoothly overrode her.

"Be that as it may, if we are going to take over recruitment for the pack, we might as well start somewhere. I think this woman could be a good fit. She already lives in the community and she's newly divorced—which means she'll be lonely and looking for a man soon enough."

Heather opened her mouth again, but this time Vera cut her off. "I'm not convinced that volunteering Charles or Lucas as a fit for this woman we haven't met is such a good idea. Make her one of the pack? Sure. Hand her over to the available men? Not unless she's breeding pups before she's turned. Which doesn't solve our numbers problem for the short term."

Alexis smirked, drawing her straw across her tongue in a playful, flirtatious bid to draw the attention of one of the men at the bar before adding her thoughts. "Divorcées are generally bitter, lonely people. Not the mothering sort, if she doesn't have rugrats already, I'm sure. She can choose someone else; perhaps one of the hopefuls that Gabriel keeps going on about inviting to those dull brunches of his. . . ."

Cassandra gave Alexis a withering look, which went ignored. Her smile was cold enough to make Vera and Heather drop their eyes submissively, knowing better than to tease her about her husband—or his parties.

"Thank you, Alexis. I'll be sure to tell him you think so," Cassandra said, her tone flat enough that Alexis finally realized she was in error.

"I'm sorry, Cassie, you know I didn't mean anything by it."

Alexis had turned her eyes down, but her tone told the lie. Cassandra leaned forward, her ample cleavage spilling from her low-cut top, drawing the eyes of several men at the tables around them as she settled her hand on the glass tabletop next to Alexis's drink. One nail had formed into a talon, etching a fine line of warning into the glass between them.

Alexis audibly gulped and lowered her head contritely, a faint sound like a whine dying in her throat. Cassandra stared at her across the table, the others keeping their eyes down as she tapped her fingers impatiently. Finally, she spoke, her words cold and biting.

"If you don't like how the pack is run, you may rise to the challenge to change it. Otherwise, I suggest you remember who is in charge before your mouth gets you into trouble."

Alexis nodded once, sharply, ducking her head further. Cassandra laughed and leaned forward enough to brush her finger along Alexis's arm, making her flinch. "Silly pup, look what you've made me do! I've just had my nails done, too."

The others exclaimed over the now cracked veneer of polish on her finger, clucking their tongues over the damage. Before long, Cassandra rose, putting the full force of her chilly smile on Alexis again.

"Let's go meet the new girl, shall we?"

CHAPTER 2

The body is meant to be seen, not all covered up.
—Marilyn Monroe

The beautiful people of New Jersey often convened on the Gold Coast or fled to Manhattan when they wanted to see and be seen. For those who wanted to do so in the relative privacy of a community too expensive for the locals and too subdued for the tourists, the residents of Saddle River often looked no further than their own backyards to the elegantly overpriced charms of the Smoke & Whiskey.

The nightclub was in good form when Cassandra arrived. She was fashionably late and prepared with a newly restored manicure as she glided down from the heights of her Navigator and passed the keys for her SUV to the valet.

She sauntered up the solar light–lined walkway to the entrance where a host held the door for her. She promptly paused to bask in the recessed spotlights and let the crowd inside take in the view of her in all her chic splendor. As was to be expected, a low murmur of appreciation started up amidst the candle-lit interior as the tall, Amazonian brunette in killer Ferragamo pumps and a sleek Valentino dress surveyed her domain, finding it wanting.

Particularly when Tiffany appeared behind her, settling into an equally statuesque pose in her Manolo strappy stilettos—making her just a smidge taller—as she came to a glittering rest in her vintage Versace beside Cassandra.

"Lovely evening for a night out," Tiffany purred. "I had no idea there was nightlife this close to home."

Said nightlife was composed of a number of men and women at low, intimate tables talking over drinks while candles sparked and sputtered in dark alcoves, and the gentle strains of soft jazz came from an easily forgettable band on the stage across the room. Smoke drifted from dry ice placed in hidden recesses and gave the place its namesake, admirably reproducing the atmosphere of a Prohibition-era speakeasy. The club tried hard to pull off the air of "upper class dive," but failed miserably thanks to the glint of crystal and glow of real teakwood from the bar and tables.

Cassandra eyed the bangles clinking on Tiffany's wrist as the blonde airily brushed her hair back, revealing equally jangly earrings. *Très* out of style, but Cassandra delighted in not telling her that.

"Quite. If it gets too dull, we can always go to Manhattan," Cassandra said, gesturing to the table where Vera, Heather, and Alexis had already settled, nursing drinks that glowed in the subdued light of the club. "Ah, there we are. Let's go have a seat, shall we? You can meet the other ladies of Still Waters."

Tiffany confidently took the lead; the other girls' expressions ranged from wary to impressed at Cassandra's restraint for allowing her to go first. Tiffany didn't appear to notice the others' discomfort as she swept around the table to shake hands as she was introduced. For her part, the alpha bitch was amused, finding this potential new blood to be the sort of headstrong woman necessary to build the Diamondfangs into a pack that might someday overcome the Moonwalkers.

". . . and so," Tiffany finished explaining her circumstances on moving to town as she shook Vera's hand, meeting the woman's eyes as her grip tightened uncomfortably. "I've only been in town for a couple weeks, but I think I'll be settled in before long. The divorce is nearly final. I do have to say, while I'm pleased to find myself in such company, I can't stay long tonight. We can meet again soon. I'm sure we'll all be fast friends."

Vera showed her teeth in the semblance of a smile, her eyes briefly taking on a glimmer of something unnatural as she held on to Tiffany's hand long past when she should have let her go.

"Is that right? You look familiar. Are you sure you've only been in town for two weeks?"

Tiffany gave Vera a tight smile of her own, but said nothing, pulling her hand back hard enough that it was obviously an effort. Cassandra made a faint hissing noise between her teeth, and Vera gradually relented, looking away. Alexis sipped her drink, her expression turned wary and calculating as she watched the exchange, while Heather's attention was focused on the band across the room.

"Quite sure," Tiffany replied. "I haven't been to New Jersey since, oh, before I was married. I used to travel extensively, so perhaps you saw me in the airport on my way to South Africa or Versailles."

"South Africa?" One perfectly sculpted brow arched as Alexis regarded Tiffany over the rim of her drink, a sardonic twist to her cherry lips. "I can't imagine what you'd be doing there. The place has nothing to offer but backward politics and savages, if you ask me."

Tiffany's smile turned murderous. "Visiting family, actually. My mother is from Johannesburg. Also, I often visit to acquire more tribal artwork and supplies for my gallery. Many people admire the richness and beauty of the culture."

Alexis reddened and muttered something apologetic into her drink. Cassandra watched all of this with the avid gaze of a cat who has spotted a wounded bird fluttering within reach of its paws.

Heather dove to the rescue, her voice sweet and sincere as she sidled her chair a bit closer to Tiffany. "Don't listen to that nonsense, she's just being her usual catty, bitchy self. *We* are glad to have you here!"

Tiffany's narrowed blue eyes slid from Vera to rest on Heather, her expression lightening considerably. "Thank you. What a doll you are!"

"Do you want to come shopping with me tomorrow? I heard there's a new store with vintage Louis Vuitton that just opened up in Manhattan." Heather's wide brown eyes were completely guileless, and the others couldn't restrain their eye rolls as she squealed in excitement at Tiffany's nod. "Excellent! Give me your address, I'll pick you up at noon."

Tiffany did, smiling wolfishly as she slid a business card across the table. "I'm looking forward to it."

Vera watched Tiffany leave with narrowed, distrustful eyes. The woman positively sauntered off, clearly pleased at how Alexis and Heather had warmed to her.

"I think we have a winner, ladies," Cassandra said as she ran her fingertip along the edge of her glass, making the crystal sing.

Heather nodded enthusiastically, while Alexis reddened. "I shouldn't have said—"

"Hush," Cassandra scolded. "I don't think you scared her off. Besides, she's taken to Heather, and I'm sure she can salvage any hurt feelings and bring the girl around to seeing things our way."

"I don't like her," Vera stated flatly. "I don't think she's what she seems."

"Neither are we," Heather replied.

The women quieted briefly, sipping at their drinks. Heather frowned, glancing back and forth between the others. Seeing as no one was talking, she broke the silence with a few chipper words.

"I think she's great. I can't wait to get to know her better. If she became part of the pack, we could set her up with one of the single wolves. Who hasn't been mated yet? Oh, I bet she'd be a great match for Travis or Damon—"

"Will you stop that prattling?"

Heather regarded Vera with a hurt expression.

"I've seen her somewhere before," Vera muttered. "I'm not sure where, but I know I have. Something about her is dangerous. We need to know more about her before we take her into the pack."

Cassandra was not amused. "If you can provide proof of whatever it is that has you worried, I'll take it into consideration. Until then, we go forward as planned. Heather will gather more information tomorrow and question her about her feelings on Others. Yes?"

Heather nodded, smiling brightly.

"There, you see? We'll get to know her better and take it from there. I doubt she'll be willing to sign a contract within a single day, anyway. We have time."

Vera still wasn't convinced, but said nothing.

"Even if she poses a threat now, she won't be one for long. I'll make sure of it."

CHAPTER 3

I've been getting some bad publicity,
but you got to expect that.

—Elvis Presley

Tiffany toyed with the curtains while she held her cell phone to her ear, staring out over the wide expanse of her backyard to the ring of trees that surrounded her property. After a few rings, a gruff voice harrumphed in her ear.

"Didn't think I'd be hearing from you this soon. Run out of money already? Alimony isn't due yet."

"Don't be an ass, Richard," she said, turning away from the window. "I want you to tell me what you know about Cassandra Sachs and the women she surrounds herself with—Heather, Alexis, and especially Vera."

He paused. Coughed. "Don't tell me you're trying to hunt on your own? Look, I know you didn't like our methods—"

"I didn't call for a lecture. Tell me what you know."

"They're dangerous, Tiff. Diamondfangs. Rich, snobbish, always looking to expand their ranks with more of the same. They've taken lawyers, CEOs, even a couple of state senators, and made them werewolves. They've got some kind of political agenda. I wouldn't mess with them. If they're sniffing around you, get out of town. I'll send over some people—"

"No, Richard."

"Come on, Tiff, this isn't like before—"

"*No,* Richard. It's not. You're not my white knight, come to save the day."

He sighed. "Damn it, babe, you always do this."

"It's why we're not seeing each other anymore. Or have you forgotten?"

"No," he replied, dull anger coloring his tone. "Of course not. How could I? You never let me forget."

Tiffany fingered the framed image of herself in a wedding dress, leaning against a much larger man in a tuxedo who had his arm wrapped tightly around her. They were smiling, squinting against bright sunlight as they stood in a field dappled with spring flowers. Happy. Different.

"I don't think now's the time to discuss this. All I called for was information."

"No. It's never been the right time. Look, we could put off filing the papers. Try this again. Why don't you just come home? You know I'm crazy about you."

She tilted the frame until it was lying facedown, turning away. "It's not *my* home. The hunting and the killing—that isn't my world anymore."

"Babe, it doesn't have to be. Let me handle it like I always did. You don't have to do anything. You never did. You wanted to come on the hunt, and you did. You wanted to stop, and you stopped. What's there to argue about?"

Tiffany's fingers clenched around the phone until the plastic squeaked. She eased up, taking a breath to calm herself, though it didn't help much. The words were still bitter, harsh, and she regretted them the moment they passed her lips.

"You really want me to just sit on my ass on the sidelines while you put your life on the line, night after night? I won't do it, Richard. Don't ask that of me."

"You went into this relationship knowing what it meant. I never lied to you. I don't get why it's a problem now."

Distantly, the sound of a horn blared. Tiffany reached for her purse, voice inflectionless. "Good-bye, Richard."

She didn't wait for him to reply before snapping the phone shut and tossing it in her purse, clacking down the stairs to meet with Heather.

*   *   *

The silver Lexus idling in her circular drive looked right at home next to Tiffany's white Mercedes. Heather waved, giving Tiffany a cheerful smile that was soon returned in kind. There was no visible sign of her anger from a moment before.

"Hey, ready to go shopping? Hop in!"

Tiffany settled in on the passenger side, slipping on a pair of sunglasses as Heather took off down the drive, sparing her a surreptitious glance now and again.

"Everything all right?"

Tiffany blinked, startled, before allowing a bitter smile to curve her lips. "Sorry. Just got off the phone with my ex. Ever since the divorce . . ."

"Oh, say no more," Heather said. "Don't worry, honey, once we hit the stores and start spending, you'll forget all about him. We'll find you someone new. Someone better!"

"I think it's a bit early for that," Tiffany replied, tone dry. "Let's stick with the shopping for now."

"Yeah. You know, who needs men? You've got us now."

Tiffany laughed. "Easy for you to say. Don't you have a husband?"

"Sure I do. One that's never home, same as the rest of the werewives."

"The *what?*"

Heather flushed. "Sorry. Just an inside joke. Cassandra, Heather, Vera, and I, we're all such bitches, we call ourselves the werewives. We've been using that nickname for years."

"Funny thing to call yourselves," Tiffany murmured, gaze focused steadily on the world passing them by.

"You aren't afraid of werewolves, are you? They aren't so bad. From what I hear, I mean."

"No, no. Nothing like that. Honestly, I can't say that I've known any. Just what the papers tell me."

Heather was scandalized. "You don't honestly believe what they print in the papers, do you?"

"Hardly. I think a lot of things get nothing but bad press, werewolves included. I'd love to meet one sometime. Find out what they're really like," she replied.

"Really? Most people wouldn't want anything to do with them."

A low, throaty laugh made Heather glance guiltily at her guest, biting her lower lip. Tiffany wiped unshed tears of mirth from her eyes, ever so careful not to smudge her mascara. "Honey, you have no idea. Despite what the papers might say, there are plenty of people out there—me included—who are curious about Others and would be delighted to have a chance to meet one in person. Vampires, werewolves, wizards—they're different. Unique. The possibilities fire the imagination."

"Maybe not that different," Heather muttered, reddening.

Tiffany arched an artificially bleached brow, then shrugged and laughed again. "You are too funny! If it bothers you that much, we'll talk about something else. Like calling yourself a bitch. I don't see why you think so. You've been very sweet to me."

Heather gave her a sheepish smile before returning her attention back to the road. She hadn't intended to bring up the subject so soon, or with such a lack of subtlety, and was thankful that Tiffany was the one who was turning the topic back to something less dangerous.

"Wait until we both have our eye on the same purse or pair of shoes, then ask me that again."

The two laughed, together this time, and the topic shifted to far more comfortable topics: fashion, favorite brands, and which celebrity was sleeping with whom. They didn't speak about Others again for the whole of the trip; not at the store where they each bought a new purse, nor at the café they stopped at for a light lunch and cocktails. The pair gushed about their purchases, stopping at a few more boutiques (each finding the perfect pair of summer sandals, along with darling sundresses and earrings to match), before ending their trek at a Starbucks.

"Are you coming to the party tonight?" Heather asked as she sipped her grande nonfat iced mocha raspberry latte.

Tiffany stirred her chai tea with a straw, eying Heather over the rim of her drink. "I didn't know there was a party. Am I invited?"

"Of course! It's at Alexis's house, everyone who's anyone in the neighborhood was invited. She must have forgotten to mention it last night. It's not a big deal, just a little barbeque. If she gets uppity, we'll go back to my place and mix some margaritas."

Tiffany laughed, the sound attracting admiring glances from a few of the men and a number of glares from some of the women cradling drinks or hunched over laptops as they worked on the next Great American Novel. She touched her hair, then plucked at one of the buttons on her silk blouse, frowning.

"Do you mind stopping at my place so I can drop off my things and freshen up a bit before we go?"

"Of course not! Let's get moving, then, don't want to be late."

"No," Tiffany said, her eyes narrowing and her smile turning sly. "No, we don't."

CHAPTER 4

Just because you got the monkey off your back
doesn't mean the circus has left town.
—George Carlin

Alexis's mansion sprawled across the verdant grounds of the property with all of the glamour and poise of a movie starlet. The trees lining her driveway glittered with twinkling lights, urging guests to come along to see the wonders of her garden. Row upon row of Jaguar, Mercedes, Audi, BMW, and Lexus luxury cars had been positioned just so, shining to advantage in the lights spilling from the house. Gabled windows and wrought-iron balconies gave the manor a European flavor, and the sounds of chatter, music, and laughter spilled from open French doors.

Tiffany followed in Heather's wake, adjusting the strap of her purse as she paused in the foyer, bright blue eyes scanning the interior.

Much like the cars, many of the people inside had positioned themselves to advantage. They cradled drinks as they chatted in small groups of four or five, clustered around the baroque Louis XIV furniture done in rich tones of red and gold that matched the marble floors and sweeping columns in the open receiving room.

"Excuse me," Tiffany said as her eyes locked on a man in a casual Tony Bahama polo and sleek J. Crew slacks. "I see one of my clients. I'll be back shortly."

Heather nodded, but Tiffany wasn't paying attention, already stalking across the room like a hunting cat on the prowl, lacquered hand extended for the surprised gentleman to take as he noticed her. "Todd, it's been ages. . . ."

The smooth way Tiffany went in for the kill drew Heather's admiration instead of her ire. Though she wasn't pleased at being ditched, she soon shrugged it off and followed her nose, trailing the distinct, musky scents of her favored pack mates. Her own stride became smooth, quiet, the stalking of a predator, leading the people around her to unconsciously move aside as she found her way to the back doors leading outside. A bright smile was soon plastered on her face as she took an empty seat beside Alexis on the patio. Cassandra returned her smile, eyebrows arching high.

"I take it things went well today?"

"Oh yes!" Heather gushed. "Ladies, we have a winner. She's curious about Others and said she *wants* to meet a werewolf. How about that? I think she might go for it. I really do."

Alexis frowned, her voice heavy with skepticism. "Are you sure about that? Most humans wouldn't be so quick to put themselves within arm's reach of a supernatural creature."

"Yes, well, we haven't exactly been forthcoming with her about ourselves."

"She's not cut out to be one of us," Vera said, dripping disdain as she lounged back in her chair and stabbed the air with her martini olive's toothpick for emphasis. "She's well-dressed and obviously has connections, but we hardly know a thing about her. I don't want her here. Not until we're sure she's not a threat." Cassandra ignored Vera, narrowed eyes remaining locked on Heather, her expression otherwise unreadable. "Don't tell me you think we should have said something to her already? She hardly knows us. No matter what she says, no one is prepared for being faced with the real thing. Not the first time. Think of the danger she could pose by knowing too much too soon."

Heather pouted. "I thought you wanted her in the pack, Cassie? I didn't tell her anything. I just asked a few questions and got her opinion."

"It just seems a bit rushed. If you're sure it's safe, I suppose we should take advantage of her interest while we can. Where is she now?"

Heather gestured back the way she had come, lowering her voice—completely unnecessarily, considering no one but members of the pack were mingling outside. "She came with me. She saw someone she recognized, so she's distracted for a bit, but she'll be joining us shortly. We should tell her tonight. We really should."

Alexis shrugged, sipping her martini before placing the glass on the table and leaning forward, her eyes gleaming with mischief. "You know, if she's really as interested as you say, I'll bet we could sell her on joining us before the next full moon. Cassie, if you can convince Gabriel to let Heather sign her, I'll bet we'll have her on a contract before the end of the week."

They were interrupted by a discreet cough, a man holding a tumbler of brandy coming to a stop next to Alexis's chair. "Ladies, I trust you're enjoying yourselves?"

Murmurs of assent and a few pithy greetings were exchanged. Alexis was not amused by the interruption.

"Darling, do you know anything about our new guest, Tiffany . . . What did you say her last name was?"

"Winters," Cassandra supplied. Vera growled softly, but didn't say anything once she caught Cassandra's warning look.

"Tiffany Winters. We're discussing bringing her into the pack."

Everyone ignored Vera's scowl.

"Oh, I don't know. Maxwell usually handles the background checks. I think he's by the barbeque, why don't you ask him?" said Samuel.

"Honey," Alexis whined, "we want to know now, not next week. Can't you ask him? Or see if Gabriel will okay us issuing a contract? We don't want to miss out on this one."

His dark brown eyes rolled heavenward, muttering something unheard. She reached up to adjust the lapel of her husband's Dolce & Gabbana jacket, frowning at a crease in the otherwise sleek lines. He waved her off before inclining his head in deference to Cassandra at her pointed look.

"All right, ladies, I'll check with Gabriel. Give me a few minutes."

"You're a peach!" Heather favored him with a brilliant smile that he was quick to return. Alexis turned that formidable frown on her, but it was blithely ignored. Cassandra's attention sharply turned on Vera when she hissed something unpleasant under her breath and shoved her chair back, stalking into the house.

"Trouble brewing," Alexis murmured. Heather and Cassandra said nothing, their eyes briefly glittering with a touch of luminescence as they locked on Vera's retreating form.

"I know what you're up to."

Tiffany, who was laughing softly at something one of Todd's companions said, quieted and turned to face Vera. Brows arched on high and painted mouth puckered in a moue of surprise, she batted her lashes and pressed a hand to her chest. "Excuse me?"

"I know what you're up to," Vera repeated, her teeth showing in a shark-like grin, "and don't play the innocent. It's *so* tacky."

Tiffany stared at Vera, her cheeks flushing. Todd and his friends—as well as a few of the other guests nearby who had "overheard" the conversation—were staring at Vera as though she'd grown another head. With a hasty "excuse us," Tiffany gestured sharply for Vera to follow her as she spun away from the group, seeking privacy. Speculative, disapproving whispers trailed in their wake, growing louder as they left the room.

Before long they found privacy in the form of a study, bookshelves lining one wall and a set of oxblood chairs placed around a low table and desk. It was all Tiffany could do to keep from slamming the door behind them once Vera marched in, right on her heels.

"What is your problem?" Tiffany snapped, eyes flashing as

she gestured back the way they had come. "I was in the middle of a very important business deal! Couldn't you have waited until I closed him before interrupting to bitch at me?"

It was Vera's turn to flush, though she wasn't dissuaded. With difficulty, she drew in a few calming breaths, settling her nerves so her eyes wouldn't glow with her increasing anger.

"*You*," she enunciated carefully around growing fangs, "don't belong here. You're not part of this community, and I can smell the trouble following you. You should go back to wherever you came from and leave us alone."

Tiffany sniffed indignantly. "Vera, I don't know where you got these crazy notions about me, but I'm not here to cause trouble for anyone. All you're accomplishing right now is embarrassing yourself."

"I don't care what the others say. You're up to something. I'm going to find out what."

Tiffany met her gaze, her jaw set and fists clenching at her sides. Her nostrils flared as she tilted her head up, causing her carefully maintained coiffure to shift, blond strands slithering over her shoulders and hissing softly against the silken fabric. Her voice took on the same whispery tones—soft, dangerous, and deadly.

"You might want to watch yourself, Vera. Dig too deep and you won't like what you find."

Vera watched her go, the door clicking quietly shut behind her as the sound of her Prada heels clacking against the marble floors faded into the hum of the party.

CHAPTER 5

Money is your servant—do not let it be your master.
—An American Proverb

The women were not surprised to see Tiffany paused on the threshold of the patio, searching the fire pits and tables for her friends. The people outside turned to watch as she passed, their eyes flashing brilliant hues of green or gold as her scent—heavy with the reek of agitation even through the cloud of citronella—caught their interest. Once they noted where she was headed, many returned to their conversations or to picking at the hors d'oeuvres, but several continued to watch her with veiled interest as she paused behind the seat Vera had earlier vacated.

"Ladies. Sorry I took so long to join you."

Tiffany's tone was light, but her white-knuckled grip on the back of the latticework iron chair bespoke her irritation. Heather, who had been nervously nibbling her bottom lip, leaned forward and put her hand lightly on Tiffany's arm.

"Are you okay? Vera didn't find you, did she?"

"She did," she replied, her smile cold and humorless, "but don't worry. We came to an understanding of sorts."

The others were clearly interested in hearing about it, but too polite to push—beyond more than overly curious, questioning expressions—and Tiffany was not budging in her silence on the topic. After a wordless conversation composed of nothing but significant looks, raised brows, and slight twitches of lips shared between Cassandra and Tiffany, they came to an understanding.

'*Don't ask. You won't like the answer.*'

'Come on, you know you want to tell us what happened.'

'It's none of your damned business.'

'You know she'll give us the details when you're not around anyway. You might as well tell us your side of it now.'

'It's my story to tell or not. Don't push me.'

'Are you sure? It might not be wise to keep so much to yourself.'

'Drop it.'

Eventually, Cassandra broke eye contact, feigning a sudden and intense interest in her drink. Gradually, Tiffany's grip on the back of the chair loosened, and she gestured at the partygoers mingling and chatting nearby.

"There are a lot of people here I don't recognize. Heather, I don't suppose you'd be a love and introduce me, would you?"

"Of course she will," Cassandra said. "We'll all join you. There are a few people I'd like for you to meet, too."

Heather shot a helpless look at Cassandra, and then pushed her chair back with a harsh scrape over the patterned brick. Alexis smirked, but didn't utter a word, setting her drink aside so she could smooth out her skirt and brush her hair back over her shoulder.

Cassandra hooked her arm through Tiffany's and paraded her through the gathered throngs in the gardens and around the fire pits as if she were a show pony. She breezed through introductions, highlighting a few interesting tidbits and assets—both of Tiffany and of the people she was meeting—before pushing her along to the next group. Once she was introduced to a few of the young men Cassandra called "terminally single," Tiffany's mood lightened considerably, as she batted her lashes and flashed dazzling smiles at the more attractive of the bunch.

Several of them returned her obvious interest in kind with heated looks and a choice turn of phrase, but she expertly maneuvered through their flirtations without insulting or abandoning her hosts.

"I do believe Travis has taken a shine to you," Alexis remarked as they paused in their rounds for drinks and to nibble a few hors d'oeuvres. "He's still watching us. Look."

Tiffany giggled, a cute, girlish sound that drew more curious eyes their way. "Oh stop. I was just playing with the boy. He's too young for me, I think."

"No harm in having a bit of fun with him, though," Heather said.

Cassandra chuckled at the exchange before popping a slice of strawberry in her mouth, and then urging the girls to continue their rounds.

They gradually worked their way deeper into the garden toward those who were clearly more familiar with the house and each other, and were more interested in talking business than showing themselves off as the people inside were doing. There were not many women this far from the lights and tiki torches, and much of the talk was hushed, muted by distance or burbling fountains. Some—but not all—were older, and all of them radiated strength and vitality that was lacking in those who stayed closer to the house. Cassandra made the effort to introduce Tiffany to each person, and her introductions became more formal and elaborate.

Lastly, they joined Cassandra's husband, Gabriel, who was speaking to Alexis's husband and a trio of older gentlemen. Cassandra drew Tiffany in front of her, settling her hands familiarly on the girl's shoulders, earning speculative looks from the men.

"Darling, this is Tiffany Winters, that charming woman I've been telling you so much about. Tiffany, this is my husband, Gabriel Sachs. I've been meaning to introduce you two all night."

Gabriel cut a fine figure in his fitted slacks and a button-down shirt that put the tailors of Savile Row to shame. He had the tanned skin and sun-bleached hair of a man who spent a great deal of his time outdoors, and proved that he wasn't afraid of hard work by his rough, calloused hand, which closed gently around Tiffany's. He inclined his head, gaze sliding to Cassandra before returning to the new girl.

"A pleasure, Tiffany. I've heard so much about you." He smiled as her cheeks colored in a blush, and extended his hand to each of his companions, introducing them in turn. "Might I introduce Arthur Norris, Basil Thornwood, Phillip Edgington, and Dr. Greene?"

A quick round of welcoming words, handshakes, and head nods set Tiffany at ease. More so when one of them asked who her husband was, noting the ring she had not yet removed. It was enough to make her laugh, holding her hand up so the gem could catch the light.

"Don't let this fool you. I'm only wearing it as a reminder."

"I can't imagine what a woman as lovely as you is doing here alone. If only I were a few years younger, so I could catch your eye as those young bucks by the house do," lamented Phillip, a silver-haired gentleman. He caught and held her upraised hand so that he could bow over it, his thumb lightly stroking her knuckles. Tiffany demurely lowered her eyes, while the other ladies were busy rolling theirs. "Do feel free to call on me, charming thing that you are. I'd delight in your company."

"That's very kind of you, Phillip. I'll be sure to look you up."

Gabriel cleared his throat. "Right, then. Well, we do need to get back to business here. . . ."

Cassandra's eyes narrowed, but she nodded, and the other girls followed her lead as she backed away. "We'll talk more later."

Gabriel didn't answer, his gaze locked on Tiffany as he spoke in low tones to his companions.

Heather and Alexis were quite pleased, speaking with carefully reined enthusiasm. Cassandra was silent, brooding, and Tiffany gave no hint as to her feelings about her introductions beyond a sly curve to her lips.

"Well, this has been rather enlightening," Tiffany said.

"I hope the whirlwind introductions didn't leave you dizzy," said a man waiting in the shadows of a nearby cherry tree. His teeth gleamed, a slash of pearl in the dark as he smiled, before he stepped forward to offer his arm to Tiffany. He inclined his head to the other girls, who were unamused by his theatrics. "I beg your pardon, ladies. I hope you don't mind if I steal Tiffany away for myself for a while."

"Not at all, Travis," drawled Heather. "I'm sure you two will have fun."

Tiffany feigned a blush and smiled up at Travis, taking his offered arm. Cassandra shook her head and the three werewives drifted off as Travis led Tiffany back toward the house.

"That's not going to end well," Alexis mused.

"For who? Him or her?"

"Both," Alexis said, gesturing for the girls to walk with her toward the woods at the edge of the property instead of back toward the mansion. "I foresee her eating him alive and spitting him out. He'll moan to the other males about what a frigid bitch she is. Then, in a few days, she'll seduce another one of them and start the cycle over again."

Heather nearly choked on the drink she was sipping, a touch of laughter in her whispered words. "Keep it down, someone will overhear. What makes you say that? You barely know her."

"Maybe. I've known enough like her to see the signs. She'll keep working her way up the social ladder until someone takes her in hand."

Cassandra frowned. "If that's really the case, we *need* to contract her—and do it before she pushes one of the boys too far."

"Gabriel didn't seem very interested. He might not let us do it," Heather said.

"I know. I'll talk to him about it after he gets home. I need to clear my head so I can think. You ladies want to go for a run?"

Heather glanced back toward the house, frowning. "I'd like to, but I'm Tiffany's ride."

"She'll make it home fine, I'm sure," Alexis said. Heather gave her a scathing, offended look before collapsing into giggles as Alexis added a leer and suggestive waggle of her brows to go with it. "Come on. The party is winding down anyway. Let's go have some fun."

Together the ladies drifted into the woods, pausing only to remove their shoes. Once they had their heels in hand, they did not stop until they reached a small clearing far from the lights and prying eyes at the party. Alexis cursed when her silk skirt caught on a thorn and tore, yanking the delicate material free so hard that she widened the rip. Heather smothered a laugh, while Cassandra busied herself with removing her blouse.

"There goes fifteen hundred dollars." Alexis sighed, tugging the offending material off and hanging it on a low-hanging branch.

Vera silently drifted out of the shadows, her eyes aglow and her feet bare, Jimmy Choos dangling from one hand. She took in the scene, the curl in her lip lessening when she noted Tiffany's absence.

"I take it Gabriel said no?"

Heather, busy removing her own clothing, huffed impatiently. "Darling, I don't know why you're so dead set against her. Even if you're suspicious of her, it wouldn't kill you to be polite."

"I'm rich. I don't have to be nice."

Heather frowned at her. "It certainly wouldn't hurt for you to try once in a while. Besides, Gabriel hasn't given his answer yet. Cassie will convince him tonight."

"With a little lip action, I'm sure," Alexis muttered. Cassandra shot her a glare that she pretended she hadn't seen. "Give the man some deep throat and he's yours."

Heather and Vera broke out in laughter while Cassandra swiped nails arched into talons at Alexis, who danced out of the way just in time. Grinning, she shimmied out of her skirt and top a safe distance away as Cassandra growled and huffed, tugging off her own clothes and folding them into a neat pile.

"I'll get you for that!"

"Got to catch me first!"

Alexis laughingly dashed off into the dark, her body changing as she ran. Her skin grew darker in tone, limbs stretching, bones and tendons cracking as the shift brought out her inner beast. Without losing a single stride, she was soon running on four legs rather than two, the gray-coated timber wolf racing deep into the forest.

Vera, who had already shed her clothing and jewelry in

preparation for a shift, set the bundle of her belongings aside and joined her. Her coat as a wolf was as dark as her deep auburn hair, a rusty reddish brown that easily blended with the forest. Cassandra raced to catch up, ghosting between the trees as a pale gray shadow, seen only briefly as she flashed through patches of moonlight that filtered through the canopy of foliage. Heather was the last to shift, a mousy brown color, smaller than the others, but much faster. She soon caught up, and they were away, a silent pack running together and enjoying the freedom of the night.

Tiffany stepped out from between the trees, tucking a video camera back into her purse before she toed the clothing the girls had left behind.

CHAPTER 6

I don't need a man in my life.
—Enya

A few days after the party, the ladies made plans to meet again. Cassandra had been attempting to corner Gabriel long enough to speak to him about Tiffany, but he was too tied up in both his company and his pack's business to discuss it. She'd put off getting together as long as she could; Tiffany had started questioning Heather about whether she'd upset Cassandra.

As they didn't want to have her snatched up by another pack or to take the lack of time spent together as a slight, Cassandra was bound and determined to make this their last social call before she put a contract in front of Tiffany.

By way of apology, Cassandra had offered to pick up the tab for dinner at a new restaurant that had just opened a few blocks from Times Square, some fanciful place with a theme of diamonds and crystals. It was all the rage, garnering rave reviews in the local papers and an excellent ZAGAT rating. Anybody who was anybody had been spotted there. It was, rather inevitably, called Star Dust.

Tiffany had gladly accepted, and the women met outside the restaurant, decked out in shining Gucci as only it had the requisite number of rhinestones to match their need to outshine the restaurant's décor.

"Good to see you all again," Tiffany said. She smiled at Alexis and Cassandra when they joined her at the fringes of the line waiting to get in. Her expression quickly turned neutral when she saw Vera bringing up the rear, trailing a few yards behind the others.

"You, too! I'm sorry it's taken me so long to get away. My husband has been an absolute *beast* these past few days, and I simply haven't had the time."

Heather, Vera, and Alexis nearly choked on their laughter at Cassandra's statement, though they quickly got it under control. Tiffany smiled, shaking her head. "Men can be such a pain, I know."

Alexis, curious, broke in. "Speaking of which, how did things go with Travis?"

Heather and Cassandra both shot her a warning look, while Tiffany simply shrugged. "Not as well as I had hoped it would. Let's discuss it over drinks, shall we?"

Cassandra took the lead, the other girls falling into step behind her as they headed to the front of the line. Security took one look at the designer clothes, the painted faces, the svelte bodies, and the killer heels, and let them pass without hesitation, drawing aside the white velvet rope to allow them inside.

There was not a single voice of complaint from the people waiting in line, as not a one would dare—until they were out of earshot, that is.

Once he spotted her, the maître d' came around his lacquered white podium to extend a welcoming hand to Cassandra, beaming. Like much of the furniture, his tuxedo was white, his tie, cuff links, and pocket kerchief of a fine silver material. Columns of white and silver marble flanked the doors. Crystal vases filled with crystal flowers sat on low silver tables, and the white couches for waiting guests were full. Against the alabaster white walls, it was much like stepping into an icy cavern, too perfect, too austere, to be welcoming.

They fit right in.

"Mademoiselle, lovely to see you again. Your table is ready. Right this way."

The rest of the restaurant was done in similar style. The music drifting from hidden speakers was soft, melodic, with chimes resonating with the crystal and silver statues that gleamed and glittered from recessed alcoves around the room. The raised ceiling was painted such a deep, dark blue that the tiny lights set into it made it feel as though one were outdoors, staring up at a velvet night sky filled with stars. Even the hum of conversation was muted, giving the place an intimate feel, as though one were lost in the icy tundra of the frozen north.

Once they were seated, Tiffany lounged back, examining the menu. "Well, this all looks very good. What do you recommend?"

"Maybe you should try the grilled salmon salad with orange-basil vinaigrette. I hear salmon is good if you need to lose weight."

Tiffany lowered her menu to give Vera a flat stare, clearly not amused at the insinuation. Vera gave nothing back, her expression bland and innocent. Heather, exasperated, gestured at the menu.

"Whatever you like. Everything I've had here is excellent. Try their house drink, though, the Starlight is amazing."

Some of the tension at the table eased, and before long the waiter came and went with their order. Tiffany surprised them all by offering to cover the drinks, looking very deliberately at Vera when she said it. No one argued, and everyone was fairly quiet until the waiter returned with their cocktails. Once they had their drinks in hand, everyone relaxed a bit more. Tiffany exclaimed over the sweet liquor, thanking Heather for the recommendation before sighing dramatically and pressing a hand to her brow.

"I need some help."

Alexis frowned, glancing at Cassandra. "What's wrong? What do you need?"

"It's Travis," Tiffany said, cradling her drink as she leaned forward. "Can one of you please get him to stop calling me? I swear, that man hasn't given me a moment of peace since the party."

*   *   *

The other women shared confused and mildly alarmed looks, and Heather sputtered something unintelligible before Cassandra held up her hand for silence. "What happened at the party? I thought you two were getting along so well."

"So did I. Until he started telling me how much I reminded him of his sister."

The other girls couldn't help it. They all cracked up.

"Oh," gasped Alexis, carefully wiping tears of laughter from under her eyes so as not to smudge her mascara, "oh, that's terrible! I'm so sorry!"

Heather, once she got her sniggering under control, put a sympathetic hand on Tiffany's arm. "Don't worry, sweetheart, we'll find you someone better. There are plenty of men in the pa—from the party who are single. There's Damon or Michael or, oh, I'll bet you'd get along great with—"

"Enough, darling, she probably doesn't remember the names of half the men she was introduced to at the party," Alexis said with saccharine sweetness, the underlying warning completely going over Heather's head as she pouted at being interrupted. Tiffany didn't seem to mind.

"I'm not so sure I'm interested anymore," she replied.

Vera smirked. "How terrible for you. No one to take care of you . . . All alone in the world."

"I don't need anyone to take care of me. I do just fine on my own."

"You say that now. I wonder why you tried so hard to pretend not to be interested at the party? Phillip and Travis certainly didn't seem to mind your attention—and no matter what you say, I'll bet the entire time you were thinking about what you could get out of it."

Tiffany's jaw clenched and spots of color rose high on her cheekbones. Vera idly traced her index finger through the condensation on her glass before pushing it away and rising.

Alexis and Heather gave Vera exasperated looks. Cassandra ignored Vera as she walked toward the ladies' room, hips swaying.

"Don't mind her," Cassandra said. "She's just PMSing because she isn't the center of attention."

Tiffany pouted after Vera's retreating form, though her icy blue eyes gleamed with calculation under the mask of hurt. "I wouldn't mind so much if I knew why she took such a dislike to me. Does she think I'm competition? I thought she was married."

"Vera's always had a thing for Travis," Alexis mused, stirring her drink as she leaned back in her chair and gave one of the waiters watching her from across the room an excellent view of her crossed legs as she adjusted her skirt just so. "Maybe she's peeved that he's given up on her and taken an interest in you."

"No, no, it isn't that. She's had a problem with her from the start. I think she's pissed because you're single and successful enough to live in our neighborhood without the benefit of a man to pay your way," Heather declared.

The others regarded Heather with new respect for her astute observation.

"But," she added, ruining the moment, "we still need to set you up with someone nice. I'll bet you an experienced man like Phillip would last longer than the playboys like Travis, anyway."

Tiffany nearly spewed her drink, covering her mouth with one hand while the other reached for a napkin to blot her lips. Cassandra and Alexis were too busy giggling over the thought to be of any help, all of them gasping and laughing. Talk turned to simpler, less dangerous topics—what was coming up on tomorrow's daytime soaps, the scandalously awful shoes one of the women wore to the party, and whether they should go shopping or barhopping after they ate. Even Vera was civil when she returned, keeping most of her snarky comments limited to her observations about the fashion faux pas several of Alexis's guests made at the party.

Cassandra came very close to pulling the contract out of her purse to slide across the table to put in Tiffany's hands. All that stopped her were Vera or Tiffany's occasional comments that cut through the air of camaraderie. Just when things would settle down, one of them would slip, and they would bristle at each other until Heather or Alexis changed the subject.

Finally, exasperated, Cassandra turned to Tiffany and bluntly invited her on a coffee date—alone—the next day so they could have a private chat.

"Oh," Tiffany said, looking uncertainly between Heather and Cassandra, "we were going to go to one of those Botox parties tomorrow afternoon."

"We'll reschedule," Heather said quickly upon catching Cassandra's look.

"Oh. Oh, all right, then."

"Excellent," Cassandra said, a sly smile curving her lips.

CHAPTER 7

If the only tool you have is a hammer,
you tend to see every problem as a nail.
—Abraham H. Maslow

Four timber wolves raced through the shadows of a New Jersey forest, hunting under a gibbous moon. Save for the occasional chirp of insects or hoot of an owl, all was quiet, the denizens of the forest knowing better than to explore with predators such as these on the prowl.

Until Alexis scrabbled over a large rock and snagged a claw, breaking it.

The others came to a halt as she tumbled to a stop in a snarling bundle of teeth and bristling fur. Cassandra padded over to investigate, sniffing as Alexis held out the offending paw, whimpering. After giving the wound a lick, Cassandra turned back in the direction of her home, where they had started their run. Vera and Heather both whined at having their playtime cut short, but after an authoritative bark from Cassandra, quieted and followed without further complaint.

Vera and Heather still frolicked on the way back, chasing after the occasional mouse or other small creature stirred up by their passing. Cassandra stayed beside Alexis, ignoring her plaintive whines and exaggerated limp.

They emerged from the shadows of the birch and evergreens bordering Cassandra's property, lying down on the smooth carpet of grass that led right up to the woods. Sleek fur rippled and twitched, and the grinding and popping of bones and sinews rearranging rang out as the four wolves began their change back to human.

Vera groaned as the last joint snapped back into place, watching with a critical eye as her claws receded. "Damn. I'm going to have to get these done again."

Alexis's fur ruffled as she gave Vera an irritated curl of her lip before completing her change. The other ladies didn't answer; they were too busy with their own shifts from wolf to human to respond. Heather chuffed, blowing like a bellows as she collapsed on her side, having run harder than the others.

The thick fur slowly withdrew into Alexis's skin, talons and paws gradually lengthening and softening into human hands again. She quickly lifted her arm, squinting in the moonlight as she examined her nails.

"Ugh, my whole nail cracked. Gross! I guess we were all due for a mani-pedi, anyway," she said. "We can go after Cassie meets with Tiffany."

Heather rubbed her jaw, popping it and speaking around fangs that had not quite finished reforming into flat human teeth. "Are you going to give her the contract this time? I saw it sticking out of your purse at the restaurant earlier."

Cassandra rolled her ankles to get the joints to set properly, ignoring Vera's scowl. "Yes. I wanted to give it to her then, but it didn't seem like the right time. I thought it might be better if I spoke to her one-on-one instead of having the whole group there to pressure her."

"You're making a mistake, Cassandra," Vera said. "She isn't pack material. I don't know why none of you are listening to me."

"We aren't listening because there's no basis for your concern! You keep saying she's a threat, but you won't talk to her yourself and don't back up what you're saying with anything that proves she has any intention of hurting us," Heather snapped.

Taken aback, Vera stared for a moment, mouth agape. She first looked to Alexis, then Cassandra for help or sympathy, and found none. Both were shaking their head at her, agreeing with Heather.

"Well," Vera said, settling back in the grass and steepling her fingers, "I'm still looking for something that proves what I already know to be the case. I told you all that I know I've seen her somewhere before. I think she has a connection to the hunters in New York. It's not easy digging up information on them, you know."

"What makes you think so, though? She said she was interested in meeting a werewolf, not killing one."

"I've seen her somewhere before. Maybe on the news, or somewhere on the Internet. Not here."

"Are you sure it's her?"

Taking offense at the tone of the question, Vera bristled, glaring at Cassandra. "Almost positive."

"Almost positive is not sure," Cassandra said, rising and sauntering to the lounge chairs where they had laid out their clothing. She shrugged on her shirt, not bothering to button it up. "We can't assume anything when it comes to the welfare of the pack."

"Then that should go both ways! We don't know for sure that she's not a threat."

"No, but we do know she has an interest in werewolves, and that our pack will grow stagnant and gradually disappear if we don't add new members to it. We can't afford to let someone interested slip through our fingers. I will ask her what her intentions are, and offer the contract. If she wants to use it against us, then I promise you I will kill her myself."

Vera subsided, mostly satisfied. Heather, now in jeans and a light T-shirt, shifted her weight and wouldn't meet Cassandra's eyes.

"Are you going to turn her right away if she signs the papers?"

"Maybe," Cassandra said, folding her skirt over her arm and walking toward the house, not looking back. "It depends on what Gabriel has to say about it."

Alexis gasped. "You still haven't asked him?"

"No. He hasn't been home."

The other ladies shared knowing looks, but didn't say a word, following silently in Cassandra's wake.

Gabriel didn't bother to look up from his desk when Cassandra appeared in the doorway of his study.

"Not now."

"Honey, I really need to talk to you."

"Give me about an hour. I need to finish reading this brief," Gabriel said, not looking up from the papers spread over his desk. It was the first time he'd been home before eleven in two weeks.

Cassandra leaned on the door frame, toying with the diamond pendant on her necklace as she considered him. He'd barely noticed her short satin robe, the one he'd taken such delight in rubbing himself against less than a month before. Gabriel hadn't joined her for dinner before her run, hadn't answered her text messages or e-mails, and had been too exhausted for the last several nights to talk to her about anything beyond kissing her good night—if she was still awake when he got home—before he crawled into bed. She hadn't asked what was on his plate, but she had gleaned from a few conversations overheard that it involved the welfare of the entire pack.

It wasn't her, she was sure. Judging by the dark circles under his eyes, she was quite certain it really was work that kept him from home and from showing any interest in sex. Aside from that, if he'd been cheating, she would have smelled the scent of another bitch on him—so that wasn't it. He really was working himself to the bone.

This called for desperate measures.

She slunk forward, putting a roll into her hips, catching his eye. He looked up, twitching a jet brow, one hand racing through dark hair starting to show the first hints of silver at the temples. Cassandra moved behind him, rubbing at the thick knots of tension in his shoulders. He gradually relaxed into her hands, eyes closing.

"You're working too hard. Come to bed."

He sighed, arching his back so she could reach his shoulder blades. "I can't, love. This needs to be done."

"It'll still be here in the morning." Cassandra leaned over to whisper in his ear, nipping his earlobe as one hand slid down his chest to the hard bulge in his pants. "Let me take care of you."

He groaned, arching up against her questing hand. It didn't take long before she'd drawn down his zipper and slid aside his silk boxers, freeing him from his pants. Deft fingers worked his arousal with practiced swiftness.

Gabriel didn't object, his fingers digging into the armrests of his chair until the leather creaked under his hands, watching as if mesmerized by the way she squeezed and stroked him, the way he grew and pulsed under her touch.

His breath hitched in his throat as she bit his ear again, tilting his head to the side to give her access to his throat. A very trusting move on his part. Trailing her lips over the stubble on his cheek, Cassandra whispered again, her voice low and throaty.

"I need something from you."

In a blur, she was suddenly on her back on his desk, Gabriel pressed between her dangling legs. Papers scattered, flying everywhere before drifting to the floor. His eyes, usually a soft brown, now burned with a harsh amber light as he bent over her, hands exploring the smooth satin of her robe before tearing it open. Cassandra returned his growls in kind, wrapping her legs around his waist to yank him forward, nails raking down his back.

"I need—" She gasped as he bit her, nails convulsing against his back.

"I know what you need," he rumbled, rough hands sliding lower on her body. Her hips moved to meet his exploring fingers, even as she made a guttural sound of denial.

"No," she insisted, grasping and pulling at his hair until he paused, looking at her. "Something else."

He slumped, then rose just enough to meet her own burning, glowing eyes. It took a few breaths for him to calm enough to answer. He had to speak carefully, enunciating each word carefully around the mouthful of fangs he'd sprouted.

"Anything. You know I'll always give you whatever you want."

Cassandra smiled, bared teeth behind those painted lips grown into dagger points much like his own.

"I want Tiffany Winters. I want her in the pack."

"Done."

And for the rest of the night, neither of them had a chance to fit in another word.

CHAPTER 8

To be yourself in a world that is constantly
trying to make you something else
is the greatest accomplishment.
—Ralph Waldo Emerson

The next day, Cassandra settled in a seat on the patio outside of one of the quieter Starbucks in the neighborhood, cradling an iced latte. Tiffany looked up from her cell phone, setting it aside with a smile as she eased back into the wrought-iron chair. Aside from the occasional patron moving in and out of the coffeehouse, they were alone.

"You wanted to talk to me?"

Cassandra crossed her legs, leaning back in her chair while one finger toyed with the condensation on her latte. She stared directly into Tiffany's eyes, taking her measure before speaking in carefully noncommittal tones.

"Heather told me that you had an interest in werewolves. Meeting them, in fact. What if I told you that I could help you with that?"

Tiffany's gaze searched Cassandra's face. "I'd say I was skeptically hopeful. Ever since the Moonwalker pack showed themselves, I've wanted to meet one. Except for Rohrik Donovan and the rest of the Moonwalkers, they don't exactly advertise their whereabouts, and he doesn't meet with people just to satisfy their curiosity."

"No. I suppose he doesn't."

"But you will?"

Cassandra paused, latte halfway to her mouth. "You knew?"

"Yes. I knew before I moved here."

"Was Vera right, then? Are you here to cause us trouble?"

Shaking her head, Tiffany held out a hand, imploring Cassandra to stay seated. Though a touch of yellow had crept into her irises, Cassandra stilled, her mouth pressed into a thin line of displeasure.

"Vera may have made the connection between the New York branch of the White Hats and myself because I used to be married to one of them."

Cassandra swiftly rose with a harsh screech of iron over concrete, her nails forming into claws. Tiffany stayed in her seat, her hand reaching out imploringly. "Please, hear me out."

"I think I've heard enough," Cassandra replied tartly, reaching for her Hermès purse.

"No, you haven't." Tiffany insisted in such a sharp tone that Cassandra stilled, eyes narrowed to gleaming yellow slivers. Tiffany pressed on, unfazed. "Just listen to me. I'm not married to him anymore. When I first met Richard, I knew he was a hunter, but I didn't take part in that business. It took me a while to see what he was doing was wrong, and I divorced him with good reason. I thought maybe—just maybe—if I managed to meet one of you I could find some way to make up the damage I caused by standing by and supporting him for so long."

Cassandra regarded Tiffany for a long moment, taking shallow breaths through flared nostrils, more interested in her scent and the sound of her heartbeat than in her words or pleading looks. There was an understandable trace of fear under the vanilla and sandalwood musk of her Shalini perfume, but no discordant undertones of a lie.

Though Cassandra did not retract her claws, some of the beast withdrew from her eyes, and she slowly settled back into her seat. Tiffany's gaze still searched her face, fingers tight around her cup and breath held as she waited for a response. It took some time for it to come, but when it did, she couldn't help but smile.

"If that is truly the case, then I am assuming you came here wanting to bolster our ranks."

"Yes. That's right."

Cassandra stared at the girl until she shifted her weight and looked away, unnerved by those yellow eyes. "Were you going to tell any of us this? Or were you just waiting for Heather or one of the men to present you with a contract?"

Tiffany had the grace to blush, though she was quick to shake her head. "No, no, it wasn't like that. It never felt like the right time. Vera was so dead set against me that I wasn't sure if I'd ever have the chance. Of if any of you would listen to reason once I brought it up."

"I see."

Cassandra regarded her for a moment longer in uncomfortable silence before coming to a decision. She reached into the purse on her arm, withdrawing neatly tri-folded documents and sliding them across the table. Tiffany's expression quickly shifted from apprehension to shocked delight as she unfolded the *Notice of Mutual Consent to Human/Other Citizen Relationship and Contractual Binding Agreement.*

"If this is really what you want—"

"Oh, it is!"

"—then fill the papers out and come to dinner tonight. My house. Dress to impress. I'll introduce you to some of the others, and when one of them is ready, they'll sign and file the rest."

Tiffany's face fell as she realized that meant that the papers weren't ready to be lodged in a court—in effect, binding her for the rest of her life to one of the werewolves and giving them the right to feed on or make her one of them—though she soon perked up at the invitation.

"Oh, thank you, Cassie. I can't begin to tell you how happy this makes me!"

"Don't thank me yet," Cassandra drawled. "You still need to find a host who will take you. And I do expect you to behave yourself and not antagonize Vera anymore."

"I'll try."

"Do more than try. Those papers include the pack privilege clause. *If* you find a host who will have you—and I assure you that it will not be easy with your past—it will leave you open to attack from any member of our pack, not just whoever signs with you. I suggest you find a way to smooth things over with Vera."

Tiffany frowned, skimming over the documents. "I'll do that." Glancing up, she offered Cassandra a sunny smile, clearly quite pleased with this turn of events. "Thank you again. Don't worry, you won't regret this decision."

Cassandra said nothing in reply, turning and walking away.

Once Cassandra left, Tiffany took her time polishing off the rest of her coffee as she read through the contract, enjoying the time in the sun. Very little of it was different from the standard contracts often available at local courthouses. The pack privilege allowed any werewolf in the pack to hurt or even kill their applicant without legal repercussions; these days, the clause was standard language in contracts for dangerous supernatural creatures who lived in groups, such as vampires and werewolves.

Tucking the papers under her arm, she rose, withdrawing her cell phone as she headed to her car. In moments, she'd drafted a text message and sent it to Richard, then drove home.

It took some time to get ready. Some of the benefits of having spent time on the fringes, getting to know her husband's profession, were the access to his connections, the combined gathered intelligence on Others by the White Hats—and the toys.

After a long, luxurious bath in scented oils, relaxing her muscles, she padded nude through her walk-in closet, choosing and then discarding a number of outfits. For the dinner, she needed to wear something both fashionable and functional; nothing so skintight as to reveal the weaponry concealed on her person. Searching blue eyes soon found the perfect outfit. She chose a Christian Dior dress with flared sleeves to make for an easy draw of her silver-coated daggers. It had a high enough slit on either side of the skirt to easily reach the guns strapped to her garters, and looked killer with a matching pair of Louboutin heels.

Her phone rang out the strains of Bach, announcing an incoming call from Richard. Again. And a third time.

She ignored the calls in favor of examining herself critically in a floor-length mirror.

The quick-draw bands at her wrists faded into the shadows of the sleeves of the black, silver, and gray fabric of the dress, but were still too conspicuous. With the addition of some thick Swarovski bracelets studded with diamonds and opals, a matching choker, and a touch of Chanel No. 5 at her wrists and throat, she felt ready to take on the entire pack.

For the thrill of it, she twisted and hurled one of the daggers in one smooth motion, embedding it in the frame of the dresser across the room, just above where her cell phone still rang and rang. A smile curved her lips when she noted the blade had landed precisely on the knot of wood she'd been aiming for.

With leisurely strides, she crossed the room, glancing down at the phone before working the dagger out of the wood. Tucking it back within its sheath, she then turned her phone off and slipped it in her purse, heading for the door.

As much as she hoped things would stay civil tonight, she would be prepared for anything.

CHAPTER 9

The first sign of a nervous breakdown is when
you start thinking your work is terribly important.
—Milo Bloom

Cassandra greeted Tiffany at the door, taking in her outfit in one quick, critical sweep. It dragged a reluctant smile out of her, for it met and exceeded every expectation for the impromptu dinner she'd arranged.

Getting Gabriel to agree to stay home for the affair had not been terribly difficult. At his word, the remaining single males in the pack, to a one, had agreed to come. Many of them had arrived early in hopes of making a good impression, and were not disappointed by the entrance of the leggy, stunning blonde who put the shining crystals and modern art in Cassandra's smallest, most intimate dining room to shame.

Tiffany sat near Gabriel and Cassandra at the head of the table, setting her purse at her side and placing the signed contract beside her plate. She accepted a glass of wine and the brief introductions of the few men she hadn't met at Alexis's party a few days before. Several of the more prominent members of the pack had come as well, including the other werewives and their spouses. Vera, thankfully, kept her comments to herself, though she was clearly displeased with this turn of events.

Though no one mentioned anything about the pack at first, after Cassandra's cook brought out the hors d'oeuvres, guests complimented Cassandra on the fare and the talk took a more serious shift. Gabriel cleared his throat, getting the silent attention of his guests within moments.

"Thank you all for coming on such short notice," he said, giving Tiffany a nod. "I'm sure you've all heard by now that we have a new applicant for membership in our pack."

"Ah, is that what this is all about?"

"Yes, Phillip. I'll thank you not to lick your chops like a big, bad wolf and scare our honored guest away." That garnered some laughter, as well as a wink and a grin in Tiffany's direction from Phillip. The laughter became more genuine at her blushes. "As most of you know, expanding our numbers has always been a priority. The Diamondfang pack has welcomed society's elite into our ranks for decades, long before humanity openly acknowledged the existence of the supernatural. Now, under the circumstances, I felt it best if we addressed some important aspects of her request as a group, rather than allow speculation and rumors to sully what should be a joyous occasion.

"Tiffany Winters has admitted to connections to a group of hunters—the White Hats—in New York."

The room exploded with dissent, exclamations of shock and outrage, several of the werewolves rising from their seats or even letting a touch of their inner beasts peek out of their eyes as they snarled their displeasure. Vera seemed especially incensed, her accusing tones laced with triumph as she rose from her seat and pointed at Tiffany, sneering as she shouted, "I knew it! I told you she was trouble!"

Tiffany scowled, but said nothing, clutching her hands tightly together in her lap. She wouldn't meet the eyes of any of the wolves, knowing better than to give their aggression ammunition by giving them challenging looks.

Gabriel watched for a few moments, eyes narrowed. Shortly, his calm, collected, and deadly quiet voice cut through the din.

"Sit down. All of you."

None dared disobey the alpha, though many of those who weren't glaring at Tiffany were giving him sidelong looks.

"Now," he said, once the low rumble of opposition subsided to quieter levels, "she has informed us that she was connected to one by marriage, but no longer. She is not part of that world anymore, and wishes to make amends for her participation in their activities by bolstering our ranks. It is not an unreasonable request—and she could be a valuable addition to this pack."

"She's dangerous," Vera sneered, "and I can't believe you're still willing to take her in, knowing what she is."

Gabriel gave Vera a flat look. She soon quieted and turned her eyes down. Phillip, who had remained silent during the uproar, cleared his throat and spoke up after receiving a nod of acknowledgment from his pack leader.

"It takes an extraordinary person to admit when they are in the wrong. More so for someone to take so little prompting to wish to be a part of our pack. Ms. Winters, I will sign the contract, if you will accept me as your host."

Tiffany gasped, her hand flying to her mouth as happy tears sprung to her eyes. Though some of the Weres maintained their dubious expressions, most showed grudging approval; a handful even clapped to show their support. Before she could answer, Vera snarled, slamming her hand on the table hard enough for the silverware to rattle.

"I can't believe you people are falling for her story! Have any of you *checked* her background to ensure she's who she says she is? That she's really divorced? That she didn't come here armed to kill us all?"

Gabriel growled, a deep, harsh sound that rolled through the room like thunder. Much to the other diners' surprise, it was Tiffany's voice that lashed out rather than their pack leader's. She rose to her full height to point an accusatory finger at Vera.

"You have no right to be saying any of those things about me. You haven't gotten to know me or given me any chance to prove myself to you!"

"There's nothing to prove. You're connected to hunters, and that makes you a menace to every one of us!"

"I'm not here to hurt anybody, you crazy bitch! Where the hell do you get off, making these unfounded accusations—"

"I'm looking out for the best interests of my packmates. Who do you think you're fooling?" Vera snarled, her eyes glowing, ignoring the horrified looks of the other guests and the tugging on her arm by her husband in an effort to get her to settle down.

"If Phillip signs that contract, I will hunt you down and kill you myself."

Tiffany's glare turned icy, reaching for a wineglass so she could fling the contents at her. Vera's face and white Burberry top was splashed with the bloodred 2006 Château Mouton Rothschild Pauillac.

Save for Vera's breaths, hissed through her teeth, dead silence reigned.

With careful, measured motions, the werewife rose from her seat, towering in her Proenza heels. No one, not even Gabriel, was ready to interfere.

Slowly, deliberately, Vera picked up a plate of crackers and Almas caviar (which, fortunately for Gabriel, was the cheaper, darker variety) and hurled it across the table at Tiffany. She ducked out of the way just in time for Damon, who was coming to her side in defense, to be beaned with it instead.

Howling a challenge, Vera vaulted onto and then across the table in one smooth motion, evading her husband's grasping hands as he shouted at her to calm down. Tiffany shoved herself backward, knocking her chair over and sprawling as she tripped on her long skirt. Most of the other wolves quickly backed out of the way. Fur sprouted on Vera's hands and arms, her face elongating as she dived off the table to where Tiffany now cowered on the floor.

She never landed. In one smooth movement, Cassandra rose from her chair and grabbed Vera by the throat, using the partially turned werewolf's own momentum to swing and hurl her across the room. Vera slammed into the opposite wall, leaving a huge dent and sending artwork and mirrors crashing to the floor. She slumped to the ground, dazed and unmoving.

Tiffany was quick to tuck her silver dagger back in its sheath, praying none of the werewolves had noticed the weapon before it was hidden under her jewelry and sleeve again.

Gabriel and Cassandra both hurried to check on her and offer their apologies for Vera's behavior, but many of the other werewolves were still too shocked and appalled by this turn of events to do more than offer incredulous stares from their seats.

Tiffany waved off the offers to help her up—not wanting them to accidentally spring the mechanism that would flick the daggers out of their sheaths—and rose rather ungracefully to her feet.

No one said a thing as she strode over to her fallen chair to pick up her purse—now spattered with caviar and crumbled bits of cracker—and stalked out, not looking back.

"Well, that was uncalled for."

Tiffany didn't say anything as Heather fell into step beside her.

"You don't have to leave. We can send Vera home."

Tiffany still said nothing, but her lips thinned as she hurried her pace and adjusted her purse strap, heels clacking on the drive as she sought her car.

"I know you're angry," Heather said with a sigh, matching her stride, "but Phillip was really impressed back there. He's asking where the contract is so he can sign it right now."

Tiffany came to an abrupt halt, smudging her mascara as she wiped away angry tears. "Don't bother, Heather. Clearly I'm not welcome here. Vera has been an utter prat ever since I came to town, and now that she knows about my past, she's never going to believe that I didn't come here with bad intentions."

Heather didn't respond, biting her lower lip. Tiffany took a few deep breaths before continuing in a calmer tone.

"I should have known it wouldn't work out. This was all too good to be true. Maybe I'll just go back to Johannesburg. Be closer to my family."

"Oh no!" Heather exclaimed. "You just got here! Don't go yet. Come on, Phillip really wants you to stay, and so does Gabriel and Cassandra. And me! We can work something out. Vera was just looking out for us in her own way—I'm sure she'll come around once you're one of us. *Really* one of us, I mean."

Tiffany dug through her purse for a tissue, sniffling and blotting at her eyes. "Are you sure? I mean, I'd love to be a part of the pack, but not if Vera's going to keep sniping at me for the rest of my life because of something in my past. It *is* the past, and what's done is done—I can't change it, but I don't want to be paying for it the rest of my life, either."

Heather put an arm around Tiffany's shoulder, giving her a comforting squeeze. She nonchalantly flicked bits of caviar off of her dress before putting her hands on Tiffany's shoulders. Heather held her there until she lifted her head and met her eyes, taking in the serious set of her jaw and clear concern in her eyes.

"Don't worry. You aren't that person. I know you're not. Everyone's a bit upset right now, but they'll come around and see it, too."

Tiffany dabbed at her eyes again, pulling away. "Vera won't. She never will."

Heather hesitated, glancing back to the house. Though Tiffany had put some distance between herself and the house, Heather was sure that a few of her packmates were listening in, particularly when she spotted Cassandra and Alexis watching from one of the bay windows overlooking the front yard. Cassandra made an impatient "get on with it" gesture, so Heather turned back to Tiffany, straightening.

"She may not, but the rest of the pack will. Eventually. We'll fix this somehow. Look, why don't you go home for now"— Heather flinched at the sound of Cassandra's angry curse, though Tiffany couldn't hear it—"and get cleaned up, and I'll call you in the morning. We'll go relax at the spa for a while."

Tiffany glanced over her shoulder at the house, frowning. "Okay. What about the others? Do you think Cassandra and Alexis are still going to want to be friends with me?"

"I'm sure they do. And if not, I'll talk sense into them. Now you go home and get some rest. I'll see you tomorrow," Heather said firmly, urging Tiffany to turn back to her car and get moving again.

Tiffany did, unable to see the unnatural yellow glitter to Heather's eyes as she watched her walk away.

CHAPTER 10

Realize that if you have time to
whine and complain about
something, then you have the time
to do something about it.
—Anthony J. D'Angelo

After that spectacular conclusion to dinner, Vera had been told none too politely to keep her head down, and to stay away from Tiffany until the matter of the contract was sorted out. She didn't argue.

Despite Phillip's protests that he was still interested and Cassandra's pleading for Gabriel to give the girl another chance, he had dismissed the rest of his pack with a note of caution to hold on any actions involving Tiffany—whether it be contracting her or destroying her out of hand—until he had a chance to investigate matters further. Cassandra knew exactly what that meant. Later, privately, even her best efforts didn't budge him. Gabriel did not want to endanger the pack, or see it torn apart over the inclusion of a member some of them clearly viewed as an enemy.

Cassandra was still incensed that he hadn't given in to her demands to contract Tiffany despite that thing she did with her tongue.

Instead, he'd enjoyed every minute of her attentions, waited until she—or rather, *he* was done—and then told her in no uncertain terms that he was not going to put the pack at risk by accepting Tiffany into their ranks until he was assured that she posed no danger.

Quite the argument ensued. By the end of it, even Cassandra

had to admit that Vera had a point. Tiffany presented a danger to their pack even if she wasn't a member of the White Hats anymore. There was no telling how close she was to her ex-husband or what he might do if he found out she had signed a contract with a werewolf, let alone become one of them. The contract would have to be filed in court, thus becoming a publicly accessible document—meaning, through the Freedom of Information Act, the White Hats could easily find out that one of their own had turned against them.

It was a substantial risk that Gabriel was not willing to take. The more Cassandra thought about it, the more she saw the inherent danger as well.

At tennis practice at Alexis's house the following morning, Cassandra confessed as to Gabriel's feelings on the matter, and that she had changed her mind as well.

"Oh Cassie," Heather said, skipping back to smoothly return Alexis's serve with a backhanded sweep of her racket, "that just isn't right. You know it's not fair to her. All she wants is to be our friend."

"And join the pack. Don't forget that," Alexis shouted from across the court.

Cassandra snorted, scuffing her shoes against the court. Heather frowned at her, unable to give a proper glare with her gaze torn between her friend and the oncoming ball. She didn't miss a beat, returning every volley and drop shot Alexis tried pulling to win the point even as she laid into Cassandra.

"Vera's just being paranoid. I know she wants what's best for the pack, but so do I—and I think we need fresh blood to revive the older stock. Considering how long it's been since the last time we contracted someone, we're never going to find anyone so easy to convince as Tiffany Winters again. Someone who fits our standards—and comes to us, no less—is unheard of, and don't pretend like you don't know what I'm talking about. We aren't the Moonwalkers in New York, no matter how badly we wish we were. We need to take advantage of this while we can."

"She can't be one of us, darling. Gabriel said no."

"You always do what Gabriel tells you?"

Alexis hurled a particularly vicious shot over the net that Heather had to scramble to catch and return. It certainly got her attention.

"Honey, I don't think you're looking at this clearly. She was married to a *White Hat*. Bane of our existence? Hunts our kind on the weekends for sport? I'm with Cassie and Vera on this. Don't question the pack leader's judgment. We all need to back off."

Heather growled softly, the sound echoing across the court, punctuated by the sharp *thock* of the ball being slapped across the court hard and fast—too fast for Alexis to keep up with, scoring Heather the first point. Cassandra rose to take her place on the court.

The two faced off as Alexis settled primly on a bench, taking a sip of Evian as she watched the pair. Cassandra prepared to serve, pausing just long enough to speak a few words first.

"Don't overstep your bounds, Heather. You don't rank high enough in the pack to challenge Gabriel. Or me."

Heather's normally warm brown eyes now glittered gold, and she said nothing while dashing across the tarmac with supernatural speed to reach the ball. The two women played a silent game, daring each other with sharp, cutting movements, each working to outdo the other.

Sweat freely dripped down their bodies, the world narrowing to one competitive moment, every action and reaction calculated to win the point and end the game. Cassandra hit the ball high and deep into Heather's court, forcing her to exercise extra speed and leap unnaturally high to reach it.

With a rush, Heather dashed forward to meet the lob, using an overhead smash to gain the point and end the game.

"Don't push too hard, Cassie," Heather said, tossing her racket aside with a clatter and rubbing the sweat off her brow with her arm. "You and Gabriel aren't the only voices in the pack."

Cassandra and Alexis watched with narrowed eyes as Heather spun on her heel and left the court, leaving them behind.

* * *

Cassandra sipped at the mai tai Alexis had prepared for her, crossing her legs at the ankles as she relaxed in the kitchen. They'd waited a few minutes before they followed Heather inside, leaving her alone as she stalked off to one of the guest bedrooms to cool down and shower in peace.

"You're not worried about what she said, are you?"

"No," Cassandra replied, not meeting Alexis's questioning gaze. "Not worried. Concerned. Vera and Heather both make good points, but I don't think now is the time to tell Tiffany that we don't want her around or that we won't be turning her into one of us. It might be better if we distance ourselves instead."

Alexis pulled her towel from around her neck and dabbed at her forehead and cheeks before picking up her own drink and leaning against the marble countertop, taking a sip before answering.

"I'm not sure if Tiffany will accept that. Do you think Gabriel will ever let one of us contract or turn her?"

"Honestly? No."

Alexis paused in lifting her drink back to her lips, brow cocked. "And do you think she'll accept that?"

Cassandra shook her head, setting her drink down and pushing it away. The two women said nothing for a time, the silence between them growing heavy.

Shifting her weight and looking away, Alexis broke the silence by turning around and busying herself with tidying the kitchen counters, even though the maid and the cook had already done so earlier in the day. In her Juicy shorts and Nikes with sparkling pink swooshes, she didn't look like much of a domestic, but she did her best impression as she banged cabinets and put the drink mixes away.

"We can't trust her, you know," Alexis said, keeping her back to Cassandra as she reached up into one of the cabinets to adjust some of the dishes.

"I know."

"You can't let her go around thinking she's still welcome, either. One of us is going to have to tell her."

Cassandra harrumphed, a low growl rumbling in her throat. Alexis was careful not to meet her gaze, keeping her head down and her arms wrapped protectively around her stomach when she turned around.

"Maybe we should do it together. We can tell her to come over to Tiffany's later, and we can sit down as a group and discuss it like civilized people. If we keep Vera out of it, maybe she'll even listen to us."

Cassandra's eyes flashed gold, matching her eye shadow, and her lip lifted in a silent snarl before she huffed out a breath of air and let fallen lids obscure her gaze. "I'm not sure if that's an option. If we tell her, she might react badly. Go back to her husband, maybe."

"If we don't tell her," Alexis countered, "she might get it into her head that she still has a chance at becoming one of the pack, and end up doing something foolish. Worse, one of the boys might go along with it, and then where will we be? You saw how they were looking at her last night and how she had them wrapped around her fingers at the party. We can't take the chance."

"No, I suppose not."

Alexis tossed her towel down on the counter before levering herself up to sit on it, reaching for her drink again. "If we tell her that we'll still be her friends, but gradually work our way out of her life and not invite her to all of the parties, maybe she won't take it quite so hard. We'll be safe, she'll be screwed, and we can all get on with our lives."

Cassandra laughed, some of the tension easing out of her shoulders. "If she accepts it as easy as that, I'd be very surprised. I suppose we can give it a shot. Maybe after enough time passes, Gabriel will change his mind. For now, I'm sure Heather can keep her entertained when we're not around."

Heather walked in, now dressed in jeans and a Gucci T-shirt, rubbing the towel through her hair. "Doubtful. I don't like it."

"We didn't expect you would," Alexis said, pushing a third drink down the smooth countertop. Heather caught it easily and took a deep pull. "But I'm sure you'll agree it's all for the best."

Heather downed half the drink in a go, earning raised brows and concerned looks from the other two ladies. She set the glass down with a clack, nearly breaking it.

"No, I don't like it. But it'll have to do."

The two nodded and smiled, glad to hear she agreed. Until she added a quiet "for now" under her breath.

CHAPTER 11

Live by the gun, die by the gun.
—Tupac Shakur

"I have something you should see."

Cassandra harrumphed as she dug through her closet, looking for a pair of shoes to wear, her cell phone tucked to her ear. "Vera, I know you just want to help, but you need to lay off. We're handling this."

"I have proof this time."

Cassandra paused, one foot halfway into her Bottega Veneta platform wedge sandals. She was already irritated at Vera for tricking her into picking up by calling from an unfamiliar number—her husband's office line—after calls from her cell went unanswered. Vera was quick to fill the silence, the urgency in her tone not feigned in the least.

"She's one of them, Cassie. Be careful."

"We're all meeting at Heather's house in two hours. Bring whatever you found."

"I'll be there."

"Vera—"

"Don't say it. I know. I'll behave myself."

Cassandra's tone was icy, commanding, and brooked no refusal. "See that you do. Another slip like the one you made at dinner, and I'll personally see to it that there's nothing left when the police come to pick you up for harming a human outside of a contract."

Vera was met with the click of a dial tone before she could reply.

Though a trifle peeved at being hung up on, Vera tossed the cordless phone she'd borrowed from her husband's office onto the bed and gathered the printouts of articles she'd found on the Internet. She was rather proud of the glossy quality her husband's printer had spit out, showing Tiffany on the edge of a pack of scruffy-looking hunters with a gun in her hand and a White Hat pin prominently tacked to the lapel of what looked like a knockoff Ralph Lauren blazer.

So tacky.

Alexis slowly exhaled, her eyes closed, one hand palm up, the other down, resting them on her folded legs. The taste of incense was heavy on the air, and the soft instrumental music and burbling water from a nearby fountain assisted her to find her center.

Since it had been cut short, and tensions had been high the entire time, the tennis match hadn't helped her to work off the excess supernatural energy of her second nature as it normally would have. With all of the stress from Vera and Tiffany's sniping and fighting, she had felt it necessary to call in an emergency session with her private yoga instructor. It took some pleading and persuading, but he had eventually conceded, and cancelled one of his morning appointments for her.

The meditation wasn't doing much to calm her. She was certain there must be something she was doing wrong—but she didn't dare speak, knowing her yogi would instruct her if he determined she was not properly following the path of Ashtanga Yoga to serenity and enlightenment. Really, the only reason she was interested in continuing the lessons was because the instructor was one of those hard-bodied men who was Alpha enough to get her to obey his instructions without question, and because the meditation did, to some degree, help her calm herself and maintain greater control over her inner beast.

"Remember to breathe," her yogi said, pressing his hand into her lower back to force her to correct her posture.

With a slight nod, she took in the scent of sandalwood and musk, taking it through her mouth instead of her nose despite the taste it left on her tongue. She didn't want to destroy her sense of smell for the rest of the day.

If there was a hunt, she might need it later.

Heather rushed about her home, getting her maid to tidy the house before sending her on an errand so the woman wouldn't become suspicious or overhear the conversation once the other werewives and Tiffany arrived. She made sure she had plenty of alcohol on hand—she thought they might need it once the news was given.

She wasn't looking forward to telling Cassandra that she'd stopped at the courthouse that morning to file the signed and notarized papers Tiffany had forgotten and left behind at dinner last night.

Tiffany had everything she intended to bring with her to Heather's house spread out on her bed.

She wasn't stupid. She knew Cassandra was reconsidering allowing her into the pack after all that Vera had said. The offer to meet again at Heather's was what tipped her off. Neutral ground; a place she would hesitate to cause a scene, because the property belonged to a friend.

Tiffany had given careful thought to what she needed to bring with her, and felt that the netbook computer to play a video on, the photographs, and the piece of jewelry she'd stolen from Vera when the ladies left their clothing behind in the woods at Alexis's party would serve her purposes admirably.

Though they had never said as much, the Diamondfangs had always worked under the radar of the press and the hunters, working through society's elite. Its members would never want to be outed as real monsters lurking under the façades of ruthless businessmen and women—but now Tiffany knew who most of them were, and had the pictures and dossiers to prove their connections.

She would get what she wanted, or the werewives would be exposed to the world for the bitches they were.

Vera arrived early, papers tucked under her arm in a neat leather portfolio she'd also borrowed from her husband's office. Heather was surprised to see her, but didn't question it, figuring that it would most likely be for the best once she delivered her news. That way she could be present to deflect any immediate attack Vera might attempt.

Alexis was next, breezing inside with a calm, collected air and trailing the scent of incense behind her. The other girls wrinkled their noses at the stink, but she ignored them, dropping into the plush cushions of a couch. She kicked off her embossed leather Alaia sandals and swung her legs up onto the couch, lounging comfortably. Cassandra was not far behind, arriving only fifteen minutes after the scheduled meeting time. She drew off her Versace sunglasses once she was inside and tossed her Yves Saint Laurent purse on the couch next to Alexis, putting her hands on her hips.

"Hmph. She's planning to be fashionably late again, I see."

"She'll be here soon," Heather said, waggling her BlackBerry. "She sent me a text that she was running behind. Had to pick something up on the way, she said."

Vera frowned, stalking over to a chair that gave her a good vantage of the rest of the room, as well as the front door, so she'd know the moment Tiffany arrived. Cassandra huffed and toyed with a few strands of her hair, giving the other girls a hint as to just how peeved she was by the whole situation.

Alexis gestured her over, tucking in her legs to make room. "Come on, Cassie. Come sit and relax. Breathe, darling. My instructor tells me that controlling your breathing is essential in learning how to control your life force. Or something like that."

The other girls stared at her blankly.

"What?" she said, frowning at the looks they were giving her.

"It's part of the road to spiritual development. That's very important, you know."

"Oh, whatever," Cassandra said, rolling her eyes before tucking her skirt under her and settling primly on the edge of the cushions. "Heather, be a love and get the drinks started, would you? I have the feeling we're all going to need them before this is over."

By the time Heather returned with the drinks, Tiffany was just pulling into the driveway. The other girls feigned indifference, but the amber glow to their irises and tension in the set of their shoulders gave them away. Tiffany brought a Claire Chase messenger bag in addition to her purse, tucking the strap over her shoulder before striding with her head held high to meet with the werewives inside.

Heather met her at the door, showing her into the room and seating her as far as was polite from Vera as was possible. The two ladies glared daggers at each other, but were civil enough to exchange tight nods, never taking their eyes off one another.

"Well," Tiffany said, pausing to sip at the Long Island iced tea—heavy on the rum—that Heather had pushed into her hand, "now that I'm here, I'm not sure where to begin."

Cassandra cleared her throat. "Tiffany, you know that we all like spending time with you and having you here—"

"All of you?"

Vera smirked at Tiffany's pointed look, her lip gloss adding an extra sparkle to that killer smile.

"You know what I mean. Now, you know what we are. By your own admission, you've known for a while. While we certainly appreciate your desire to join us, I'm sure you can understand why we might be hesitant to let someone with your . . . background . . . join our ranks."

Tiffany turned her disapproving look from Vera to Cassandra, her frown deepening. Cassandra didn't give, meeting her gaze without flinching, and holding it as an uncomfortable silence stretched out between them. Tiffany would neither acknowledge nor deny that she was a threat, while Cassandra wouldn't let her ignore the possibility any longer.

While their bodies tensed and gazes narrowed, Alexis sat up, and Heather chewed on her lower lip as the two had their stare down.

As it seemed neither was willing to break the silence and put an end to the silent contest of wills, Vera cut in by dropping her file folder on the coffee table with a crack sharp enough to draw all eyes.

"I believe what she's trying to say is, your past history does not make you a suitable candidate for our pack."

Tiffany ground her teeth, setting her drink aside with some care and leaning forward in her seat to point an accusatory finger at Vera. "You don't know the first thing about me, Vera, and don't pretend otherwise. None of you, not even Heather, knows me well enough to make that kind of assumption."

"Oh really?" Vera purred. "Then, by all means, enlighten us about these."

With that, Vera opened the file and spread the newspaper articles and accompanying photographs over the coffee table for all to see.

The headlines of the articles screamed about the injustices and property damage caused by illegal battles between humans and Others. The anti-Other groups had picketed Other-sympathetic businesses, destroyed entire buildings, and killed several vampires and werewolves without valid warrants. Interspersed with the articles were pictures. Irrefutable pictures of Tiffany showing her allegiance as a White Hat, with the trademark white cowboy hat pin attached to her lapel in every one.

Protest marches. Riots. One even showed her with several other White Hats on the run from police dressed in full riot gear, a flaming building in the background. Surrounded by others like her, all wearing the same pins or logo emblazoned on their shirts.

Tiffany whitened under the bronze shimmer of her foundation, her lips pressed into a thin line as all eyes turned to her.

CHAPTER 12

Wanting to be someone else is
a waste of the person you are.
—Kurt Cobain

"I've said before that I've made mistakes," Tiffany said, avoiding the accusatory looks from the rest of the ladies by staring down at the photos spread on the table in front of her. Heather was particularly incensed, her balled fists and clenched teeth betraying her raw anger and hurt. "I have no good excuse for those pictures. They were taken while I was still married to my husband—"

"So you admit you hunted us before?" Vera's tone was triumphant and poisonously sweet, her nail polish fracturing as the tips of her fingers grew into claws.

Tiffany looked up and met Vera's yellow eyes with her own icy blue ones, baring her teeth in the semblance of a smile. Slowly, deliberately, she reached down to the messenger bag at her feet. The others tensed, ready to react if she pulled a weapon—but all she withdrew was a tiny laptop.

"Vera, I've said a number of times already that I haven't participated in that lifestyle for quite a while. Though I suppose that's not entirely true."

As Tiffany spoke, she booted up the netbook, searching for a file. Though wary, the other women watched her without interrupting, four pairs of glowing amber irises focused with single-minded intensity on her every move.

"You see, I realized early on that you were going to make things difficult for me. I prepared for this eventuality the only way I knew how—using skills I earned while working with my ex-husband. I do want to caution you all that this is not the only copy, and that if something happens to me or you do not reconsider your actions and my future place in your pack, this video will be uploaded onto YouTube and forwarded to every TV station in the country."

Though that last statement caused some confusion, in moments, all four of the werewives were on their feet, growling and snarling in rage. The video quality was far from that of a high-definition movie, and the playback of the audio was choppy, but there was no mistaking Vera, Cassandra, Alexis, or Heather's faces taken from some nearby vantage point in the trees—or their shifts in the woods outside of Alexis's home into werewolves.

They all watched, stunned, silent, as their banter was captured on film, as was their undressing and their change into their inner beasts. Tiffany didn't have to tell them what a danger this video posed to them. They knew. To a one, they knew that they could be connected to their husbands, some of the richest and most influential businessmen in the state—if not the country—and that it could bring the livelihoods of their families and fellow pack members crashing down around them if it ever went public. Cassandra in particular went cold, considering her husband, who was running for office next term, would likely flay her and the other werewives alive if he ever caught wind of the existence of that video.

After the wolves had rushed off into the woods to play, it showed close-ups of the clothing and jewelry left behind by the women, then faded to black. As soon as it ended, Tiffany snapped the netbook shut and tucked it back in her bag, ignoring the bared fangs, the glowing eyes, the twitching claws, and the deep rumbles emanating from their chests. Crossing her legs and folding her hands primly in her lap, she raised her chin and regarded Cassandra expectantly.

Heather was the one who spoke first, her voice deep and guttural as she fought to get a handle on her rage.

"How could you? That isn't fair, Tiffany! Why would you do such a terrible thing?"

Tiffany was startled into a laugh, though there was nothing funny about the situation. "Fair? You call this fair? Heather, you're the only one of the Diamondfangs who has listened to me from the start. I've got nothing against you. The rest of you need to listen to me, this time, and believe me when I say that I don't intend to cause you any harm unless you decide against honoring my request. All I wanted when I came here was to find a home in this pack. Nothing has changed. File the papers, do what you need to do to initiate me, and that video will disappear."

Alexis, trembling and white in the face, raised a clawed finger that still sparkled with the crumbled remains of her Gold Pearl nail polish. "You have no right to demand anything from us. Videos and pictures can be doctored. You have no way of proving that it's really us."

"That's right." Cassandra, who had been too stunned to react immediately, showed her fangs in a fierce and humorless grin. "You can't possibly believe we'd give you what you want or let you walk away from this. Bravo for the attempt—but there's no way you could ever prove to anyone that your film is real."

Tiffany smiled slyly, reaching for her messenger bag again. "That's why I saved some other evidence."

Alarmed, the four girls watched with slack jaws as she withdrew a glittering diamond tennis bracelet, dangling with a "VK" charm—Vera's missing jewelry, taken the same night Tiffany recorded them in the woods after the party.

One that had been clearly visible mixed in with the clothing at the end of the video.

The other girls shot Vera a look. She was pale, her fists clenched so tightly that spots of blood were pooling under her fingernails.

"You little thief! How dare you!"

Tiffany smirked. "Don't get any ideas. This isn't the only

thing I took—just the most obvious. Travis told me how often you forgot and left jewelry behind when you went hunting with the pack—or stayed the night at his place. Tsk, Vera. I doubt your husband would approve."

Vera's reaction was immediate and intense. With an enraged howl, she leapt toward Tiffany, closing the distance between them with supernatural speed, hands arched into claws.

Though Cassandra and Heather moved to stop her, Tiffany was on her feet in no time, ducking behind furniture and flicking her wrists to dislodge daggers from sheathes hidden under the cuffs of her Marc Jacobs peasant blouse.

Everyone froze at the unmistakable gleam of silver.

"Vera, sit *down!*"

Cassandra's voice, usually smooth and sure, cracked on a high note. Aside from the unbelievable fuck up of leaving evidence of her shift behind, she was terrified that Vera or Tiffany might actually attack one another. Free of a contract, Tiffany's injury could mean a death sentence for all four of the women if Vera didn't back off. Plus, the silver weapons Tiffany was holding were deadly weapons—even a small nick could do enough damage to incapacitate or kill them.

Vera stayed where she was, straining against the solid hold Cassandra and Heather had on her arms. Her glittering gaze, maddened with rage, never left Tiffany's.

Alexis moved to take Cassandra's place restraining Vera, whose skin was starting to darken with fur and muscles were now bulging unnaturally under her clothing. Moving slowly, carefully, palms up to show she meant no harm, Cassandra edged closer to Tiffany. With any luck, she could draw close enough to incapacitate her without risking injury.

"What does a hunter want with our pack? Did someone send you?"

Tiffany's gaze didn't waver from Vera, though one of her hands shifted so the weapon was now pointed at Cassandra, making her flinch and stop in her tracks.

"Like I told you before, I'm not a hunter anymore. If I show myself in Manhattan after dark, the vampires will kill me. If I show up in Central Park, the Moonwalkers will kill me. If I show up anywhere the White Hats are planning a raid, *they* will kill me."

Tiffany was met by incredulous stares. All the while, she maintained her fighting pose, poised and ready to strike at a moment's notice. After giving her statements time to settle in, she continued, very slowly lowering her weapons in a bid to show she wasn't about to attack—but would be ready to defend herself if need be.

"I want what you have. I want your strength, your speed, your stamina. Your ability to heal. I've had too many trips to the hospital, and too many brushes with death to kid myself. The only way I'll ever be able to survive in this world, particularly with my past, is with a supernatural edge."

Heather, Alexis, and Cassandra were stunned speechless for the second time in as many minutes, hardly able to believe Tiffany's motivations.

"You don't deserve what we have!"

Vera gave voice to a thunderous growl, the glasses rattling on the table nearby as she bumped into it when she struggled against Alexis and Heather's hold. They managed to keep her from breaking free, but just barely.

With a contemptuous sneer, Tiffany finally shifted her gaze to Cassandra, whose mouth was working soundlessly as she tried to find the words to speak. Vera used the distraction, forcing a quick shift and using her superior strength to slide out of Alexis and Heather's grasp, yanking her arms free with an audible rip of clothing. They stumbled forward, and then fell to their knees when she slammed her fists down on their shoulders.

It took a talented shifter to rearrange the bones and tendons in their body so rapidly without being crippled by the mind-numbing pain of the change. Rather than assume the form of a wolf, she'd chosen the half-man, half-wolf shape that all were-wolves were forced to take during the height of the full moon, her body reformed into the dog-headed beast of legend. Her clothing fell in tatters at her clawed feet, the leather bands of her sandals groaning and snapping, and she shook her muzzle hard enough for her earrings to give a discordant jangle. The jewels at her ears and throat glittered obscenely against her pelt, a mockery of the fashionable image she'd projected only moments ago.

Now towering over the other women, Vera's sleek fur bristled, dagger fangs dripping saliva as her lip lifted. She stalked forward with murderous intent, clawed, furry arms outstretched to wrap Tiffany in a crushing embrace.

Cassandra stepped in her way, shouting at her to stop, but Vera batted her across the room hard enough to send her careening into an end table, shattering the furniture.

Tiffany stood her ground as Vera came on, staring up and up into the massive Were's murderously glowing eyes. Defiant to the last, Tiffany curled her own lip, tossing her hair back as she raised a dagger in invitation.

"Bring it, bitch."

With an ear-shattering howl, Vera sprang forward.

CHAPTER 13

Life contains but two tragedies. One is not to get
your heart's desire; the other is to get it.
—Socrates

Gaping jaws and talons snapped and clacked as the twisted, furred creature that was Vera pressed the attack. Despite her size and bulk, she moved with supernatural speed, though her paws slid on the smooth marble tile and prevented her from launching into a full charge.

Tiffany moved with the grace of a dancer, arching, twisting, skipping back from swiping claws. She wanted to be turned—but not crippled in the process.

For her part, Vera didn't take any care as to how sloppy and uncoordinated her attacks were until after the first burning swipe she received on the inside of one massive, hairy arm. She yelped, dropping onto all fours and backing up, tail between her legs.

Tiffany circled around, balanced on her toes, ready to spring away if she needed to. The other girls were only just struggling to their feet when Vera sprang with catlike agility, diving in low so talon-tipped fingers could close on the hunter's ankle, yanking her off her feet. Tiffany was unable to compensate and lost her balance, crashing onto her back and sending one of the daggers clattering across the floor to slide under a couch, far out of reach.

Before any of the other werewives could stop her, Vera was on top of Tiffany's sprawled form, one paw on her shoulder to keep her down and massive jaws diving for her throat.

Tiffany didn't hesitate to bury the remaining dagger in Vera's side, the sharp metal sinking between her ribs with the ease of a hot knife through butter. Vera's head snapped back and she howled in pain, her talons ripping through Tiffany's silk blouse, and then her skin as she convulsed and jerked away. The knife came free as she pulled back, and Tiffany dropped it in favor of scooting back across the slick floor as far from Vera as possible and grabbing at her bleeding shoulder, crying out in pain.

By then Cassandra and Alexis had regained their feet. Heather, the weakest of the three, was still clutching at the back of her neck and moaning on the floor. Cassandra was a little unsteady, but she put herself between Vera and Tiffany, her jaw tight and a muscle ticking in her cheek as she placed her fists on her hips. She glared down at Vera, who was whimpering and rolling on the floor, writhing against the silver burn now racing through her bloodstream. It wasn't enough to kill her—the blade hadn't struck anything vital or damaged any internal organs—but she'd be in a great deal of pain for the next few days, and left with a permanent scar.

Assuming Cassandra let her live, that is.

"I hope you're happy," Cassandra said, a scowl twisting her features as she kicked Vera's bleeding side, drawing another choked yowl of pain out of her. "You've just signed our death warrants, you moon-crazed, silver-tainted, imbecilic whore!"

Heather's head jerked up, her eyes widening. She gasped when she spotted all of the blood now pasting Tiffany's shirt to her chest, then dragged herself to her feet using a nearby chaise as leverage. "Cassie—"

"If I told you once—"

"Cassie!"

Cassandra turned a withering glare on Heather, and she shrank back from the heat in her gaze, voice a low whisper.

"I filed the contract."

Everyone—Alexis, Tiffany, Cassandra, and Vera—turned their attention on Heather, who wrapped her arms around her stomach and looked away so she wouldn't have to meet the incredulity and anger in their gazes.

"I filed it this morning. Before the meeting. I knew none of you would ever do it, and I didn't agree with Gabriel saying no."

Tiffany gave voice to a raspy, triumphant laugh, sitting up and tossing her hair back over her shoulder, though some of the longer strands were now red with blood and clung to her chest and shirt. Cassandra sucked in a breath through her teeth, her gaze torn between Tiffany and Heather, who was busy hugging herself and trying to look as small as possible. Alexis simply ran her palm over her face, though she was admittedly relieved that it now meant there was no liability connected to herself as far as this unbelievable fuck up on Vera's part was concerned.

Tiffany used her free hand to grab a nearby lamp pole to lever herself to her feet. The wounds weren't too deep, but they stung when she moved around, dragging a wince out of her. Cassandra tensed, but made no move to help, not wanting to risk being struck by another silver weapon she might have hidden in her clothes.

"Well," Alexis ventured, hoping to defuse some of the tensions between the women now that the worst seemed to be over, "I suppose that means you're *really* going to be one of us, now. Congratulations."

Tiffany's sunny smile was at odds with her pallor and the way she swayed on her feet. Despite the pain, she stood tall and proud, arms folded in front of her chest. Lifting her chin, she turned that pleased grin on Alexis, her look just as predatory as any of the werewolves could have pulled off.

"Don't worry. None of you will regret the decision. I promise."

Vera growled, the low rumble cutting off into a pained whine when Cassandra shoved her again with her foot until she subsided. Cassandra whirled on Tiffany, eyes narrowed and brows furrowed into tight knots as she stalked forward, though she still left a healthy distance between them.

"You may have gotten your way, but you'll have to rise through the ranks just like the rest of us did. Gabriel isn't going to make it easy for you, and neither will the rest of the pack.

What you did was inexcusable, and hardly fitting behavior for a member of the Diamondfangs. I have the feeling you'll be spending the next couple of years proving yourself to the rest of us."

Tiffany's smile faded, and she inclined her head by way of apology. She was still far too pleased to be terribly sorry. "If that's what you wish, so be it. I suppose I have nothing but time now, so I'll spend as long as it takes to prove my worth."

Heather paused in rubbing the back of her neck, still sore from Vera's blow, to turn a puzzled look on Tiffany. "What do you mean?"

"You know that's why I came to you instead of the vampires, don't you? I wanted immortality without the nighttime limitations, and I got it. Under the circumstances, it seems to me being furry for a few nights out of the month isn't such a bad deal. Now that what's yours is mine, I'll do whatever it takes to earn the respect of the pack. We can start with my overseas connections—which should help the pack expand its influence enormously. It's only a fair trade, considering."

Cassandra snorted, leaning back on her heels and eyeing Tiffany with a sly twist to her lips. The other girls were staring blankly now, even Vera, too surprised to contradict her.

"Really, now. That's why you wanted to join us so badly? Immortality?"

"Of course. You think I like the idea of being a monster? What's the point if you don't get something out of it—like living forever?"

Cassandra startled everyone by throwing her head back and laughing, covering her eyes with her hand. Her shoulders shook so hard with mirth that she couldn't speak right away. Irritated, Tiffany huffed, looking at Heather, who was watching her with wide eyes, her hand over her mouth.

"What's so funny about that?"

Heather shook her head, not wanting to be the one to break the news. So Alexis did it for her.

"Honey, you should've stuck with the vampires. Werewolves

aren't immortal. We have *decreased* life spans because of our nature."

Tiffany blinked. "Come again?"

"Decreased. Life. Span," Alexis repeated. "We're destined to die young. Well, relatively."

Already pale from blood loss under the bronze shimmer of her makeup, Tiffany grew whiter still. She staggered a few steps to collapse into a nearby chair. Heather grimaced when she saw the bloody handprint left behind on the furniture, but felt it was the wrong time to caution her guests about keeping the place tidy.

". . . but . . . but I thought . . ."

"Wrong, obviously," Cassandra said, lacing her tone with as much sympathy as she could muster. Under the circumstances, it wasn't much. "Sorry, sweetness. I'm surprised you didn't know. I thought the White Hats were better informed than that."

Tiffany shot her an angry look, though she was still too shocked and weak to do more than raise a shaky fist at her. "I didn't care about the details, I just went with Richard when he went on hunts. No one ever told me!"

"Get used to it," Heather snapped, her own patience at an end. "You're one of us now. Welcome to the werewives."

EPILOGUE

If you want to know what God thinks of money,
just look at the people he gave it to.
—Dorothy Parker

Six Months Later

Alexis stirred her martini, watching a woman ordering one of the cabana boys at the hotel pool to get her a towel and something from the bar. The werewives had decided a vacation down to Atlantic City was in order, and were making the most of the time away from their husbands by shopping, gambling, visiting the local clubs, and soaking up sun by the poolside. Now, resting at a glass table with a view overlooking the rest of the patio, the pool, and the ocean in the distance, the ladies were relaxing after a long, hard day of wearing out the magnetic stripes on their husbands' credit cards.

Alexis studied the woman with interest. She was dark-haired and golden-skinned, probably from out of town. Her bikini and matching sarong were ones Alexis had considered buying herself when she was shopping at Saks Fifth Avenue earlier in the week. The rock on her finger shone brightly enough that Alexis was glad she'd remembered to bring her Christian Dior sunglasses with her.

The lady said something so sharply that the boy taking her order was quick to pick up her purse for her when she gestured for it, and then rushed off to fetch her drink. Though the sight of the tight butt as he bent over to pick up the bag was distracting, Alexis used the excuse of plucking the olive garnishing her drink out and shaking it in the woman's direction to turn the attention of the other werewives her way.

"What do you think?"

Heather glanced over the rim of the oversized piña colada she'd ordered, then shrugged. "Not bad."

Cassandra nudged her Prada sunglasses down to rest on the tip of her nose and tipped her sunhat up. She watched the girl snap her fingers as she made demands that the hotel personnel scurried to carry out, catering to her whims as if she were the Queen of England.

"She looks like she'd be a pain in the ass to break in," Vera commented, not bothering to crane her neck to take a look.

Tiffany slid behind her, giving her a hug as she put one of the two cocktails she was carrying down on the table in front of Vera, giving her an air-kiss on the cheek. "That's why I love you. You're always so positive about these things."

Vera gave Tiffany a vicious, toothy grin, which was soon returned in kind. Tiffany slid into her own seat, crossing her legs so that her Zac Posen floral skirt rode up high on her thigh, distracting several of the men working and lounging near the pool.

"We've taken chances before," Cassandra said, smiling wryly at Tiffany and toasting her with her drink. "What do you think, darling?"

Tapping her cheek with one French-manicured fingernail, Tiffany made a big production of thinking about it, taking her time while the other women rolled their eyes and sipped at their drinks. Lips curved into a Cheshire grin, she curled her fingers around her glass, hairline cracks appearing in her polish as her nails began forming into talons.

"I say it doesn't hurt to give her a chance. After all, she looks like she'd fit right in."

The woman, thanks to the Bulgari sunglasses shading her from the sun's glare, failed to notice five pairs of glowing, golden eyes simultaneously focused upon her with predatory intent.